WOMAN of the CLOTH

WOMAN
of the
CLOTH

by

Roger E. Herst

SHENGOLD BOOKS

Woman of the Cloth
by Roger Herst

Published by:

Shengold Books
an imprint of Schreiber Publishing, Inc.
Post Office Box 4193
Rockville, MD 20849 USA
1-800-822-3213
www.schreiberpub.com
spbooks@aol.com

First Printing

Publisher's Cataloguing-in-Publication

Herst, Roger.
Woman of the cloth / Roger Herst. -- 1st ed.
p. cm.
Preassigned LCCN: 97-61910
ISBN: 1-887563-41-5

1. Women rabbis--Fiction. 2. Judaism--Fiction. 3. Washington (D.C.)--Fiction. I. Title.

PS3558.E79W66 1998 813'.54
QBI98-170

Dedicated to clergywomen and clergymen
who serve selflessly
with little recognition and small reward

Chapter One

July 8th

Rabbi Dr. Seth Nehemiah Greer is a *shmuck.*

He is smart, articulate, and so uproariously funny that his sermons fill the synagogue sanctuary every Sabbath, whether or not there's a Bar or Bat Mitzvah. For Jews, his humor is a relief from the repetitions of the weekly liturgy; for Gentiles, it is an entertaining glimpse into the Jewish psyche. No less compelling are his personal charms, which make people feel he is their personal confidant and close friend, which in most cases he isn't. Yet despite such talents, he's still a first-class *shmuck*.

These aren't the kind of thoughts Gabby enjoys having about anyone, least of all her senior rabbinical colleague, but then, thoughts have their own natures and we can't always control them. They come and go inside our brains with dependable irregularity, acting as though they enjoy complete independence from us which, of course, they do.

It is 7:37 a.m., and Gabby is in Rabbi Greer's study. To be more exact, she is seated in his chocolate-brown leather chair in a room lined with empty bookshelves already collecting a veneer of dust. Six weeks before, he had packed his belongings late Saturday evening when the synagogue was closed, then disappeared. Nobody knows where, though his congregants hope it's as far away as Israel or, better yet, Tasmania. No forwarding address. No phone number. And no suicide note. The fact that nobody knows his whereabouts isn't a tragedy since these days even his close friends have nothing to say to him. In the course of one month this demigod who had ascended Jacob's ladder spanning heaven and earth has toppled, leaving behind many angry, puzzled, and ashamed admirers. People are electrified when a man of stature stumbles. The rabbi's followers have lost their innocence, and that's not shed without a measure of mortification. No one enjoys being deceived and the once-adored Seth Nehemiah Greer deceived not only the women he screwed (literally and figuratively), but those who for long years believed he was sleeping with no one but his wife, Emma. Not only did his name become grist for the rumor mills of his home town, Washington, D.C., but the media broadcast his peccadilloes for the amusement of a national audience. In the end, God's ordained shamed not only the Jewish community in the Nation's Capital, but Jews throughout the country. Gentiles who didn't particularly like Jews to begin with suddenly found a bona fide leader to bash. The Evangelical Christian Right quickly seized from his carcass the abandoned standard of sexual rectitude.

People openly ponder how a creep like Seth Greer could have bamboozled so many for so long. It's easier to blame the dissembler than to admit one's own naivete, so everyone just points the finger oblivious to his own blindness in this matter. And of course, the Internet bristles from coast to coast with fresh jokes about sex and the clergy (the rabbi/priest/minister type) which bear tedious symmetries. Three clergymen reacting to the same situation, then a punchline, harpooning one or all of God's servants, along with the faith(s) they espouse.

Gabby is inclined to be more charitable toward the senior rabbi with whom she has worked for seven years and who after her graduation from the rabbinical seminary provided much of her on-the-job rabbinical training. He proved to be a patient and engaging instructor who expected her to learn by practicing what she knew and experimenting with what she didn't. During these apprenticeship years, she noted a progressive shift in his attitude toward religious practice. Contrary to most rabbinical colleagues who tend to become more permissive over time, Seth Greer seemed to add rituals on a scheduled basis. His fastidious observance of Jewish rites propelled him beyond the traditional boundaries of Jewish thought into the less-traveled domain of Kabbalistic mysticism. Gabby thinks he is intellectually brilliant and enviably creative though quite unworldly—connected to the earth by little more than gravity and his Italian designer shoes.

Knowing the rebellious, sometimes caustic, and judgmental side of Seth's wife, Emma, Gabby would not have been surprised to discover him in a discreet sexual affair—one distant from Washington and with a mature woman who might enjoy his endowments between bedsheets and leave it at that. What astonishes her is the scope of his affairs. As soon as one accuser complains to the congregation's Board of Directors, three more jilted paramours come forward. And, one assumes, there are still others who remain silent in the shadows. Because the Board refuses to make public the victims' identities, the number of women Seth rolled in the hay is a matter for speculation. In an attempt to ensure privacy for the four accusers, the Board issues pseudonyms to the press. The problem is that Seth's affairs captivate the media, and over time these fictitious names take on real identities. People refer to Elizabeth Silversmith, Amanda Caen, Michelle Tickleman, and Dorothy Kogent-Weiner as real ladies of the flesh done in by a slick clergyman selling more than access to the Almighty. In a town where rumors disseminate like spring pollen, this strategy is surprisingly successful. Silversmith, Caen, Tickleman, and Kogent-Weiner become household personalities who, it turns out, appeal to women feeling victimized by sex-driven men.

Gabby had no idea her boss possessed such a libido. She spent many hours with him at professional conferences, often in hotels at distant cities. At home in the District of Columbia, they enjoyed private lunches and dinners, usually in Italian restaurants, delighting in the inventive ways which chefs prepare pasta. In their spare time they played mind games of nearly every variety, from crossword puzzles to whodunit mysteries, competing with each other for wit and ingenuity. In quiet moments, alcohol freed their inhibitions to talk forthrightly about their profession, as only people who share it can. Between themselves they could complain and commiserate without fear of gossip or misunderstanding. To one another, their fears and aspirations were very personal, leaving little to the imagination. Seth told about extreme stress in his marriage while the unmarried thirty-three-year-old Gabby revealed anxiety about not finding a mate or having children of her own. Yet despite the potential for intimacy between them, never once had Seth Greer crossed over the line and suggested that he might become *her* lover—either for a casual after-lunch *shtup* or for a more permanent secret alliance.

In the early morning quiet of the Temple offices, she wonders if she might have consented to sex with a married man or violated a professional code and slept with her boss. Seth is not overweight or nerdish as are so many of her over-dined and under-exercised rabbinic colleagues. His dark, penetrating eyes seem to dance and it is impossible not to be absorbed by a smile that sucks you into his mirth. Yet she concludes that his chances of seducing her were next to nil. Not nil, mind you, but close to it. A temptation, yes. But submission, no. No!

Though women's organizations to which Gabby belongs express their outrage over the rabbi's behavior, she withholds public judgment. To remain silent and let others voice their shock is sound professionalism and good politics. What adults do in the privacy of their bedrooms should be of no concern to others, though laymen make an exception for the clergy, who when it comes to sex are held to a high moral standard, perhaps because they spend so much time preaching about it. Or perhaps because parishioners have difficulty imagining their ministers grunting and groaning under the bedsheets like normal couples. Gabby is so busy defending her profession from poisonous arrows that she fails to acknowledge her feelings about Seth's affairs. Something gnaws inside her. She knows she is an attractive woman—slender, athletic, with all her facial features in symmetry, including a nose which was successfully altered at fifteen with a gentle curve downward at the tip rather than the customary plastic surgeon's ski-jump moored between flaring nostrils. When she smiles, her nose snuggles comfortably between punctuating dimples. After conjuring up an image of the mares in Seth's stable, she wonders how their physical endowments compare with hers. A chill of rejection possesses her. The thought of hopping into bed with him never crossed her mind until she learned that at least four other females were more resourceful than she.

The truth is that he never gave her a chance to say no. And that's infuriating as hell!

"The foolish *shmuck*," she mutters—to ruin a wonderful career for nothing more than vaginal juice. She is certain that though he seduced these women, he never raped a single one. Seth does not force himself on others, either intellectually or emotionally, so in each seduction there must have been an element of mutual consent. The way women fawn over him, that is not far-fetched. She believes that his paramours should bear a measure of responsibility for their liaisons, but in this case that's not likely to happen. Wide attention by the media produces communal self-righteousness. Noting Rabbi Greer's abuses, not one female commentator on television suggests any female complicity in the matter. In Gabby's mind that paints women as victims, rather than accomplices. This picture ultimately denigrates feminism rather than honors it.

To Seth's credit, he did not deny the accusations. That would have been like swatting mosquitoes at twilight on a hot summer night. For every insect killed, three more attack. His timely resignation from the congregation minimized humiliation for everyone but himself and his family. Emma Greer proved a consummate actress, skillfully playing the role of jilted wife, simply upstaged by sexually aggressive women. It happens every day of the week, perhaps more than we think. During the brief ordeal, Seth's two children, Jeremy, a graduate student at the University of California in Berkeley, and Margarie, a laboratory technician in Frederick, Maryland, stayed away from the community in which they had grown up. That spared everyone additional pain.

So how would *you* like being the Associate Rabbi at Washington's Ohav Shalom Congregation and have to fill Seth Greer's shoes?

GABRIELLE IS HER GIVEN NAME, BUT NOBODY CALLS her that. It's *Gabby* in all but the most formal circumstances, such as her ordination as a Reform rabbi seven years before, made official by the laying on of hands and a *smicha* certificate which reads in Hebrew *haRav Gabrielle Batya Lewyn—Toreh, Toreh, Tadin, Tadin*—Ordained to Teach and Adjudicate in Rabbinical Matters. She seldom introduces herself as Rabbi Lewyn in order to avoid inevitable and tedious discussions about female rabbis in what, until recently, has been a male club. Pioneers in any field must justify themselves, and women in the male-dominated rabbinate are no exception.

Gabby is in Rabbi Greer's study where she shouldn't be. For legal purposes, the congregation's Executive Director, Harold Farb, circulated a memo to all synagogue personnel declaring the Rabbi's office off-limits. In an attempt to obliterate his memory and get on with the business of running a synagogue, he removed Seth's private notes and papers. As Associate Rabbi, Gabby enjoys special privileges, as well as a master key to all offices. Still, she doesn't believe that exempts her from Harold Farb's decree.

At this early hour, the administrative offices at Ohav Shalom in the Woodley Park neighborhood are quiet. She had never planned to enter Seth's study and sit at his desk, but was driven there by curiosity. The congregation buzzes with theories about the motives of their ex-Senior Rabbi. Gabby knows him with professional intimacy and few explanations make much sense. In his study she hopes to glean a clue or two, at least to stimulate her own thinking. But once there, another urge seizes her. When she drops into the soft cushion of his chair, she feels like curling into his lap. Yet nothing is so innocent. Deaths and resignations provide career opportunities. Joshua succeeded Moses; Lyndon Johnson, John Kennedy; and Shimon Peres, Yitzhak Rabin. Somebody will eventually fill the now-vacant position of Senior Rabbi. New leaders replace old leaders and the world's business goes on. The congregation is in shock, and it is only natural for the Associate Rabbi to fulfill Seth's rabbinic duties for a time. But how long will that continue? No American Jewish congregation with more than five hundred families has a woman in the senior post. Feminism hasn't achieved that much, at least not yet. Still, Gabby's ambition compels her to ask, why not?

No one seeks her opinion about the future. Board meetings she routinely attends suddenly occur behind closed doors. A conspiracy of silence hovers over an institution normally riddled with gossip. Tom-tom drums circulate coded rumors in the background, but Gabby can only surmise their meaning. All the while, everyone expects her to fill Rabbi Greer's rabbinical shoes —to conduct services and life-cycle ceremonies, supervise the religious school and the Bar/Bat Mitzvah program, teach adult education classes, counsel the depressed and lonely, as well as serve on numerous committees. Whenever he is booked to speak at affairs outside the synagogue, she fills in—with or without a new invitation. Rabbi Greer is scheduled to teach an evening course on Medieval Jewish Thought at Georgetown University, and Gabby is a natural substitute. She'll never be as funny as Seth, who could have made a handsome living as a standup comedian in the Catskills, but she loves teaching and her preparation is impeccable.

To the best of her knowledge few congregants are uncomfortable with these arrangements. In the short term, what alternatives have they? Several congregants praise her calming composure in a time of extreme stress. Others go out of their way to compliment her abilities.

A rumble from the direction of the administrative offices down the corridor distracts her. Her heart rate increases. Is this her imagination? If synagogue employees have arrived earlier than scheduled, there should be additional noises. But for the moment all is quiet.

She jumps up in preparation to leave and gazes at Seth's leather sofa. Rumor has it that two of his dalliances occurred there, after hours when synagogue employees had left for the day. Such scuttlebutt is without substantiation. One accuser testified that Seth fucked her on the boardroom conference table, the very table around which the congregational Board of Directors later gathered to deliberate his fate. Gabby imagines them pushing back from the table and settling their hands in their laps, no longer wishing to make contact with this infamous love bed. The meeting adjourns to an adjacent lounge where the members feel more comfortable. Two days later, workmen arrived to resand and restain the elegant mahogany table. Executive Director Harold Farb claims this refurbishment in the Boardroom had been scheduled for more than a year. Timing of the repair amounts to nothing but mere coincidence. If you believe that, friends, there's a bridge you'll want to buy.

Still, no additional noise from outside the offices. Gabby concludes that her imagination is playing games.

She circles Seth's sofa. The room is cold, slightly musty, with a pervasive silence from the dead air circulators. He has left behind on the bookshelf a thick volume which she recognizes as the *Biblia Hebraica*, edited by Rudolph Kittel, a scholarly reproduction of the Old Testament, with editorial marks and endless footnotes—the most authoritative Hebrew rendition of the ninth-century Masoretic text. She is intrigued by the symbolism in what Seth has chosen to discard. Is he throwing away his faith along with his career? The arcane side of his personality is fascinating. By now it's clear there are secrets in his life which make a physically attractive man all the more intriguing. How could she have missed such signals before?

She finds herself again seated at his desk, swiveling thirty degrees off center, and testing the fit of her rump into the cushion. She likes the sensation or, more properly, believes the chair fits her. Seats of power such as thrones, corporate CEO chairs, and law court benches possess mystic qualities. Seth's chair produces a tingle in her spine. Her fingers sweep over the textured binding of the *Biblia Hebraica*, then open the cover. The prolegomena is in German, the notes in Latin, and the text in Hebrew. Her eyes fall on the yellow tail of a square Post-it stuck to the frontispiece. It is in Seth's handwriting.

> *For my colleague, Gabby Lewyn,*
> *who is seldom stumped by a puzzle.*
>
> *Seth*

She leans back in the chair, thunderstruck. What puzzle? She isn't aware that the situation presents any challenge. What occurred seems straight forward enough. Why did Seth choose to communicate in such an odd manner?

Her speculations are interrupted prematurely by sounds of heavy footsteps from the corridor outside. This time there can be no doubt. Somebody is approaching the administrative offices! Her heartbeat now stampedes. It is unseemly to be discovered usurping the Senior Rabbi's office, even if she is Acting Senior Rabbi. Of course, she could say she entered in order to fetch the Kittel Bible. But she isn't good at lying. Even white lies produce redness in her nose, which she feels grows like the fabled Pinocchio's. She believes that, were she to practice the craft of prevarication, she might become as good as the next lady, but why bother? There are more productive ways to spend a lifetime.

An impulse to escape possesses her. It is impossible to tell where other staff are and to dash down the corridor might attract the attention she hopes to avoid. In the end there is nothing to do but act natural—ease slowly into the corridor en route to her own study.

LIKE A HOUND ON SCENT, HAROLD FARB IS DRAWN toward Rabbi Greer's office and approaches as Gabby exits. He's the last person on Planet Earth she wants to meet. She expects a nasty greeting, but it doesn't come. The scowl on his face softens as he recognizes her. She reckons he may be relieved to discover her rather than someone else. Still, there is confusion in his rumpled brow and clipped greeting.

Her dark hazel eyes lock on his, distorted behind thick glasses to correct for astigmatism. "Sad, so utterly sad," she improvises in her signature voice, deep and husky. "I know you don't want people in there, yet something compels me. I need to feel Seth's pain, if that makes any sense. He gave up so much for so little."

Harold's eyebrows rise at the same time as his eyes appear to narrow behind the lenses. There's a fire burning inside him, yet he is controlled, a political animal from his crown to his toes. No executive director of a large congregation can afford to be anything else.

She turns down the corridor and puts her hand on the small of his back, guiding him in direction of her own study. "You know, Harold, whenever I see something like this, I think: 'there but for the grace of God go I.' I could have made the fatal fall just as easily as he."

He cants his shoulder and eyes her with skepticism. "Oh, I think not, Gabby. Not a woman like you. Seth's a gambler. This might sound like Monday morning quarterbacking, but I always felt he was testing himself; he enjoyed living dangerously. That's why he did it under our very noses. He could have accomplished the same goal with a minimum of discretion. Gone off and satisfied his lust in some other city. I'm sure rabbis do things like that, though I don't pretend to have proof. But that wasn't Seth's style. He had to tempt the Devil in his own backyard, if that isn't an offensive metaphor. But you, Gabby. You're made of different stuff."

She believes Harold is a savvy observer who must perceive her ambition for Seth's job. No one understands congregational politics better than he. While pausing outside the Ladies Room, she says in parting, "Thanks for the compliment."

"Well deserved. I've been watching you these past weeks. Here at the crack of dawn and out late in the evening. It's not fair dumping so much work on you. Must feel like the Vice President when the President has a heart attack."

"One day at a time. I think to myself, if I can just make it through this day, the rest will be sailing. Unfortunately, each new day seems to be no less taxing. By the way, how was the special Board meeting last night?"

Farb, who seldom hesitates before offering an opinion, hesitates. "I'm not sure what you're referring to."

She presses against the spring door to the Ladies Room and holds it open a crack. Out wafts the scent of bathroom disinfectant. "Oh come on, Harold. Nothing happens in this palace of rectitude without you. They tried to conceal the meeting from me, but I wasn't born yesterday. Still got a few loyal spies around."

"Delicate times," he half-whispers. "People wear their feelings on their sleeves. Lots of subjects are off-limits."

"Well then, Harold, I'm about to step into a place out-of-bounds to you." She glances at him in a wry manner and pushes the Ladies Room door open enough to slip through and lets it snap back in his face.

THE TELEPHONE RINGS AND RINGS. THANK GOD Gabby's secretary, a holdover flower child from the sixties who "got religion" late in life and is therefore willing to accept modest secretarial employment at Ohav Sholom, defends his boss with the bulldog tenacity of a Redskin linebacker. Charles (Chuck) Maximillian Browner originally worked for Seth Greer but, in a personnel shift before Seth's departure, became attached to Gabby. Always courteous and diplomatic, he's more at ease working with women than men. Or perhaps better put, women have fewer problems with him than straight men. He is neither strongly masculine nor particularly feminine, which suits his position as secretary. The subject of homosexuality seldom comes up with Gabby, who believes sexual orientation is a private matter. Chuck's secretarial work is largely unobjectionable to members of the congregation. Whether these same congregants would be as tolerant were he to teach their children in Confirmation class on Sundays or the Bar/Bat Mitzvah classes on weekday afternoons is another matter.

Since he knows Gabby is alone, Chuck pokes his head into her study to announce a telephone call. The phone began ringing at 9 a.m. and hasn't stopped for more than a minute or two. Some uninformed callers still want to speak with Rabbi Greer though the number diminishes daily. Meanwhile, the number of people wishing to speak with Rabbi Lewyn has almost doubled. So too have the private conferences with those seeking rabbinic counseling, Bar/Bat interviews, funeral and wedding arrangements. If there is a moment free, Gabby jots outlines for her two *Shabbat* sermons on a yellow legal-size tablet. She uses a computer for editing and drafts, but prefers to outline a sermon the old-fashioned way, with pencil and paper.

At the moment, Chuck Browner catches Gabby working over notes for a monthly newsletter. Desktop publishing has transformed many readers of fine books into readers of newsletters. She detests writing columns for them almost as much as reading them.

"Ephraim Rothman." In the mocking tone of a medieval herald Chuck announces the ex-president of the congregation and a personal friend to Gabby. "Shall I tell him you're in conference and can't be disturbed?"

Gabby exhales a gust of air through her front teeth, puffing her cheeks as though inflating bubble gum. Demands upon her time and energy are ceaseless. The pace is exhausting. Every moment of privacy is invaded by a petitioner who wants her to write a letter, make a phone call, pay a visit, or promote a cause. Each petition is not without reason, but they accumulate faster than they can be dispatched. She feels herself drowning in work and occasionally thinks about giving up. Just stop and let herself slip beneath the water's surface to drown. Impulse is overruled by a counter-impulse. She gasps for air, and life. "Tell Mr. Rothman, tell him..."

Chuck puckers his lips, a sign he knows that Gabby is improvising.

"Tell him that the rabbi is *thinking* and cannot be disturbed. That should give him pause for thought."

"I most certainly hope shẹ is," says Chuck.

"Or should we say *praying?* Sounds more impressive, doesn't it?"

"He won't believe that."

"Then put him through. I'll save that for someone else. Eph deserves better treatment."

As soon as Chuck transfers the call, she hears Ephraim Rothman's familiar baritone. "Hello, Gabby. Did you jog this morning?"

"Is the Pope Catholic? You bet. 5:30 a.m. on the dot."

"Have you read *The Washington Post* yet?"

"No, my schedule's crazy. Are you calling to say I won the lottery? Sorry, I don't play. What would people say if I won? Can you imagine the jokes? Rabbi wins without even buying a ticket! Now there's a true miracle for you. What have I missed in *The Post*, Eph?"

"Story about Jonathan Zentner's son, Noah. He's been accused of raping a woman on a sailboat on the Chesapeake Bay. Seth officiated at Noah's wedding."

The Zentner family is a pillar of Washington's Jewish community. Real Estate Development—office buildings and shopping centers, in days when fortunes could be made investing other people's money...and were. But to the Zentners' credit, only a portion of the wealth earned stays at home; they dole out a healthy share to philanthropies, both Jewish and communal. The University of Chicago, Sloan-Kettering Memorial Cancer Center in New York, the Big Brothers, the United Jewish Appeal, the Hebrew University in Jerusalem. Big gifts as though they were buying entry into heaven. That's not to say they donate their way into poverty. Most charitable contributions come from the top of the pocket, not the bottom.

Seth Greer and Noah Zentner hung around together, that is until Seth flew the coop—tennis, Redskins games, and skiing in season. Noah and Morgan Zentner vacationed with Seth and Emma Greer on Nantucket and occasionally in Jerusalem. When scandal over Seth's affairs hit the press, the patriarchal Jonathan Zentner immediately offered to protect him. Many folks believed that was wrong, though public criticism never seemed to deter him. His son's best friend was in trouble and he possessed the resources to help. Whatever Seth needed. Lawyers, therapists, or just time to pull himself together. Instead of accepting this help, Seth resigned from the congregation.

The minute Ephraim Rothman mentions the names, Gabby has a feeling she will be swept into their world. She doesn't mind rubbing shoulders with the wealthy, but resents doing so by default. "Seth, you *shmuck*," she thinks to herself, "Why the hell have you abandoned me for a few vaginas? You didn't even try unzipping *my* jeans."

She trusts Ephraim to keep their conversations confidential and therefore feels comfortable saying, "Noah Zentner's a newlywed. I can understand what happens when petals fall off the marriage rose. But he can't be married more than two years. Besides, a hunk like him wouldn't have to rape anybody. For just a whistle, half the girls on the East Coast would jump in bed with him. Married or not."

"Apparently one did. Someone famous. You must have seen Eli Waller on television? That feisty financial commentator on CNN?"

"No. Don't watch programs about the stock market. You know I only watch wrestling and car races. Demolition derbies are my favorite. But I do know Eli from the Women's Movement. She's a mover and shaker on a dozen boards. Big crusader for feminist causes. Chatted with her on several occasions at cocktail parties."

Ephraim responds, "That's what I'm worried about. Crusaders annoy me. They think they're born in log cabins and mangers. You can't tell what's bigger, their egos or their causes. Just for your information, this Waller woman is also a power on Wall Street."

"She's a bit aggressive for my taste. A man would have a better chance surviving in a bunk with a boa constrictor. Most rapes go unreported. If this goes to trial, she'll become a role model for other women. You think Noah did it, Eph?"

"My gut tells me no. But the papers report there were witnesses. Read page two of *The Post*. The media will have a heyday with this. They love to chronicle the fall of a rich boy. Publicity won't do him any good. Hopefully, the District Attorney won't press for an indictment."

"I'm sure he's got a good lawyer."

"Not one. A battalion. No—a full division. Best that money can buy. There's a bevy of attorneys around Jon Zentner at all times. A click of the fingers and they take over for the Zentner family. Money buys that kind of help, you know. It cushions the rich against life's tumbles. That's not to suggest Jon isn't feeling this. Noah could go to prison."

"Can I help?" Gabby asks.

"Noah wants Seth. His father asked me to locate him. That's why I'm calling. Nobody knows where Seth is. I won't violate any confidences you have with him. I told Jon that up front. But still, I promised to ask you for Seth's whereabouts."

"I don't know," Gabby says. "I'd love keep in touch but I must remind him of what he sacrificed. I'm probably the last person in the country he wants to see. I can ask our colleagues, but I'd be surprised if Seth's in contact with any rabbis."

"I'm recommending that Noah come to you. Not certain he'll take my advice. He may need you for a character witness in court. You know him, don't you?"

"Of course. But he was Seth's friend, not mine."

"Rape's a terrible crime. When the child of a close friend commits it, the lights go out, if you know what I mean."

"That's not a fact yet, is it? The rape, I mean?"

Ephraim pauses for a long while. "Well, I guess it isn't. Or rather, I hope it isn't. There must be mitigating circumstances. Nothing is black and white. But I get bad vibrations. The congregation doesn't need another scandal."

"Sounds as though we've got it, whether we need it or not."

Ephraim interrupts, "I called to ask you about Seth, but also to remind you that we have a lunch appointment tomorrow. I hope you haven't forgotten."

"I've got it down in my electronic organizer. A couple of key punches in the daytimer and *Shazam!, Ephraim for Lunch*."

"You know my private number at the office. Ask my secretary, Dorothy, to pull me out of any meeting. And I mean *any meeting*. Don't stand on formality. Dorothy will make a reservation for us at La Piccola Roma, say 12:30. I know you like Italian."

"My favorite. Something nice to look forward to."

Elisheva Waller
July 9th

Though she cannot say it publicly, Eli Waller thinks the host of MSNBC's financial talk show, *Your Money*, C. Claude McMillian, is a jerk. With only thirty-four minutes to go before air time, he has the audacity to drop a fresh set of questions on her desk. Benjamin LeVell, the program's guru on investment stocks, telephoned that his taxi has just been rammed by an ambulance en route to another accident. Two minor injuries, but the police won't release him until everybody's testimony has been taken. McMillian now expects Eli to pinch hit for LeVell. Normally she would kill for extra minutes before the camera, but she's an expert in Finance and Real Estate Invest-ment Trusts, and possesses only pedestrian knowledge about stocks. McMillian's new questions deal with companies she doesn't even know exist so she'll have to spin from a subject she doesn't understand to one she does. Politicians do that all the time and she considers herself a savvy politician. Plans to handle these questions are interrupted by a rap on the door of her studio office.

Sidney Hines and Sylvia Junqueira from the Baltimore Office of the District Attorney wait outside. When she tries to explain last-minute pressures of live-time television, they respond with bulldog resolve. Reluctantly, she permits them to step into her office where they halt beside her desk. She's impatient and in a dramatic gesture strips bone-rimmed designer glasses from a nose that is slightly irritated where the frame pads rub against the skin. Light lipstick on her lips and professionally mascaraed eyes with long artificial eyelashes accentuate her Plain Jane features. She wears absolutely no jewelry on her ears, neck or fingers. Her gray suit is tailored with simple elegance and her white blouse with a high collar touching the base of her ears is still starched firmly, though it has endured a long business day at her investment firm.

Sylvia Junqueira introduces herself and her colleague as designated prosecuting attorneys should the State of Maryland indict Noah Ventner for rape. She opens a worn leather-bound note carrier and withdraws a document. In contrast to Eli's conspicuous lack of jewelry, her embroidered gold earrings and two necklaces, one hanging inside her blouse and the other outside, provide a Gypsy flair. There are three gold rings on the right hand and a modest-sized engagement diamond on the left. "Sorry for the interruption, but New York is the only place we can be private. The press hounds us day and night in Baltimore. Women's rights organizations clog our e-mail with demands to prosecute. Bags of mail block corridors of our office. The Fire Department is on our backs to do something about the clutter. Now I have a sense of what it's like to be famous. Not for me, Ms. Waller."

Eli rustles Claude McMillian's questions before their eyes. "You people don't lose any time. I'd love to talk, but my show begins in less than a half-hour. I'm afraid I've got to review these questions before I go on."

"We'll be brief. We need to ascertain if there's sufficient evidence for the state to prosecute. Then the District Attorney must decide if there's a reasonable chance of conviction. No sense trying a case we can't win. We've got to go before the Grand Jury to get an indictment. I'm sure your attorney has told you that no matter what our determination on the criminal suit, you're free to pursue civil action against Zentner."

This abruptly changes Eli's attitude. "Are you suggesting the State of Maryland has doubts I was raped?"

Sidney Jefferson Hines is partially balding and easily thirty pounds overweight, with a prematurely puffy chin covering a portion of his frayed collar. During the train ride from Baltimore to New York, his necktie slipped from his neck and the collar button snapped opened, then both managed to remain that way. "Absolutely not. We're convinced you were raped—fair and square, as it were. But circumstances leading up to and during the crime might give a jury pause for thought. I've been in this trade a long time, Ms. Waller. Seen many battered and raped women. If we go to court, we win. And the bastards we prosecute end up in the slammer, not in some white-collar detention facility like Allenwood. The law says we'll have to prove our case and for that we'll need a lot of help. To understand what you told the police in Easton we've scripted a timeline of events. It's important to account for every minute before and after the crime. If we don't get the sequence right, Noah Ventner's defense team will. And they'll beat us right there."

Junqueira hands a document of several pages to Eli. "Here's what we've drafted. Errors and all. Your job is to make it accurate. They say the Devil's in the details and, Ms. Waller, I can assure you he is. The side that doesn't master the details, loses. It's just that simple."

Eli scans the papers, reading every other sentence. She has no intention of doing more before her broadcast. Her rump eases into the chair and shoes she has had on all day slip from her feet and hit the floor. One foot takes a position on an open lower drawer; above it is a shapely calf that would attract most male eyes. "I'll give this my attention as soon as possible. Certainly not until after the program. You need to know up front that I'm under pressure. Rape embarrasses my male partners at the firm apparently more than me and, please keep in mind, I'm the dame who got screwed. I've tried to explain how Noah Zentner was against us from the beginning. I was always skeptical about winning Pyramid's business. My associates loathe the publicity this has engendered. That's because they're men and have never been violated. They'd have a different view if they were sexually assaulted by a wild Amazon threatening to bite off their cocks."

"Every male's dream," Hines remarks offhandedly and, when no one chuckles, adds, "Sorry, I didn't mean that."

Junqueira tries to evaluate Eli's switch in tone and concludes she is a mercurial personality. She throws her hands out, palms up, fingers outstretched. "If you're having second thoughts, we haven't a song in hell. No prosecutor will risk a trial without the prime witness, especially in a rape case."

Eli snaps, "I didn't say I was bailing out. Only that I've got far more to lose than gain. A wise woman would probably try to put this pathetic episode behind her. Do what she can to forget it. Move on with her career. If I were the only dame screwed like this, I'd probably bag it. But I'm not. Thousands of raped women will look at this case. These are weak and frightened women. Silent women. I represent the strength they don't possess. One shouldn't walk away from this responsibility. Noah Zentner took a little piece of my body and a God damn big hunk of my pride. It's time for women to speak out against this kind of abuse."

"I admire you," Junqueira states in a sympathetic tone.

Sidney Hines' pudgy, smiling face belies his love to beat his competition in court. "You understand, Ms. Waller, the media will play a major role in this case. There's talk about televising the entire trial on the Legal Channel. Our department has been approached by a major network. Others are certain to follow. Somebody will want to dramatize it in the movies."

"Women need publicity, but as you can see for yourselves, I personally have more than I need."

"The trial will divide over gender issues. Women want rapists punished. Men excuse them. It's that simple," Hines says.

"Are you trying to discourage me, Mr. Hines?" Eli asks.

"Our case is compelling but with as many holes as Swiss cheese. Zentner's hired Greenwald, Molletz, Steiner, and Mavenhouse. If they lead with Zoe Mountolive, we'll have our hands full. She's a pro at exaggerating the gray areas, maximizing the ambiguities, nurturing doubts among jurors. Talk about a pit bull."

Lawyers and their work often bring out sarcasm in Eli. "I suspect some day you'll both be defending rich clients like me and there will be another junior team representing the government. Defense is where the real money is, isn't it?"

"You don't see many old, silver-haired prosecutors, do you?" Junqueira questions with a grin. "But that's why you need youth on your side. Someday we may become rich and fat on the law, but we won't get there unless we establish ourselves as good prosecutors first. Unfortunately, this case is likely to be fought in the media as much as the courtroom. The press will hound you. It's absolutely essential not to speak about it. Reporters will talk with anybody and everybody you have contact with. Family, friends, acquaintances. Old school chums. Long abandoned heartthrobs and adolescent dates. Laundry men, cab drivers, garbage collectors, anybody. They'll try to portray you as a promiscuous lady, bedding everything with pants on."

A rap on the door by Eli's assistant director deflects their attention. "Time to get you miked up, Ms. Waller. Ten minutes to broadcast."

She slips her feet back into her shoes. "I'm on two financial shows a week. While on camera it's going to be hard to deflect questions put directly to me."

"Reply with the words 'no comment.' Stick to your professional field. And, before we scoot, one last question. What does your firm actually do?"

"The Hawthorne Group syndicates large loans and underwrites real estate securities. Real Estate Investment Trusts, for example."

"Is that how you came to know Zentner?"

"His firm approached us to refinance its debt."

"In layman's terms, what's that mean?" Junqueira asks.

"Borrowing money for building and maintaining large real estate complexes, such as office buildings, shopping centers, apartment complexes, is normally done by pension funds and insurance companies. Many buildings have lost so much value since 1986 that the rents can't pay back what's owed. In brief, the income doesn't support the debt. So instead of looking to traditional lenders to lend more or transferring ownership back to the lender, developers come to us to work out their debt problems. Pyramid Development is highly leveraged and approached us to alleviate the burden. That's a dead issue now. I'm afraid I must get on the set immediately."

As she steps toward the door, Hines throws in a final question. "Were you two dating?"

"Are you crazy? He's a married man. I don't go around busting up families."

"Of course," Junqueira says while looking at her watch. "Please review our timeline. Make notes. Make amendments. See how finely you can tune it."

Hines moves into the corridor. "Unfortunately, by the time we get a conviction, you're probably not going to like us. You might even come to look on us as the enemy, not Noah Zentner."

They are almost at the studio door through which only authorized personnel are permitted to enter. "I hope not. Staying for the show? I'm sure there's room in the audience. We can always use extra faces out there. Not many people want to watch a bunch of talking heads discussing a dry subject in front of a camera."

"Already picked up tickets," Sidney says.

Chapter Two

July 9th

La Piccola Roma on Connecticut Avenue, north of Washington D.C.'s Dupont Circle, is an unpretentious restaurant with simple Northern Italian decor, excellent pasta, and efficient but not officious service. Straight-back mahogany chairs flank tables set with white cloths and fresh summer flowers. Italian antipasti—eggplant, spinach, anchovies, and sliced tomatoes—languish on serving carts, and in the corner a dessert exhibition features regional chocolate pastries. Out of the way for the power lunches of Washington lawyers and lobbyists, it is only a third full when Gabby arrives and takes a seat at the table Ephraim Rothman has reserved, then orders a bottle of mineral water.

Ephraim has been around rabbis, of one persuasion or another, all his life and is realistic, even generous in his appraisal of them, though many congregants are mistrustful of their mysterious motivations. Eph, as she and Seth Greer refer to him, is from an old school of communal leaders which respects rabbis and considers them the rightful leaders of their congregations, not boards of elected or appointed lay officers. During his tenure as President, he scrupulously honored his conviction that the synagogue should take no action without first consulting its rabbis or do anything to displease them. The week before monthly Board meetings, he made a habit of taking Seth and Gabby to lunch to discuss the upcoming agenda. Once the congregational presidency passed to Doris Silbert, these lunches ceased.

When Ephraim's secretary called Gabby's office to arrange lunch, she wondered why. Since Eph rarely does anything without an agenda, she has a premonition of trouble. Worrying that bad things will happen is a character trait she despises yet cannot shake.

Eph Rothman takes Judaism seriously and his service to the congregation as a matter of filial duty. His family roots in the District of Columbia date from the Civil War and nurture an unbroken chain of communal leaders—some working for the Jewish Welfare Federation and others in their respective synagogues.

Eph had inherited his father's and grandfather's furniture manufacturing business when it was moderate in size and built it into a corporate giant, then took the business public and amassed a comfortable fortune. Wealth, as he likes to point out, came after his tastes for material things were already grooved. With the exception of a single indulgence, a four-passenger Cessna 182 aircraft, used primarily for weekend jaunts to the Eastern Shore of Maryland, he never purchased a big house or luxury car. His tennis is played not at a country club, but on public courts in Rock Creek Park or at Sidwell Friends School on Wisconsin Avenue. As far as Gabby can determine, he considers himself nothing more than a moderately competent furniture merchant, however lucrative the trade had become.

Money failed to shelter the Rothman family from life's sorrows. An alcoholic wife and the death of a second son to testicular cancer sensitized Ephraim to the world of suffering. Seth Greer once confided to Gabby that in the china shop of other people's feelings Eph is no raging bull.

Gabby often glances at her wristwatch, a large, unstylish sextagonal timepiece with old-fashioned Roman numerals. She loves this watch, a keepsake from her grandmother who made the fatal mistake of saying goodbye to her daughter at the dock in Bremerhaven, Germany, then returning to the family home in Hamburg to await the inevitable fall of Nazism. Gabby's mother, Hilda, presented it to her own daughter when she was accepted into rabbinical school. She never believed Gabby would wear it, nor that it would actually keep time. How much her daughter paid an expensive Austrian watchmaker in New York for repairs and service remained a secret.

Ephraim arrives at the restaurant eight minutes late, locates Gabby, and moves through scattered tables with powerful steps. His dark striped suit is immaculately pressed; his light blue shirt and silk flowered necktie well matched. He drops into the chair opposite the banquette and reaches across to receive Gabby's hand, damp from holding the glass of iced mineral water. They exchange greetings until a waiter brings lunch menus.

"I finally reached Jonathan Zentner this morning." He seems eager to pursue this as first business. "He's disappointed I can't locate Seth. I recommended Noah call you himself, an idea that didn't seem to go very far. I've known Jonathan for half of my life. We're like brothers. Suddenly, he seems unreachable. Complained he wasn't feeling well. He suffers a urinary problem and has been postponing the inevitable male plumbing job. Now he has to worry about his son. He's angry and feels Seth abandoned him in his hour of need. There is a healthy chunk of narcissism in Jon. Tends to view things in terms of how they affect him personally."

"I can sympathize with that." Gabby is not yet focused on Jonathan Zentner's problems. "Seth didn't do me any favors by leaving without so much as a goodbye. No transition. No instructions. Just vanished in the dark of night. Lots of people feel hurt at what he did. But they don't have to pick up the pieces after him. I feel like I'm following circus elephants down Main Street with a broom and bucket. It doesn't sound as though Jonathan Zentner wants my assistance. Perhaps Noah will."

Gabby decides on a *salade niçoise* and puts down her menu to study Ephraim's face, still reading the selections on his own menu. His hair, richly salted with gray, is cut fairly close to the scalp. Round glasses with thin rims, the kind often worn by lawyers, become bowls for his eyes. There is an unnatural roll to his lower lip. He looks as though he is holding back something. She tells herself that perhaps he has just finished reading a popular self-help paperback titled *How to Deliver Bad News*, by Gladys Goldstone, Ph.D.

Actually, someone had recommended Goldstone's work to her years before, thinking how rabbis are often conveyers of bad news and could use tips how to be artful in the role. The book is full of pithy wisdom but thin on psychological research, written to fill a commercial niche in the growing library of *How To* titles.

She imagines Ephraim checking off chapter titles from Goldstone's book.

Chapter One: *Create a Sense of Concern for the Recipient's Welfare*

After making a lunch selection, Ephraim talks a little about his wife, Gloria, and their grandchildren. No mention of her drinking. Nor of the three grown children, all of whom suffer from maladjustment, probably related to their alcoholic mother. There's talk of the second son, David, coming to work at Contemporary Designs Furniture Inc. and someday managing the firm. Gabby perceives this discussion as a mere digression.

Chapter Two: *Set the Groundwork to Reduce Shock*

"No doubt, you've heard that the Board at Ohav has convened several extraordinary meetings," Ephraim says.

"To which I was not invited. I don't like being left out, but then I say to myself—let's look at the bright side. Some meetings are worth missing. Perhaps the majority. So I just called a friend from the Old Biddies Confederation—that's a club of single women like myself who accompany each other to nice places—restaurants, movies, the ballet. Occasionally basketball games. Funny thing; Eph. The congregation usually buzzes with rumors. Not these days. My spies are mute. Not a peep from anyone. Whatever it is, I reckon people don't want me to know. I won't fib; it hurts."

"Yes, of course. That's only natural."

"The congregation's got decisions to make. Selecting a rabbi is usually a spicy issue."

The waiter removes a place setting to make more room on the table. From a note pad, he recites the luncheon specials as if auditioning for a TV sitcom and is visibly disappointed when his recitation produces no takers. Both selections come from the regular menu.

When alone again, Ephraim is businesslike. "The Board's asked me to communicate with you."

Chapter Three: *Make the Recipient Feel Good About Him/ Herself*

So this is it, Dr. Goldstone! Gabby prepares herself. From the dour look on his face, it can't be good.

"A congregation's board is a strange entity, Gabby. In reality, it's nothing more than the sum of the individual opinions of its members, yet it is supposed to reflect the will of the membership. As you know, few of its decisions are unanimous, so there's always a majority and minority view. As with the law, there's no right and wrong, just differing interpretations."

Gabby doesn't like what she hears yet is momentarily distracted when the busboy arrives with a basket of freshly baked breads and rolls, accompanied by a vial of yellow-green olive oil. Her glass of mineral water needs refilling. Ephraim orders iced tea for himself.

He tries to pick up his lost momentum. "First of all, the Board and the Trustees have asked me to convey deep appreciation for the work you're doing. Everybody recognizes that Seth's resignation put a lot of pressure on you. When things settle down they're probably going to reward you. Financially, I mean. Real shekels, not just commendations. The matter hasn't yet come to the agenda, but it will in due course."

"You said first of all," Gabby interrupts, for she senses the shoe has not yet dropped.

"Well," he says after considerable hesitation, "The Trustees have appointed a Rabbinical Search Committee to find Seth's successor. We're going to bring several candidates here for interviews. Maybe some trial sermons, but that is not yet settled and I know your rabbinical association takes a dim view of pulpit auditions. None of this can be accomplished behind your back."

Her eyes fall, but only momentarily for she ratchets them up to glare across the table. They are colder than she would like, but accurately reflect her disappointment. Acid flows into her stomach and she does not know if there's anything she wants to reply. Until that moment she had entertained hopes for an automatic promotion to Seth's post. No rabbinical search. Just a field promotion, like a colonel becoming a brigadier when the general is injured. The next-in-command just steps up. Everybody knows she can do the job. But obviously the Trustees and Board of Directors do not share this thinking. An interlude of silence. Ambient noise from the restaurant abhors the vacuum. It is Gabby who finally says, "Will I be a candidate before this Search Committee?"

He takes an audible breath which is broken when the waiter arrives with their entrees. Bad timing. Neither has much appetite for food, but the waiter doesn't know this and sets the plates before his diners. Nothing can happen until he finishes.

Ephraim resumes at a slow pace. "You know, I've always held you in the highest esteem as a rabbi and, I hope, a friend. In my judgment, you're the best rabbinic mind this congregation's ever had, male or female—and my family's collective memory goes back several generations."

Gladys Goldstone writes several paragraphs about what comes before and what comes after the pivotal word *but*. "You're the best employee the Allied Can and Rust Company has ever had on its payroll. No firm in our industry has ever enjoyed more loyalty and commitment. *But* unfortunately we're forced to make some personnel changes. You know, modernize the plant with new talent and strike out in a new direction." Praise and accolade precede the *but*. Then the ax falls. Gabby has always believed there's a certain cruelty in the formula. Spirits are lifted high so the fall becomes more precipitous.

"Yes," he continues, "I've watched you function with an insightful mind and a good heart. We watched you grow from a raw, unseasoned rabbinical graduate to a mature, thoughtful woman. A perfect complement to Seth's flamboyance and that's meant as a compliment. Personally, and here I'm speaking for myself and not the congregation, I wish the Board would appoint you our Senior Rabbi. And I am not alone, though our opinion is far from the majority. The Board has its reasons—not unreasonable ones, I should add."

Of course there are reasons. Gabby believes there is only one. Gender. She's a woman and no major American congregation has a woman in the senior post.

She carefully positions her fork to signify that she has eaten all she desires. A busboy viewing this would conclude she wanted her plate removed. But it's too early for that. Saliva sticks in her throat. "If no one else will, I would like to tender my own name to the Search Committee. With a little luck, somebody in the congregation will second my nomination."

He imitates her with his own fork. His hand strokes his chin, then does what surprises her. It reaches across the table and drops over her wrist, patting it against the tablecloth. "If Seth had only kept his fly zippered this wouldn't have happened."

"So I'm not going to be considered even as a candidate?"

"That's not final. The Board can't and won't just overlook you. I won't let that happen. That's a personal promise."

"Will you recommend me, Eph? You know I'm up to the job."

He pauses too long. "If you wish."

She pulls her hand from under his. "That's not very enthusiastic. I guess I shouldn't ask you to give the keynote address when I run for the Senate."

He fumbles. "Are you sure you want me to? Nobody would deny you're qualified. But there are compelling reasons why a man would be preferred. Seth did this congregation a lot of damage. Some members argue that Ohav Shalom cannot return to health until there's a strong male leader to restore our tarnished image. If a man doesn't succeed in his position, nobody will ever trust another spiritual leader on our pulpit."

"So it's because I'm a woman, is it?"

"You could put it that way."

Her lips tighten and her fingers dust the silverware. "What else, Eph? All my life I've been on the outside track. No matter how hard I try I don't seem to run along the post. Seems I must run farther and longer than the next guy just to make the finish line."

He reaches out a second time to make physical contact. She pulls back. "You want the truth or pap?"

"Straight. Unadulterated. You might as well pile it on thick."

"This will hurt, Gabby. Are you prepared?"

"Give me a second to adjust my armor, then pull the trigger."

"Truth is, the gender question arises only indirectly. We're a mature congregation. Women work in the majority of our families. I don't know of anybody who doesn't respect professional women and want them to succeed. We have two female Trustees and five more women on the current Board of Directors. The presiding President is a woman. Most large congregations in this country have yet to appoint women to their senior post, but if there's any congregation prepared to pioneer, it's Ohav Shalom. Washington women are expected to work, to succeed and, most of all, to lead. There's absolutely no reason why a woman cannot be appointed to Seth's job." He pauses to emphasize the congregation's commitment to gender equality. "The issue is not that you're a woman, Gabby."

"If it isn't gender, what is it?" She sounds like a prosecutor trying to capture the truth by smothering it.

"You're single and without children."

"Because I'm not married that doesn't make me barren!"

"But you're thirty-three years old, if my reckoning isn't wrong. No one on the Board thinks that you have a significant other in your life. If you do, it would be helpful for us to know. But to our knowledge, you're not engaged. Even if the right man should pop into your life tomorrow, it takes time to court. Time to romance. Time to get married. And time to conceive a child."

"So Ohav Shalom won't appoint a single, childless woman as Senior Rabbi?"

"I didn't say that. Who knows, when push comes to shove, the Search Committee may not be concerned with this. Of course, the appointment of a Senior Rabbi takes a vote from the full congregational membership. A Special Plenary Congregational Convocation will be called. That's how Seth was appointed. It's spelled out in the congregation's bylaws."

"I don't understand this thinking. Or maybe I understand it too well."

"We're a family oriented organization. For each single member, we have close to five hundred families. The vast majority are young families with children in our religious school and Bar/Bat Mitzvah program. Half of these have young girls. These families see their daughters eventually entering the work force as professionals, but they also see them as mothers of their grandchildren. And that's important. Everything they value is centered around the family and children. A single woman as Senior Rabbi is a very good role model in one respect, but a bad one in another."

Gabby curls her lips. "I can't believe what I'm hearing. These people you talk about, who are they? On what planet do they live? And in what century? How can they expect me to go through college and rabbinical school, then work my fanny off Monday through Sunday and still have anything that resembles a normal family life? Who else works seven days a week? And is on call twenty-four hours a day, both in the synagogue and at home? How can they be so rigid?"

He sighs, starts to respond, then pauses and starts again. "I'm sorry. I knew this would hurt. It isn't nice stuff and you, of all people, deserve better treatment. But the Congregation is bigger than those on today's Board. Ohav Shalom is ninety-six years old and will be in operation long after all of us are six feet under. It must live both for today and tomorrow. And to do this it must constantly recruit new families. If all its members were single, it would immediately decay. Without families, without children matriculating through our various schools, there won't be a future. Today's Board must guarantee the endurance of the institution."

She conceals moisture forming in her eyes. A napkin would remove it, but she doesn't want to give Eph the satisfaction. "You people don't understand the trade-offs for being a female rabbi. Dating isn't normal. Why would an eligible American male want to date a rabbi?"

"For the normal reasons, I guess."

"If you're implying sex, then think again, pal."

"The majority of our members expect you to enjoy a normal private life. You're entitled to privacy like everyone else."

"I don't think you really mean that. There's hardly a daughter in the congregation past puberty who's still a virgin. Parents have learned to accept sexual norms of the day. But that doesn't mean their rabbi has license to live by these new norms. The congregation wouldn't tolerate its rabbi in a extramarital affair. Look where it got Seth."

"You're in a fishbowl. The price for celebrity. You're an absolutely sterling model for our youth in every respect but one. There isn't a family in town that wouldn't be delighted to have a daughter as well-educated, dedicated, and successful as you. But to a point. The single flaw is your marital status. The Search Committee will want the Senior Rabbi of Ohav Shalom to fit a mold. Particularly after what Seth did."

Gabby's stomach is a tumultuous sea of gas, placing any attempt to eat her *salade niçoise* out of the question. She tries to keep the message and the messenger separate but for the moment she doesn't like either one. How can the congregation be so insensitive? How dare it exhibit so little gratitude!

Lunch ends on a sour note. Food is left uneaten. The warmth of friendship with Ephraim is chilled to the bone. He makes several attempts to bring them together again, but fails on each occasion. She offers to pay her own bill which he absolutely refuses to consider. It would have been better, he thinks to himself, if someone else had delivered the bad news. It's too late; the damage is done.

DURING THE SUCCEEDING DAYS, GABBY BELIEVES THAT Ephraim will call to apologize, perhaps change his view—at least to become her sponsor as a candidate for Seth's job. He doesn't. That makes her suspicious. Perhaps he isn't the friend she believed him to be. Or there's a congregational agenda she doesn't appreciate.

The moment the congregation contacts the Rabbinical Placement Commission in New York regarding candidates for Seth's job, Gabby's telephone rings with inquiries from rabbinical colleagues. Ohav Shalom in the Nation's Capital serves many in Washington's Jewish political and diplomatic community. The aura of the Potomac rests on her pulpit. Consulting with colleagues about the job is humiliating for it is obvious she is being passed over. She would like to explain the predicament, but no colleagues ask. Even female colleagues fail to make inquiries about her status. The general insensitivity drives her into further isolation.

A colleague in Ohio who graduated from Gabby's seminary three years ahead of her, and who subsequently served a congregation of 260 families, initiates several discussions. His family is growing up and, with education costs well above his ability to pay from his salary, he's looking for a larger congregation that can provide more income. His wife grew up in Alexandria, Virginia, just across the Potomac from the District of Columbia. Ohav Shalom might be a perfect fit. The conversation inevitably leads to Seth. A rumor circulates in Ohio that he had been seen in Safed, Israel, writing a book on the doctrine of *Zimzum* in the *Kaballah*. Gabby ends the discussion by promising additional information that might help his candidacy, then hangs up and sits gazing at the opposite wall, feeling hollow. That afternoon, she fields calls from four other rabbis currently serving congregations in New York, Rhode Island, South Carolina, and Texas.

WITH THE HELP OF CHUCK MAXIMILLIAN BROWNER, she sequesters herself in her office on Friday morning in order to polish two sermons, one a speech for the short *Shabbat* evening service and the other, a full address for *Shabbat* morning during the Bar Mitzvah of Jeremy Sylvan Meir, the third and last Bar Mitzvah from a distinguished family of lawyers and judges.

Chuck keeps callers away from Gabby until 10:35 a.m. when he pokes his head into her study. "Noah Zentner's on the phone. Wants to speak with you. Says its urgent."

She has expected a call to come from his father, Jonathan Zentner, and is relieved Noah has taken the initiative himself.

It's an inconvenient moment, but then she's not sure of a better time until Saturday afternoon at the earliest.

The call is forwarded to Gabby's desk.

"Rabbi Lewyn, this is Noah Zentner. Seth Greer's friend. I guess you've read about me."

"I have. I know your father's been looking for Seth. I'm afraid I can't help. Seth doesn't want to stay in contact with me, at least not for a while."

Silence intervenes while Noah Zentner seems to process that disclosure. "I understand," he replies in a tone of resignation. "Seth and I are in the same boat. I thought he'd stay in touch with me. Apparently not. I was sure he'd call when this nasty business about me hit the papers. Wrong again. Not a peep."

"Rumor says he's in Israel and he may not know."

"I doubt that. He's too close to his children. One or both of his kids would tell me."

"I guess you knew him better than I. We talked a lot. Sometimes very personally. What happened was a great shock."

"Then you didn't really know the true Seth," Noah responds. "He's very complex. Lives constantly in a danger zone."

"I didn't appreciate that until now. I feel like a tortoise creeping along the roadside. Missed the important clues. On another subject, I never wanted to interfere in your relationship with him. What you don't know is that at your wedding, Seth had the flu and, for a while, it looked as though he might not be able to officiate. I was standing by to fill in. Of course, in the end, he rallied. He was a pretty sick puppy. You could say I'm almost the rabbi that married you and Morgan."

"We're separated these days. I couldn't hold my marriage together with charges of rape leveled at me. Troubles seem to multiply. Get in one pickle and before long you're embroiled in several more."

"I'm sorry, Noah. If there's anything the congregation can do, it will."

"Not the congregation. I have a personal favor to ask you. I'll need a character witness if the District Attorney indicts me. My attorneys said it's important to have a rabbi talk about my background. You're my rabbi now."

"I don't know you that well."

"A trial won't happen for months. There's time to get

acquainted."

"I won't rule that out."

"The immediate favor I need to ask is this. I'm calling from New York. I'm meeting with my lawyers on Monday morning to map out an overall strategy. Is it possible for you to fly up and meet with them? I'll take care of your expenses. Put you in a hotel on Sunday night."

She flips open her electronic scheduler and taps the screen for Monday's schedule. Full. Two community meetings in the morning. Lunch with the Washington Board of Rabbis at which she must provide a *drash*, a rabbinical interpretation of the weekly Torah portion. A wedding consultation at three in the afternoon, followed by two conferences which Chuck has scheduled without providing names of the individuals involved. When he does that, he usually fills in details first thing in the morning.

"Sorry. I'm fully booked Monday. Too many appointments to shuffle around. Perhaps another time?"

"Saturday morning?"

"I've got services. With Seth gone, I've got to be there. No backup."

"If necessary, I think I can get the lawyers to meet on Sunday morning. Fly up the evening before. I know you probably have social plans for Saturday evening, but this is important to me. If you stay at the Pierre, could you make a Sunday meeting at 9:00 a.m.?"

Gabby mocks the myth about herself. People immediately jump to the conclusion she has a million dates when the reality is just the opposite. Single men don't know what to do with a female rabbi, so they take the course of least resistance and avoid asking her out. She wonders if God ever intended for his clergy to suffer such an injustice.

"Yes, if it will help you, Noah," she says, "Sunday morning in New York might work."

"I'm grateful, Rabbi Lewyn. I know this is an inconvenience. Is Hotel Pierre all right?"

"More than just all right. Absolutely elegant."

"I'll reserve a room and will leave a message about the exact time and place with the lawyers. For the present, I'm in a state of limbo, a suspect but not yet indicted. My father is here to help. We're staying at our Manhattan apartment on 82nd Street. Our New York number is 212-657-9889."

"I look forward to seeing you again, Noah."

GABBY STOPS EVERYTHING AND LEANS HARD AGAINST HER desk chair. There are compelling reasons why she should have declined. She is booked late through Saturday afternoon. And she has already made a movie date with a girlfriend for Saturday night. Moreover, she has no rabbinical backup in the event of sudden sickness or death in the congregation. But she didn't say no. In fact, she quite eagerly accepted. There is a special draw in the Big Apple.

She dials a 212 number known by heart and waits while a phone rings in New York City. Eventually a machine answers: "You've reached Timothy Matternly. Leave a message and I'll call you just as soon as possible."

Gabby declines to leave a message that can be heard by anybody at the Presbyterian Office of Community Affairs on West 18th Street. She has reasons for wanting privacy.

An hour later she tries again to make contact with the Reverend Timothy Matternly. No success. A third attempt before leaving her office is equally unproductive. Then, while driving home along Massachusetts Avenue she connects from her cellular phone. The tenor voice on the other end resonates with crisp clarity. Like the voices of people known for many years, it is comforting.

"Tim, it's Gabby."

"The nicest thing that's happened today. All week, for that matter. Great to hear from you, Lovey."

"Know why I'm calling?"

"You usually come up with great ideas. There are three things your uncircumcised Philistine cherishes most in this world: Jesus Christ, Gabrielle Lewyn, and linguine with white, not red, clam sauce. Yes, exactly in that order. So when it comes to calls from the thing I love second most, I'm all ears. Incidentally, if you don't already know, I've got a secret for you. My first love never telephones. For that matter, He rarely bothers to answer my prayers. Don't even know if He listens."

Gabby is accustomed to Tim's banter, sometimes irreverent, sometimes caustic, but always witty. It can be downright offensive, but for the most part is entertaining. He is inordinately verbal as New Yorkers tend to be. "I'll be in the City this Saturday night. Staying at the Pierre. Are you free?"

"Saturday night. Got dinner reservations in a new Mongolian restaurant on Second Avenue. Seedy but the food's supposed to be outstanding. Can you join us? Company's guaranteed to be good. Someone special I'd really like you to meet."

"I'd rather do something hormonal. Alone…with you."

"Now that's an invitation to take seriously. But I've already made an engagement."

"Break it, Tim. I'll be at the Pierre with a surprise. I'll leave the hotel room number on your home machine. Don't ask at the desk. Just come up. Our usual knock." She punches the phone to stop transmitting over a cellular network. This gives her something to look forward to on the weekend.

GABBY ARRIVES AT NEW YORK'S LAGUARDIA ON THE U.S. Airways five o'clock shuttle from Washington's National Airport and takes a taxi to the Pierre Hotel on Fifth Avenue at 61st. After telephoning Tim's phone machine with her room number, she works out for forty-five minutes on Nautilus equipment in the hotel exercise room then orders from Room Service a Heineken beer.

The workout produces a film of perspiration down the spine, on her neck, under her armpits, and in the groin. She pauses momentarily before the bathroom mirror on her way to the shower to admire a trim figure with breasts that have not yet begun to droop or hips to spread. Her legs are her best asset—lean and shapely with the calf muscles of a ballet dancer. She likes what she sees and sighs with a humorous gust of self-deprecation. Why such a body doesn't attract a permanent male partner of equal or better physical attainment seems a terrible waste of Nature. She'd like to believe God takes some interest in her personal welfare but knows She, He, or It doesn't.

There is a chasm between what she does and what she believes. The liturgical prayers she faithfully recites from the pulpit refer to an omniscient god who watches over the affairs of individual worshippers. To her mind this type of divine providence is a wish rather than a reality. Ethical or unethical, selfless or selfish, people seem to share earthly rewards and punishments quite randomly. No fairness. No equity. No underlying rhyme or reason. The best she can commend to her inquiring congregants is a deity who somehow watches over the human species and (despite wars, disease, and an inequitable distribution of the earth's resources and wealth) somehow permits humanity to flourish in increasing numbers. But as far as individuals are concerned, hey, they're on their own.

Her nipples cry out for a baby to suckle and remind her it's time to examine her breasts for potential malignancies. With hot shower water coursing over her shoulders, she raises her left arm and tucks it behind her head to expose the left breast.When satisfied there's nothing to worry about she performs a similar test on her right breast, thinking what a health freak she has become.

A passion for daily exercise is just the beginning. One aspirin tablet every other day because the *New England Journal of Medicine* published two scientific studies showing how an aspirin three times a week proves a powerful inhibitor of bowel cancer and cardiovascular disease. Red meat and fatty foods vanished from her diet years before. Self-improvement starts with the body but spins beyond it. Biweekly cooking classes teach her enough culinary skills to prepare a respectable meal, if or when Mr. Right breezes into her life. Mr. Right, she jokes, doesn't seem to know the gastronomic pleasures he's missing. Tennis lessons she takes to play near the top of the Tuesday Night Tennis Club ladder haven't helped her volley, but have provided many good laughs and one reasonably attractive date. Unfortunately, the blond-haired Gentile Apollo-types with big white teeth, enveloping smiles, and hair floating over the ears who dominate the courts with their confident strokes and big serves, never give her the time of day. Gentile men are intimidated by her rabbinical status; Jewish ones, simply puzzled. Men looking for a tumble in the hay disregard her entirely.

Alternate Monday nights she devotes to the Professional Women's Book Club, a gaggle of female physicians, lawyers, accountants, and teachers scratching the Glass Ceiling for career recognition. These are serious professionals who support an active female network to counter the Old Boys clubs that exclude them. This puts her into a frame of mind for Thursday nights—her favorite community service which promotes feminine self-respect among high school girls in the besieged public schools.

What's left of her free time is devoted to the Temple. Meetings of Jews multiply like bacteria: committees, subcommittees, and sub-subcommittees, some formal, some ad hoc in which business and pleasure often merge.

Before turning off the shower, she works a healthy lather along her legs and thighs and shaves away soft body hair. Once the water is off, she removes small scissors from her traveling kit and crops away errant hair growing around the groin.

An oversized bath towel promotes a sense of luxury. She wraps it around her torso and moves to the bed to repaint toenails whose crimson has begun to chip. There is still a half hour to dry before Tim's arrival.

She met him nine years before when they were divinity students at distant and quite different seminaries, both in their final year of training. The occasion was an ecumenical conference on gay rights in New York City. About twenty percent of the attendees were clergy, the rest were gays and lesbians along with human rights advocates. At the time, the nation was just beginning to confront the legitimacy of sexual diversity and its champions shared an unpopular yet pioneering spirit.

In a small breakout session, Gabby found herself at a table with three Protestant clergymen, a handsome, strong gay athlete who looked like a model in *The New York Times Magazine*, and two lesbians with hermaphroditic appearances. The subject under discussion was biblical authority for homosexuality. A white-collared Catholic priest in a rumpled black suit passed around a handout of relevant excerpts from the New Testament then opened the discussion. No one mentioned the Old Testament since societal attitudes before the Common Era were notoriously homophobic.

Tim Matternly possessed flowing rusty-blond hair he pulled together in a ponytail and a manicured beard. Gabby immediately recognized in him a breed of young Presbyterian ministers, aggressive and well-schooled. She was mesmerized by the clear, musical quality of his voice and the fluidity with which he delineated his ideas. Within a half-hour other participants deferred to his authority. Until he referred to the Hebraic attitude toward homosexuality as barbaric, she had been satisfied to listen. But an anti-Semitic remark forced her to take issue.

In the introductions, Tim had obviously overlooked the fact

that she was a rabbinical student, not a community organizer. He took strong issue with her, citing a string of Old Testament references. But Gabby was the better student of history, particularly the Inter-Testamental Period about which they found themselves debating. He tried to rebuff her arguments but simply lacked the information, a fact which soon became apparent to those around the table. Eventually, others broke up a nasty argument.

Tangling with Tim Matternly caused Gabby to fear the cultural and spiritual gap separating Jews and Protestants. During the refreshment break, she was surprised when he worked his way through the milling crowd and addressed her. "That wasn't what I expected. Nor did I intend to sound so hostile. Please forgive me."

"I'm not sure why I should. I believe you meant exactly what you said. And your scholarship is flawed. I can forgive you for being a bad pedant, but not for spreading anti-Semitism."

Tim smiled widely to reveal a fine set of teeth with a marked cleavage between the incisors. "I stand corrected in my facts and humiliated in my intention. I had underestimated you, Gabrielle Lewyn, or Rabbi Lewyn."

"Not yet. In a year if I pass my exams."

"Oh, I'm certain you will. I would imagine you could teach your professors a thing or two. You certainly gave this seminarian a trouncing. I'd like to make amends. Allow me to get down on my knees and plead for pardon, then let me stand and invite you to a sleazy saloon on 28th Street. Sorry, I just remembered that Jewish people don't think much of kneeling."

"True enough, but we've got a healthy reputation for drinking. You don't merit it, but I'll accept your apology. I could use some alcoholic refreshment. The pursuit of gay rights is exhausting."

ONCE YOU CRACKED THROUGH THE MANUFACTURED charm that emanated from Tim like cheap perfume, he was exceedingly good company. Conversation at Tyler's Pub was a relief after the righteous talk at the conference. Tim proved to be a devout Christian who believed profoundly in the spirit, as well as the discipline of Christianity. Upon ordination, he intended to avoid combat in the church ministry and attach himself to the

Presbyterian Social Action Commission working in New York City slums. There, as he put it succinctly, he could practice what he did not preach, and keep his faith in Jesus to himself. No proselytizing and no evangelism. That spirit appealed to Gabby.

The next night they skipped the evening session altogether and ate in a Basque restaurant, then walked up and down well-lit Manhattan streets. Tim kissed her goodnight and, what was more astounding, she kissed him back. When the conference ended, he invited her for dinner in his apartment before her flight back to the rabbinical seminar in the Midwest. After a meal of stir-fried chicken and salad, they made love, concurring that there was no harm in a consensual act of sex that had no chance in hell of maturing into a lasting romance.

Time proved them both dead wrong. What began as a one-night stand continued for eight years. The relationship worked for no other reason than it was destined not to work. In the course of the years, they made love, fought, made love again, broke up and then reunited, only to start the process again and again. Every time they came together they renewed the same pledge—never, never to fall in love.

Easier said than done. Gabby withheld full emotional commitment. Tim didn't, but was mature enough to accept the inevitable. Romance between a Presbyterian minister and a rabbi was simply preposterous. No one would take it seriously, especially their respective professional associations. More importantly, conversion of a devout Presbyterian to Judaism was out of the question, as was the thought of a rabbi converting to Christianity. What worked about this unholy alliance was that both parties understood the limitations, or thought they did. Naturally, they spoke of their dreams for the future. Someday, Gabby would find a Jewish husband and Tim, a Protestant wife. Both would become parents. They agreed that when the time came, one sign from the other would signal the end of the relationship, at least the sexual part. No hard feelings and a zillion wonderful memories. Seldom did they fail to compliment themselves on their wisdom and maturity. The mind may be disciplined, but the heart knows no governance.

IN HER ROOM AT THE PIERRE, GABBY BRUSHES HER teeth and blow-dries her hair whose errant gray strands, emissaries of the future, she has begun to recolor to the original brunette.

During a rabbinic convocation in St. Louis, she managed to steal away from the meeting and shop in Union Station Mall. Though totally out of character, she browsed through Victoria's Secret and bought herself a diaphanous nightgown and see-through panties. At home in Washington, she tried them on before a dressing mirror and concluded she looked uttterly ridiculous. It would take truckloads of seductive props to transform this modest woman into anything even resembling a sex kitten.

Tim Matternly sees things quite differently. "Ravishing," he says inside her hotel room when she opens the front of her robe to reveal the see-through underwear beneath. She stands high on bare toes, now brightly painted, to draw herself up to his bewhiskered chin.

"Brought a bottle of Scotch," he says as she leads him into the room, her arm interlocking with his.

They sit on the bed, holding hands. It is an awkward moment. The pace of sex is difficult to set. Tim slows things down.

"So tell me now, what brings you to the Big Apple?"

"What if I told you, you did?"

A nervous giggle he immediately regrets slips from his lips. "I wouldn't believe you. This is Saturday night. You'd have to miss your religious school in the morning. I don't get that kind of billing. Besides, I can't see you booking into the Pierre when we've always used my pad in the past."

"If I tell you the truth, you'll have to keep it secret. Professional confidentiality."

"I can handle that."

"You've read about Noah Zentner in the papers? The fellow accused of raping Eli Waller on Chesapeake Bay?"

"Who hasn't? Everybody loves a juicy rape. There's no TV or newspaper without the gory details. Looks like they've got Zentner as naked as a parading nudist on Fifth Avenue. How are you involved in this?"

"The Zentners are old-time members of Ohav Shalom. Seth Greer and Noah Zentner are close personal friends. Their families were always together. Now that Seth's no longer on the scene, I'm their rabbi—by default. They've asked me to meet tomorrow morning with his lawyers about being a character witness. I hardly know Noah."

Tim takes both Gabby's hands in his and cants his torso, fixing his light-brown eyes on her. "Gabby, listen to your friend Timothy and listen good. Be careful. They're using you to further Noah Zentner's defense. They'll expect you to stand before a jury and say nice things about a man everybody knows is a first-class prick. Prosecutors will discredit not only what you say but who you are. They'll demean you and your profession. To use a tired expression, ask yourself not what you can do for your country, but what you can do for Gabby Lewyn. There's nothing in this for you but abuse. They won't compensate you for being a character witness. Lawyers get fat fees; the expert witnesses get full compensation, but character witnesses get zilch. This will also destroy you in the feminist movement."

"My career's already flattening out. I've been told that my advancement in the congregation is limited. They don't want an unmarried thirty-three-year-old childless woman as chief. I'm the wrong role model for young girls."

"Bastards. If they weren't running an upstanding Jewish congregation in Washington, I'd say they'd be perfect for a Presbyterian parish in New York. So they've already given you the 'We Love You But' treatment?"

"You got it, pal. Bull's-eye."

"You gotta fight right from the start. No Gabby Lewyn as Rabbi Number One, then no Rabbi Lewyn as Number Two."

"It might come to that. But not yet."

"Tell them in the meantime you're not gonna be a character witness for Noah Zentner or anybody else."

"He's entitled to a fair trial and character witnesses are part of his defense. It wasn't his fault that Seth Greer disappeared."

Tim disengages his hands from hers and stands up. He snatches the paper bag with the bottle of Scotch and looks around for a bucket of ice usually found in New York hotels. Glasses are produced from the bathroom. "Not in your job description, Lovey. Read your employment contract. Where does it say you must testify for members of the congregation just because they pay annual dues?"

"Not in so many words. But service to the members is implied. Especially when they're in trouble."

On the bed, her knees are arched high in front, exposing her painted toes on the bedspread. He sits before them and massages the upper portion of her foot rising above the ankle. As they talk, his massage slowly moves higher to the well-defined, athletic calf and strokes the relaxed muscle. She likes him to touch her just about anywhere, except when she's ticklish and that only happens when she's anxious, annoyed, or cold. A desire for his fingers to migrate along the leg toward the pelvis is frustrated when he stops short of her knee.

"When you called me on Wednesday, I invited you to dinner with a friend," Tim says.

"If this friend is female, I don't want to talk about her. I'd only get jealous."

"It is, Gabby. A woman I've been dating now for several months."

"Why didn't you say something?" her voice gags. Words which usually flow from her mouth with ease suddenly don't.

"Because the relationship caught me off-guard. Sally's a divorcee with two young daughters. She's had a hard time since her divorce. The most unlikely woman in the world to affect me like this. I'm aware it's a dangerous relationship, so I'm going easy."

"Serious? I mean real serious?"

"Probably more so from my part than hers, but yes, it's serious. Real serious? Well, only time will tell that."

"Do you sleep with her? You don't have to withhold from me. I'm tough. I wouldn't like it, but might be able to countenance a one-night stand. But if you say you're sleeping with her on a regular basis, I'll just find a bridge to jump off. What are we talking about here in uptown, the Queensboro, or is it the Tri-Boro? So are you sleeping with her regularly, Tim?"

He nods affirmatively.

Her eyes begin to glaze with tears which are resisted. "She better be a great screw because, if not, I don't want to have to give her lessons. God, how I've dreaded this."

His tone is low and without its usual joviality. "I've dreaded this too, Love. I never thought I'd be delivering such news to you. For all these years I feared you making this speech to me. You're the most desirable woman in my life. I fell in love with you from the day we met and never stopped loving you. And I continue to fall in love each time we're together. When you leave me, I can hardly see through the tears and I go through terrible, terrible withdrawal. One, two, sometimes three or four days. I used to wake up with a nightmare that you were sitting in a hotel room just like this, telling me that you found a wonderful man who's crazy about you, with a dick three inches longer than mine. Rich and famous and smarter than you are, which is somewhere between a double and triple genius. In the nightmare I'm the one looking for a bridge to jump off."

Her eyes fall over the painted toenails then focus on the beginning of a bunion behind the big toe where her foot rubs against her shoes.

"There's anger inside me, Gabby. Directed at you. You've managed to screw up every relationship I've had with other women. Every time I meet a decent woman and matriculate through the get-to-know-ya phase I compare her with you and nobody, I mean nobody, matches up. I'd think about you and drop my dates like a hot potato. Every time I met someone decent, I became more depressed. What I always wanted was you and what I couldn't have has always been you. Sure, we make wild, wonderful love together. It's always great until one of us has to leave. Then it feels like cascading over a waterfall. For years, I've known that if I couldn't break the deadly cycle, I'd go crazy. Sally's my only chance. I hope you understand that."

Gabby untangles her feet and rotates forward on her knees. Her bath robe falls open revealing the semi-opaque bra. With both hands she captures Tim's head, draws her lips close and kisses his eyes. Once, twice, then smothers them with her lips. She sighs in her throaty voice, "That's the same speech I've been rehearsing for you, Timmy. Once, I put it on tape and replayed it so that the words would be perfect."

He stretches himself to plant his lips on her neck and kisses.

"Tim, have you passed the point of no return with Sally?"

"No. Absolutely not. Anything can happen. We haven't had our big blowup yet. You know, boy meets girl, boy loses girl, boy regains girl. We haven't gone through the second stage."

"Are you prepared to take on her children?"

"The father's very active. It's a responsible divorce. No acrimony. The girls are great. I never thought of myself as an instant father, but it's easy. And without the financial responsibility. When they reach the terrible years of puberty I'll probably regret everything. But so far, so good."

Gabby stands, opens her bathrobe and, with a dramatic movement from a sex film she saw on pay-TV in a hotel, lets it slip from her shoulders to the floor. "Hey, sailor, what d'ya think of my new outfit?"

"I think it barely covers the most beautiful woman I've ever known."

"I appreciate that," she replies. "If I didn't believe that we'd be in the same pickle a month from now if we don't come down to reality, I'd strip off these shreds of nothing and jump you. But that would only make me cry and, God damn it, I'm not going to cry, Timmy. You're sole witness to this extraordinary act of bravery. I want you to testify to the fact that I'm not, repeat, not crying. And if anybody asks, you must tell them, Timmy boy, that Gabby Lewyn didn't shed a single tear."

"Want some Scotch?" He feels enfeebled.

"No. Absolutely not. But I want you to leave the bottle behind when you leave. Forget about me jumping off a bridge. Old Gabby has too much invested in this world to check out when a good friend follows his brain rather than his heart. I'm going to pour myself a stiff and I mean stiff drink. Then I'm going to sit on this bed and maybe have a second and third. I'll probably cry long and hard until there are no more tears left in me. Eventually I'll fall asleep. And when I wake up tomorrow morning, I'm going to my meeting with Noah Zentner's lawyers. No red eyes. No self-pity. No sorrow. I'm going to walk away and move on."

"You'll find someone soon. We've prevented each other from finding the right mates," Tim says with half-hearted conviction.

"Perhaps," she replies with an equal measure of skepticism.

BY 10:35 P.M., GABBY HAS A HEADACHE FROM THREE Scotches. She is not tipsy, though her memory cannot reconstruct a long, silent descent into sadness. Not only does her head ache, but there is a throbbing spasm in her stomach. Accompanying this involuntary contraction comes weeping—not a cry or wail, but an upsurge of sorrow from deep inside. It begins in the gut and wells up to a pitch, then recedes. She has observed this response in mourners standing beside the open graves of their loved one.

Until Tim stepped out of her life, she never had to acknowledge how important his friendship was. For his replacement, she will be forced into what her girlfriends dub *the meat market*. For the eligible men in Washington, she will be competing with women whose biological clocks are ticking away the final years. Single women facing the prospects of not becoming mothers are consummate daters and even more passionate lovers. One finds them in restaurants seated with their dates, their eyes blazing with animation, their smiles open and toothy, their hands searching for flesh to fondle.

She is dozing on her bed. Her body is heavy and her insides feel as though disemboweled. At first she does not hear the telephone ring. When she eventually becomes attuned to the sound, it occurs to her it is Timothy—wanting to repair the breach between them. She lifts the receiver and manages a faint, dispirited hello.

"Rabbi Lewyn." She cannot fit the voice on the other end with anything in her memory. "Noah Zentner here. I promised to call in the morning, but just had an idea. Hope this is not an inconvenient time."

"It is, but that's certainly not your fault. Will we be seeing each other in the morning?" she says, gathering strength from her professional persona.

"That's what I'm calling about. We're scheduled to meet the lawyers about ten. Four of them. As sour a bunch as I ever met, but when you need killer lawyers, you need killer lawyers."

"I haven't agreed to anything yet, Noah, except to listen to you and your attorneys."

"Well, that's why I'm calling you now, Rabbi. I know you're a jogger and wondered if you brought your shoes and sweats with you. I jog, too. And if you're willing, I could come to your hotel early tomorrow morning. We can run in Central Park. Around the reservoir. That is, if you're not frightened to jog with an accused rapist."

The invitation catches her off guard. Usually quick with repartee, she feels caught flat-footed. He asks a good question. Is it wise to run with an accused rapist, even one whose family has long been associated with Ohav Shalom? "I was planning to get up early and run," she says. "A ritual with me on Sunday mornings."

"From what I hear, on Monday through Fridays as well. I suppose you know folks refer to you as the running rabbi. It would be a good chance for us to get to know each other. I'm at a loss without Seth. If he hadn't gotten into trouble, I might have stayed clear myself. That's what my therapist suggests."

"I wouldn't know about those things, Noah. What I do know is that I don't know you. And I can't be of help if I don't."

"If you would feel more comfortable, we can have breakfast at the hotel."

"I like the idea of running better. Can you be here at 7:30? That will give us enough time for the lawyers at ten."

"Great. In the lobby at 7:30."

Chapter Three

MEMORANDUM

To: Ms. Sylvia Junqueira, Esq.
State of Maryland Office of Prosecution

From: Eli Waller, CFO
The Hawthorne Group, Ltd.

Re: Rape, Sunday, July 4

In my testimony to the police at Easton, Maryland, a copy of which your office has forwarded to me, I have already provided the sequence of events aboard the chartered sailboat, *Dame Cynthia*, on the evening of July 4. Please be aware that the rape took place at night, on a chartered boat in unfamiliar waters. Due to circumstances that can be confirmed by Captain Alexander Danberry, we had little or no light aboard. Few of the passengers, officers of The Hawthorne Group Ltd. and Pyramid Development Corporation, wore watches. During a normal business day we are constantly consulting watches to make appointments and meet deadlines. Not so when the rape occurred on Sunday evening. We had no deadlines to meet and therefore took little notice of the time.

THE INN AT PERRY CABIN,
St. Michaels, Chesapeake Bay: Saturday, July 3rd

While marketing my company's financial services, we became aware that Pyramid Development Corporation in Washington, D.C. was considering securitizing its debt in the form of a Real Estate Investment Trust. I made two trips to interview CEO,

Jonathan Zentner, at Pyramid's headquarters on 19th Street in Washington, one meeting of which Noah Zentner attended. Both father and son met with me again at The Hawthorne Group, Ltd. (hereafter referred to as HGL) in our New York office. At that time, I suggested that in order to design a program for going public the staffs from our respective firms should meet. Because interruptions during a routine work day can be so disconcerting, I proposed that HGL host a weekend retreat near Washington where our people could mix in an informal setting. The Zentners were wary, but eventually conceded the plan's wisdom. In the meantime, they sent us confidential financial information regarding Pyramid's debt and income. My assistant later came up with the idea of retreating to the Inn at Perry Cabin, a luxurious conference center outside St. Michaels, on Maryland's Eastern Shore. The only date that worked for the senior people involved was the holiday weekend of July 4.

The following members of HGL went to St. Michaels:

St. John Lutkins, Senior Analyst
(212) 447-1923
Arlene Houston-Gephardt, Director of Finance
(212) 447-1919
Douglas Wurtzel, Director of Securitization
(212) 447-1944
Gil Brillenbourg, Director of our Real Estate Appraisal Unit
(212) 447-1923
Charlene C. Murphy Esq., Attorney
(212) 447-1925
Robert Crane, Financial Assistant and Records
(212) 447-1918

The meeting opened with a false start because Jonathan Zentner arrived late, forcing us to repeat HGL's multimedia presentation. Though unapologetic about his tardiness, he was cordial and enthusiastic. We were warned in advance that Jonathan Zentner's personal charms belie his iron toughness. Pyramid had just emerged from two lawsuits with major pension funds. With the prospect of a litigious client, we approached this opportunity very cautiously. Still, the size of the trust and the potential fees could not be overlooked. We devoted the morning meeting on Saturday to introductions and the upcoming agenda.

After lunch, my analysts began asking hard questions about the financial information provided. Gil Brillenbourg is an expert at establishing the underlying value and cash flow of properties. He ran a five-year projection of the Accumulation of Wealth, the Internal Rate of Return, Financial Management Rate of Return, and the Net Present Value of Pyramid's real estate portfolio. Arlene Houston-Gephardt came to the meeting armed with knowledge about Washington tenants, the competitive market for similar projects and the bottom-line cost of operating the real estate in question. Discounting for a basket of assumptions based on statistical standard differentials, HGL possessed a fairly accurate handle on the value of the assets, perhaps more accurate than Pyramid itself.

On Saturday evening, we focused on the risks associated with this securitization. Disagreements arose. This is common and healthy. The session broke up at 11:30 p.m. on a sour note. Both teams moseyed separately into the bar for a nightcap but later intermingled. In the informality of the bar they agreed that their differences were by no means insurmountable.

Sunday morning was devoted to more questions posed by the HGL staff. To sum up our views on the securitization, we presented the Zentners with a bound reference book filled with diagrams, graphs, spreadsheets, and time lines showing how the trust would take form.

To reward HGL and Pyramid personnel for giving up their Fourth of July weekend, HGL hosted a Sunday afternoon sail on the Chesapeake Bay and had chartered a 90-foot skipjack sail boat, launched in 1924, one of two such historic vessels remaining from the Chesapeake's fishing heritage. The *Dame Cynthia* was once used for oystering and crabbing, but was later refitted for day charters and parties. In addition to my people from HGL, thirteen from Pyramid joined the sail. They are:

Noah Zentner, Hugh Simpson, Bill Pell, Karla West, Wendy St. Clair, Joan Bradford, Chin Wei, Tom Knapp, Zantovska Vin, Stephen MacNeille, Martha Low, Wedall Leake, and Dina Seiman.

Jonathan Zentner excused himself after lunch to be with his

wife at another engagement in Washington and did not join us. With a comical gesture of his arm, he humorously delegated his son to represent the firm's commercial interests at sea.

EXCURSION ABOARD THE *DAME CYNTHIA*, On the Chesapeake: July 4th

Summer heat and humidity on the Chesapeake was brutal. Fortunately, the crew of the *Dame Cynthia* passed out souvenir T-shirts, short pants, and sandals in a wide assortment of sizes. We set sail down the Miles River and headed for open water in a mild northwesterly wind. The skipjack possessed a large mainsail with a boom that spans most of the cockpit and a short stubby jib. She has a shallow draft for navigating the bay's sandbars and a wide beam, designed for fishing, oystering, and hauling cargo.

To benefit from the light breeze, passengers congregated in the cockpit, near the stern. We rapidly became dehydrate and took advantage of abundant beer, wine, and soft drinks from well-stocked coolers. Jokes began to flow. Skipper Alex Danberry pumped music through a loudspeaker, which forced everybody to shout. As we entered the wide expanse of Eastern Bay, off Tilghman Island, the music stopped abruptly. We took special note of this because we could suddenly talk in normal voices. Bill Pell threaded his way forward to speak with the skipper and returned a few moments later to relate that the *Dame Cynthia* had been suffering from a minor electrical problem. At the time, we were told it was nothing to worry about. Captain Danberry left the tiller to his mate and scampered below to reroute the electrical circuitry. Many of us were unhappy when the music resumed some thirty minutes later.

By this time, thunderclouds darkened the eastern sky, blocking the afternoon sun. This, I am apprised, is a common occurrence on the Chesapeake during summer months. Humidity and heat on the earth's surface engender fierce electrical activity in the clouds. The skipper predicted there wouldn't be rain until after nightfall. Despite this, the wind picked up and drove the skipjack south. By six o'clock, day cruisers and yachts from Annapolis had all but disappeared.

Approximately 6:15 p.m., the crew set up collapsible tables for a traditional Chesapeake Bay seafood dinner. On a plank over the cockpit they placed bowls of blue crabs, spiced shrimp, corn on the cob, coleslaw, and corn muffins. A second plank served as a bar, well stocked with white wine and a half-dozen different beers.

Throughout the afternoon, Noah Zentner and I spoke to each other intermittently. We had an agreement not to talk business. In an effort to bridge two corporate cultures, we asked routine questions about family and hobbies. When it was time to eat, the others insisted we serve ourselves first, then find seats together near the stern.

Thunderclouds moving overhead failed to produce rain. The sun, still burning hot as Hades, dropped toward the western horizon. The heat and humidity we experienced during the afternoon returned and the wind slowed, then ceased altogether. The skipjack's sails bobbed listlessly in irons. It was clear to everyone that there wasn't enough wind to sail back to St. Michaels. We'd have to use a diesel motor for the return journey.

After dinner, the crew cleared the deck for dancing. Music wafted through the loudspeakers again. By this time, Pyramid and HGL employees felt comfortable in each other's company. Gil Brillenbourg from HGL and Wendy St. Clair of Pyramid started to dance. Zantovska Vin and St. John Lutkins followed. Off came the sandals. Folks were still drinking beer and Cokes. Our bodies were wet with perspiration. The music got louder and wilder, then stopped suddenly in the middle of the Electric Slide. More trouble with the electrical circuits. Final rays of sunlight passed from gray into black. Thick clouds above screened away starlight. The skipper threw a few switches and a single emergency light illuminated the foredeck and cockpit. It flickered on and off for a few minutes, then died altogether, plunging us into total blackness. Though specks of light dotted the shoreline far in the distance and we could see occasional bursts from Fourth of July fireworks, the only light aboard came from the skipper's flashlight. Soon that disappeared as he went below to restore electricity.

Waiting for the skipjack's lights to return, Doug Wurtzel and Bill Pell from Pyramid took advantage of the darkness to relieve themselves on the forward deck. Both are controlled and disciplined professionals, but a combination of alcohol, music, and heat made them a bit tipsy and they abandoned self-restraint. Nobody would have known what they were up to had not laughter and sounds of their streams hitting the water drawn attention in the cockpit. By this time, just about everybody had a full bladder and there was only one head below and no light with which to reach it. I heard St. John Lutkins and Gil Brillenbourg on opposite gunwales also relieving themselves. Since it was too dark to see, Hugh Simpson and Wedall Leake didn't bother going forward and simply urinated from the cockpit. Their behavior made everybody conscious of swelling bladders. Women, of course, are more inhibited and relieving themselves became a problem. Someone suggested the men go forward to leave the women free in the cockpit. But female physiology makes urinating over the side difficult. A few expressed fear about climbing onto the gunwale and hooking their feet into the railing.

I think it was Dina Seiman's idea for everyone to take a swim. Karla West pointed out the advantages. The skipjack was in irons and everybody was hot as hell. Furthermore, it would be an easy matter to relieve oneself in the water. No mess, no embarrassment. Nobody conceived of straying more than a few feet from the skipjack. In retrospect, going over the side of a sailboat at night was a very foolish thing, but a full bladder is a powerful inducement.

Wendy St. Clair, asset manager from the Pyramid staff, escalated this stupidity. She lifted a bare foot onto the gunwale and invited the rest of us to dive overboard. At first there were no takers. Disappointed, she challenged us to follow her into the water. We were hesitant, perhaps because the dark water looked so foreboding. Somebody stated that despite the lack of wind, the skipjack was still moving in the current and reboarding might be difficult. The next thing we heard was a splash in the water.

Doug Wurtzel, from my team, tried listening for the swimmer. I think he believed Wendy was in danger, for he quickly kicked off his sandals. Moments later, we heard a splash as he dove overboard. Instead of calling for help, both swimmers invited us to join them. Gil Brillenbourg jumped overboard next, followed by Martha Low and Karla West. Zantovska Vin and Hugh Simpson eventually plunged over the side. The mood captured the rest of us, including myself and Noah Zentner. Tom

Knapp and Joan Bradford protested how dangerous it was to get separated from the boat, especially without light aboard. By the time Captain Danberry clambered topside and realized what had happened, it was too late to exercise his authority. I heard him yelling at us but couldn't make out the words, and I don't think anybody else heard him over their splashing.

It was dark and sort of creepy in the water, but voices nearby provided a sense of security. Noah Zentner hailed the skipper to shine his flashlight onto the water so people wouldn't stray. There was no response, for presumably he needed the flashlight for other things. Shortly thereafter, I estimate about two minutes, the deck lights came on, bathing the sailboat in bright light. A cheer arose from the water because we were beginning to sense our predicament. Swimmers immediately regrouped, preparing to return.

There was a cry of alarm as *Dame Cynthia*'s beacon lights suddenly died again. I later learned that the skipjack's first mate had used his battery-powered shortwave transmitter to raise the Coast Guard. Apparently, the battery was low on voltage and his signal went unanswered.

Sailing an old skipjack is cumbersome under normal conditions. Under emergency conditions it was nearly impossible without full attention of the crew. The mate left his radio and concentrated on maneuvering the vessel. To those of us in the water, *Dame Cynthia* had all but disappeared. We looked around for additional lights but there were none except faint flashes from the Eastern Shore, three miles away. Though none of us were far from each other, the darkness created the illusion of distance. Our only contact was by voice. The water baffled sound and it was difficult to discern who was near and who was far away. People shifted their positions by swimming toward what they believed to be *Dame Cynthia*. It dawned upon us that the skipjack had been drifting from the time we had jumped overboard. Fortunately, we were in the same current and likely to drift in the same direction at the same speed.

Under normal conditions when a sailor inadvertently falls overboard, a skipper will notify the person in the water and circle back under close haul reach, then turn into the wind and pluck his victim from the water. Textbook stuff. But how was the skipper to identify his swimmers in the dark? Instead of attempting a risky procedure, he ordered his crew to drop the mainsail in the event of an unexpected gust of wind, then sounded a compressed air horn to assure us that his vessel was nearby. With no lights, we'd have to make our way to the skipjack by sound alone.

Someone had the presence of mind to suggest a plan. First, call out names to ensure that everyone was safe. Then, find the closest buddy and stick with him or her. Two-person teams should join with other teams and make their way back to the skipjack.

Someone aboard *Dame Cynthia* circled the skipper's flashlight. A comforting sight, though it served no purpose other than to give us the sailboat's location. It took several roll calls to form the teams. No one panicked, but panic was just a question of time. Eventually, one or more swimmers would tire, then lose their wits. A male voice counseled others not to swim, but to turn onto their backs and float. The water was warm and had not yet begun to draw heat from our bodies. Everybody expected that in the course of this exercise the crew of *Dame Cynthia* would correct the electrical malfunction. It didn't happen.

Voices cried out at different locations. Several swimmers made their way toward the flashlight beam, encouraged by voices from the crew. Tom Knapp and Joan Bradford flicked a cigarette lighter on and off from the bow. Crewmen hovered on the gunwale to spot swimmers. Those near the vessel were guided to a platform rigged near the stern. They hauled themselves onto it, exhausted from the ordeal. Once on the platform, swimmers scrambled into the cockpit to make room for additional folks to come aboard.

Of the fifteen people who jumped into the bay, thirteen found their way to the *Dame Cynthia*. Chin Wei from Pyramid and Arlene Houston-Gephardt from HGL remained unaccounted for.

The skipper howled over excited voices, "Pipe down so we can hear them." He gave two sharp blasts from his air horn, then added a third for good measure.

We strained our ears but heard only water lapping against the hull. Responsibility for what was transpiring had begun to weigh heavily upon us.

At two-minute intervals, Bill Pell utilized a bellowing voice to call out. Meanwhile, the skipper tried unsuccessfully to contact the Coast Guard by shortwave. A crewman produced an SOS launch gun and flare and asked the captain's permission to fire.

The mate commented that it had not been inspected in years and would likely fail to ignite. The skipper granted permission and a few moments later the crewman launched it into the darkness. We held our breaths waiting for the second stage. If and when the flare ignited we would have about thirty seconds of light. Everybody selected a patch of water to watch.

Waiting was tense, but eventually rewarded as the night sky exploded in bright luminescence. We scanned the water. Nothing. On its path homeward, the flare flickered, then began to gutter out.

At the very last instant, Tom Knapp yelled, "Over there! I think I saw something on the water. Not sure."

The skipper had been using the skipjack's diesel engine with great caution. He didn't want to wander from immersion point. Nor was it possible to hear a swimmer in the water over the din of the engine. Still, if Arlene and Chin were not in the immediate area, the sailboat would have to move toward them. He switched on the ignition and waited for the diesel engine to turn over.

Tom Knapp kept his eyes fixed on the spot where he thought he had seen something. It proved to be inordinately difficult since that point was buried in darkness and the skipjack's movement changed the coordinates. When the skipper shut down the engine to listen, observers on the port side heard a scream. Two blasts from the air horn. Another scream from the water. A male voice.

Chin Wei was exhausted by the time the skipjack moved into position to pluck him from the water. He had given up hope of a rescue and didn't believe he had the strength to stay afloat until daybreak.

"I heard a muffled sound about ten minutes ago," he said, pulling a soaking T-shirt over his head. "Not sure it was Arlene or even human. Just that it was a noise."

A caucus clustered around the wheel to confer with the skipper and there was unanimous agreement that the skipjack should power up again and move towards the area where Chin Wei heard the noise. Only silence greeted us there. Bill Pell called out Arlene's name at regular intervals. His tenor voice penetrated the darkness, followed by a period of silence. It was on the sixth attempt that everyone heard a faint response. Not necessarily a human voice, but a sound. It happened only once, though Bill tried to elicit a second response.

Forward, near the bow, two fellows dove headfirst over the side. We could hear splashing and occasionally their voices directing each other. The darkness was suddenly punctuated by two yells. At first they sounded like groans of distress, but in fact they were cheers. Arlene was treading water. *Dame Cynthia* altered course for a successful pickup.

The skipjack's diesel was small and never designed for extended travel. Her return to St. Michaels was slow. We dried ourselves off and sat in dark silence, privately contemplating how close our frolicking had come to disaster. We might have been hot stuff in the world of finance, but we were amateur sailors. Most of us were city people with infrequent exposure to outdoor dangers. We acknowledged that we had underestimated the vastness of the bay and the darkness of the night.

The somber mood eventually changed to exhilaration. We chattered, exchanging experiences.

As the euphoria began to wear off, I realized that in all the excitement I had failed to achieve the original purpose of the swim and empty my bladder. There was no way on God's earth I was going back into the water. To use the head below required navigating through the dark compartment below by feeling my way. Urgency was so great I had no alternative. I banged my shins and tripped over just about everything. When I finally crawled into the head, it was difficult sitting on the small toilet seat because the skipjack had entered a patch of turbulent water and was rocking in the swells. When I left the head that I heard breathing in the compartment. Noah Zentner heard me shut the door and identified himself. The thought dashed through my mind that he had come below to use the head after me. While feeling my way through the cabin clutter, I said, "Well, it's free now. The head is all yours."

He waited in the darkness until my hand brushed his thigh. His hand swept forward and snatched my arm. I was sure he would step sideways to let me pass, but he didn't. Instead, he barred my path and stepped closer. I could smell brackish bay water on his skin.

At that moment, the skipjack rolled to starboard and we were both jostled, brushing one another. Off-balance, I found myself falling over a bunk cluttered with the crew's foul-weather gear and other unidentified paraphernalia. Zentner fell in the same direction and the next thing I knew his body was on top of me, pressing me deeper into the bunk. I tried to right myself but his weight made that impossible. I was alarmed, but at the moment believed he too had been thrown off balance and would immediately roll off me onto his feet. He didn't. I struggled but couldn't get any traction. His lips were on my neck, groping for my mouth. I managed to twist away. By this time I had no illusions about his intentions. The way I thrashed, there could no doubt that I was resisting him.

His hand pawed my shoulders and his lips pressed against my neck. The moment he forced himself on me he was no longer my client. Not even a potential client. It was just that simple. Despite our investment in time and money, as far as I was concerned, The Hawthorne Group was no longer interested in Pyramid's business.

Wet from the bay, the T-shirt and bra I was wearing stuck to my skin. Zentner's hand slipped under the shirt to my breast. I had no free hands to prevent this. One of my arms was buried beneath my waist, the other restrained by his. His lips covered my mouth, making it difficult to scream. I struggled to tell him to stop, but his lips covered mine. For a moment, I thought I might die for want of air. When his tongue forced a passage through my teeth, I attempted to bite it. But he was quicker than I.

Before I knew it, his hands were on my pelvis, then inside the elastic trim of the shorts. The underpants stuck to my skin. His fingers stroked for my genitals. If I couldn't stop him, I certainly wasn't going to provide any pleasure. When he eased off my wrist, I fisted my fingers to deliver a blow to his head. It missed and plowed into his chest without deterring him for a single moment. He coughed, then laughed at the feebleness of my resistance.

The skipjack's rocking kept me constantly off-balance. I could feel him tugging my shorts. My thrashing made it difficult to clear my backside, but he was persistent. Elastic in the waistband ripped (I later submitted these torn garments to the police in Easton as evidence). He kept my mouth covered with his lips so I couldn't scream, though I knew a pair of hatches above were open to the deck.

He pried my legs apart with his knees. While I could see nothing, I felt him poking my pelvis. My struggles prevented penetration. My free hand grabbed for something and finally fell upon a chrome grinding winch used for hauling in the sheets. I guess I could have brought it down upon his skull and possibly maimed or killed him. But however violated I felt, I could not make myself do such a thing. Instead, I threw the winch across the compartment where it collided with the bulkhead.

Zentner's head lifted for an instant and freed my mouth. I yelled as loud as I could "NO! NO! NO! GOD DAMMIT, STOP, STOP!"

Attracted by the sharp bang from the winch, the hatchway opened. I repeated, "NO! NO! NO! GET OFF ME! GOD DAMMIT!"

While I couldn't see who was entering the compartment, I later learned it was Doug Wurtzel from my staff and Steve MacNeille from Pyramid.

Zentner immediately rolled off. I am told that Karla West and Wendy St. Clair followed into the compartment.

In the darkness, Zentner stepped away from the bunk and pulled up his pants. Nobody could see if he was naked anyway. I pulled my shorts back over my hips and fastened them at the waist with a snap button.

"Everybody all right?" a female voice asked.

"Absolutely," Zentner answered, as if nothing had happened. I couldn't believe he could lie with such facility.

"What happened?"

"Slipped," he said. "When the boat rolled, we bashed into the bulkhead."

"Anybody hurt?" a male voice asked. I think it was Steve MacNeille.

"I'm okay," Zentner replied. "Elisheva is, too. You all right, Eli?"

It was at that moment I made a quick decision. I calculated we were at least an hour from St. Michaels. I had more to lose than gain by pressing charges of rape and needed time to consider my right move. A final decision could wait until we were all safely docked at St. Michaels. I needed time to think about what to do.

One thing was certain—the business relationship between HGL and Pyramid was dead.

Chapter Four

July 14th

Gabby wishes she had not drunk so much Scotch, which not only gives her a mild headache, but also feeds the suspicious side of her character. By the time she descends to the hotel lobby to meet Noah Zentner, her guard is up. His invitation to jog in Central Park is probably a con job. After all, he needs a character witness and, in order to get it, he must first sell himself. Moreover, abusers of women are known to beguile their victims. Raped women are notoriously gullible. Like hunting carnivores who instinctively select the weak, young, and lame for their prey, cunning men stalk unwary women to exploit. She must not fall into that trap.

When she enters the lobby, he is waiting nearby dressed in a blue and white jogging suit. A Stanford undergraduate, he matriculated through Yale Law School which facilitated a two-year clerkship with a Federal Appeals judge in Boston and ultimately provided access to prestigious legal firms on the Eastern seaboard. He joined a Philadelphia partnership representing corporations in technical and costly federal disputes with the Environmental Protection Agency, Departments of the Interior and Commerce. Philadelphia closed the distance to his father's Pyramid Development Corporation in Washington which Jonathan Zentner often boasted would someday be run by his lawyer son. When Noah showed little interest, his father was forced to consider the sale of Pyramid. Before that happened, Noah's law firm lost a major suit and, while no one blamed him for the defeat, he assumed responsibility for tactical errors committed during the trial. His subsequent resignation facilitated an appointment as General Counsel and Deputy

Executive Operating Officer at Pyramid Development. Once resettled in his home town, he married Morgan Claire Blau, an editor and literary agent from a patrician family of Washington journalists, most of whom made their marks writing syndicated columns on American politics.

In the Pierre Hotel lobby, he walks toward Gabby on long, athletic legs. He wears round, steel-framed glasses fastened to the skull with an elastic headband and a black Baltimore baseball cap embroidered with an orange oriole, turned backward so its visor drops down over the nape of his neck. She judges his age to be a couple years younger than herself, which means it will be a challenge to keep up with him when running. Heavy drinking from the previous night will not help her stamina.

She makes it a general practice not to engage in sports with congregants, though just about everybody knows she's an exercise freak. For this meeting she shuns her customary running briefs in favor of full-length mauve-colored sweat pants. Her sole concession to informality is to pull her hair into a short ponytail.

After brief introductions, she and Noah slip out of the hotel and across Fifth Avenue, then walk together on the pavement bordering Central Park. Urban noises make conversation difficult. An entry path leading into Central Park is blocked by a recently installed sign:

> **RABIES ALERT!**
> **BEWARE INFECTED RACCOONS AND SQUIRRELS**
> —Do Not Feed or Play with
> Raccoons, Squirrels, or Opossums
> Report Sighting During Daylight Hours to Park Police
> N.Y.C. Department of Health
> (212) 667-9800

Noah jogs in place, twisting his torso with hands on his hips then, in an arching movement, clasps them behind and above his head to stretch. A moment later, he bends forward almost touching the ground in an effort to extend muscles at the rear of the thigh and leg. Gabby imitates with a deep bow forward but stops short of his full routine.

When she straightens up, they move forward onto a path surfaced with crushed rock. He says, "I'd rather be running along the C&O Canal. Sunday is normally my day to run there. Usually start in Georgetown and go as far north as my legs will carry me. My wife, Morgan, would sometimes pick me up in a car at Carderock, but those days are gone now."

"I don't follow," Gabby assumes an easy, warmup pace alongside him.

"My running from now on will be in a prison yard. Maryland's a lousy state to be indicted for rape. Juries there are usually composed of females who have a penchant for convicting rapists. Judges hand out long sentences."

"Sounds as if you've already given up. The papers say you might not be indicted."

He starts to increase the pace but then holds back. Their shoulders bump innocently and separate just as fast. "The District Attorney's under pressure from women's groups. Slim chance there won't be an indictment. You must know, Rabbi, how hard it is to prove a negative. I didn't do what Elisheva Waller claims. I admit to having sex with her. But what occurred on the Chesapeake was as much her doing as mine."

"You don't sound as though you believe in our legal system."

"In some matters, but not rape. Too emotionally charged. There's a chasm between the genders on this issue. The moment the story hit the papers, I was convicted."

Gabby kicks her legs a little harder and reaches just a tad farther with her lead foot to attune her stride with his. This puts her slightly ahead of him. "I hope that's not true. For you, and for the women's movement of which I'm a member. We can't build a case for women's rights on false accusations."

"I want you to know the truth, Rabbi. I promised myself I wouldn't withhold anything. No matter how embarrassing or incriminating. Elisheva consented to have sex with me and I with her. In my book that's adultery, not rape. The law will probably punish me for what I *didn't* do, while overlooking what I *did*."

"Seems unfair to me, if that's what happened and, of course, I'm in no position to make that judgment. Still, I'm glad to hear it from your lips. Are you comfortable with your lawyers?"

"If one can feel comfortable with pit bulls. You'll meet the team in a few hours. Between you and me, I wouldn't choose them for friends, but they're supposed to be the best money can buy. Lots of experience defending rich men accused of forcing themselves on unwilling women. I'd rather have them for me than against me."

The pace increases and they start to pass strollers and pet lovers who vie for space on the narrow pathway. When the path clears, Gabby takes a modest lead and flaps her arms to keep circulation at the extremities of her limbs. "You said on the phone Seth Greer is partially responsible for what happened. I don't understand."

Noah angles onto a detouring service road circling the Central Park Reservoir. A NO ENTRY sign obstructs the path. Day-Glo orange police barrier tapes stream from it to adjacent trees where they are secured. The couple comes to an abrupt halt and jogs in place.

"Think this is because of the raccoons?" Noah asks, turning to Gabby. "Hard to believe a few little creatures can close down Central Park. How dangerous could they be?"

"People say if you see them after sundown, they're harmless. The ones you see during daylight are probably sick."

Noah takes this as a sign they can bypass the DayGlo tape and head through a wooded area, still moving up an incline in the direction of the reservoir. The rising morning sun casts a warm glow through the trees. Fellow joggers work the path ahead, the majority women, some in pairs or threesomes.

The number of runners increases as they sweep through the last trees and onto a gravel path separated from the reservoir by a chain-link fence. Noah jogs left, almost stumbles, and stabilizes himself by grabbing Gabby's arm. He comes to a quick halt and she almost plows into him. They laugh, begin again, then fall into a parade of joggers, each at different paces, sloughing counterclockwise along the circumference of the reservoir. It takes a few hundred feet for them to re-establish a comfortable pace.

"Something I've wanted to say to you, Rabbi," Noah tilts his head to look at her. "I couldn't tell this to anyone but you, not that it makes any real difference. Yet I need to clear the air before we get to know each another."

She regards him for only a brief moment, acknowledging permission.

"I'm not sure I like rabbis," he says. "What I mean to say is that they're partly to blame for the pickle I'm in."

Like ice water splashed across the face, that gets Gabby's attention. The connection between rabbis and rape eludes her.

"I don't mean this to be personal. That's why I brought it up now. I can't tell you how pissed I am at Seth."

"You're not alone. There's a regiment of jilted lovers who'd love to string him up the highest tree in Nottingham Forest. He had the good sense to hightail it out of town before one of his paramours slipped a kitchen knife into his gizzard."

"Seth and I were good friends. I mean real good friends. We talked about everything: family, politics, sports, our beliefs, and fears. He spoke often about Ohav Shalom. I suppose he talked a lot to you too."

"Yes. But he apparently left a lot out. I learned about his womanizing when it was too late to be of help."

Now in perfect step with each other, they run side by side, their gait like ice dancers, kicking an easy pace.

"I knew about Seth's romancing," Noah says, knowing this is bound to produce shock. "He told me about his women, all in strict confidence, you understand. At first, I thought his affairs were nothing but innocent liaisons. Everybody knew that his marriage was in trouble. I regard him as a henpecked husband who should never have become a rabbi in the first place. Too restless a mind for the rabbinate. Later, I came to regard his sexual exploits as a sickness. He was driven by something inside. I'm sure it wasn't hedonism or lust. Something deeper than that."

"Some males are dedicated seducers," Gabby adds, "but then no babies would be born without female collaboration."

"I hope you don't think I'm a womanizer like Seth. Elisheva was the only time I cheated on my wife," he interjects.

"I'll give you the benefit of the doubt, but why the anger with Seth?"

"The fact that he was sleeping around gave me license to

cheat on Morgan. I permitted him to set an example. In some convoluted logic I argued that if a rabbi could sleep with other women, so could I. What chumps. He's in disgrace and I'm about to be indicted."

"Sounds like you're angry with yourself. That's still no reason to be irate with me."

"If you're going to help me, I can't afford to be."

They come full circle around the reservoir and start a second circuit. Bright sunlight shines through the trees to make the morning sparkle with July freshness.

Ahead on the path, a half-dozen fellow joggers are clustered near the chain-link fence, no longer running. Until Gabby and Noah approach it is unclear what attracts their attention. Hunched against the fence is a heavy, bewhiskered raccoon, a swath of black across its eyes and snout. Blood from an open gash behind the shoulder oozes onto its fur. The creature looks as though seeking an avenue of escape but is trapped between the fence and spectators. It hisses and exposes small, menacing teeth.

"How'd it get injured?" Noah inquires from fellow joggers.

"Kids threw rocks. They thought it was rabid and tried killing it. Several rocks must have connected."

Gabby steps back, putting extra distance between the danger and herself. She is a cautious woman and prefers to take as few chances as possible.

"A cornered creature will strike something much larger than itself," Noah warns.

Gabby takes hold of his arm to guide him past the bystanders. Most have already reached a similar conclusion.

Noah resists and instead drags her through a screen of joggers to face the creature. For a long moment, he studies its position, making friendly gestures which appear to mesmerize the beast. "There's no saliva around the mouth and his eyes are clear. My bet is he isn't rabid."

"Don't touch him," somebody warns. "The park's teeming with sick animals. He'll give you a terrible disease."

"He's gotta bite me first," Noah responds while keeping his eyes firmly locked on the raccoon's. He speaks to it directly. "Now, you wouldn't do a thing like that, would you, fellow?"

"Not too close, buddy," another runner cautions. "I heard the treatment for rabies is horrible. Injections in the stomach for a month."

Noah disregards the advice and steps still closer as though prepared to tame the creature. He resists Gabby's tugging. The raccoon is less agitated the closer he gets. Now everybody is voicing advice about the dangers. He stands foursquare before the animal, then suddenly does what causes everybody to gasp. His arm juts out at the same moment the raccoon recoils. The hand darts through the animal's defense zone and grabs fur behind the ears. With a fluid motion he lifts the creature into the air removing traction for its feet. The creature screeches with a sickening whine, but dangling in the air, cannot twist its head to bite the restraining hand.

Noah's free hand supports the animal under the rump. Paws are scratching nothing but air. Observing that the danger of being bitten has passed, spectators express their relief. Noah examines the wound and thinks better of attempting any treatment. He searches for place to release the creature and decides that the bystanders, whose numbers have swollen, would panic if he just set it on the ground. Instead, he lifts it above the fence and with a powerful arm, releases the startled animal on the opposite side. The landing is not smooth, but the creature scampers to its feet. A few seconds later it disappears amid bushy reeds along the shore.

"Well now, Rabbi," Noah addresses Gabby, "shall we continue running? If we're going make our mark, we've got to set a faster pace. You'll need time for a shower before we meet the lawyers. And maybe a quick breakfast."

Once they are jogging again, she says, "I can't believe you'd do a thing like that. Why take such a chance? If that raccoon is rabid, it will die soon anyway."

"I'm an inveterate cat lover."

"I can see that. It still wasn't prudent."

"Very perceptive, Rabbi. It's clear I'm not a prudent man, otherwise I wouldn't be in the present predicament."

"If you're innocent the truth will come out."

" I wish I were as confident. Half the women in this town would lynch me if they could. Forget about evidence. That isn't in the equation."

"Which leaves the other half for whom evidence is critical."

"And you're in that half?"

"I would hope so. I don't understand how a man who would help a wounded animal could rape someone."

"He didn't." Noah is uncompromising.

THE ZENTNER FAMILY COLLECTS SECOND HOMES like a philatelist collects postage stamps. They branch out from Embassy Row in the District of Columbia. The family has a vacation home in Gingerland Parish on the Caribbean island of Nevis in the West Indies. Nothing pretentious, but for a pad visited no more than a fortnight at most each winter season, it's impressive. Members of the family are obliged to let it compete with another vacation condo, this one on the ski slopes of Vail, Colorado. Again, modest in size, but an expensive luxury when other ski aficionados stay in hotels or lodges. A fishing cottage on Vancouver Island, British Columbia, was sold after the matriarchal Jeannie Zentner died of chronic emphysema. Jonathan maintains an apartment in Jerusalem's Yamin Moshe District, overlooking the Jaffa Gate of the Old City. This pied-à-terre he uses when visiting the numerous philanthropic institutions he supports in Israel. Seth Greer once told Gabby that cocktail parties there include Israel's who's who, both in government and the arts.

The Zentner Manhattan condo is on the forty-second floor of Sutton Place Tower, a block north of the United Nations Plaza, with a panoramic view of the East River. Jonathan Zentner, in casual Sunday sport slacks and a cotton navy-blue pullover, greets Gabby at the door with a warm, friendly smile. Behind him, Noah steps from the vestibule to shake her hand like an old friend. After the jog in Central Park, she feels moderately comfortable in his company. She is pleased that he, not his father, leads into a living room where three attorneys from the law firm of Greenwald, Molletz, Steiner, and Mavenhouse are waiting for an introduction.

As a concession to the Sunday morning venue, the lawyers wear sport jackets with neckties, while the woman, a blouse and dress slacks. Jonathan Zentner, a consummate host, seats Gabby in a swivel lounge chair which permits excellent visual contact with the attorneys who share a black leather sofa and two adjacent reading chairs. Noah drops onto a Naguma chair brought from the dining room. His father offers coffee from a Russian samovar while they are making introductory small talk about the US Airways shuttle between LaGuardia and Washington National Airports. Coffee cups cause a logistics problem since yellow legal pads are already on the lawyers' laps.

To Gabby's surprise there is yet a fourth lawyer. From the bedroom emerges Zoe Mountolive, a tall, thin- waisted brunette who moves with large, purposeful steps toward Gabby, a thin hand outstretched in greeting. "Sorry, Rabbi Lewyn. My daughter's been in a small biking accident. Just got a call from the emergency room at St. Agnes."

"I hope it's not serious. If you need to scoot off, I can wait until the afternoon."

Because she looks determined to proceed, two colleagues make room on the couch. "No. No. I've left the telephone number here. As soon as an orthopedist reads her X-rays, they promised to call. Clementine's a big girl. I try not to mollycoddle her." As soon as she's seated, she points to the second female attorney, "Rabbi Lewyn, we're hoping to head off an indictment but, given recent press coverage, that might be wishful thinking. We must be prepared for a trial. I'm going to take the lead on Noah's case and Andrea Delagnes will be my first back up. Mortimer Steel is our man for jury selection and monitoring, while Norman Kwan over there specializes in technical legal issues and investigation. Of course, in practice nothing is delineated so precisely and we'll be overlapping. We have associates in the firm who will be assisting us upon demand. So...," she pauses with a smile that reveals teeth straightened by orthodonture, "we like to think of ourselves as the unbeatable A-Team."

Gabby is impressed and glances at Noah to see if he's satisfied with the Greenwald, Molletz specialists. He appears detached and inattentive.

Zoe Mountolive exhibits signs of stress. Afraid she may be interrupted by a call from the hospital, she abandons preliminary banter and plunges immediately into business. "Rabbi

Lewyn, Noah has told us that his primary relationship at Ohav Shalom Congregation has been with Rabbi Greer. Mort, our guru on juries, advises us that in most rape cases, the testimony of clergy has a profound influence. And often these cases are determined not by matters of evidence, but how juries *feel* about the defendant. With that in mind, we're obliged to seek your help in establishing Noah's character. Even if Rabbi Greer were available, which I'm told he isn't, we probably wouldn't want to put him on the stand. The prosecution would use his own troubles to discredit his testimony."

Gabby interrupts, "You'll have to spell out the role you would expect me to play. Under no circumstance can I testify to a better relationship with Noah than what actually exists. Our jog in Central Park this morning lasted longer than all of our previous meetings put together."

Gabby watches how this disclosure affects Zoe Mountolive who raises an eyebrow but tries to conceal it by looking over her half-frame reading glasses perched low on a slim, almost Egyptian nose. She observes Zoe's colleagues scratching notes on their yellow pads. Everything is significant. Everything is recorded.

"We won't ask of you anything that you feel uncomfortable about providing. Juries often miss a lot of what goes on in the courtroom, but not this. They have special antennae for phonies. We're not asking that you commit yourself at this point. You're absolutely free to decline. However, if you decide not to be available, we ask that you tell us at least a month in advance so we can make alternate plans. Can we get an agreement on that much now?"

Gabby considers the proposition. No backing out one month before the trial. This sounds fair enough and, for the moment, commits her to little.

Zoe looks at Jonathan Zentner. "We'd like to encourage a relationship between your family and Ohav Shalom. I understand that you were once on the Board of Trustees."

"Still am a Trustee," Jonathan adds as though very proud of that fact. "But no longer on the Board of Directors. I leave that to younger and more energetic folks."

Gabby's glance brushes off Noah and back to Zoe. "Doesn't

this create a conflict of interests? How can I be expected to be objective about a congregant when his father is my boss?"

"Good point, Rabbi," Zoe is quick to respond. "We will be sensitive to that conflict."

Jonathan is on his feet. He approaches the samovar and fills a stainless steel thermos with hot coffee, from which to offer refills.

Zoe waits until he's reseated, then dips her head, once again glancing over her reading glasses to Gabby. "We've done some preliminary intelligence on you, Rabbi Lewyn. Nothing secretive, of course, but it's our job to be thorough. And what we find is a very dynamic professional who appears to be deeply committed to the feminist movement. So am I. And I invite you to ask my colleagues with the firm about me. Some think I'm loony on the subject of gender equality. Testifying is bound to bring you into conflict with organizations that deal with feminist rights. My male colleagues may not appreciate what I'm going to say, but I believe you will. Defending Noah might make you more enemies than friends. There are many who already believe he's guilty and don't want to be confused by the facts. If you stand up for a person accused of a sex crime, they're going to hold it against you. How do you feel about that?"

Gabby immediately likes Zoe Mountolive, who she feels has correctly assessed her dilemma. She senses a kindred soul, a professional woman like herself who is very much in the feminist movement and yet somehow outside it. "To tell you the truth," she states, "I haven't had time to give it much thought. I don't yet understand details of the case and," here she looks directly at Noah, "I haven't resolved in my mind whether I think he committed rape or not. I'll say unequivocally at this point that I *hope* he's innocent and I *want* him to be innocent."

"But what will your friends in the Women's Movement think? What about female members of your congregation? Fellow rabbis? Will their opinions sway you? Will they make you worry at night? Keep you from sleeping?"

"I don't know."

"This is why it's important we meet today when we still have time to maneuver. There's no purpose saving one career and ruining another. We know of your reputation. We think helping

Noah could damage it. People who respect you today may not once you take the stand. And there's no way to compensate you for your testimony. My colleagues and I will be paid very handsomely for our services. We're worth it because we intend to see that Noah is not convicted. But we can't compensate a character witness."

"Clergy are not supposed to think of themselves," Gabby mutters without conviction.

Zoe emits a quiet, mocking laugh. "Then perhaps someone else ought to. I'm enough of a cynic to believe that clergy are just as self-conscious as the rest of us, yet perhaps better packaged. But Rabbi Lewyn, I've been there and know how other women think of people who defend rapists. Noah has become a lightning rod for grievances he didn't commit. I think you have a good feel for what I'm saying."

There is a long silence in which Gabby senses the lawyers trying to size her up. Their approach is encouraging. Facing problems up front has always been her policy and she knows Zoe is not pulling punches. Political fallout is a certainty. "Have you got a strong defense strategy?" she stares at Zoe. "No lawyer bullshit. Have you got the facts now or do you expect to have them in the near future?"

To this Zoe remains silent. She looks first to Norman Kwan who makes a strong nod of affirmation, then to Andrea Delagnes who winks like a private detective in a bad murder movie. Lastly, to Mort Steel who gives a thumbs up sign. "Well, there you have it," Zoe says. "These are the best legal minds in the state of New York and we believe we have the facts on our side. Does that make you more comfortable?"

"Let's say it's encouraging."

"I'd like to say something," Noah interjects. "I want everybody here to know my respect for Rabbi Lewyn and how difficult this might become. As far as I'm concerned, I'd be obliged for her testimony so long as it isn't paid for with personal anguish. We've already talked this morning. If she chooses not to testify, that will be all right with me. No hard feelings."

"I share your sentiments," Jonathan Zentner insists. "We'll live with her decision, whatever it may be."

Gabby remains silent. They're making it either very easy or

very difficult for her. She feels manipulated though she is not certain it is intentional. "There's a lot to think about."

The apartment telephone rings. Jonathan Zentner allows it to ring twice before stepping over to take it. The interruption upsets the rhythm of the interview. His eyes survey the others. He looks glum, nodding, then talks directly to Zoe. "It's for you. The emergency room. There's a phone extension in the bedroom for privacy."

"I'm sorry." Zoe rises to her feet. Her slacks cling close to her body, outlining her backside. She is in too much of a hurry to adjust them.

None of the other lawyers know how to fill the void and the silence is awkward.

"The jury is likely to be composed mostly of women," Mort Steel intones. "That's why we need female witnesses. Any jury is likely to accept the word of a rabbi without much questioning. Most prosecutors don't like pressing the clergy under cross-examination. There's a built-in protection. This is especially true if there are Jews on the team."

"Do you know who will represent the State?" Gabby asks, also making conversation.

"Too early yet. But I wouldn't put it past Baltimore prosecutors to use a woman lead."

Zoe re-enters the living room looking pale and slightly off-balance on her feet. "Very sorry. I'm afraid I must cut this short."

"Is she all right?" Noah asks, suddenly standing.

"A bad sprain of the ankle. No broken bones, thank God. Something like this always happens when you try to work on Sundays. I'm afraid I must go to St. Agnes."

"Of course," Jonathan Zentner says. "We understand. How old is Clementine?"

"Ten. She is a great jock so falling off her bike shouldn't have hurt her too badly. Don't know how hard she fell."

"We'll carry on here with Rabbi Lewyn," Andrea Delagnes adds.

Gabby stands to shake Zoe's hand as she passes briefly along with perfunctory goodbyes.

"I'll be in Washington toward the end of next week," Zoe

announces. "We've got a preliminary meeting at the District Attorney's office in Baltimore. The team and I will be in DC Thursday or Friday. There are still several issues yet to discuss. I'd like to call you, Rabbi Lewyn. May I?"

"Of course. I'll see Ms. Delagnes gets my numbers at the synagogue and at home."

After Zoe's departure, conversation focuses on technical issues of the upcoming trial. Once Zoe is no longer present, her assistants talk more and listen less. They remain addicted to their notepads, jotting down almost everything said. Gabby's attention wanes; her mind is on other things and she is glad when Andrea Delagnes declares the interview ended.

Back at the Pierre Hotel, she must pack her overnight bag for the flight home. When she folds the see-through bra from Victoria's Secret, sadness captures her. She sits silently on the bed. After several minutes she dials Timothy Matternly's apartment. The phone rings many times without an answer. That is not surprising, for he is one of the few clergymen she knows who sincerely enjoys attending religious services he does not personally conduct. Midday on Sundays will usually find him in church. Or eating brunch with friends. Gabby is about to hang up when, on the last dial tone, someone picks up the receiver.

"Hello, Tim," Gabby wrenches herself from depression and barks with disingenuous cheerfulness.

A female voice, sonorous and with crystal clarity, responds, "Sorry...Tim isn't home at the moment. May I ask who's calling?"

Gabby wants to snap back, *Who the hell is this?* but she doesn't because she knows who it is. This is Sally, Tim's new lover who stole him from her. Her first reaction is to say something rude but she controls herself. For a long moment she doesn't know what to say. Impulse, not reason, governs. Her left forefinger acts without consulting her brain and presses down on the disconnect button. The receiver clicks dead. There's nothing worth saying anyway.

As she remains seated on the bed, her panic recedes and, for a moment, she wants to talk with Sally—he never provided her family name. She wants to tell her about Timothy's lovable idiosyncrasies, sharing intimate secrets. Sally is destined to learn in time. She wants to establish a claim, though she knows it is foolish. Losing him is more difficult than she imagined.

She debates telephoning Sally Whatever-her-Name, but in the end finds it easier to lie back on the bed, regard the ceiling and let her eyes cloud with tears.

For years she rehearsed this event. Now that it has arrived she finds herself ill-prepared. She feels sorry for herself though she detests self-pity. No one to talk with. There's no rabbi for a rabbi.

The emptiness inside seems to grow, expanding from her chest into the throat. Loneliness causes her to utter a name. It's a public name she uses quite often with her congregants. Still, in private it seldom passes her lips.

"*Elohim*, God?"

The name stirs an insight. Maybe prayer is nothing more than words of a wounded heart spoken to One who must listen because He has nothing better to do.

GABBY RETURNS TO HER GARFIELD STREET CONDOMINIUM near the National Cathedral on Sunday afternoon. Several telephone messages await on the answering machine. She takes notes to return the calls until there's a rather long message from Ephraim Rothman.

"Gabby," he says in the inimitable sharp clarity of a banquet toastmaster, "I've been trying to get you at the synagogue but they said you were in New York. Sorry about being so rough at lunch last week. I was trying to protect you, though I know you are perfectly capable of protecting yourself. To make amends, I've placed your name as a candidate for Seth's job before the Rabbinic Search Committee. That raised some eyebrows but I think the overall reaction was favorable. I've learned to be skeptical about first impressions. People can be subtle and often canny. The bottom line is that Gertrude Swidler, who chairs the Search Committee, will be giving you a call in the next few days to arrange an interview. In my opinion, nobody deserves the chance more than you. Welcome home."

Chapter Five

July 23rd

Friday morning, the synagogue is under siege from the moment it opens. The air-conditioners circulate nothing but hot, humid air. Working is nearly impossible. Harold Farb cajoles, then throws a temper tantrum in order to get repairmen to save his staff from heat prostration or asphyxiation, whichever might come first. By 10:00 a.m., the hallways are filled with workmen searching through ceiling tiles for blockage in the ducts that distribute cool air. Their commotion disrupts the normal Friday crunch, just when everyone is rushing last-minute preparations for Sabbath events.

Charles Maximillian Browner doesn't function well in heat and is temperamental. He barely gives Gabby a chance to settle herself at her desk before demanding they review the day's agenda.

"Harold should have fired his air-conditioning contractor long ago. This happens two or three times a year, always on the hottest days. Men come; men work. The bloody system operates for a week, then breaks down again. The yahoos they send from Central Casting don't seem to know the difference between an elevator motor and an air-conditioning chiller."

"Tolerance was never your virtue, Chuck." Gabby feels exasperated, too. "Before my brains get fried in this heat, refresh my memory. Who's coming today? And remember, I need a minimum of an hour and a half to polish weekend sermons. If you're feeling lousy, I'm feeling washed out. Two sermons a week is more than any rabbi should be asked to produce."

"Have they offered you hazard duty compensation yet?"

Matters of money are personal and Gabby usually avoids such questions. But she feels close to Chuck. His question warrants an answer. "Nothing material, if that's what you have in mind. A few have expressed appreciation for the extra effort made. I hinted that if they wanted this exhausted old mare to plow another field, they better put some more oats into her basket. She needs more sustenance. I'm told that's the way it's done in the business world."

"What was the response?"

"I don't think they understood the metaphor."

He steps toward her desk. "Well, just so you don't think today will be slow, here's a list of people coming. And don't forget, you agreed to meet briefly with Morgan Zentner at 4:30, before the *Shabbat* service this evening."

She receives the list. "How did I agree to such a foolish thing? It sounded like a reasonable thing at the time. I'm not sure now. I'm going downstairs to work in the boardroom which usually feels like a damp dungeon. Send my visitors there. If these yahoos, as you so delicately dub them, get this place cool enough to work here, call me."

GABBY IS USED TO SEEING THE BOARDROOM FILLED with a long, polished mahogany table to seat twenty, with accompanying leather chairs in buffed black leather. Since the table was removed for refinishing, it no longer looks like the boardroom of a Fortune 500 Corporation. Collapsible chairs, appearing quite incongruous, are dispersed around three portable dining tables normally used for Bar/Bat Mitzvah banquets in the social hall. Somebody had deposited tablecloths to hide the crude, composite-wood surfaces, but nobody had yet gotten around to spreading them.

Morning interviews are routine. Two conferences about a religious school teacher some believe incompetent to teach youngsters. One family confers about a son who is engaged to a Gentile girl whom the parents don't like. Whether these parents dislike their future daughter-in-law because of her personality or her Gentile status, Gabby cannot tell. They want their son to marry a Jew and blame the Jewish community for its failure to provide a Jewish mate. Is there anything that can be done in the eleventh hour? Gabby is sympathetic and stoic. The issue of religious identity confronts her daily and plays havoc with her personal life, though no one but Tim Matternly knows it. Part of the responsibility lies with parents; the other with an open society in which Jewish youngsters come in close contact with Gentiles of the opposite sex during the mating phase of their lives. Jews want their children to attend the best universities and graduate schools yet don't want to pay the intermarriage tuition.

Just before lunch, a telephone call from Zoe Mountolive is patched through the receptionist to the boardroom.

"Rabbi Lewyn." Zoe is formal and Gabby believes overly impressed with titles. "I'm at my firm's Washington office. I'd like to see you, if possible."

"Absolutely." Gabby's enthusiasm is apparent for she admires the attorney. "God knows, my schedule is packed and If I don't squirrel away time for preparing my weekend sermons, it's going to sound as if everything I say comes directly from God's mouth, not mine—which, of course, it does."

Zoe laughs modestly. "I can't get away until the end of the day. I know this is your Sabbath, but is there a chance I could come to your service this evening and we can talk a bit afterward?"

"You really want to attend our Sabbath worship?" Gabby is dubious of the motivation.

"Sure. I grew up in New York. Most of my friends are Jewish. They call me their *shiksa* mascot. Exposure rubs off."

"The service begins at six and usually ends at seven so people can go home to their families. If you'd like, we can go to my condo afterward and I'll put together a little *Shabbat* dinner. Nothing fancy, you understand, but I've been taking cooking classes and would love to put some of this impressive training to use."

"I'd like that. I'll return to New York sometime tomorrow midday. What did you learn in cooking classes?"

"To make *sushi*."

"Sounds marvelous. Can I be the beneficiary of this talent?"

"I doubt we can pick up the necessary fresh fish at that hour. *Sushi* isn't the traditional *Shabbat* dinner, you know."

"I'll take a raincheck. Wait until friends learn. You're probably the only rabbi/*sushi* chef in America."

"You know where Ohav Shalom is located?"

"No. But I'm sure a good cab driver will."

"Discuss the fee first. Drivers in this city are infamous for fleecing out-of-towners. It's a scandal."

"Not to worry. The Zentners are paying my expenses. And this is official business."

BY 4:30 IN THE AFTERNOON THE AIR-CONDITIONING is working, but the building hasn't cooled sufficiently for Gabby to see anyone in her office. Chuck Browner ushers Morgan Zentner, Noah's estranged wife, to the boardroom. She is a dusty-blond understated woman who lets her natural beauty speak for itself. There are no traces of makeup around her eyes, or on her cheeks or lips. Her ears, over which her hair is drawn back with a simple bone buckle, lack earrings. That no necklace dangles from her narrow, sculpted neck is in keeping with the statement she is attempting to make. No wedding ring either. Her eyes dart from side to side avoiding contact.

During an opening conversation, Gabby learns that Noah met her at a boating party when she was an editor with Paradigm Books in New York. Shortly after their marriage, she returned to Washington where she had grown up and founded a small but successful literary agency, representing what the book trade calls Washington books, because they are usually authored by ex-government officials with inside savvy about how things really work in the capital.

Morgan Zentner appears to hesitate as she takes a seat opposite Gabby. Her eyes scan the room as if looking for something. "You're probably wondering why I want to speak with you."

"The thought crossed my mind. But now that you're here, I'm sure you'll tell me."

Morgan's eyes drop to her lap, but immediately rise to meet Gabby's. "It has to do with loneliness, particularly now that I'm separated from my husband. I'm sure you've read about Noah's troubles in the newspapers. He did me in pretty bad. Infidelity isn't a victimless crime as liberals in this town would like us to believe. I'm now a bona fide member of the Betrayed Wives Club."

Gabby usually practices the art of listening without interruption, but an urge she doesn't understand compels her to interject, "From the little I know of him, he doesn't strike me as the raping type."

"You're perceptive, Rabbi. Eli Waller is lying through her

teeth. Noah didn't rape her. I don't think he has enough imagination for something as unconventional as that. Besides, he could hop into bed with just about any woman he wanted by waving a wallet at her. He screwed Eli. He admitted that much. But I doubt he raped her."

"We'll have to let the law sort that out. I know this hasn't been easy on you. I try to imagine how it would be to be married and have someone around all the time, then suddenly be alone again. Like a death in the family, I suppose."

Morgan doesn't reply. Instead, she adjusts her position in the chair and allows her hand to pass over the top of the table, tapping it with her forefinger. Only after a long, uncomfortable silence does she re-enter the conversation. "Rabbi Greer was a wonderful counselor and friend. I'm sorry to see him leave. I never got the feeling he was trying to pry open my soul. 'That,' he once said, 'is private property. No man should trespass therein without express permission.'"

"And did you give him that permission?"

She yawns in the late afternoon heat and fights a second yawn. "Not really. I never sought him for therapy in the traditional sense. I edited a book he was writing which I hope someday to publish for him. I also took his courses at Georgetown. Rabbi Greer taught me how to talk to God."

"You probably know he was scheduled to teach Medieval Jewish Thought this semester. The administration's asked me to substitute for him and I've agreed to give it a whirl."

"I'm enrolled, Rabbi Lewyn. I didn't know who would take his place. I look forward to hearing a few of your lectures."

Gabby notes how she has committed herself to only a portion of the course. To move from the subject, she asks, "Were Seth Greer's instructions useful?"

"He introduced me to prayer for a starter."

"Not revolutionary, but prayer is the most popular pathway to the Almighty. If this is too personal, feel free to remain silent, but I'm curious to know why God is so important to you. To people who feel they know God, He's very important. To those who do not, He isn't. People seem to be in one or the other camp. Where do you fit?"

"I want God to be my friend. Someone to talk to."

Gabby's eyebrows rise in approval. "Sounds wise to me. It

isn't a good idea to burden families and friends with our fears and anxieties. They have their own troubles. God, in contrast, is supposed to be a patient listener. Conventional wisdom has it He likes to listen, especially if our thoughts are uttered in the form of prayer."

"Rabbi Greer encouraged me to attend worship services."

"Good advice. If someone prays with a congregation on a regular basis he or she usually feels comfortable approaching God privately. Even if just to vent angers or frustrations. There's a credit system involved when asking God for favors. Putting in the time and effort at public worship adds credibility to private petitions. If you've punched the right tickets, you don't feel like a silly hypocrite when you ask for divine help."

"Seth once said that God must listen because that's His job. Nobody would come to the Temple if He stopped listening."

Gabby notices that Morgan is more comfortable now. She has dropped the formality and called Rabbi Greer, Seth. This informality triggers suspicion that Morgan was among his paramours. Just about every female is suspect these days. Seth, Emma, Noah, and Morgan were close.

Gabby says, "Sounds like something Heinrich Heine said on his deathbed. His friend asked him if he believed God would forgive his sins and he replied, 'Why, of course, that's God's job.' Speaking of forgiveness, how do you feel about it?"

"I don't understand," Morgan answers.

"Can you forgive Noah? Forgiveness seems to be in the genes. I don't mean that literally and I have no scientific proof for this, but I've noticed that some people have the capacity to forgive and others do not."

"It's not my specialty, if that's what you're suggesting. Have you given a sermon about forgiveness?"

"More than people want to hear. I've been accused of repeating myself."

"Occupational hazard?"

"Absolutely. Particularly when I have to deliver two new sermons each week, which brings up an immediate problem. I'm afraid I must excuse myself to prepare for this evening's service. If you're staying, it would be a good time to practice talking with God."

"Then I won't be able to hear your address."

"Better you should talk with God than listen to me," Gabby says as she stands to end the conversation. "Of course, you're welcome to come back when I'm not so pressed. I'm no Seth Greer, however."

"Close enough in a strange way," Morgan says as she also rises. They walk toward the door where she pauses. "What happened to the beautiful conference table that was here?"

Gabby puts her hand on Morgan's spine, ushering her through the door to the hallway. "You might say it's at a hospital for sick furniture. It has been removed for refinishing. Rather ironic, nobody seemed to take particular notice until workmen carted it away. Now, it's on everybody's inquiry list. Perhaps we should auction off visitation tickets."

"I'd like to see you again, Rabbi," Morgan says a moment before they break company. "You've opened a possibility I hadn't entertained before."

"Then you're welcome to call."

"I know this might sound strange but I have a small request. Will you say a prayer for Noah?"

Gabby hesitates for a moment in surprise, then quickly rallies. "Of course, but it would be better if offered by you. If I were God, I'd be very pleased to hear from a betrayed spouse."

"God has left me to face my troubles alone. He's abandoned me."

"Sorry." Gabby has cultivated a didactic manner of speech. "In my experience, it's not God who abandons people, but people who lose faith in God. Reach out, Morgan. If you find nothing in response, then come talk with me. I promise not to say that God listens when you don't believe it. Feeling abandoned is like getting slugged in the gut with a baseball bat. See you in the chapel."

AT EXACTLY 6:00 P.M., GABBY STRIDES ONTO THE raised platform ahead of Cantor Blass. Her smile greets the congregation, mostly composed of senior citizens and people who have dropped in to say *Kaddish* for a deceased relative. The organist is playing a musical adaptation of the 41st Psalm of David. The short, balding Cantor possesses a crystal-clear tenor voice of extraordinary amplitude, a fact which fuels speculation he's a frustrated opera singer. His range among the octaves is so wide it discourages congregants from joining him in song. Gabby fears that restricting him will hurt his feelings. Seth Greer once commented that accompanying Reuben Blass was like singing along with Yma Sumac, the legendary Inca voice of the Andes with a five octave range.

When the music ends, Gabby steps to the lectern and, for an instant, scans the congregation. The question arises in her mind—why are they there? She hides an internal giggle. Well, Mrs. Garfinkel in the second pew comes to talk with God. And Mrs. Cohen seated on her right and whispering into her ear, has obviously come to talk with Mrs. Garfinkel. The congregation is invited to stand, at which time the cantor and organist break out into a traditional version of the Sabbath Bride whose refrain most congregants can sing. Its poetic lyrics from the seventeeth century liken the Sabbath to a bride entering the marriage canopy. Gabby mouths the words while identifying Morgan Zentner. Three rows in front stands Zoe Mountolive, reading glasses on the bridge of her nose, studying the prayer book as though a legal brief. During the cantorial recitations her eye catches Morgan Zentner seemingly contracted into her own thoughts.

Later, when congregants gather to bless the *Shabbat* wine and bread in the synagogue foyer, Gabby circulates among them, exchanging greetings. She feels uncomfortable at the prospect of introducing Zoe to Morgan and is relieved when the necessity doesn't arise. Morgan elects not to stay for the blessings. Zoe, on the other hand, steps forward and extends both hands in greeting.

"Hungry?" Gabby asks.

"Famished."

"Then what are we waiting for? Let's head to my pad where we can get you something stronger to drink than Manischewitz Concord."

"If we can't get *sushi* at this hour, how about *gefilte* fish *kakumachi*?"

Gabby likes her wit. "Not from my fridge. Nothing but a jar of spaghetti sauce, months old. We'll pick up something else on the way home. After dinner, I'll take you to your hotel. Where are you staying?"

"The Willard."

"My favorite. Did you know that President Grant used to walk there from the White House to smoke cigars in the lobby and watch Washington society parade by?"

"No. But I'm not surprised. People-watching was a favorite pastime. These days people just see others on a TV screen."

SABBATH DINNER AT GABBY'S CONDO IS A MAKESHIFT affair. They stop at Sutton Place Gourmet for a selection of pre-cooked dishes: cold Oriental sesame chicken, roasted peppers and green beans and a loaf of *challah*. Gabby arranges *Shabbat* candles and a *Kiddush* cup, then places the *challah* on a silver tray. Though she has already recited the blessings at the synagogue, she likes to duplicate candle lighting at home when she has guests This presents something of a religious dilemma, for Jewish law forbids the duplication of identical ceremonies on the grounds that the second fulfillment depreciates the first. But then, she reasons, rabbinical scholars never anticipated a female rabbi who would come home to have a Sabbath meal with a lawyer friend from New York City—now did they?

Gabby assembles the food while Zoe shepherds it to the dining room and fusses with table settings. The peace of Sabbath descends upon them as they sit in quiet, looking at each other through soft candlelight. Gabby pours for her guest a glass of Sauvignon Blanc, then arches back, sipping from her own glass.

"So how's Clementine getting along after her injury?"

"Had to hobble around on crutches for three days, but I think it was an adventure. She was a hero among her friends, and that's important for young girls. Her walking cast has so many autographs it looks like a souvenir baseball. Thanks for remembering her. One imagines that with all the troubles you hear about you'd forget something as insignificant as this."

"On the contrary, when you deal with problems all day you tend to remember even small ones. God help me if I forget that Sarah Goldstein is in the hospital for a tonsillectomy. Or that so-and-so is having marital difficulties. By the way, I don't recall you mentioning your husband. I'd like to meet him."

"In a prison yard, perhaps." Zoe takes a long slip and smiles playfully. "Separated, just a hop, skip, and a jump from final divorce. If I say anything about that S.O.B., I'd tarnish this Sabbath."

"Sorry to hear it. I take it then that Clementine is living with you."

"Yes, but she visits her father on weekends, that is when he can make time in his busy social life. He's a lousy role model for a female adolescent."

"Why is that?"

"My soon-to-be ex acknowledges only two parts of the female anatomy—the jugular and the vagina. Clemmy is the most discreet child I've ever known. She never says a word about the women in Peter's life, though I know they're always fluttering about his home or, should I say, our old home."

"Kids are like that. Born politicians. They keep secrets far better than adults. So how is your social life?"

"Stinks. Between work and Clemmy there isn't much time. No, that's not true at all. Clemmy sort of takes care of herself. There is time for dating, but no dates. It's a desert out there. Not sure why, but my telephone barely rings. Other women in my situation seem to have the same complaint. The good men are taken."

"But you must meet fascinating lawyers."

"Only nerds and creeps. Having dinner with a lawyer is like dining with Father Torquemada, the Grand Inquisitor. First, he tells you how busy he is, which is a code word for how good a lawyer he thinks he is. Then, he boasts about how he outfoxed a judge, a jury, or both. And you, Rabbi? Have you a significant other?"

"First of all, it's Gabrielle, or Gabby. No reason why you should call me Rabbi when none of my friends do. And no, there's no significant man at the moment. There was someone in the shadows. Somebody I cared a lot about, but he's moved on to another lady."

Gabby pauses to pass the peppers and green beans sautéed in olive oil. They busy themselves with their plates, then cast empathetic eyes on one another.

Zoe pours more wine into Gabby's glass and refills her own.

"Is there going to be a trial?" Gabby asks.

"Yes. Got confirmation from the grand jury this morning. A team of prosecutors has been selected. Sylvia Junqueira will lead it. Smart, with a specialty in rape cases. Wins more than she loses."

"Sounds like your firm should hire her."

"When she gets tired of representing the government and wants to make more money she'll probably take a job with a big Baltimore firm. We may see each other at conferences of the Bar Association. But for the next few months, she's my enemy, the Wicked Witch of the East. Which brings us to a new development in Noah's case."

Gabby puts down her fork. She senses there's an agenda which takes a long time to come out.

"You've noticed our case has stimulated media attention big time. The Women's Movement is responsible for stoking small embers into a roaring bonfire. There's nothing like a celebrity rape case to captivate national interest. To make matters worse, the press is attracted to Eli Waller like the Mafia to money. We'd prefer this publicity go away, but it won't. The case is already being tried in the media."

"Sounds like a rush to judgment."

"Hopefully a jury will weigh the evidence carefully. I must tell you that we've been approached by the Legal Channel to cover the trial on live TV. Judge Cauldfeld, who probably won't hear the case himself but who has temporary jurisdiction over the pretrial proceedings, has no objections. Both prosecution and defense are being consulted."

"Why drag Noah through hell? Can't you prevent it?"

"We might, but it's dangerous. A jury will think that we had something to hide. Our team, some of whom you met in New York, thinks we should agree. I personally concur. But that will have implications for our witnesses. Publicity may be good for the lawyers, but not for rabbis."

Gabby remains in contemplation. She is unprepared for this. Indeed, it puts her in a difficult position, yet she knows how to deflect with a counter-question. "How important is my testimony?"

"Things might change as we approach the trial, but for the moment it's very important."

"Discrete testimony is one thing, but testimony before the eyes of the world is something else. My friends in the Movement will fricassee me for dinner."

"Not this one. But I know what you're saying. We're asking a lot."

"If a rabbi supports an accused Jewish rapist, people might say that Jews condone one of their own while condemning Gentiles for the same crime."

"True, but unfair," Zoe comments. "I don't believe anybody will hold you personally responsible."

"Gentiles can think what they want. Jews will blame me for exposing them to accusations of favoritism. If they go on a frenzy of self-righteousness, nothing will assuage their wrath. This rabbi will probably have to turn in her yarmulke. I won't even get a job teaching kindergarten."

"Sorry, friend. We've got to fight with all the ammunition at our disposal. We can't afford not to be on TV. But we also need you on the stand. I know this complicates your position, but hopefully you'll see your way clear."

Gabby stops eating. What Zoe suggests will require much thought but for the moment she's too tired to think clearly. "I assume that your team will be making preparations in Washington."

"Some, but not all. Our headquarters will remain in New York. I plan to be in D.C. biweekly until the trial begins. I hope we'll see each other. And talk about things other than work."

Gabby is silent again, lost in thought. Nothing is simple. When she emerges from her contemplation a single word escapes her lips. "Asshole."

Zoe doesn't understand and shakes her head.

"Nothing," Gabby rejoins the conversation. "This has nothing to do with you. Or Noah. I was referring to a colleague who left me in the lurch. I wouldn't be in this pickle if Rabbi Greer had kept his pants on."

July 27th

Despite Ephraim Rothman's notification, Gabby hears nothing from Gertrude Swidler or the Rabbinical Search Committee for several days. That's hardly what one would call enthusiasm. The Committee is obviously occupied with other candidates. It is difficult for Gabby to persevere when she feels slighted. In its own blundering and blind manner, the congregation takes but does not give back. No one is particularly at fault. Gabby's rabbinical colleagues complain of the same occupational hazard. She believes that clergy set themselves up for mistreatment. Congregants keep asking for more and more; clergy love to be loved and therefore fail to say no. Soon they feel abused.

By the time Gertrude Swidler's invitation arrives, Gabby feels like someone invited to a Saturday night dinner party late on Saturday afternoon. You know you were not the first choice among invitees. Delay is proof Gabby is running behind others for Seth's job. The Committee works overtime, sometimes meeting three times a week—shuffling interviews, correspondence, recommendations, telephone calls, and of course, gossip. Most meetings occur outside the synagogue to minimize disruption in daily routine. Since the announcement of a search in the Rabbinical Association's newsletter, Gabby has been inundated with inquiries from colleagues, seeking insider information she does not feel comfortable providing. The callers are, after all, her competitors.

Before leaving her condo for the Tuesday evening interview, she checks her e-mail for a message from Timothy. There's always the possibility that something will go wrong in his romance. She's not proud of that hope, but neither can she extinguish it. Perhaps Sally will be good for Tim. Were she his therapist, she would deliver a Dump-Rabbi-Gabby-Lewyn-and-Get-on-with-Your-Life speech. Limbo is the worst ground to hold. And were she her own therapist, she'd advise the same damn thing. Fortunately, she is neither. It would be wholly wrong to try sabotaging Tim's ticket to happiness. She is nevertheless free to hope for a breakup. There is no e-mail from him.

She does not recognize the address of a new message on her screen. It turns out to be from the Pyramid Development Corporation. The message is slightly longer than the abbreviated communications one usually receives.

> *Since my arraignment I am supposed to remain in the District of Columbia. For the time being I'm staying in an apartment at the Watergate owned by business partners. Can you jog with me late Saturday afternoon after you're finished with your rabbinical duties? We could run at Hains Point, opposite National Airport. Trying to keep in shape in order to keep my spirits up—not an easy task these days. Waiting for the law to run its course is horrible. If you're free, I'll pick you up at the synagogue or your home.*
>
> *Noah Zentner*

Gabby checks her appointment schedule, then asks herself if jogging with Noah crosses a professional line separating a minister from her parishioner. Mixing work and leisure can be dangerous, especially with someone hounded by the media. Running together in Central Park was one thing. But Hains Point in their hometown could be quite another. Television cameras and aggressive reporters are ubiquitous in the Nation's Capital.

She is about to reply negatively, but hesitates. The jog with Noah in Central Park was enjoyable. She sensed his reserve strength and endurance, yet he avoided taxing her at an impossible pace. While he has cause to feel angry, she discovered in him few signs of self-pity or, for that matter, outrage. His attitude seemed positive, yet resigned. And that she admires.

On the keyboard her fingers act with their own independence, responding more from impulse than reason. They type a simple reply:

OK, Rabbi Lewyn

She does not send the message until it becomes necessary to log off the network, but at the last moment presses the SEND key, dispatching it into cyberspace.

THE VENUE FOR HER INTERVIEW IS THE SWIDLER'S Kalorama home, among ambassadorial residences along Embassy Row. The Search Committee is composed of past movers and shakers of the Washington Jewish community. However friendly their greetings at the Swidler home, she nevertheless feels isolated. Ephraim Rothman has purposely absented himself. By phone, he confided that he had made his position clear and did not wish to prejudice the Committee's judgment. His presence is missed.

Nine interviewers sit around Gertrude's glass dining room table, now stacked with folders and notepads, all closed to prevent Gabby from glimpsing their contents. No one is particularly at ease for they are interviewing a rabbi whom a previous search committee hired seven years before. Two of the presiding members, along with Seth Greer, served on that committee.

Gabby is seated at the foot of the table in easy eye contact with four individuals on each side and Gertrude at the far end. As chairperson, Gertrude is aware how the selection process has demanded more of everybody's time than originally anticipated and she is eager not to waste more of it this evening. "You know, Rabbi Lewyn, how grateful we are for your service during this difficult period. The fact that the Temple is running on all cylinders while we're searching for Rabbi Greer's replacement is a credit to your rabbinical skills." She glances to the left and right for approbation and notes three bobbing heads. "That you are functioning so well cannot be overlooked by this committee when it makes its final recommendation to the Board and ultimately to the members. I feel compelled to state that regardless of our final recommendations, you have our admiration and gratitude. Yet those seated here tonight agree unanimously that for the congregation's welfare we must separate the present from the future. We hope you understand this delicate matter."

To Gabby that sounds like a writeoff. "It's been a busy time. Rabbi Greer left behind much unfinished business."

Nathan Pearl, an accountant by training and President of the congregation a half-dozen years before, shuffles notes before him. He is Deputy Secretary of the United States Department of the Treasury and is comfortable dealing with personnel matters. "Rabbi Lewyn, we're trying to place all candidates on a level playing field so we can properly evaluate their qualifications. We recognized that candidates might dissemble a bit in order to tell us what they think we want to hear. Since you are known to us, that isn't so easy."

A round of muffled chuckles emanates around the table. When it subsides, Nathan Pearl continues, "That's not to say you would, only that you wouldn't get away with it because we know you too well. In a bizarre way, that's not fair to you."

Gabby opens her hands parallel to the tabletop. "I didn't go into this trade in order to dissemble. Life's too short, as the saying goes."

Gertrude interrupts. "Gabby, there are subjects we've agreed not to talk about this evening. That's not to say they won't come up later, but for the time being they are of secondary interest. And to put you into the picture, they are the gender question and your past service to the congregation."

Steven Blau, a cardiologist at George Washington School of

Medicine, a sitting Trustee, smooths his manicured goatee. "So there's no misunderstanding, there are two women among the candidates we're interviewing. One has three more years experience than you; the other, two years less. Ohav Shalom is not against hiring a woman to fill Seth's post. If we exclude women from our search, the members would probably drag us before a firing squad."

"That's gratifying. Women have come a long way in this profession since I entered the field."

It is Sadie Meyerson who intones, "If you think we've come far in your day, there were times in mine when women couldn't make *Aliyah*. No Bat Mitzvahs either. Ohav Shalom is and will remain a leader in the equality field, despite what the Orthodox say about us."

Kenneth Michaels is a litigating partner in the prestigious law firm of Drew, Morrison, Denning, and Stevens which represents client interests before the various federal agencies in the Nation's Capital. His Hermès silk necktie fits perfectly against the white starched collar of his shirt, though he has removed his jacket in the informality of Gertrude's dining room, revealing wide scarlet-red suspenders. His hair thins in the front which he manages to disguise by pulling forward thicker hair from the sides and crown, providing the appearance of an aging Roman consul. He's been employing the Socratic method of interrogation in litigation so long he's unaware how aggressive his verbal interaction is.

"If I may..." He elbows his way into the conversation. "Rabbi Lewyn, you force us to face a significant dilemma with respect to your candidacy. On the one hand, you're well respected in the congregation. In the course of your tenure with Ohav, we conducted polls and evaluations. As I understand it, you were originally appointed for a two-year stint, and the fact that you're still with us is a credit to your skill. Seth Greer was one of your strong supporters."

Someone across from Michaels mutters, "*Alav ha-Shalom*." May he rest in peace, the traditional Hebrew phrase for referring respectfully to a departed loved one. Applied to Seth it was meant to be humorous yet only one other person manages a chuckle.

"The problem area I referred to," Michaels continues, "deals with your position about not officiating at interfaith marriages. The congregation did not have to face the issue when you were originally appointed. Since Seth Greer was prepared to officiate at these ceremonies, we understood that the two of you worked the matter out between yourselves."

Gabby expected this question to arise and is prepared. The propriety of rabbis to officiate at interfaith marriages has been a contentious issue for years—on legal, religious, and pragmatic grounds. No decision has been rendered except that each rabbi has the right to make his or her own decision.

"Rabbi Greer and I talked about this endlessly," Gabby says, sensing her body temperature rising and fighting to remain calm. "We had an honest difference of opinion and both of us thoroughly understood the complexities. There is not a single word on the subject that hasn't already been said. When it comes to the do's and don't's, the scales of reason are dead-center, fifty-fifty. It is incumbent upon each rabbi to make her or his own choice. Seth came down one way; I another. So he graciously agreed to handle the interfaith weddings for our members' children. Since his resignation only one situation has arisen which I referred to a colleague in Bethesda. The family seems quite content."

"As a practical matter, Rabbi Lewyn," Michaels continues, "do you regard this situation as one that can be handled satisfactorily on a long-term basis by other colleagues, say in Bethesda?"

"I don't see any reason why not."

"Well, let me provide one. If my own daughter were to fall in love with a Gentile boy, I don't think I'd be comfortable with a stranger officiating. Families form special affections for their rabbis and want them to participate in the important life-cycle events. Weddings are very special. People wear their emotions close to the skin."

Gabby holds back her fury. Her rabbinical association has already taken a strong position on the matter. The fact that Ephraim failed to mention this issue causes her to wonder if it is a smokescreen. Is the Search Committee hiding its true agenda? She answers Ken Michaels in an artificially slow cadence. "The question has arisen many times at Ohav Shalom. Both Rabbi Greer and I have dealt with it in seminars and on the annual retreats. I doubt that anyone who has been at one of these sessions will misunderstand my persuasion. I'd delineate it for you now, but I think that would be repetitious and pointless."

Sadie Meyerson, sensing an adversarial tone, interjects with the mature, elderly voice of a peacemaker. "Gabby, were this congregation to promote you Senior Rabbi, would it be within your principles to reconsider your stand on this issue? We wouldn't want you to compromise what you believe in and we're not asking you to do so. My question is—is there room to revisit your past position?"

Gabby's fist is against her lips and she is exhaling warm breath into the cavity created by her fingers. She becomes aware a fist is a hostile symbol and immediately lowers her hand. "Is this a condition of promotion?" She directs her question back to Meyerson.

"We have not come to that conclusion yet. We're exploring."

"Reconsidering means, I guess, that I alter my position."

"If that suggests violating your principles, the answer is, absolutely not," Gertrude adds. "The congregation thinks too highly of you to require that. We have no right to do so."

"Then I take it," Kenneth Michaels says, "that you do not feel the inclination to revisit your position? Is that correct?"

"There are no new arguments. The matter has been debated. *Ad nauseam*. I cannot believe someone will discover a fresh argument or unearth a lost *Halachic* ruling that will turn the debate on end. If that occurs, I'll be happy to reconsider. I doubt I will."

"She's made her point, everybody," Gertrude scowls at Ken Michaels who has a pedantic tendency to beat a dead horse. "So let's move on to another issue and that's one of theological orientation. Over the years, we've noted a marked difference between you and Rabbi Greer over the concept of God. While this is perhaps unfair, he seemed more traditional than you. Would you say that's a fair evaluation?"

"Everyone comes to Judaism in his or her own way. Rabbi Greer was raised in an Orthodox home and comes from an older school. I was not. To use jargon from our profession, he is a Theist and I'm a Deist. He conceives of God as an omnipotent judge, and I as a remote cause. His notion leads to personal relationships; mine, to philosophical concepts."

Daniel Krone, obviously less affluent than the others yet

revered for his selfless devotion to the Temple's daily needs, speaks for the first time. In contrast to the others' fastidiousness, he wears a rumpled shirt, open at the collar with an old-fashioned tie that never made it closer to his neck than three inches. "Is that why he was so good with the prayers?"

"Perhaps. He loves the liturgy."

"And apparently many women, as well," another voice adds in jest.

This jibe catches on. Chuckling is contagious.

Ken Michaels uses the opportunity to elbow back onto center stage. "Well, if that's true, Rabbi Lewyn, would you consider yourself left, right, or center of mainstream Jewish theology?"

She notes the interrogator in hot pursuit and proceeds with caution. "Hard to pigeonhole beliefs as left, right, or center. There are just positions. Or feelings, if you will. And they are subject to change. I've watched people alter their views about God with age. What seems appropriate at one age seems inappropriate at another."

"Sounds like a school of pragmatic thought to me." Michaels exposes a grin of victory. "But clearly, I don't hear anything to make us believe that you're a mainstream thinker on the subject. Your mind is so creative, I wouldn't expect humdrum from it. Eph Rothman thinks you possess the best rabbinical intellect we've had at this congregation in many generations. Better, yes, than Seth Greer and whatever his shortcomings in the flesh, nobody ever accused him of a slothful mind. Yet Ohav Shalom is an institution not unlike the Vatican, however more modest in size. It sits on an institutional bedrock of time-tested beliefs which provide stability, and stability is what our members expect from their rabbis. There's a danger in moving too far and too fast from the bedrock of tradition to make accommodation with the modern world."

"That's what our Orthodox brethren argue and look where's it brought them!" Gabby replies.

"A loyal following." Ken Michaels is lightning with repartee. "And that's what Ohav Shalom must seek for the future. Rabbi, I'm certain you know more about the internal dynamics of congregational life than we; still, we are the appointed guardians of this institution. In a year or two, nobody will remember our deliberations and certainly nobody will thank us for them.

Nevertheless, the fruits of our selection will endure for a long time, like a Supreme Court Justice. A careless choice might have disastrous consequences."

Gabby senses the souring mood of her inquisitioners.

"Seth Greer never had any doubts about the prayers he recited," Glenda BenNachmon enters the conversation. She is a petite, rather attractive widow who serves several congregational committees and is active in city politics. "But you do have doubts about God, is that not true, Gabby?"

"Yes." Gabby is blunt. "But no more than what I discern in the hearts of many members. Often our congregants voice their doubts and reservations about God."

"Good," Glenda BenNachmon blurts, "then can you tell us how you respond?"

"With great difficulty."

Gertrude interjects. "Don't you learn the answers in rabbinical school?"

"If I did, I have forgotten them by now. Besides, I don't believe members of this congregation expect me to provide canned answers learned in rabbinical school. Were I to try, they'd howl me off the pulpit."

"When you go to a doctor you expect him or her to know how to heal your disease, not share your pain."

"True enough, but Judaism can't be quantified and measured like medical science. We're trying to establish a climate for individual judgment. If I'm not wrong, our members object to rigid dogma. There's a delicate line between tradition and dogma and I, for one, advocate flexibility in drawing it."

Glenda BenNachmon again: "Wouldn't you think that a congregation wants its rabbi to possess a powerful commitment to God?"

Gabby is quick to respond. "I would, indeed, yet there's danger in believing we're God's emissaries, that somehow rabbis have stronger convictions than others. It tends to make us arrogant and pompous."

"Well put," Ken Meyerson interjects, his cheeks softening as he tilts his head to peer at his cohorts over the upper rims of his glasses. "Still, we must keep our mandate in mind as we evaluate the liberality of your position."

Gabby shoots back, "Let me make an unequivocal statement

lest anyone misunderstand my position. I don't believe the rabbis at Ohav Shalom should establish core beliefs that will exclude members of our community. We can't afford to lose those who are struggling at their own pace and in their own ways. The pursuit of a belief is just as important as the belief itself."

When committee members begin to glance at their watches, Gertrude Swidler knows the interview must end, otherwise the focus will be lost. Given the first sign of adjournment, they begin packing their belongings in preparation to stand up. Gertrude is pleased questions have focused on Gabby's theological views and not her private life.

"Of course, this session is only preliminary," she reminds everybody. "While we know more about Rabbi Lewyn than the other candidates, there are still many questions we haven't explored. We all thank her for coming this evening."

On the way down the walkway to her car, Glenda BenNachmon catches up and places a hand on Gabby's shoulder. When she is alongside, she says, "Good job, Gabby. You've earned a lot of support in the congregation. Lots of good feeling."

Gabby likes what she hears but is skeptical. Yes, she has many friends, but only a handful will stand up and be counted. And as for a job well done at the interview, she thinks not.

July 24th

Warm summer rains clear Washington's muggy air and satisfy the thirst of its semitropical vegetation. The pavements are slick with puddles, reflecting bright sunlight which peeks through fleeting rain clouds and reveals patches of blue sky beyond.

Unlike her jog with Noah in Central Park, Gabby now feels more comfortable revealing bare legs below nylon shorts. They are well-toned from running—with excellent muscular definition. No ripples of fatty tissue and no varicose veins. Low-cut socks cover only the lip of her jogging shoes and expose the top of narrow ankles. A T-shirt embossed with a collage of drums and cymbals covers the outline of a crossed-strap jogging bra.

Noah is less concerned about his running attire. His T-shirt has been washed so many times the printing is faded beyond recognition. The shoes he wore in New York are soiled from extensive use and the stitching is beginning to fray. He parks his Acura near the 14th Street Bridge and they trot along the Park Service road. Previous rains and a high tidal swell of the Potomac River flood the low-lying lawn beyond the embankment. She inches in front of him just far enough to decide how they should navigate pooling water. Puddles splash their shoes and calves. Since staying dry is impossible, they plow through the water with abandon.

"I've met with Zoe Mountolive," Gabby tells him as they find a comfortable stride and move south, the Potomac and Washington's National Airport on their right. "She was in Washington and we talked about your case."

Noah steps up the pace as they move from a gravel path to an asphalt road. "We speak daily. Never did any criminal law myself and had no idea how complex this case is. I want you to know what I said in New York still stands. If you choose not to testify, I won't be angry. If I were your attorney, I'd advise you not to."

The new pace is faster than her training speed. Experience has taught her to run through this initial fatigue to find a second wind, then adjust into a cruising rhythm. "I appreciate the honesty, Noah."

"You've got other things on your mind, Rabbi. I'd be surprised if you didn't want Seth's position. Why shouldn't you? Testifying will bury your career in Washington. Zoe Mountolive concurs with me."

Warm air causes Gabby to sweat heavily on the back of the neck and on her chest. Drops of perspiration begin to run from her forehead into the eyebrows. "Lawyers see everything as adversarial; consequently, everybody operates for self-interest. Rabbis don't fit the stereotype."

"Sounds idyllic."

"We're not exactly selfless. We're trained to be teachers, not saints."

"Well, in my book anybody who runs as well as you deserves to be Senior Rabbi at Ohav Shalom."

"I'll take that as a compliment. Maybe I can get the Search Committee to let me race my competition."

"You'd run them into the ground—if that's not contrary to your view of self-sacrifice."

Gabby tilts her head to smile and finds him smiling at her. She enjoys the banter. "I suppose it is. But don't be deceived. I'm not conceding and intend to run as fast and as hard as I can."

"Then drop the idea of helping me." His voice is now authoritative.

"Sounds as if you don't want my help."

"What I want is not what I deserve. There's no purpose to compounding tragedies. I've made my mistakes. You shouldn't have to pay for them."

They continue south as flocks of herring gulls head north into wind gusting along the Potomac. Scattered black-headed Canada geese rest on the water, facing the wind. Occasionally, they launch themselves into the air with powerful wings, only to join their cohorts on the water some distance away. As he strides through the pools of water, Noah is sure-footed; Gabby is more cautious. When puddles deepen, her speed decreases. Being off-balance upsets her stride.

Within view of a bronze sculpture of the sea god Neptune emerging from the lawn as though from the ocean bed, Noah cuts to the east, just as two white-and-olive-colored presidential helicopters rise into the air from Bolling Air Force Base, across the Washington Basin. They move in unison, one two-hundred feet higher than the other, and turn north in the direction of the White House Lawn to meet the President. Noah's eyes follow as the noisy aircraft claw for height and, for an instant, he loses awareness of his feet. During this lapse of attention his lead foot drops into pooled water hiding a discarded beer can. His shoe smashes into the tin surface, twisting the foot inside. He hops instinctively with his other foot to reduce impact. Too late. Ligaments in his ankle send pain shooting from the foot through the calf.

Gabby is slightly ahead and for a few moments does not notice. When she finally glances back, he is stopped, bent over, massaging his ankle.

"I'm all right," he says as Gabby scampers in his direction. He drops his lame foot for a test and immediately recoils with pain. The second attempt is less shocking and he manages a limp.

"Sprained my ankle like a damn fool. Wasn't watching where I put my foot. Serves me right."

He hobbles a few feet on the lame foot, but this time Gabby snatches his arm to help distribute weight.

"Give me a few seconds and I'll be as good as new."

She studies the pattern of his footsteps. "The way you're moving, that's not likely."

"As soon as the pain leaves, I'll be able to move again. I usually run through minor injuries."

"Can you walk?"

He does, but has to keep his weight off the injured ankle. She plants an arm around his waist as he moves slowly forward. "If I were you, I wouldn't run on that. Short-term bliss, long-term doom. No need to impress me. I know an injury when I see one. The best athletes get hurt. Smart ones take the time to heal. Foolish ones end up on the waiver lists."

"Is that a rabbinical edict, Rabbi?"

"Absolutely not. Just coach talk. I'll get your car."

"Know how to drive a stick shift?"

"I can drive a five-ton truck, a Humvee, a CAT, a Harley-Davidson, and a ten-speed bike. Your Acura's a cinch. I can also fix a flat tire and change the oil. Don't ask me for anything more complicated."

They turn together and start hobbling in the opposite direction. "I'm impressed. Lady of multiple accomplishments. You've got to be the most talented rabbi alive."

"A few twentieth-century skills, but I'm no scientist. Damn near flunked Beginning Algebra."

He moves easier now, with each step placing more weight on the injured foot. When they near his parked car, he hands over the ignition keys. "Okay, Rabbi, you drive. It's 4:30. Got time for a beer?"

"Sounds great to me, though we didn't run enough to deserve it. I know a colonial tavern in Alexandria with some pizazz."

"Is that in the Washington Metropolitan Area?"

"I guess so."

"Good, because the terms of my release restrict me to the Washington Metropolitan Area, New York City, National and La Guardia Airports."

"Alexandria is close enough to National Airport. Besides,

you're with a rabbi which should count for something, although I'm not sure what."

WELLINGTON'S TAVERN FIRST OPENED ITS DOORS to the likes of George Washington and his crowd in 1769, almost a decade before the American Revolution. Over the years, the tavern opened and closed a dozen times and was reopened in 1987 after major restoration in the colonial style. Waitresses and barmen dress in colonial costumes. The dark, colonial-style ale served in crockery tankards is produced in a local Virginia microbrewery.

Alexandria yuppies cluster around Wellington's beer taps as they get an early start on a Saturday evening pub crawl. Gabby and Noah sit on opposite sides of an oak table in the shadows where they are not likely to be noticed. Nobody in Wellington's puts the face of a jogger together with what they see on television.

"How's your case going?" Gabby asks after determining they're not to be overheard in the bar room din. "I try to follow it in the *Times*."

"The incident has escalated. It's taken on a life of its own. Hard to understand how people could make so much from so little. The media exaggerate everything. Over and over, station by station, the same drivel. If you want my opinion, what happened on the Chesapeake is nobody's business but Eli Waller's and mine. The public thinks it owns a part of us. What it actually owns is 10 percent fact and 90 percent invention."

"I've seen her on TV. She seems to be on one channel or another every night. New hairstyle. New chic clothes. She's wearing jewelry for the first time. Somebody's managing a fantastic press campaign for her."

"That's the plan. At first I couldn't believe she'd accuse me. But she must have weighed the publicity value verses loss of Pyramid's business. Overnight she becomes a crusader for feminist causes. Unfortunately, I'm on the wrong side of this political correctness."

"The final chapter hasn't been written yet. Hopefully some good will come of it."

"I'm not against that. And I'm not against prosecuting guilty rapists. But only with evidence."

Gabby sips her ale thoughtfully. A small residue of foam remains on her upper lip. "You believe you were set up for this?"

"Not at first. But as I watch Elisheva exploiting every opportunity to publicize herself, I have difficulty resisting the temptation. Normally, I don't believe in plots. Most people just bump along, muddling through the day. Elisheva's a walking advertisement for sex. She certainly doesn't groom herself like that to sit at home and play bridge. There isn't a red-blooded male in this country who wouldn't find her an enticement. She initiated our little tryst, but turned against me for some reason I don't understand."

"Sounds as if she's the aggressor. Did it ever occur to you to press rape charges against her?"

"The thought never even entered my mind. Has there been such a conviction? The truth is, she didn't rape me. How could I accuse her of what she didn't do?"

"Rape's a delicate line."

"Tell me about it. In the end, it will come down to her word against mine."

He looks uncomfortable with this. In an awkward gesture he glances at his watch. "I promised not to monopolize your time, Rabbi. I'm sure you have plans for the evening. Tell me when, and I'll scoot you home."

"That's all right," she says.

"Is there a time you must be back?"

She laughs at herself, a smile just budding on her lips which she hopes he doesn't notice. "No. Truth is I have no plans tonight. So we'll go when you're ready."

"Then maybe you'll have an early dinner with me. Dressed in these clothes we can't go anywhere fancy, but there are some informal places nearby where I might not be recognized."

It is past nine o'clock when they finish eating Chinese food and he drives her home. His ankle is now swollen and walking is still painful. He isn't worried. A few days and he will be jogging again.

In the car outside her condo, he says, "Rabbi, there's a matter of some delicacy I haven't brought up. I could have said something earlier, but the idea sort of gets caught in my throat. It's not something that I'm comfortable with." He fondles the steering wheel nervously. "You know that Ephraim Rothman and my father are like brothers."

"I know they're close but not exactly how close."

"Ephraim is almost an uncle. He cares a lot about the Temple. He cares a lot about Judaism. And he thinks you'd be a great Senior Rabbi. He would exert his influence on the Selection Committee, but he respects the process and insists on letting it evolve. He gives service to Ohav; my family gives money. If we wanted to, we could make things happen there for you."

The suggestion catches Gabby unprepared. "Are you trying to buy my help as a witness?"

"Absolutely not. One is unrelated to the other. I already told you I don't think testifying is in your interest."

"I don't think I believe you, Noah Zentner. But I'm flattered nevertheless." She pauses, gathering time to think. "Thanks for the offer, if that's what it is. I can only give one answer and that's no. Between you and me, I'd love to become Senior Rabbi. I hope I will, though I believe my chances slim. Still, I have no right to be shoehorned in. The congregation must make its own selection because it must live with its choice for a long time. Eph is right about the process. If the truth be known, he's the one they should appoint. Eph's the saint here."

"Personnel decisions ultimately come down to influence."

"I won't quarrel with that, only I don't have to condone it. Can't imagine standing in the pulpit and looking at people who didn't elect me to be their rabbi."

"I thought you'd say something like that. After what Seth's done, I was beginning to lose faith in your profession."

"Elu v'elu, divray Elohim," she remarks in Hebrew.

"What does that mean?"

"There are people who see an issue one way, and others just the opposite. That's what makes ball games."

"You get all that from a few Hebrew words?"

"Well, let's say I added a little commentary."

Chapter Six

August 2nd

Katherine Klein came to Washington from a patrician California Gold Rush family as a political appointee in the Department of Commerce and caught Potomac fever, an affliction of the wealthy who lust to govern. She married and raised three children in the District of Columbia, continuing to take appointed jobs in the Federal City when the Republicans were in power. In years when Democrats ruled, she worked the TV circuit as a government affairs commentator and wrote a book about financial mismanagement in various Democratic administrations. Political hibernation allowed her to devote time to family and the arts—always waiting for a change of administrations and a new appointment to office. Unfortunately for the elegant and social Katherine, time was limited.

Surgery for ovarian cancer at Sloan Kettering in New York, followed by a crippling regime of chemotherapy, tested her mettle. Her doctors claimed they could do no more than carefully monitor her health, which they did at Georgetown University Hospital. Her final years of life she devoted to communal and philanthropic causes, one of which was Ohav Shalom's vocational training program in Tel Aviv for immigrants from Morocco and Tunisia. Pain in her left hip was her first clue that the old tumor had metastasized. More chemotherapy, more doctors, more time in Georgetown Hospital, with trips to Johns Hopkins in Baltimore and Sloan Kettering in New York. At each stage she became weaker.

Seth Greer had been a superb rabbi to the sick. Before offering the infirm counsel or prayers he would first educate himself thoroughly on the nature of their disease. Few rabbinic colleagues could match his medical knowledge, and some humorously referred to him as Dr. Seth, swapping an M.D. degree for his earned Ph.D. It was not unusual to see him reading the *New England Journal of Medicine* for state-of-the-art treatments. And unlike many clergy, he was seldom uncomfortable at the bedside of dying congregants. His words of solace were never laced with cliché. He gave willingly whatever time the sick required. When it became clear Katherine's physicians could not restore her health, the family looked to him for mediation with the Almighty. He didn't believe God would intervene in the natural process of disease but comforted the family anyway.

When modern medicine could do no more for Katherine, her suffering ended. Her extended family from the suburbs of San Francisco attends the funeral, as well as innumerable friends and associates from Washington, including a half-dozen Congressmen and the newly-elected female Senator from California. So large is the gathering it is necessary to forgo the funeral home chapel and utilize Ohav Shalom's 1,700-seat sanctuary.

Under normal conditions, the Klein family would have wanted Seth Greer to officiate, thus Gabby knows she is second choice. While Seth was definitely a better counselor to the sick, she feels better at conducting life-cycle ceremonies. Seth is florid and sentimental; she, terse and pragmatic. At funerals he stresses the eternal life of the spirit, while she the hard-core pain of loss. He yearns for the future; she grieves for the present. Seth tends to dramatize and sometimes glamorize the life of the deceased. Gabby's eulogies simply trace the prominent deeds of the dead and fit them into a family profile.

Dressed in a black suit with a broad cream-colored collar that contrasts with her brunette, almost black hair, she wears no *tallit*. A simple black *yarmulke* is pinned to the crown of her head. Demure gold earrings. She studies those who stand in the pews. They come to pay respect to the deceased, yet seem to come for another purpose—perhaps to rehearse rites for their own deaths. Gabby often reminds herself how time alone, not wealth, station, or power, separates those in the pews from the corpse in the coffin.

She is unfamiliar with many mourners, yet her eye catches the face of Emma Greer. This is the first time she has noticed her at Ohav Shalom since her husband's shame became her shame. Emma was always a partner with him, attending the major events of congregational life, as well as a fair proportion of Sabbath and Festival services. It was only natural for her to identify with his fall from grace though few in the congregation would concur. Her presence at Katherine Klein's funeral triggers the memory of committees and charity fundraisers they shared.

Gabby must now recognize how she has been avoiding her. Many a time the thought of calling crossed her mind and just as many times she managed to procrastinate. Emma knows how many hours she and Seth spent together on out-of-town trips. How could she not suspect an affair with him? During Seth's ordeal the congregation buzzed with such suspicions. Yet as far as Gabby knows, she never lent credence to the gossip.

After the funeral service, the burial of Katherine Klein's remains takes place at King David Cemetery in suburban Virginia. A long motor cortege snakes through Washington and over the American Legion Bridge spanning the Potomac River. In order to return to the Temple for interviews after the interment, Gabby elects not to ride in the family hearse but to travel in her own navy-blue Volvo. Policemen on motorcycles escort the procession through traffic lights, stopping cross-traffic where necessary.

Northern Virginia skies are overcast. A previous shower has dampened the cemetery. Only rarely does the sun peek through windswept cumulus clouds. There is an unseasonable chill in the air. Who can remember a burial in bright sunshine?

Cemetery employees usher Gabby and the others to the family grave site, preselected with plots for her husband, Joseph, a syndicated political analyst for *The Los Angeles Times* and three children, two in graduate schools of medicine and law, one an undergraduate at Princeton.

Emma Greer is among those who have arrived with the cortege. Though before Seth's fall she had many friends and admirers in the congregation, she appears to be alone, infrequently nodding demure greetings to passers-by. In a social gathering, her isolation would be patently uncomfortable. At a funeral it is not unusual for one to stand apart, secluded in meditation.

Emotion erupts when the coffin is lowered into the grave. All thought of holding on to the deceased vanishes. Gabby honors the ritual of throwing dirt upon the coffin once it is on the floor of the grave. There is nothing more humane and more dignified than helping to bury the body of a fellow human being. Animals do not bury their dead but leave them to decay or be eaten by carnivores. The physical act of burying the dead is sacred pledge to the deceased.

People often comment how difficult it must be for Gabby to officiate at funerals. Nothing could be further from the truth. There are few times in her professional life when her skills are absolutely essential. No other professional is as qualified to organize final rites of passage. No other professional is better suited to link the corporeal with the spiritual, to bridge the here with the hereafter.

The Klein family and close friends circle the open grave. Now is the time for the recitation of two more Hebrew psalms from the writings of King David, after whom the cemetery is named. Then a simple utterance from Job: "*Adonai natan, Adonai lacach, yehe shem Adonai m'vorach*, The Lord gives and the Lord takes, blessed be the name of the Lord."

Gabby adds a prayer in English associating God with the hope of existence for the spirit after death, then steps toward the gravediggers for a shovel. With an athletic movement she drives the blade into a pile of fresh-turned dirt, then hands it to Katherine's tearful but dignified husband who wails aloud and drops the dirt into the grave. It pounds the coffin top with a loud thud. One after another of the family follows his lead.

After all have taken their turn, Gabby gathers the family to the head of the grave, placing her arms around Joseph Klein and his eldest daughter. They hold cards with a transliteration of the *Kaddish* prayer. Their eyes are fogged with tears and reading an Aramaic text is difficult. Voices are weak and throaty. Gabby's is soft but firm, as she guides them in this communal prayer for the dead.

The interment concludes abruptly without further ceremony, mirroring the abrupt disjunction between life and death. No Hebrew blessings and no supplementary eulogies. There is a point in every burial where nothing more need be said, nothing more done. As soon as the deceased is in the ground and the mourners have fulfilled their duties, the process of separation begins. Mourners step back from the grave and silently cluster in small groups.

Gabby kisses Joe Klein on the cheek with a brief phrase in Hebrew, "She'll be in peace now." Despite her rabbinical training and years of apprenticeship, ministrations of the *Malach ha Mavet*, the Angel of Death, are as much a mystery to her as to any of her parishioners. She voices only what she believes is true. Death is hell.

In clusters, people walk slowly along a gravel path toward their vehicles parked out of sight behind stone mausoleums. A wet wind whips along the gravestones.

Normally, Gabby would move quickly to her car to beat traffic from the cemetery and return to the synagogue. But for reasons she does not understand, this time she hesitates beside the open grave. Katherine Klein is about to begin the eternal sleep alone. A sadness wells up inside as she gazes upon soil covering the coffin. She tries to withhold emotion from her congregants, but now that she's alone, the floodgates open. Part of what she feels gushes up in a sob. A second upheaval of sadness follows.

"Hello." A voice surprises her for she believes all have left. She knows the voice and turns to watch Emma Greer approach, her hand outstretched to shake. Gabby has eaten many *Shabbat* meals at the Greers' home and stayed with them for two weeks when her condo was being painted. Though she had long believed Emma to be dubious about the partnership she enjoyed with her husband, Emma never exhibited jealousy. A strong feminist, she appeared to be happy for Seth to have a female colleague.

"I'm glad to see you, Emma," Gabby says, taking the gloved hand offered. "I've picked up the phone a dozen times to call, then put it down again on the receiver. Once I dialed your number completely, but hung up after the first ring. You must have lots of calls."

"Not many. I'm a leper these days. Like Seth, I'm a bad smell everybody hopes will blow away. I feel as though people expect me to leave Washington. Go anywhere, just far away."

"I don't hope that, Emma." Gabby closes the distance and plants a kiss on her cheek. "Now that you've had the courage to approach me, rather than me doing what I should have done weeks ago, I can say what I've long wanted to tell you."

"Yes, of course. But could we walk a little? I need the

circulation and Katherine's grave makes me cry. We were very close. During the ordeal she remained a friend, though God knows, she had her own troubles. We became kinfolk in pain. There's commonality in suffering, you know. Let's walk."

Gabby takes the lead, turning Emma with a hand on her arm as they proceed along a path between old gravestones whose Hebrew lettering is weathered thin, almost unreadable. Soil erosion causes a few older head stones to lean over, breaking the symmetry.

"I didn't sleep with Seth," Gabby blurts without further introduction. "I know you've thought about that. And you probably believed it. Certainly, Seth and I had many opportunities. But I want you to know that whatever Seth did, he never suggested we go to bed together. He never laid a finger on me. Never intimated or led me on. Never tried to compromise me with alcohol. And as far as I can remember, he never even told me a dirty joke. I know he has a fabulous repertoire of jokes he wouldn't tell in public. How he draws out a shaggy dog tale. But except for a few ethnic gags, nothing was crude or suggestive."

"The thought had crossed my mind," Emma says, "but I wasn't suspicious, even after his women started coming out of the woodwork. Seems he slept with just about everything with a female orifice. But I never believed he was doing it with you."

"Glad to hear you say that, but I can't think of a good reason why you wouldn't be suspicious."

"Simple. With all Seth's flaws, he possesses a strong moral compass. He loves the rabbinate too much to dishonor a colleague. He could screw women who weren't rabbis, but I don't think he'd touch a colleague and demean the profession. He respects you. Did from the day you came to work at OS. Seth recognized your talents. If anything, he was a bit envious. He loved your directness. He felt he had to embellish everything and you didn't. He often said it took him ten words to say what you managed to convey in three. And when he talked about retirement, he wanted you to be his successor. Once he told me it was his responsibility to lay the foundation for your succession. No one could carry on better than you. I'm afraid he made a botch of it."

Gabby takes Emma's arm to steer her ninety degrees into a new path. "Your trust makes it easier for me, especially if you intend to remain a member of Ohav."

"I doubt I will. Too many memories. Too much hurt. Too much to explain and too few facts with which to do it. I make people edgy. I know that."

"What's a congregation for if one can't go there in trouble?"

"Do rabbis and rebbitsins go to their congregations for help? I think not."

"Perhaps you can help me."

Emma stops and faces Gabby for a moment. Gabby is a bright, independent woman who seldom needs help from anyone.

"I'm exhausted, Emma. I'm running as fast as I can. I'm trying to be the rabbi Seth was. I can do his job, but not half as well as he. And I don't think I'll ever get better at it until I understand one thing. And there's no one to explain it except you. Tell me why the hell Seth did it? It doesn't make sense. He had to know someone would snitch on him. He had to know it would finish his career."

Emma's eyes fall to the ground and she tightens her lips as if sealing them. Her head turns away and she regards the silent tombstones, each marking a life lived and life spent. "I don't know myself," she finally says.

"Were things that bad between you two? Your marriage didn't look any worse than many I see."

Emma pauses again, debating whether to be drawn into a discussion that might be misunderstood, then mumbles. "It wasn't like Seth's accusers said. That's not to suggest he didn't screw those women. What they reported must have happened, except the part where he used his rabbinical position to satisfy his lusts. They had to be wrong on two grounds: first, he wouldn't have abused his rabbinical post, and two, he wasn't lustful. Don't get me wrong, Gabby, I hate the bastard's guts, but he loved his profession too much to tarnish it. And, as far as I know, he wasn't sexually frustrated. Our marriage failed in many ways, but not in bed."

Gabby is at a loss for an appropriate response to this personal disclosure.

"Yes." Emma fills the void in conversation. "That much of our relationship was excellent. You read in women's magazines how men only want to satisfy themselves. That wasn't him. And it wasn't always easy, especially when I entered menopause. He never, never rushed me, even when I became ticklish. Seth avoided doing anything that would trigger a spasm of ticklishness."

Gabby exhales a gusty breath, washing out preconceived notions. She is humbled by Emma's openness and honesty.

"I won't say I never tried to fake it for his sake. Especially during the menopause phase. But he always knew. He could feel things like that. He knew my voice and breathing. He knew my rhythms. It was no use. When I begged him to satisfy himself, he refused. For him, it was both of us or neither of us. He possessed a mystical belief about orgasms. I never understood it, but he said it dealt with nexus, the bonding of souls, where male and female leave themselves for an instant and bond some place between. That's why he believed that conceiving children was so sacred. *Godly* was the way he put it."

Gabby is speechless. In all the acrimony over Seth's misdeeds, she never suspected this dimension of his personality. She assumed sexual frustrations at home drove him to marital infidelity.

"You'll have to face menopause some day." Emma looks drained.

"I hope I'll be as successful as you," Gabby responds.

"I don't condone what he did. Seth isn't evil; he's just a jerk."

They come to a stone wall, turn, and head back in the direction of the cars, walking slowly in silence.

Near her cream-colored Toyota Camry, Emma pivots so that Gabby must stop in her tracks. "You're the only one I could tell. It took me a long time to muster the courage. Seth trusted you and so do I."

Gabby says, "That damn fool abandoned both of us. He left you in the lurch and me wrestling with a bucking bronco of a congregation. If the truth be known, becoming Senior Rabbi at OS isn't really my first choice."

A smile dawns on Emma's cheeks for the first time and corresponds with a shaft of warm sunlight filtering through the broken clouds.

"I wouldn't like to hazard a guess what is."

"To be Seth's associate once again. With this nightmare past."

"Noble, noble. You rabbis are all dreamers."

"I know," Gabby says, as Emma pulls open the driver's side door of her car.

August 6th

For a change, Gabby is invited to a special meeting of the synagogue Board, though the invitation is for only a portion of the meeting. The time for her participation is set for 9:30 p.m.

Twelve members of the Board are seated around the freshly restained conference table. They shield confidential papers from her vision. All smile with warm greetings as she enters. Four gentlemen stand. A seat is made available for her along the left flank. Doris Silbert maintains the premiere position at the head of the table while, according to custom, Recording Secretary Cecilia Block, M.D., is seated to her right.

"We're sorry for the late hour, Gabby," Doris opens, "but you're aware of the extraordinary schedule facing this Board. The search for Rabbi Greer's replacement is only the beginning. We must also face financial questions, dealing with his family. And Rabbi Greer himself. You know, matters of pension, salary, et cetera. A terrible tangle."

Around the room there are grunts of approval, providing Doris with confidence to introduce a sensitive matter.

"I'm afraid we're going to have to enlist your patience a little longer. We are very much aware of the additional burdens Seth's departure has put on you."

"Hear, hear," Sally benHoran says loudly, seconded by David Swerlin and Alfred Maitland, both past presidents of the congregation.

"And," Doris continues, "we want to express our gratitude for the professional manner in which you're coping. When Rabbi Greer left town, I feared the whole place would fall apart. We believed members who were disgusted and humiliated would cancel their memberships and trot across town to Beth Ami. Our financial reserves would dwindle and the long, proud tradition at Ohav Shalom would grind to a sad end. Fortunately, none of these forebodings have come to pass. A few members dropped out. Some wrote nasty letters. Telephone calls were even meaner. But the bulk of members have stayed loyal. And that, Gabby, is partly a credit to you. You've given everyone confidence in the future."

Such words reflect the thinking of the Board, for the instant Doris finishes, those on the opposite side of the table stand in tribute, clapping their hands. Members flanking Gabby accept the signal and also stand to join the applause.

When they settle back into their seats, Doris says, "Gabby, we feel that for your extra effort you're entitled to additional compensation. This evening the Board has voted you a special, one-time bonus of fifteen thousand dollars."

Gabby smiles with appreciation. She didn't think anybody was noticing, or was that her natural cynicism? Pats on the shoulder with the obligatory compliments are numerous in her trade. Financial rewards are far less common.

Now that this housekeeping matter is concluded, Doris glances around the table to signify that she is ready to move on to the next item of agenda.

"So that we have a uniform approach to this selection, our Search Committee has designed a series of questions for the rabbis. In your case we already have a sense of where you stand on matters of ritual and theology, but there's an area in which we need clarification. The Selection Committee has asked us to bring this up."

Clarification is a code-word for a problem. Gabby smiles as though willing to enter any subject. Thinking before a crowd is her specialty, yet she is wary of getting sand-bagged.

"We're surprised by the high quality of those seeking Seth's position." Doris Silbert fills the pause. "We were all a bit naive. We had gotten used to Rabbi Greer and you, and we failed to notice how the job changed before our eyes. You're probably aware that there are numerous men and a couple of women seeking the post. We had never given much thought to how desirable this congregation is. Perhaps because it's in the Nation's Capital. Or its size, or age. Rabbi Greer's departure has been a wake-up call."

From across the table come nods of agreement.

"What surprises us," the President continues, "is that several Senior Rabbis with extensive scholarly achievement have applied. Ph.D.s and publications. Several are authors of significant books on Judaica. One by a doctor of psychology about families under stress. Another has published two novels, though none of us have heard of them. Applicants have sent along published material for us to review. And I don't mind telling you, Rabbi, there's a lot here to read. Of course, we must look at this favorably. It brings prestige and depth to this rabbinical pulpit."

Gabby's eyes drop over the tabletop. Nothing could imperil her candidacy more than her lack of publications. She is suddenly vulnerable.

Cecilia Block senses the need to soften what she knows will be painful. Her melodic accent fails to hide her childhood in North Carolina. "You see, Rabbi, we fully understand how busy you've been with the congregation. You probably don't have time in the day to eat a bagel let alone write books and study for a doctoral degree. We wonder, however, if you have anything planned in this direction. Something to eventually bring you on par, so to speak, with the other candidates."

"This is a demanding congregation," Gabby states in a voice that staggers for a moment before being brought under control. "There are different kinds of rabbis. Some are scholars; others, ministers to their flocks. I make no pretense; I'm more a people rabbi than a scholar, though I'm often at home curled up with a book. I'd like to remind you that Rabbi Greer didn't get his Ph.D. while Rabbi at Ohav Shalom. He finished his work well before assuming this pulpit. From the day he was appointed at OS his writing slowed down. He's been working on a manuscript about Jewish mysticism in the sixteenth century for as many years as I can remember."

"We certainly don't demand that you publish," Cecilia Block interjects. "We're not like a publish-or-perish university."

"We'd just like to know if you are planning to seek a doctorate. Or perhaps write a book," Doris says.

Saliva in Gabby's throat is a reminder the Board has struck her Achilles' heel. She swallows. "Everyone in my field has plans. We all map out a strategy. But most of us become inundated with rabbinical duties. They come like bullets from a machine gun. One of my colleagues in town says that rabbis die from accretions. They keep accepting new responsibilities until they burn out or have a heart attack. Few congregational rabbis have time for serious studying. We talk a lot about its virtues, but then don't follow through. Professors in the university have more time for this and usually do a better job. They're paid to publish."

"So what are we to infer from this?" Gideon Berkowitz enters the discussion.

"That I have long-term plans," Gabby responds. "I've inquired at the Department of History at Johns Hopkins. I have some notes about a possible thesis on medieval Hebrew poetry of Spain, but that's as far as I've gone. Nothing immediate. Since Rabbi Greer's been gone, I haven't even had time for dreaming."

"Any books in the word processor?"

"Nothing more significant than an outline and one chapter, once sent to an agent in New York. He didn't even bother to reply."

"How about articles? Are you writing anything at this time?"

"Two columns for *Ohav Shalom Newsletter* every month. I contribute to the *Jewish Week* every month or two. Also I've published two small articles in the *Rabbinical Journal*, one on Hebrew poetry."

"Sounds pretty damn impressive to me," Cecilia Block intones. "Besides all the duties we demand of our rabbis, any scholarly production is a miracle."

"But other rabbis manage," George Kahn jumps in from the far end of the table. "True, they might not be as busy as those at Ohav Shalom. But scholarship gets done somehow. Others we've interviewed say they can write while also fulfilling daily responsibilities of a congregation."

"They'll write if the Associate Rabbi performs ministerial functions for him or her," Gabby says.

"Well then," Doris cuts her short and fumbles with her pencil, appearing to consult notes she's been taking. "I think Rabbi Lewyn's answered forthrightly the questions we put to her. Is there anything you want to add, Rabbi?"

Gabby shakes her head. She sees her candidacy slipping away. On the one hand they compliment her work and dedication, yet on the other, pound away at her vulnerability.

"Then we'll call this subject closed for the time being. But before we return to the agenda, Rabbi, we'd like your cooperation on a little matter. This selection process is far more complex than we initially anticipated. To be fair and yet respectful of people's feelings, we must enter a very delicate field. One such issue is bringing potential candidates before the congregation at services. But since you're also a candidate for Rabbi Greer's post, that's awkward. We've deliberated over this for some time and come to the only practical conclusion."

Gabby's pulse quickens and she feels heat around the temples. Her throat is dry, but the water pitcher is at the far end of the conference table.

"We're going to give you a series of weekends off, Rabbi. August twenty-first and September fourth, to start. We tried to figure out a diplomatic way around this dilemma and failed. There's no alternative but to be up front. It will be uncomfortable for everyone if you're on the pulpit when the rabbis are here. Everything would be different if you were not a contender."

She smirks. What choices has she? "Of course," she responds without conviction.

"Sounds like you could use some old-fashioned R&R." Somebody tries to be helpful and isn't.

"Yes, of course, rest and recreation. Just what I need."

The atmosphere is suddenly chilled. A heavy silence hangs in the room.

"You'll be pleased to know," Doris adds, "that the first candidate we're bringing to Washington is a very qualified woman whom you probably know. The gender issue at this pulpit cannot be overlooked. And I proud to say Ohav Shalom is facing it up front."

Gabby manufactures a sympathetic smile, but does not respond. Her brain floods with the names of female colleagues.

After courteous goodbyes, Gabby passes through the conference room door to the hallway and mutters, "Whoopee, I'm off two weekends! Enough time to author a fuckin' book, write three lousy articles on esoteric subjects nobody is interested in, and get a Ph.D. Free at last. Free at last. Thank God, Almighty … "

Chapter Seven

August 17th

Though she has no compelling reason to hear from Timothy Matternly, Gabby nevertheless checks her home answering machine twice daily. In the past, he would leave messages at all hours of the day and night, seldom expecting an answer. They were sometimes short and sometimes long, but always witty. The sound of his high-pitched boyish voice which never mellowed into adulthood reminds her of a clarinet's dancing notes. A giggle which inevitably erupts amid serious conversations reveals that to him the world's a comedic stage, inhabited by people caught in inextricable webs of intrigue and coincidence. His world is peopled by hack actors muddling through poorly cast stage roles. No one is worth taking too seriously. His sanity is moored in humor.

Gabby, in contrast, is inclined to be serious and often dour, emphasizing the sinister side of human behavior. While Tim is trustful, she is suspicious. While he is naturally optimistic, she is pessimistic. One treats life as a game, the other as a deadly minefield. They know instinctively that their personalities complement each other which makes their parting all the sadder.

No message from Tim on the phone machine. She can conclude only that his romance with Sally isn't falling apart as she secretly hopes. Boy meets girl. Boy apparently doesn't lose girl. Boy gets girl. Something is wrong with this plotline. Her mood darkens.

Each day she checks e-mail on her computer. Tim's work with the inner city ministry requires him to navigate cyberspace on a daily basis, but after hours he is too social to be isolated in front of a computer screen. No e-mail from him either. There is, however, a message from Noah Zentner.

> *Would like to talk with you, Rabbi. The trial is a dark cloud hovering above and my optimism is waning. I know now what Seth Greer must be going through. When you're on top, everyone wants to be your friend. When you fall, you face a wall of silence. Please let me know when I can see you.*
>
> *Noah Zentner*

She neither types a reply nor deletes the message. Rather she saves it to an electronic file which periodically alerts her that future action needs to be taken. The note, terse as it is, is suffused with loneliness. Many of her congregants talk about being alone, wanting her to be their friend. Widows and divorcees, mostly. She feels herself a gregarious person, still she personally knows loneliness face to face. Seth must be wallowing in it. His roots in Washington are suddenly gone. Either he must slink around his home community disguising his movements or, more likely, begin establishing roots in a new place. Even for a man of his charms and talents, that can't be easy.

After shutting down the computer, she enters the kitchen for something to eat. These days her appetite is all but gone. Her skirts sag at the waist and her breasts fail to fill the cups of her bras. Two scrambled eggs and a dry bagel serve for dinner, washed down by a stiff drink of Glenfiddich single-malt Scotch. CNN news on the television screen for company. An advertisement for tourism in Jamaica causes her to consider a delicate subject—what to do with the two free weekends the congregation has bestowed on her.

Under normal conditions, she would use free time to catch up on life's chores—postponed car repairs, clothes that require tailoring, replacement of a soiled bedroom carpet. Leisure can also be a burden to a single woman with no one to spend it with. Work is a refuge. Above all, she does not want to be near the congregation. The thought of visiting her father in Los Angeles has appeal, yet flying such a long distance is impractical, though there are deeper reasons. Since her mother's death, Sam Lewyn is obsessed with his daughter's unmarried status. Like many Jewish parents he believes that words of wisdom on the sore subject will miraculously produce a suitable husband and a family. It is inconceivable to him that men don't line up for dates with his talented offspring. Though a retired primary care physician with excellent common sense, he just doesn't get it. Even less does he understand the dating subtleties of her rabbinical occupation. She detests the excuses she finds herself making in his company. She also toys with a visit to her younger sister in Cleveland but that could be equally depressing. Terry's husband and three children make her envious, another emotion she detests. These are not weekends to stir one's feelings of envy.

CHUCK BROWNER NOTICES GABBY IS LOSING WEIGHT and invites her for dinner after work on Wednesday evening and, to his surprise, she accepts. They rendezvous in a restaurant/bar called Hugo's Palace, off Dupont Circle where affluent gay males are seated at small tables in animated discussion. Chuck is no stranger here. As they move between tables, he proudly introduces *his rabbi boss* to numerous acquaintances—well-groomed men in elegant clothes. Smiles are open. Introductory banter flows. Though no other females are visible, she doesn't feel uncomfortable.

Chuck nods at a lean waiter with small gold earrings in both earlobes who hands them menus and adds wine glasses in anticipation. A black busboy, barely out of high school, pours ice water and adds a basket of multigrain breads and thin Italian breadsticks. No butter. Olive oil on small plates. When he moves away, Chuck asks, "Feel uncomfortable here?"

"Absolutely not. This is arguably the safest spot in the city for a heterosexual like me."

"Good, because I wouldn't want our congregants to gossip about the bars you frequent."

"Some wouldn't be surprised at all. Because I'm single and without children they deduce it must be by choice. Rumors circulate that I'm a card-carrying lesbian."

"No rumors about me, Rabbi Gabby. There was a time in my life when I tried to hide what I was, even from myself. What a waste. Truth eventually catches up to us all. I know fellows who get married, sire children, and act as heterosexual as the next guy, but inside they know they're living a lie. They detest their sexuality far less than the deceit required to mask it. Eventually, they turn their disgust against straight society, riding a merry-go-round of accusations and counteraccusations. For them it's a perennial war of attack and defend. I matriculated through each stage. Took my lumps; paid my dues. And here I am—all grown up."

The waiter returns for their beverage choice. Wine for both. Chuck surveys a list and selects an inexpensive California Merlot from Monterey, not from the venerable and more expensive Napa Valley. Insider's knowledge.

"Scuttlebutt has it the Rabbinical Search Committee's been rough on you, Gabby."

"Now how would you know that? Deliberations are supposed to be confidential."

"Jews are constitutionally unable to keep secrets. Things like that leak. It doesn't have to be a member of the Committee. My dear lady, there are other sources of information."

She brushes off disbelief with a shake of the head.

"Notes have to be taken and transcribed. Committee members pay secretaries like me for that stuff, you know."

Gabby chides her own naivete. "Are you in that secretarial pool?"

"I meet with secretaries in Harold Farb's weekly staff meeting. We're expected to cover for each other when somebody's sick or on vacation."

"How often is that?" she asks in a conspiratorial tone he does not recognize.

"It varies. On average I'd say once every two weeks. Why?" She pauses before launching into a delicate subject. "Do I have your confidence?"

A wide grimace enlarges his lips and exposes teeth bleached extra white with peroxide. "Rabbi Greer lectured me on the importance of confidentiality in rabbinical affairs. Comes with the territory."

"Glad to hear it from your lips because I assume you also possess a firm moral backbone."

"I like to think so. Toilet training in early childhood. The Browner family has excellent values in just about everything except sexual orientation. Before we get started on that, let's order something to eat. If I'm going to be compromised, I must do it on a full stomach. I can see you're hardly eating these days, but I can't let you die of starvation on my watch."

As usual, Gabby isn't hungry. To be sociable she orders a plate of spinach sautéed in virgin olive oil with fresh garlic.

Chuck is more adventuresome and selects a bouillabaisse soup and a tossed green salad with balsamic vinegar dressing.

"Think I could pervert your moral compass, Chuck?" she says, once the waiter is out of hearing distance.

The suggestion surprises him. Gabby is ethical bedrock. She doesn't give him a moment to recover.

"I'd like to look at Rabbi Greer's old appointment books," she says without waiting for an answer. "Harold Farb cleared official documents from his office. But he's a packrat. He must have stored those records somewhere. Any idea where?"

"Not offhand, but I'm a born sleuth. If they're in the building, I should be able to place my hands on them. May I ask why you're interested?"

"A hunch, Chuck. Just a hunch."

"Appointments from what years? Rabbi Greer goes back thirteen or so at OS."

"The last two."

"What are you looking for?"

"Not sure yet. Something bothers me about what's happened with him. Don't ask me what. I'll know more after I have a look at his appointments."

A tall handsome man with narrow hips and well-developed muscles bulging from a tight T-shirt sidles by the booth and greets Chuck.

A moment of hesitation elapses before Chuck extends a hand in welcome. "Hello, Terrance. Someone here I'd like you to meet." He stands and makes a formal introduction, using Gabby's rabbinical title.

Terrance cannot sit without sliding into the booth, so he remains standing. "Well now, Rabbi Lewyn. Chuck's spoken of you. I've tried to imagine what you'd look like. Had the vision of someone matronly and buxom, rather untidy, bordering on masculine. He didn't prepare me for what I see. It's clear now why he works overtime."

He nods at Chuck and absorbs a hostile glare in response. That convinces him to return to the bar where a couple is arguing. "Pleasure to meet you, Rabbi. A good Catholic boy like me isn't likely to attend your temple, still I'd bet you're a damn good rabbi. If I were Jewish, I'd come in a heartbeat."

"I'll take that as a compliment." She half-lifts herself to reach for his hand. When he's out of hearing, she says to Chuck, "Terrance keeps in shape, I see."

"Don't get any ideas. A pretty woman isn't going to get to first base with him. He's got a dozen guys in pursuit at all times."

"You among them?"

"Once. But he's a floater. Always on the move, like a fly fisherman testing new streams. He's decent, egregiously disloyal and hopelessly narcissistic. Bad combination for me. Of course, you don't know those things from the get-go. You have to learn how to keep distance from people who can hurt you."

"Sounds like good advice to me. When I need a therapist, I'll know who to come to."

"Good idea, Rabbi Gabby. Nobody observes you as closely as I do. I know succeeding Rabbi Greer is important. I'm more objective than you and can see what's going on. You're in the sweet-talk phase of the selection process. At this time, all the horses are running nose to nose. Sooner or later one or two will emerge from the pack. The congregation adores you. I hear things they'd never say to your face. But don't let that go to your head. Adoration isn't enough. There's a deeper agenda in finding Rabbi Greer's successor."

"How come you know so much?"

"Because I'm gay. Societal pariahs develop acute sensitivities. People are constantly judging us. To survive a gay man must be ruthlessly honest about the world around him. He must know his own limitations and be sensitive to those of others."

"So you think they'll reject me, do you?" She reaches across the table and touches the back of his hand with her fingertips in a gesture of friendship.

"I think you're too good for this congregation, Gabby Lewyn. Some rabbis are saints, and others scholars. And some are politicians and scholars, like Rabbi Greer. The politicians and scholars prosper. The saints don't. That's why in Christianity most of them got crucified. Tell me, do you think they would appoint a gay man or gay woman as Senior Rabbi?"

She hesitates, not wishing to offend.

"Come on. I can take it. No bullshit."

"That depends."

"No bullshit, lady. You know damn well they wouldn't

appoint a gay man or woman. Homosexuals don't fit the mold. And what's even crueler, you don't either."

She squirms and hopes he doesn't notice. It's easier to change the subject than follow logic which makes her uncomfortable. "I need another favor from you, Chuck. It's a favor, not an order. If you feel you can't oblige, I'll understand. No hard feelings." She leans forward and lowers her voice though this is hardly necessary. "Deliberations of the Board are normally entered into the official minutes which are available to the membership for review. I doubt anybody takes the time to read them, but theoretically they have every right. Do you know who takes the minutes?"

"The recording secretary, I presume."

"The recording secretary is responsible for putting minutes in writing and distributes them to the Board. They're transcribed from a tape recording. But everything from the tape isn't transferred to the recorded minutes. Some matters are deleted."

"What matters?"

"Personnel issues. Deliberations over salaries and wages."

"And you want to know what the Board is saying about you? Should I be shocked?"

"No. I know there have been deliberations about me. I don't expect you to believe this, but I don't give a damn what they say. I want to learn what was said about Rabbi Greer. I was purposely excluded from those meetings. Now, I'm curious."

"And you want me to get those tapes for you?"

"If you can."

"Why not ask Harold? The dust is settling now. He might lend them to you."

Gabby shakes her head. "I don't want anybody to know about this."

"If I'm going to be a thief, I've got to know where my crime will take place."

"I presume Harold's got them stashed away in his office. You're a resourceful fellow. Figure it out."

"Dangerous for you at a time when you're being considered for Greer's job."

"You just said I haven't a chance, didn't you?"

"Not in so many words. I'm more politic than that."

She smiles with artifice. "But that's what you think, isn't it,

Chuck?"

"Yes, Rabbi. That's what I believe. In a metaphorical way, I've been there."

A sigh escapes her lips which she eventually draws closed. The waiter arrives in the nick of time with their entrees. Just as well. There's no purpose defending her optimism. Chuck is probably right, anyway.

BEFORE BED THAT EVENING, GABBY CHECKS HER computer for e-mail. Nothing from Tim. She fumbles through a stack of business cards and eventually discovers what she's looking for—Zoe Mountolive's address. It's too late to phone New York, but definitely not too late for sending e-mail.

To Zoe Mountolive: ZoeMount@compuserve.com

I'm off duty this weekend and would like to visit you in N.Y., for professional and social reasons. Love to meet Clementine and I know you spend your weekends with her. Let me know.

Gabby Lewyn

Before logging off the network, she is reminded of the unanswered message from Noah Zentner. He is much on her mind, but seeing him is awkward. Pressure from her female friends. Sentiment against him is strong, particularly because Eli Waller seems to be on television every evening. She avoids talking about what happened on the Chesapeake, but her very presence makes a powerful statement.

To Noah Zentner: NoahbobZ@aol.com

I know what you're going through, Noah. Cruel world and you're in the maelstrom. Would be happy to meet with you at the Temple. Call my secretary, Charles Browner, for an appointment. Will be off in New York this weekend while the congregation auditions a candidate for Seth's post. Hope to see Zoe Mountolive sometime Saturday or Sunday.

Rabbi Gabrielle Lewyn

When Gabby pulls herself awake the next morning, there is an e-mail response from Zoe Mountolive.

Delighted to see you this weekend. Clemmy is spending half of it with me and half with her father. I've got a tennis court in Queens reserved for two hours Saturday afternoon at 1:00. I've heard you play a neat game, so bring your racket. Clemmy's got an hour lesson first, then Peter, Clemmy's dad, is scheduled to collect her in Queens. We can play the second hour together. I'll drive because the club is located in a rough neighborhood. Can't think of anybody I'd rather see.

Zoe

AFTER CHECKING INTO THE LYNDEN GARDENS HOTEL on East 64th Street near Central Park, several levels below the Pierre for luxury but adequate for her needs, Gabby takes a taxi to Zoe's apartment on 86th Street, off Second Avenue. Together with Clementine, they travel in Zoe's Lexus to North Queens, where loitering men huddle beside brick siding of aging warehouses in soiled pants and beaten shoes, some hiding wine bottles in paper bags. They eye the car distractedly as Zoe cruises up one street and down another, hunting for a parking place. Trucks and trailer hitches parked for the weekend fill the spaces. Zoe is forced to leave her car in a narrow alley off Parsons Avenue a block and a half from the renovated warehouse complex housing the North Queens Sports Club.

The first hour of tennis time is devoted to a lesson for Clementine Mountolive, who is tall and lean for her ten years of age. All her limbs seem to have sprouted at different times with their own independent designs, but beneath the physical chaos of adolescence, Gabby discerns the makings of a beautiful young woman. Her legs are long and well-shaped, the waist slim. Her auburn hair is pulled back with a bright yellow headband holding long locks away from her face. Her tennis instructor, a stocky, freckled redhead, reminds Gabby of the hulks who hang around single women at the Tuesday Night Tennis Club in Washington.

Dressed to play, Zoe and Gabby sit in an open gallery and observe the lesson. The crack of balls bouncing from rackets reverberates in the indoor court and they must raise their voices to be heard. Gabby notes the intensity of purpose on Zoe's face. She recognizes the look of an anxious single parent. In contrast to the spontaneity married couples enjoy with their children, single parents often force a parenting agenda. Time is precious. Attention they once focused upon their spouses is now concentrated on the children. There is reciprocal anxiety from the child.

"I'm beginning to get a hold on Noah Zentner's case," Gabby reports in between Zoe's monitoring of her daughter's progress. "Had my secretary make a file of press clippings. Since we met at the Zentner's apartment, I avoided reading the details. Too much hype in the media. I wanted to stay out of the whirlwind and maintain objectivity. But it's hard to live in the twentieth century and not get bombarded with coverage. Click one channel off and you find commentators discussing the case on another. There must be an audience for this. Every detail's dissected. One wonders what's left to do in court."

A tolerant smile enlarges on Zoe's lips as she rotates in Gabby's direction. "My team's got its work cut out. We must build a case before the jury step by step, detail by detail. Can't let the prosecution dictate the field. We want them to argue on our territory not theirs. What do you make of what you've read?"

"Confusing. I drew myself a timeline in order to get the events straight and I think I now have a reasonable understanding. Noah seems contrite about cheating on Morgan. I don't get the impression he's lying about Eli Waller."

"The State of Maryland isn't accusing him of infidelity." Zoe's eyes remain locked on her daughter, who is now at the net practicing backhand volleys. "Or of having sex with Eli. The crime of rape has a precise legal definition. We're going to prove that he did not meet that definition."

Zoe jumps to her feet in approval as Clementine reaches over her head to blast an overhead past the instructor, who is caught flatfooted. Dropping back to her seat, she says with acrid bitterness, "Womanizing husbands are not uncommon."

"Is that what happened with Peter?"

Zoe hesitates and, for an instant, glances away as if seeking counsel from some distant power, then returns to Gabby. "Multiple affairs behind my back. Guess I could have suffered a one-night stand or a momentary lapse into fantasy. There have to be women less inhibited in bed than I am. For Clemmy's sake I would have taken my lumps and gone on. But Peter's not like that. He's a roamer. It came to a point where I couldn't manage the deception anymore. Cheap, sleazy lies. Phony excuses. Fatuous stories. The guy should have been writing science fiction.

You wouldn't believe his imagination. Each new lie eroded my trust in him. Each prevarication demeaned me a little more. He's better off now, free to go bed-hopping all he likes, that is until he breaks one heart too many. Someday, perhaps not this year or next, but someday, one of his jilted lovers will nail him with an arsenic canapé."

"And you, Zoe? Are you better off now?"

"Absolutely. Well, if the truth be known, I have periods of despair."

She stands as her daughter's lesson draws to a close and the coach hands Clementine a basket for retrieving balls scattered over the court. She calls out congratulations. To Gabby, Zoe says, "You're going to have the honor of meeting Peter shortly. Mussolini should be here soon to pick up Clemmy."

"Look forward to meeting him."

"I'll spare you the fireworks. We no longer talk, just snarl at each other. He brings out the worst in me. I've vowed not to get sucked into childish fights with him but the moment he gets in range they break out anyway. I hate myself like this."

Once balls are collected, Clementine calls from the court to her mother. Time for them to play together. Zoe insists that she and Clementine rally against Gabby who agrees only if they consent to rotate after a few minutes. They begin at the net with practice volleys. A few volleys provide evidence that Zoe is an accomplished player. Grooved strokes with fine preparation and excellent follow-through. Her balls sail back with pace and control. In competition she will be a tough adversary.

With youthful abandon Clementine tries to show off and hit harder than her control warrants. When they rotate on the court, Zoe's skill shines as she squares off against Gabby and Clementine. She has little difficulty dividing her returns equally. Eventually, the two adults team up to hit against Clementine and the pace slows. The youngster is driving a forehand into the net when Peter Mountolive throws back the protective canvas at the rear of the court and, without seeking permission from the players, walks onto the playing surface, effectively terminating further play.

"The hour's not over yet, Peter. Please wait in the gallery until it's up." Zoe trumpets in an outburst.

Peter Mountolive is not what Gabby anticipates. She imagines him tall, dark-haired and as handsome as Zoe is attractive. In the flesh, he's square and muscular, a heavy bull neck and with blond hair prematurely balding in the front. "I drove from the City through goddam terrible traffic to convenience you, Zoe. The very least you could do is return the courtesy and convenience me for a few lousy minutes." Without pause, he marches toward the net and places an arm over his daughter's shoulder, then plants a kiss on her cheek which she acknowledges with a confused counter-kiss. "Time to go, honey."

From the opposite side of the net, Zoe's eyes burn laser holes into her husband. When she recovers, she introduces Gabby.

At close range, Gabby is struck by the color and intensity of blue-green eyes which Peter knows how to use in conjunction with a gracious smile. He thrusts forward a thick, hirsute hand and holds on to Gabby's for an instant too long. "I saw a few of your strokes. Pretty nice work. You're obviously a jock. Perhaps one day you'll play with Clemmy and me."

"Sports are my therapy. Your daughter's got great potential if she sticks with it. Her mother's no slouch either," Gabby answers.

Uncertain why her affections have to be divided at all, Clementine searches for a middle ground between her parents. Peter's nervous eyes regard the pile of rackets, towels, and athletic paraphernalia strewn on the nearby bench. "You've packed an overnight for Clemmy, I presume." He baits Zoe with a remark certain to provoke.

"Presume nothing, Peter. Absolutely nothing. Everything she'll need for tonight should be in her bag. Tomorrow's clothes. Toothbrush, slippers, and a couple of books to read between your spasmodic attentions. I'll expect her home at the apartment at 6:30."

Peter snaps back from a search for Clementine's over-nighter. "Too early, Zoe. We have dinner plans. Back after dinner. Say about 8:30 or perhaps nineish."

Zoe steps in front of Clemmy, blocking her path. "No, Peter. No eights or nines. That's not our agreement. She's got to be back before dinner to prepare for school on Monday. She needs time to review her homework. Bathe. Get ready for bed. Don't change our arrangement at the eleventh hour. If you want to talk about an exception to the rule for next weekend, call me at the office. I promise an objective discussion of the merits. But not now."

"You know how I detest calling you at Greenwald, Molletz. The receptionist thinks she's Chief of Staff to the Pontiff, and instructions on your voice mail are more complicated than launching a space shuttle. The phone's probably bugged."

"That's illegal and you know it."

"Never stopped your partners before. Greenwald, Molletz is notorious for using the law as a weapon of combat. I'd rather wrestle with a python than talk with one of your partners. Get real, Zoe. 8:30 won't harm Clemmy one iota."

He finds the overnight bag and stands erect, signaling to his daughter with an outstretched hand. "Come on, honey. Let's not throw a good afternoon at a bad argument."

"Then I'll see Clemmy at 6:30?" Zoe hugs the net as Peter and their daughter traipse toward the backdrop.

Peter halts and turns to glower at her. "Expect Clemmy home when she gets home. I'll do what I can to be reasonable, but I can promise you it won't be at 6:30. Dinner doesn't start until six."

When Peter and Clemmy disappear, Zoe turns toward Gabby. "Asshole! Peter could pick a fight in an empty room."

Gabby is cautious about saying something inane or patently insincere. In such circumstances she doubles her efforts not to use disingenuous clichés. "Glad I've met Peter. Clementine seems very attached to him."

"You probably won't believe me when I say I hope so. She needs him as much as me. No matter what's happened between us, he's still her father. But about her affections, I'm not certain. She's a diplomat and fears his anger. Chip off the old female block—afraid to offend a man. It's our training, you know. In the genes."

Gabby places her hand on Zoe's shoulder and gives an affectionate squeeze. "Seems you avoided that gene. I didn't see you backing down."

"Takes practice. I train every day. At the firm and at home. Let your guard down and Peter will clobber you. Talk about a manipulator."

"So what time will he bring Clementine home?" Gabby inquires.

Zoe shakes her head in disgust. "When he damn well feels like it. Could be 8:30. Nine or even 10:30. Let's play tennis, Gabby. No sense ruining more of the afternoon."

Gabby takes Clementine's side of the court, then puts a ball deep to Zoe's forehand. Zoe moves into position on well-trained feet, planting the racket in position behind her right hip and ripping under the ball with topspin. It travels over the net toward the back line with double Gabby's velocity. The trajectory appears to sail long, but topspin forces it down inside the back line. When Zoe returns her second ball equally well, Gabby concludes she is up against a formidable opponent. Her backhand is classic in form, but contact with the ball is not as forceful as the forehand. The more she boils over the incident with Peter, the harder she hits. Gabby plots to turn this misdirected aggression into errors on the court. Her gameplan is only partially successful.

At 15-30 in the ninth game, the buzzer sounds to indicate the end of the playing hour. It takes only a second before new players duck their heads through the canvas backdrop and begin entering the court. They have the right to take possession of the court immediately after the buzzer. New Yorkers don't allow those on the court to complete the final point.

The game is so hard fought neither Gabby nor Zoe speaks as they gather their belongings. Tennis is a means to size up personalities and both are uncertain what to think, except that the other is a damn good player and competitive as hell.

"You didn't learn those strokes on a schoolyard court," Gabby observes as they move into the locker room for a shower. Zoe is equally impressed. She expected Gabby to be a moonballer. "New Haven Country Club," she says. "We had a dynamite pro who drilled me twice a week for as long as I can remember. At one time he thought I might play the circuit, but I had other ideas. University of Michigan tennis team. Played in the lower range of the ladder. Lost more matches than I won and learned that the good Lord intended other things for Zoe Miller. I came to terms with my limitations early. If I wasn't going to be a great tennis player, at least I would be a decent lawyer. No regrets on that score. And you, Gabby? You've got great strokes."

"Lots of lessons. My father put a racket into my hand and got me started early. We didn't belong to a country club, but we did have access to public courts. On vacations we went to places with a tennis program where I got more lessons. Unlike you, I never entertained fantasies about being a star. Just a recreation which has proven compatible with my work schedule. Golf would have been a disaster. If there is any free time it's only in one- or two-hour segments and you can't play golf in two hours."

"Guess you're not a skier then," Zoe adds.

"Occupational hazard. No weekends, no skiing."

Zoe stops at a stainless steel water fountain and drinks hard. Gabby follows, but with less thirst.

"They have a juice counter at the lobby canteen," Zoe says. "How about something with more bite. Treat you to a Coke if you're decadent enough for sugar-water. For health freaks they have iced chamomile tea."

"Nope, I'm game for an ugly Coke, sugar, caffeine, the whole catastrophe." Gabby is enthusiastic. "Bad for your teeth, bad for your heart, probably causes cancer, but just what I want after being run from one corner of the court to the other."

IN THE CANTEEN, THEY SIT ON STOOLS BESIDE A long bar. Fruit and health foods are stacked on the counter to entice the clientele. Aerobic instructors staff the concession between their normal duties, which means the service is slow to nonexistent. Eventually, a slim-waisted dusty-blond with short pants and a Polo shirt shows up to take orders.

"I need to ask a professional question," Gabby says after she quaffs a healthy portion of her Coke. "Don't know if Noah said anything to you about what's going on at my congregation in Washington."

"Bits and pieces, but I'm not sure I comprehend temple politics."

"You can imagine I'm hoping to fill the post left by my predecessor. I know I can do it, but I won't be offered the job though I'm fulfilling all the duties now."

"From what I witnessed at your Sabbath service, I know you can do it. The synagogue would be foolish not to promote you."

"It won't. I'm a woman. Too many members want a man to restore the tarnished image my colleague left behind. Does that look like gender discrimination to you?"

"Could be."

"You sound like a lawyer. Wait, I'm going to do some research before I render a judgment."

Zoe paws at her lips with the left hand, looking unsettled. "Sorry. I should be more sympathetic. What you describe looks, sounds, and probably is gender discrimination of one form or another."

"Is there anyone in your firm who handles cases like this?"

Zoe exhales a gust of air through her teeth. "Thinking of suing Ohav Shalom?"

"Perhaps if I'm passed over. That's not my first choice. The congregation's been good to me and I've been good to it. A suit would make us adversaries."

"Has anybody said anything about being rejected?"

"You bet. The Rabbinical Search Committee questioned my academic achievements."

"Which I would bet are numerous."

"Wrong, counselor. I'm a damn good pulpit rabbi, but no Talmudic scholar. The other candidates have Ph.D.s and publications. I don't."

"Those are pretty objective criteria. Academic degrees tend to separate women from the girls, as they say."

Gabby downs the rest of her Coke, then pounds the bar top with the glass. "Only a smokescreen. In the seven years I've been at Ohav they've never encouraged me to take a higher degree, publish articles, or write books. Now suddenly it becomes a selection criterion. What they don't want is a female Senior Rabbi. Especially a single woman without kids. Is that the kind of case you might take?"

"Not my expertise, Gabby. Claudia Frenilli, a senior associate of the firm, has had success representing women with promotion claims. If you want, I'll be happy to introduce you to her."

"I'm not ready quite yet. Just exploring options. I don't think anyone would enjoy suing a synagogue. Certainly not me."

Zoe finishes her iced tea, then fishes her pockets for currency to pay. Gabby is there first with three dollar bills.

"My treat," Zoe objects.

"Let's just say this is token payment for legal advice. It's nice to know I have an option."

"Don't wait too long. If Ohav Shalom appoints a male, you may sue, but it won't get you the post. You might want to put the congregation on notice of your rights. Claudia Frenilli can help with the initial contact. If it were me, I wouldn't wait until they provide you with a *fait accompli*."

"I'll take that under advisement." Gabby smiles. She likes Zoe Mountolive, who strikes her as a lady who doesn't get pushed around—except perhaps by her husband.

Zoe glances at her watch and declares that she must complete a series of chores in Manhattan. "I'm free this evening if you'd like to have dinner together. Saturday nights are not much fun these days. Clemmy is usually with Peter. Single men, if they're not an extinct species, haven't gotten word that I'm available. How about you? A date tonight?"

Gabby responds with a sympathetic grin. "The creep I've been in love with has run off after another lady whom I have never met but, of course, hate. That also makes me a free agent and I'd love to have dinner with you. I promised to visit with old friends in Brooklyn this afternoon, but I could make it into the city after seven. How about making a reservation?" She eases from the bar stool. "Shower time."

They walk together for several feet until Zoe says, "I'm out of time. Will have to smell like a skunk until I finish my errands." She stops at a pay phone and fishes in her athletic bag for a wallet and change. Gabby is quick to supply a quarter.

"Come to my place around seven. I'll call Contraputo's for an eight o'clock reservation. Like Italian?"

"My favorite. I should be able to be there by seven. But not in anything fancier than what I wore this afternoon."

AFTER SHOWERING, GABBY REPLACES HER TENNIS clothes with a beige cotton sweater and pleated linen skirt, appropriate clothes to visit Orthodox friends who observe the sanctity of the Sabbath by staying home, eating, and relaxing. They will not be insulted when Gabby violates a prohibition against riding on the Sabbath and arrives by taxi. To make the date with Zoe later that evening, she will have to depart by taxi before sundown.

On the street in front of the North Queens Sports Club, she is struck by the seediness of the neighborhood and considers returning to the reception desk to telephone for a cab. She does not heed her own advice and elects to walk in the direction of

Parsons Avenue, a major thoroughfare likely frequented by roving taxis. Men—white, African-American, and Native American—appear to have nothing better to do but stand against buildings and scrutinize intruders passing through their territory. She is suddenly conscious of her isolation. Her pace quickens. The tennis racket dangling from her left shoulder provides a measure of security. With her free hand she reaches back to unzip the carrying cover and expose the grip. The sound of feet pounding the pavement behind her, amplified by the weathered brick siding of the warehouses, makes her wary.

As she crosses the alley where Zoe parked her car, she glances down a line of trucks and utility vans for a possible escape route. Too bad she changed her tennis shoes to leather flats in the club locker room. Her eyes search for Zoe's cream-white Lexus, expecting it to be gone. But to her surprise the vehicle is exactly where originally parked. No sign of Zoe, though farther down the alley she observes two men hanging against a warehouse loading dock. They are facing the dock and, on first glance, they appear to be relieving themselves against the concrete leveler. But they are not stationary as one would expect of men urinating. Their arms and legs are moving. An impulse to hurry along Parsons Avenue courses through her, but it is neutralized by a sense that something is wrong—perhaps with Zoe.

She diverts into the alley, creeping forward cautiously for a better view. Footsteps behind her slip from her consciousness. Her fingers tighten around the tennis racket grip, though the strings remain hidden in the vinyl cover. As she approaches the docking area, she becomes aware that what she believed to be grown men are really two adolescent boys, tall and heavy. Her pace increases. The sounds of her own feet clatter on the roadway surface. The youths are doing something to a third person, who is hunched over, arms flailing.

At that moment Gabby hears a female scream. She whirls around to survey the entrance to the alley and her possible escape route. A man is silhouetted against the opening to Parsons Avenue. Too late for a retreat. Her feet propel themselves, walking fast and then scrambling. On weathered cobblestones near the teenagers is an abandoned tennis racket cover and beside it Zoe's racket. The identity of the third youth is now clear. Not a kid being pummeled by his contemporaries, but Zoe!

"Stop!" Gabby yells at the boy as she comes within range and can identify Zoe's tennis warmup jacket. She is pinned against the loading dock, unable to maneuver. The assailant has pulled her jacket down over her arms to restrain them, yet she is nevertheless clawing to protect herself. He is trying to pull her sweatpants past her hips.

"Get off her!" Gabby howls.

A tall youth with disheveled hair and an adolescent beard turns on Gabby. His underpants are exposed through the open fly of his trousers. "Mind your own fuckin' business, Lady. This got nothing to do with you."

The youth grabbing at Zoe assumes his accomplice will take care of the second woman and presses Zoe hard against the loading dock. Gabby knows instinctively that the moment to respond is quickly disappearing. Her fist tightens over the grip of her tennis racket. The youth who snatches her left arm inadvertently facilitates her freedom with the right. The racket slips free of the jacket.

"Stop," she threatens, holding the racket like a weapon. The youth is not impressed until she slams it forward with all the force of her powerful first serve, rotating the neck to expose the graphite rim. It slashes through the air with a swish and cracks against the skull of her molester, behind the ear. The blow strikes with such force that it throws him off-balance. As he stumbles, his head bounces against the steel bed of a parked delivery truck. An expletive escapes his lips just as Gabby delivers a second blow to the neck, cutting his wind. The youth's body collapses on a slick of oil soiling the cobblestones.

The tall, heavy youth holding Zoe reacts immediately. He abandons his victim to jump on Gabby and trap her upper arms. Zoe is quick to take advantage of her sudden freedom and hauls herself from the dock. The sleeves of her jacket still bind her limbs until she can wrestle her right arm free. Gabby manages to hold onto her racket until Zoe is within distance, then lets it drop from her fingers to the cobblestones.

On the road, the first youth's knees are forward in a fetal position and his hands cradle his head. A moan of pain curdles the air. Blood oozes through his fingers. Zoe ignores him and snatches Gabby's racket. The youth who is manhandling Gabby curses and rotates his captive before the threatening club in

Zoe's hand. She feigns a blow to catch him in the wrong position and swings at his head. But he is too fast. Meanwhile, Gabby kicks and wriggles, keeping him off-balance. Finally, when he yanks her around to face Zoe for a second feint, he releases her arms long enough for her to slip away. That lapse proves to be his undoing. As he strives to restrain his hostage, he exposes his head long enough for Zoe to strike. The graphite edge of the racket clips him across the bridge of his nose, instantly breaking the cartilage. His eyes fill with tears while excruciating pain burns his face. He can no longer hold onto his captive. Zoe's second blow lands on his ear, leaving a large gash. As his hand jerks up to cover the wound, he releases an animal yelp of pain. His fingers become red with blood. He looks to his partner for help but finds him still on the pavement, coiled in pain and unable to reenter combat.

"I'm fuckin' bleeding to death!" he exclaims.

Zoe winds up like a baseball pitcher, ready to strike a third blow.

Gabby snatches Zoe's racket from the cobblestones and stands above the first youth, threatening to swing again if he attempts to get up. "Are you all right?" she asks Zoe.

"Roughed up. Punks were trying to get my clothes off. Never expected to be rescued by a gladiator with a tennis racket."

"Fuckin' cunts," the large youth curses.

"We'd better get an ambulance. Got a phone in your car?"

"Gone. Ripped it out in Manhattan. Haven't had time to get it replaced."

"Think you could make it back to the Sports Club?"

"I'm not leaving you here alone."

"Don't think these punks are prepared to start again."

"Fuckin' animals. Wild bitches." The smaller youth swears but does not raise his hand to resume. He rolls onto his knees and remains there like a puppy dog, gathering strength to stand. He needs the loading dock for support, but as he clings to it more blood flows from his wound.

Meanwhile, the pursuer from Parsons Avenue materializes. During the scuffle, he remained at some distance, but the moment it is over he dashes to the scene. Street grime thinly masks desiccated skin from overexposure to the weather. An ill-fitting, soiled baseball jersey hangs from his shoulders and a red knee pokes from a hole in his overalls. The butt of an unsmoked cigarette clings to the corner of his lips. "I seen everything what happened here, ladies," he introduces himself. "Seen these two youngsters taking a short cut through this alley when you two jumped 'em. Can't understand why women want to batter youngsters to death with tennis rackets, but rich people like you are unpredictable. Must have something against kids mindin' their own business. Malicious battery is what I seen. Law's tough on child beaters."

"Jesus Christ." Zoe turns to Gabby with a sneer. "All we need now is a vulture. Looks like we're going to have to level this asshole, too."

"Don't even contemplate it, lady." In a swift motion he moves within Zoe's defensive zone, smothering her arms and immobilizing her racket. He spins her around in an exhibition of strength.

Gabby barks, "We're going to get the Rescue Squad. Prevent us and we'll press charges against you, too. We're moving back along this alley to the Sports Club to get help. If you want to be useful, stay here and tell the police what really happened."

Gabby raises her racket head as if lining up for a high forehand volley, face open, wrist down and slightly cocked for maximum power. The newcomer glowers at her, suddenly aware that so long as his hands are holding Zoe, he cannot defend his head against a blow from a second person. Seeing what damage tennis rackets inflicted on the youngsters, he holds Zoe in front as a buffer. Gabby keeps her distance so he cannot grab her.

"Make a deal with you, ladies," he says while releasing Zoe who instinctively clutches her racket and steps behind him to batter from the rear. Her racket remains cocked at shoulder level. "Twenty bucks and I'm out of here. Twenty bucks and I didn't see nothing that happened."

Zoe glances over the first youth who pulls himself up against the brick wall and sits with his knees buckled up in front. His moaning has stopped. His eyes are downcast and he is weeping. She concludes there will be no further trouble from him. To the stranger, she says, "No money for lies. Tell the police whatever you damn want."

In stressful situations, Gabby is inclined to be pragmatic. The idea of rewarding extortion is repugnant, yet she senses ceaseless complication with the way she and Zoe handled the youngsters. There will be a police inquiry. False testimony will only complicate the story. She picks up her athletic bag and rummages it for a wallet. "Twenty dollars," she declares, sorting through the travel currency she brought from Washington. "For some food. And maybe a bath. A bottle if you want. But not for silence. We don't buy false testimony, Mister."

Her willingness to wave a twenty-dollar bill in the air confuses him. Rich people are often doing confusing things. In the end, it is the twenty that wins his acceptance. A hand, swollen and pocked with open scabs, darts forward to snatch the bill.

Gabby says, "Stay with these boys until we get help. Don't let them move away. It shouldn't take more than a few minutes."

Zoe is uncomfortable leaving her attackers and thoroughly skeptical that the witness will stand by after they leave. On the other hand, she is not about to remain behind alone or let Gabby keep watch. *The New York Times* recently ran a series on the poor response time from the Metropolitan Police and Rescue Squad. The Borough of Queens won no prizes.

THOUGH IT IS TWO BLOCKS AWAY, THEY DRIVE ZOE'S car to the sports facility. As they circle to enter a one-way street, Zoe speaks in a hushed voice. Until that moment she has been in a state of shock. But now the significance of what happened causes her eyes to water, impairing her vision. Saliva rises in her throat and her breathing becomes uneven. She hides the physical reaction by clasping her hand firmly on the steering wheel and forcing vision through squinted eyes. Her voice is strong and unaffected. "Thanks for rescuing me back there. I resisted as much as I could, but it's tough against two."

"Lucky timing," Gabby responds, also feeling a disjunction between her limbs and her mind. A familiar sensation of shaking overwhelms her, making her fingers tremble and her teeth chatter. But unlike Zoe there are no tears. "I almost missed you in the alley. I noticed your car hadn't moved and went in to investigate. Then I saw a bunch of bodies clustered together. For an instant, I told myself not to get involved. I thought it was just two guys in a fight or a police shakedown. But when I got closer I could see the two guys were huddled over someone. Then I saw you against the wall."

"They had their hands all over my body. Everywhere on my chest but couldn't get through my sport bra. There were fingers in my crotch. I fought as hard as I could."

Gabby feels drained and is trying to prevent Zoe from seeing her shake. That takes some doing, for it is necessary to keep her arms out of sight and speak very slowly. "I didn't know my strength. Lost my senses. Didn't have to hit that kid as hard as I did. Hope he pulls through all right."

The Lexus enters the passenger loading zone at the club entrance. Gabby is ready and jumps out, dashing through the double glass doors to the reception desk. Thank God her legs aren't wobbly. Two receptionists are issuing courts and athletic equipment to other players, but Gabby interrupts. "There's been a bad incident outside! Need an ambulance! Emergency! Get the Rescue Squad on the phone!" To the second receptionist, she orders, "Call the police."

Both receptionists look to each other for direction and ultimately rally, as Gabby finds herself with a phone receiver at each ear, one connected to the local police precinct, the other to the Rescue Squad at the Fire Department. Her shaking stops almost as fast as it began. In the background, she hears a buzzer ring, alerting the rescue team at the station. On first impression, that's far better response than was reported by *The New York Times*. She has difficulty describing the exact location and eventually does so not by addresses, but by streets north and east of the North Queens Sports Club.

"Mugging or rape?" the police dispatcher asks.

"No mugging, if that means stealing money or jewels."

"Rape or assault?"

"Both. But the rape wasn't successful. There was resistance."

"We'll dispatch a car immediately. Go back to Parsons Avenue to guide the officers, but don't get near the suspects if they're still there."

"They're hurt and can't move."

"Don't be naive, lady. What did you say your name was?"

"Rabbi Gabrielle Lewyn."

"Right, lady. And I'm Pope John Paul."

WHEN GABBY AND ZOE SEE THE RESCUE SQUAD arrive, they point down the alley to the crime site and, as the vehicle snakes between parked trucks, they follow on foot. Pope John Paul from the police precinct was right. The two youngsters are gone, along with the witness. Police arrive on the scene a few minutes later, their sirens blaring. As they approach, it is apparent the suspects have fled and there's no further need to rush. They sit in their squad car for a long interval until Gabby and Zoe walk up to their open window and try to explain. That the suspects are no longer around comes as no surprise. What did the two daffy women from Manhattan know about the criminal mind? Felons don't usually wait for the police to arrest them.

The police officers are detached and skeptical. Maybe this call was just a figment of fertile imaginations. This kind of thing happens every day. Or maybe they're reporters manufacturing something to write about in their newspapers. Fresh blood on the rubber bumper of the loading dock eventually convinces them the victims are credible. More blood is discovered on stones where the first youth was floored. They take Polaroid pictures and scribble in their note books.

Gabby and Zoe follow the officers to the police station to make a statement and give descriptions. There are promises to post alerts at regional medical facilities. The lieutenant who conducts the debriefing asks if they need medical attention which they don't.

"From what you tell us," the lieutenant states, "these kids have been punished already. We'll try to find them, but it will take time. You're free to call me for a report."

"Will you catch them?" Gabby is sometimes innocent with her questions.

"Maybe," he deflects.

"That means no, doesn't it?" Zoe pursues.

In the parked car outside the station, Zoe closes her eyes and weeps, a low, quiet release of tension from deep within. The toughness she showed in resistance is spent and in the shell left behind is a fragile girl. She brought the battle to the enemy's shore and, with her tennis racket, wounded her adversary. But when it was over, the shame and horror of violation wells up, releasing a torrent of emotion. It could rise as anger or fatigue, but instead emerges into the world as sorrow. Zoe weeps aloud. Under normal conditions she would have hidden this emotion, but the eruption is too violent. Gabby plants a hand on her shoulder and listens to her weeping. From time to time, she squeezes a little, just to let her know she's still there.

GABBY'S ORTHODOX FRIENDS IN BROOKLYN DO NOT answer the phone on *Shabbat*. They do, however, have a phone machine whose messages she knows they check soon after sundown on *motzey-Shabbat*. She does not explain why her visit must be canceled but promises to call in the next few days with an explanation. A shame, because she was looking forward to celebrating a portion of *Shabbat* together. So much for a Sabbath of Peace and Rest.

Zoe also abandons plans to complete weekly chores. She wants a shower and time to regenerate. In the car traveling over the Queensboro Bridge into Manhattan, she says to Gabby, "I can still hear the sound of my racket striking that kid. Don't think I'll ever forget it. Or the sight of his blood. I have no idea where the strength came from."

"You were protecting me," Gabby responds.

"And your strength came from protecting me, I suppose?"

"Something like that. People often talk about being possessed by an external power. In my case it arose from within and was wild and uncontrollable. Don't believe I thought about what I was doing because if I had, I wouldn't have done it. If I thought hard first, I might have let you get raped or robbed or whatever those kids intended to do, and submitted to a similar fate myself. Now I have to worry that some underprivileged kid is living his life with chronic migraine headaches. Maybe worse."

Zoe laughs aloud, a prelude to her thoughts. "I'm not as forgiving, but then I'm not paid by the legal profession to forgive my enemies. I bet we scared the shit out of those punks. They underestimated our resistance. We took 'em by complete surprise. They'll think twice about attacking women again."

Gabby does not respond but descends into her own thoughts.

"Feel the same way I do?" Zoe tries to return her to the conversation.

"In part. But I'm ashamed of myself. Not sure why. I guess you could say we were fantastic warriors. But we were also wild.

Out of control. Our resistance was primitive, almost uncivilized."

"No less than those kids."

"Little boys, overflowing with testosterone. We have a legitimate quarrel with them. But we also have a quarrel with God. He put that testosterone in them and let it explode during adolescence. I don't mind telling you, Zoe, I'm angry and humbled at the same time. And when you take your shower, I'm going to sit in your living room, drink a double Scotch and have a good cry just like you. But not until we get to your place."

"Were you scared, Gabby?" Zoe inquires with a rhetorical ring in her voice.

"No. Not then. But now that it's over, I'm shaking inside. And you?"

"I was too angry to be scared."

GABBY FEELS COMPELLED TO SEE TIMOTHY MATTERNly while in New York, yet she is fearful of what she might find. Though she tries to be objective about their breakup, it is not easy to disengage from the relationship, hopeless as it was from the outset. Too many wonderful memories. Too much human fulfillment. Too much good sex with a giving, patient lover.

When she called him from Washington to arrange time Sunday morning, he was courteous but somewhat reticent. It wasn't just a conflict of scheduling or a conflict with Sally and her daughters. She could feel he wasn't enthusiastic and yet neither did he want to dismiss the idea altogether.

As usual, he masked discomfort with jest, stringing together a series of one-liners that got Gabby chuckling, though she didn't feel like laughing.

"So what are the plans, Timmy?" She talks on the phone while Zoe is taking a shower. And before he can answer, she adds, "You wouldn't believe what happened to me and a friend this afternoon."

"My Lord, Jesus, appeared to you in a vision while stuck in traffic at Forty-Second and Avenue of the Americas. There He was, hanging between two marquees advertising all-nude girlie shows."

"Nothing so mundane, Timmy. I see visions like that every night after I down a nightcap too fast. My friend and I were accosted by two kids in Queens. I helped her and got into a brawl. Quite a scuffle."

"Sounds like those kids are more industrious than I. I've been trying to get my arms around you for years."

"Don't think you'd want to trade places with them."

"Try me."

"We floored 'em. Flattened them on the pavement. Almost incapacitated."

"Sweet. That's what I always admired about you, Lovey. A model of patience and tenderness."

"You don't understand. I'll explain everything tomorrow. Where do we meet?"

"At home. I'm fixing brunch."

"Jesus, Tim. You know how to hurt a girl. I can forget all about you, forget you ever existed on this planet, but damn it, I can't forget your cooking. Every time I smell garlic, I see my Timothy and taste his artichokes. Your asparagus with thyme and basil has the same effect." There is a slight hesitation before she gets serious with a question she fears. "Is Sally coming?"

"Yes. With her daughters. I want them to meet you. I hope you don't object. You're an important part of my life, Lovey, and if they're entering it, they've got to know what's important to me."

"What about our secrets?"

"Sally's discretion incarnate. If her girls break this confidentiality, I'll break their beautiful little necks. When you meet them you'll understand the kind of people they are."

"Will there be time for us to visit alone?" Gabby petitions as well as asks.

"They're coming at 10:30. Come at 9:30 and help cook."

"Do I have to keep my hands off you?"

"God damn it, Lovey, you could tempt a saint into hell. If you lay one finger on me, I'll clobber you with a blintz."

"It's your call, Tim."

There was a long, engulfing silence in which Gabby could hear him sniffling. "Don't break my heart again. I'm just starting to feel whole again. No more wounds, please."

She absorbs his entreaty as Zoe enters the living room in her bare feet, her body draped in an enormous towel. Before she realizes that Gabby has a phone receiver to her ear, she says, "That's better. Feel much better, now. You may want a shower yourself."

Gabby is distracted for only an instant. She says to Tim, "Promise you, Tim. You're the last fellow on earth I'd ever consciously hurt."

"Good. Cooking starts at 9:30."

"DO I REALLY WANT TO DO THIS?" GABBY ASKS HERself the following morning as she approaches Tim's apartment on Mercer Street, near Washington Square in Greenwich Village. She is perplexed by the conflicting emotions that propel her both toward and away from him—on the one hand regarding him as an intimate lover to be possessed and defended and, on the other, a close friend, to be supported and promoted. As the roller-coaster of emotion rides high, she feels the wild urge of an alley cat to protect her territory and Tim Matternly is definitely hers to protect. But when her mood plunges, she sinks into depression. The predicament is impossible. Neither she nor Tim can endure such emotional swings.

Meeting Sally is not what she had in mind when she called him from Washington suggesting a rendezvous. She had hoped for personal time alone, when they might bring resolution to raw, open-ended feelings—perhaps find a formula for making the break more tolerable, and assuring each other that when the dust settled they might resume as close friends. Sally's presence makes that impossible. Gabby does not like her and she chides herself for this prejudice. After all, she has never met the woman. They share good taste in men. And besides, Sally is apparently making Tim happy, no easy task for one who masks the black terror of his life with humor. Someone has to do it. Gabby is gratified that it is not a gorgeous New York fashion model with popcorn for brains, flashy white teeth, exploding tits, and a 22-inch waist.

Tim meets her on the fourth-floor landing, dressed in a chef's apron, short-sleeved polo shirt and open sandals, revealing strong, straight toes. His wet hands cannot manage an embrace. His kiss avoids her lips and lands on her cheek.

"Feeling guilty already," she observes as they enter a kitchen with the appearance of a neighborhood delicatessen, stuffed with boxes, cans, and bottles of packaged foods. Baskets of tomatoes, eggplants, squashes, and mushrooms rest on the butcher-block island workstation. Along the sideboard is crockery stuffed with bananas, apples, a pineapple, and bunches of purple and green table grapes. Open cabinets reveal rows of condiments and spices of sufficient variety to stock a suburban restaurant. Tim returns immediately to a pile of diced onions he has left to answer the doorbell and, with a wide butcher knife, moves them to the corner of the chopping board to make room for a mound of parsley.

There is an awkward interval of silence in which neither knows what to say. Finally, Tim looks up from the parsley he has begun to chop. “I’m trying to think of something funny and can’t come up with anything except I’m glad to see you.”

“Me, too.” She works a smile to her lips. “When you left the Pierre, I was miserable enough to reconsider jumping from a bridge. Then I asked myself if the Tri-Boro or the Queensboro bridges are high enough for a clean suicide. The only bridge I could be certain possessed the obligatory height was the Verazzano and that meant a long and dangerous subway ride through south Brooklyn. You know, one can get killed riding a subway at night.”

Tim keeps his eyes on the knife he uses with quick, practiced chops, moving the parsley into a pile with the blade. “Maybe that’s a better way to go than off a bridge. You exaggerate the danger riding our mass transit,” he teases.

“Maybe the subway, but not New York. My friend and I almost bought the farm in Queens yesterday. Two young hoods tried to get their hands under my friend’s clothes. I bet they wished they hadn’t.”

“You said on the phone you flattened them. What does that mean?”

“Exactly what I said. Both of us had tennis rackets and we have hard serves. I knocked one of them to the ground with a blow to his skull. No powderball blow either. I think he suffered a concussion because he went down and stayed there. Blood all over his neck.”

“Jesus, Lovey. Better mind my manners. Give women the vote and before you know it they’ll be toting lethal weapons. What did the police do?”

“Nothing. Arrived too late. By the time we got an ambulance to the scene, the attackers had fled. Along with a stranger who extorted twenty bucks from me not to give false testimony. I figured better to give him twenty up front than to pay thousands to the lawyers later."

"That's my Gabby, practical to the core," he says while moving a pasta machine into position. Next come semolina flour, water, and eggs. "You seem to have recovered."

"On the outside. You know me. Inside, I feel like Jello. I might have hit the kid too hard and made a bad juvenile into something far worse. Could have made him into a permanent basket case."

"Kids are all bad at one time or another in their lives."

"That's why I feel like a shit. And there's no way I can find out the real damages. Maybe I don't really want to know. Unless the police locate these punks, I'll be haunted by the thought."

"You need somebody to talk to," Tim says, measuring semolina into a measuring cup and lifting it high to inspect the faded red measuring line.

She inches close to his side, wants to put a hand around his waist but refrains. "For years I had someone wonderful to talk to, but he eventually got tired of waiting for me and found somebody else."

He puts down the measuring cup and turns toward her. "I mean a psychiatrist. Somebody professional. Not a hack minister of the Presbyterian faith."

"Rabbis have hard times with mental health professionals. You know who I really miss beside you?"

"Norman Vincent Peale. Maharani Gaheeta Punjami."

"No, silly. Seth Greer. Whatever people might say about him, he was a great listener. An insightful counselor. We used to talk a lot."

"Did you tell him about us?"

She takes her time and slowly shakes her head. No.

"And he told you about his love affairs?"

Her head continues with the same horizontal motion. "Not a word. When I heard, I felt cheated. Fact is, when the word got out I was as surprised as everybody in the community. But there's one small clue after the fact, one that still puzzles me. I went to his study. It's empty now and waiting for his successor."

"You, of course. I cast my vote unequivocally for Rabbi Gabrielle Lewyn. Many others will, too."

"Dreamer. In his study he had left a copy of the Kittel Bible in Hebrew, you know, with the Masoretic text and all the comments and footnotes. He must have figured they'd deliver it to me for safekeeping. Inside the cover there was yellow Post-it with a note. It said, 'For my colleague, Gabby Lewyn, who is seldom stumped by a puzzle.'"

"That's almost tautological."

"Not if you begin with the premise there isn't a puzzle. Lusty rabbi screws four or five women. Lusty rabbi resigns from big congregation. End of story. But why refer to a puzzle, Agatha Christie style?"

Tim turns back to his cooking. "Is there one?"

"I'm not sure. I know the crimes, but not the motives. I think I know who's responsible, but not why he did what he did."

"Which comes full circle. You need somebody to talk with."

"Like you, Timmy. I couldn't have gotten through these past seven years without somebody on the outside. Now my confidant is dating someone else."

"But that doesn't preclude discussions, Lovey." He glances at her looking injured.

"If this Sally is the kind of woman I think she is, she won't permit it."

"Then why tell her?"

"Because that's not the kind of relationship you're looking for. I'm not about to be a saint and sacrifice my beau only to sabotage his relationship or his marriage."

"Who said anything about marriage?"

"I did," she says. "Because if it isn't leading in that direction, then ditch the broad and come back to me so we can grow old together screwing secretly in sleazy places and lying to our families and friends."

He ponders that with an artificially serious expression on his face, then manufactures an equally phony smile, exposing teeth. "Well now, that's an attractive proposal that will take some time to reject. And just so we don't get bogged down for another decade, how about making yourself useful and setting the table."

"Now that's the most practical idea we've had yet. Setting the table was my job as a youngster. My mother was very fussy. It had to be perfect. And so it will be for Sally and her daughters. By the way, what are their names?"

"The six-year-old is Becky. The eight-year-old, Shira."

"Sounds biblical to me," Gabby replies as she lifts a tray of silverware from a dining room breakfront. "Say, you never told me Sally's last name."

"Goldwater."

Gabby drops the tray of tableware back into the drawer with a loud bang, then pivots around to face Tim at the kitchen sink. "Jewish? Tim, what's with you and Jewish girls? Isn't one enough?"

He throws one of his mirthful smiles across the kitchen to the dining room. "Experience with my first Jewess was so good, I thought I'd try again."

"You're jumping from the pan into the fire, my boy. You're better off dumping the Goldwater family and coming back to me."

"Not quite, Lovey. There's a world of difference between you and Sally."

"You could hurt my feelings, Tim. So don't."

"Nothing personal. Only Sally's not a rabbi and you are."

Chapter Eight

August 19th

Gabby is uneasy when she returns to the Temple a few minutes before 8:00 a.m. on Monday. Chuck Browner left her the name of the rabbinic candidate who auditioned at the Temple on Friday and Saturday. Rabbi Toby Deutscher, Associate Rabbi of Congregation Sherith Israel in Glencoe, Illinois. He learned that she had been wined and dined throughout the weekend by the Search Committee. Rabbi Deutscher had graduated from the seminary four years prior to her own ordination and has been active in rabbinic affairs, chairing a rabbinical committee on the promotion of family values. From time to time she publishes articles in Jewish publications, usually dealing with the stresses of life-cycle events upon the family, a subject which earned her a Ph.D. from the University of Wisconsin. While Gabby is always careful not to make disparaging remarks about colleagues, she has long regarded Toby as a pedestrian thinker with the imagination of a garden slug. She doubts she possesses sufficient wit to crack one joke, certainly not several in rapid sequence like Seth.

At a little past 8:30 a.m., she hears Chuck Browner moving about in the secretarial station outside. A moment later he sticks his head through the open door to say good morning and get a report on her weekend. She keeps it general and purposely skips the brawl outside the tennis club in Queens. That will come soon enough. He appears uninterested in details and she notices a mischievous grin parting his lips.

"And what did you do, Chucky boy?" she asks.

"It's not what I did that's important, but what I got." He flashes four tape cassettes cradled between his fingers, whirling them in a circle to catch her eye.

At first she does not appreciate what she sees.

"You asked to hear what was said in the Board meeting about Rabbi Greer. Here are the tapes."

This compels her to stand up. "How'd you do it? I know you're good, but I never expected you to succeed in this. Were they in Harold's office? Talk to me. How? When?"

He steps forward to set the tapes on her desk. "You don't really want to know, Rabbi."

"Oh, yes I do. Tell me."

"I don't think you heard me, Rabbi Gabby. So I'll repeat: you don't want to know."

"*Au contraire, chéri.*"

"I'm an out-of-the-closet gay. The majority of men like me are still locked up and living a hellish masquerade. You wouldn't believe how many. We have developed our own currency for the exchange of property and favors. People call this a network. More information isn't necessary. Spend your time listening to these tapes."

A look of comprehension captures her face as she struggles with her imagination. It's time to ask if she commissioned Chuck to go beyond the call of duty. She would like to think she hadn't, but she put no boundaries on his invention.

"There are two messages from Noah Zentner on your weekend voice mail. Wants to come here at noon and take you to lunch. You know I've booked him for Wednesday. What should I tell him about today?"

She flips open her scheduler and taps commands on the screen with a stylus. "I'm swamped, dead under water. Haven't got enough free time to eat a pretzel. But Mr. Zentner's hurting. If I'm free on the synagogue docket, we can eat here in my office. Phone Snyders' Deli and have them deliver a couple of tuna sandwiches on kaiser rolls. Lettuce and tomato. Pickles, no mayonnaise. Hold the coleslaw; no potato chips either."

"There's another important call," Chuck says. "The Rabbinic Search Committee has asked you meet with them at 8:30 Thursday evening, Gertrude Swidler's home. Schedule for an hour and a half."

This is a surprise. She has tickets for Arena Stage with two girlfriends from the Old Biddies Confederation. Though she feels like snubbing the committee, she doesn't possess the confidence.

"Okay, confirm at Gertrude Swidler's. Ask if there's an agenda I should prepare for."

"Remember what I told you about the sweet-talk phase." Chuck registers a snide curl of the upper lip.

"My resident Cassandra. Thanks for your vote of confidence, partner."

"I'm protecting my friend, that's all."

"Okay, then while you're doing it, how about preparing this Power Point presentation. I'm beginning Rabbi Greer's summer school class at Georgetown. I made a slide presentation on my PC at home. Made transparencies from numbered documents on this disk. Georgetown said they'd have an overhead projector available in the classroom."

Chuck examines the 3.5-inch disk. "Woman of innumerable talents, Professor Lewyn. I didn't know you were an expert on Medieval Jewish Thought."

"I wasn't until I got this assignment. Most teachers are just a chapter ahead of their students."

"Expecting a big turnout?"

"Absolutely. Seth Greer had them standing in the aisles and auditing from the corridors. His name is in the class catalogue. At least a portion of the students won't know there's been a substitution. Once they learn he's not on stage, the majority will vanish."

"Promise them all *A*s from the get-go. That'll inspire them."

"SORRY ABOUT NOT BEING ABLE TO EAT IN A RESTAURant, but my schedule's crazy." At noon, Gabby greets Noah Zentner at her office door and ushers him to upholstered chairs fronting a glass coffee table usually piled with journals and monographs. Chuck has cleared it to make room for the deli sandwiches.

"Seth once told me you're a workaholic," he replies. He is in a gray Italian business suit, bleached white shirt with stiff collar that reaches high along the back of the neck and a navy-blue silk Hermès tie.

Out of habit, Gabby sits herself in the armchair next to her desk phone. "I hope he didn't tell you all my secrets."

"Only the admirable ones. Never heard him say anything but good things about you."

"I envied your friendship. Rabbis don't often make good friends from these congregations. How sad it's come to this."

"I've known Emma Greer throughout their marriage. Seth's kids used to think of me as their uncle. When the scandal broke, I met Jeremy in San Francisco for lunch and went to see Margie in Frederick. Emma's a difficult woman, but beneath her abrasive skin she's really a pussycat. Her only flaw was that she refused to be a model rebbitsin and play second fiddle to her husband."

"I hope you like tuna sandwiches, Noah." Gabby breaks the thread of his conversation. Yes, she's curious about an insider's view of the mysterious Seth Greer yet, at the moment, there are more important topics. "I had Chuck Browner supply Diet Pepsis."

"*Poi-fect*," he responds in a Yiddish accent, mimicking comedian Jackie Mason while examining the sandwich to decide which end he will first introduce to his mouth. "I'm glad to see you, Rabbi. Hard to talk to people these days. My affair has escalated beyond imagination. It's repeated over and over in the media, and each time there's a new variation on what happened. Publicity is responsible for making a mundane encounter into a national event. In the process, fiction eclipses history. Nineteen people were aboard the *Dame Cynthia* and there are nineteen differing stories of what happened. I've heard CBS has commissioned a re-enactment drama for late-night television. Can't wait to see how they'll handle the fact that the incident occurred entirely in the dark."

Gabby rests her sandwich upon a paper plate. As usual, she has little appetite. The piquant dill pickle irritates her taste buds. "I only know what I read in the papers; I think it's better if we keep it that way. If I become a witness, the prosecution might ask me under oath about my relationship with you both before and after. Of course I can argue client privilege and refuse to answer. But that might influence a jury negatively. Better if I don't have insider information."

There is a distant abandonment in his eyes. He wants to talk about it with her.

"I do know this is a nightmare for you. It must be very painful."

He pauses to wipe a particle of tuna from the corner of his mouth with a paper napkin. "More than anyone can know. What hurts is the stupidity of it. Nothing horrible happened out there. I didn't kill anybody. All I did was react to instinct. Too much testosterone, I guess."

"I hope you get support from your father."

"Of course, but he's getting on in age. I'm the one supposed to take care of him, not the other way around. He has his own worries."

"Something wrong with him?"

"The usual male plumbing problems. They've recently diagnosed a small tumor on his prostate. He's got a battery of doctors at Johns Hopkins sorting out the therapy. Some argue for surgery and chemotherapy, others radiation. He's confused."

"Nothing can be more confusing than medicine." Gabby leans back into her chair and regards him studiously. "What remains a mystery to me is your relationship with Morgan. It's hard to understand why you'd want to cheat on such an attractive and accomplished woman. I meet her on the tennis courts from time to time. She's a good athlete."

Noah's complexion blanches. He puts down the remains of his sandwich and appears to contract into himself, saying nothing. Gabby is sensitive to his reservations and knows she is on fragile ground. "I'm sorry," she finally says, "I don't think anyone has the right to invade the privacy of husband and wife."

"No," he shakes himself from mental drift, "my hesitation isn't because of you. The truth is I'm ashamed. I wasn't raised to cheat on a wife, especially not Morgan whom I cherish, though I won't pretend that our marriage was working. It wasn't. Something went wrong almost from the beginning and the tragedy is I don't really understand it. Isn't that pathetic?"

Gabby is more reserved now, fearful of venturing where she is not wanted, yet curious. She is constantly surprised by the complexities of marriage. How easy it is for an unmarried woman like herself to sit on the sidelines and watch others make a hash of marital life.

"Morgan and I barely argued, certainly not more than average couples, if there are any average couples left these days. During the first year of our marriage we had our tiffs, heated but easily worked out. My therapist said most healthy marriages go through an adjustment stage. Last year, arguments stopped altogether, probably because we both sensed their futility. Neither one of us could foresee victory in changing the other, whether the arguments were about politics, money, or family. We just hunkered down into a form of trench warfare. Neither side attacking; neither side retreating. We became mere roommates, not lovers."

Noah twists his body toward Gabby and plants his hands atop his knees. His posture is now more relaxed. "Sometime in the second year, Morgan began to withdraw. You read about things like this in novels, but somehow don't believe they can strike at home. Psychologists call this *disengagement* and say it is quite common. We learned to avoid not only arguments but conversation. I don't mean we stopped all communication. We spoke when necessary to organize life's chores, pay the bills, maintain the semblance of a functioning marriage before our families and friends. But friendly conversations died."

"A lot of energy for little reward," Gabby comments.

"Tell me about it. The dirty part is that as Morgan withdrew, so did I. For a while I tried continuing as if nothing had changed. I hoped things would get better and return to normal, but they didn't. I became a stranger in the house, and she must have felt likewise. She maintains an office at home and is often there during business hours. But after hours, we both avoided the place."

"You got counseling, I presume."

"I did. But she didn't feel the need for it. You'd think that when a marriage is collapsing, she'd acknowledge the problem and seek help to repair what's broken. But the puzzling thing is that she didn't seem to care. She didn't care whether I was in therapy or not. Never asked me about it."

"Maybe she didn't recognize or acknowledge your marriage was broken."

"Her mind was elsewhere."

"Any clues where?"

"She worked six, sometimes seven days a week in her office at home. In the late afternoon she would go out and not return until almost midnight. Once I searched her desk, clothes drawers, and closets to find out what she was doing. Nothing.

Not a clue. If I called her office during the day, she was usually there. So I don't think it was another man."

Two rings on Gabby's phone interrupt the discussion. She waits until there are two more rings, a signal from Chuck Browner the call is important. She excuses herself and steps behind the desk.

"Meyerson Memorial," Chucks reports. "The family of Hildagard Sacks is there now making final arrangements for Mrs. Sacks' funeral on Wednesday morning. They want to know if eleven o'clock is open on your schedule. I tried to put them off until you're finished, but the family's insistent. They have relatives to notify on the West Coast."

Gabby is exasperated by the intrusion, yet she doesn't want to complicate matters for the Sacks family. It takes a few seconds to consult her electronic organizer.

"All right, Chuck. Tell them eleven o'clock. See if you can find some biography. I think Seth knew the Sacks family."

"Speaking of Rabbi Greer," Chuck interrupts, "have you listened to any of those tapes?"

"When exactly did you have in mind? When I'm in the Ladies Room?" she replies and hangs up.

She apologizes to Noah upon returning to the table. "Story of my life. Always interruptions. Hard to keep focused. Some days I feel like an iron nail being pulled in different directions by multiple magnets."

"A lot of people look to your services. If you were a doctor you'd be rich."

"Perhaps not. If I charged the fees doctors do, people might not come. How did you compensate for the distance from Morgan?"

"How do professional men and women usually cope? With work. I entrenched myself at the firm. There's always another building or shopping mall to develop. And not without financial results. Since I started with Pyramid, funds from our operations have grown by a third. The equity side of our portfolio is twenty-three percent higher. Fees for management services and consultations also increased by about nineteen percent. Our partners have nothing to complain about."

She releases an adolescent giggle. "But of course if they're Jews they complain anyway."

"How did you know?"

"Complaining is a Jewish legacy passed down from generation to generation."

At the end of the interview, Gabby leads Noah toward the door. "I'm glad you came to talk."

"I am, too. I wanted you to know that I'm not your run-of-the-mill sex deviant. I never made a practice of cheating on Morgan."

"Were you seeing women other than Eli Waller?"

The question unnerves him and he hesitates, searching for an answer. "No. She caught me off-guard. With my pants down, you could say." Then he laughs at himself.

Once the door is open to Chuck Browner's office, the confidentiality of the session is broken. Gabby smiles. "Well now, I like a man who can laugh at himself. Even when there's not much to laugh about. I believe Chuck's got you booked for another appointment. Looking forward to it. And by the way, say hello to your father for me. Keep me posted on his health. We have a lot of men in the congregation with prostate disease. It's no picnic."

"His invitation to help you with the Search Committee is still open." Noah seizes an opportunity to bring up a subject that had been on his mind.

She touches his arm and applies a bonding squeeze. "I've thought damn hard about it. Sort of wish I could tell your dad okay, I'm game. But somehow that isn't me. Never got shoehorned into a position in my life. Too late to learn new tricks. Tell your father I find the invitation enormously flattering. Many thanks for the support." Her hand moves along the arm to take his in a formal farewell shake.

IT IS FIVE MINUTES PAST FIVE IN THE AFTERNOON when Gabby tears herself from the office and dashes to the parking lot. Before entering her car she looks around to see if anyone is nearby and is happy to be alone. That makes extracting the stack of cassette tapes from her briefcase less conspicuous. The top cassette she places into the tape deck and turns on the ignition.

The Georgetown campus is three miles distant through heavy commuting traffic. Students tend to size up their new professors during the first ten minutes of a class and Gabby is determined to command their respect on the first night, especially with respect to promptness. That will make future sessions easier. Fortunately, she is driving against commuter traffic which is beginning to stream from the District of Columbia in the direction of suburban Maryland, but unfortunately, there is no direct route to the university. She decides to head west along Garfield Street, then travel south along 37th Street and enter the campus from the north. She shoves the tape cassette until it engages inside the port.

Except for the scratchy swish of the tape mechanically moving over the speaker heads, there is no sound. Eventually, she hears the noise of people talking in the background with no conversation dominant. Voices jumble and she is unable to discern more than individual words. If this is when the Board is discussing Seth Greer's tenure with Ohav Shalom, she isn't going to learn much. A voice belonging to Doris Silbert commands the microphone for a few moments. The subject is not Seth Greer, but rather Harold Farb's pension. Nathan Pearl, accountant on the Search Committee, is going over figures.

ON THE OUTSKIRTS OF GEORGETOWN, TRAFFIC FUNnels into narrow colonial streets. The need to pay attention at the wheel makes careful monitoring of the tape impossible and she gives up for the time being. Valuable minutes are eaten up waiting to pass through various intersections. By the time she finds a parking place, all thoughts of grabbing a bite for dinner must be abandoned.

Georgetown University is perched on a promontory over the Potomac River in the southwest quadrant of Georgetown, the original pre-Georgian settlement which the nation's Founding Fathers selected to serve as a federal city. Modern red brick buildings complement the original Gothic stone. The hilly, uneven campus is linked by a matrix of outdoor stairways, bridges, and walkways, bordered by black wrought-iron fences. Gabby's eye for design is satisfied with a pleasing sense of horizontal and vertical lines. From almost every vantage point, the eye is rewarded with a vista above the Potomac River.

She asks students for the location of the Intercultural Center. First stop is at the Office of Continuing Studies to collect a roster of students. The size of the lecture room surprises her. A quick glance at the roster explains why. Seth Greer's reputation draws not only Jews with an ethnic interest in Jewish subjects, but students from the Departments of Philosophy, Religion, and English. Sixty-six have enrolled, though she cautions herself that after the first lecture that number will dwindle. To keep at least twenty students sufficiently amused she must dust off as many jokes as she can remember. Moments before class begins, she nervously fiddles with an overhead slide projector.

At 6:00 sharp, she turns on the lapel microphone and maneuvers through a quick test program ready to begin. Students talking to one another settle into their seats. Many more remain standing.

Gabby's stomach churns, yet she is forceful, conscious not to appear uncertain. The microphone assists in this conspiracy. "I have a few short introductory remarks and then we'll dive immediately into the syllabus. Let me begin by solving a puzzle in your minds. Where is your professor, Dr. Seth Greer? Answer: I'm afraid he is not available for this course and I have been asked to pitch in."

She is expecting a revolt and signs of disappointment from the audience do not alarm her. In the din which follows, she slips the first transparency over the glass which reflects her name in bold characters on the front screen.

"Question two in your minds is, what's happened to Dr. Greer? I know many of you are so busy with your studies and jobs that you haven't got time for current events. Those of you who read the newspaper know that Dr. Greer resigned from his appointment at Ohav Shalom. After class some of you are going to ask me what really happened. I'm telling you now that I don't know. I have private suspicions, but I'm too political to broadcast them. You can ask me about just about anything but that. Now then, item three: Rules of the Road, so to speak."

She pauses to let those who have really come to hear Seth's jokes get up and leave. Oddly, while there is rumbling, none do. Timing is everything in teaching and she knows to maintain a fast pace.

"I'm a busy woman and you're very busy students. Time is short, therefore punctuality is essential. The class begins at 6:00 p.m. sharp and that doesn't mean 6:03, or 6:20. Those of you who are Jewish will ask what's happened to 'Jewish Time,' that is, twenty minutes late for everything. Well, 'Jewish Time' died with this rabbi. I respect you too much to have you waiting for me. You or your parents pay a lot of shekels for these classes; last time I calculated it was more per hour than a ticket to a Redskins game, and NFL football isn't cheap."

There is mumbling of respect in the audience.

"And just to give you a little incentive, I'll let you in on a secret. Unlike many professors who talk about tests at the end of their classes, I make a practice of divulging tips and information likely to be on my tests during the first four minutes of each class. I reckon those courteous enough to be prompt should get a reward. Understood?"

She finds the lecture hall in something of a stir, none of the students certain about the person conducting their class, but none prepared to challenge her either.

"Next," Gabby keeps on the pressure, "I like to teach by engaging my students. What that means is that you won't be able to sit back, take notes, and read the assignments. I'm going to haul you kicking and screaming into the learning process by asking questions, by demanding your involvement in preparing materials and by soliciting your views. My roster says there are sixty-six students aboard. I'll be asking all of you questions from time to time. You may not know the answers. That's okay. I probably didn't know the answers either, until I dreamed up the question." Faint laughter ignites the hall and travels from row to row. "It wasn't many years ago when I was sitting in your seats, hiding behind my clipboard, too. Will I embarrass you? Absolutely. Should you be embarrassed in the learning process? Absolutely not. So be warned. I shall be calling on you in class. The more active you are, the more you'll learn and the more you'll retain.

"So ladies and gentlemen, please refer to the assigned readings that have been collected into an anthology, available in your bookstore. Reading Six is an excerpt from a translation of a late professor of mine at the Hebrew University in Jerusalem, from the *Guide of the Perplexed* by Moses Maimonides. The translator, Professor Solomon Pines, Book Two, Chapter 32, on the Nature of Prophecy. Incidentally, the way you pronounce Professor Pines' name in Hebrew is *Penis*, just like the male sex organ. So for next week, I want all you ladies and gentlemen to grab your Penises and read Chapter 32."

The ripple of humor that begins in the first row shoots like lightning backward to the rear. The fact that a cleric can joke about a penis is to her credit. She might, after all, be able to deliver some of Dr. Greer's humor.

A transparency suddenly replaces Gabby's name on the overhead screen.

—*The Satanic Verses* of Salman Rushdie
—Mind/Body Dilemma
—Prophecy
—Heresy

She turns a red laser-pointer onto the words. "Here, ladies and gentlemen, is your introduction to Jewish thought in the Middle Ages. Four notions. Who among you can tie them into a coherent theme? Your course outline will provide you a reading list. My style is not to lecture, which might exercise my cerebral matter, but it won't stimulate yours. I prefer to make opening remarks, then let you develop the theme in groups. Each week we'll address a different philosophy, then see how your author of the week handles it. After a few sessions, I'm going to ask you to prepare ten-minute presentations, taking a second author and showing the class how that author tackles the same issue. But for the moment, let's return to our four notions on the screen. What was the author of *The Satanic Verses*, Salman Rushdie, charged with by the fundamentalist Government of Iran? Anybody remember?"

"Saying bad things about the Moslem religion," a dark-haired, plump woman in the fourth row says aloud while raising her hand afterward.

"Close. Real close. And what do we call defamatory remarks about a religion or cult?"

"Heresy," someone from the middle rows shouts.

"Excellent. So you've got one of four concepts. Now I'm going to paraphrase for you the sexy part of *The Satanic Verses*. The novel itself is turgid, very difficult reading, but the passage that put Rushdie on Ayatollah Khomeini's hit list or shit list, whichever you please, goes like this. The characters are Muhammed of Mecca, supreme prophet of Islam, and his loyal scribe.

Muhammed suffered from what physical malady?" She stops to survey the lecture hall over the rims of her reading glasses. Of sixty or so students, not one can offer an answer.

"Syphilis," an unidentified voice offers and is rewarded by chuckling. The majority of students sense this is a tasteless guess with a malicious intent and do not respond. They are curious how Rabbi Lewyn will reply.

"No. There is absolutely no evidence that Muhammed suffered from syphilis, but the Koran describes physical fits which contemporary physicians diagnose as epilepsy. Muhammed was also illiterate and depended upon his scribe to write down the prophecies he received from Allah. Similar prophetic phenomena are purported to have occurred with Moses and Jesus of Nazareth. And you've all heard about Isaiah, Jeremiah, Ezekiel, additional prophets from the biblical period. Now in Salman Rushdie's book, one morning the Prophet Muhammed dictates the divine revelation received from Allah. His scribe decides to play a very small, innocuous trick on his master. That evening, after writing all day, the scribe brings his manuscript for Muhammed to review. It's exactly as dictated, but with one exception. And herein lies the trick. In a playful mood, the scribe changes a tiny and insignificant preposition. Nothing big, mind you. Not a verb or a subject, but a tiny preposition. Muhammed does not catch this change and accordingly verifies that the scribe has faithfully rendered the revelation. Can you see where this is going?"

An attractive, dusty blond woman in a business suit stands. "Rabbi Lewyn. If Muhammed verifies the changes made by his scribe, how can the Koran be the true and perfect revelation from God, or Allah?"

"Precisely." Gabby recognizes the smartly dressed woman to be Morgan Zentner. No surprise, but she had forgotten that Morgan was planning to attend. "So what happens next? You can probably smell this one coming. The scribe expands his little game. The next day he transcribes more of the prophecy, but when he commits it to parchment, he changes a little more of the dictation. Say two or three prepositions. And does Muhammed recognize these alterations? No, he doesn't. The scribe is curious now. When will the Prophet notice the changes? Before long, the scribe is fabricating more and more. The true and perfect revelation, as the student in the fourth row observes, is now thoroughly corrupt. You might ask, how is that possible? Doesn't Muhammed know the revelation he is providing?"

"I don't buy it," a young male student with thick round glasses and a four-day growth of beard, blurts. "Muhammed would have to know."

"But what would happen if he received the revelation from Allah while in an epileptic condition? Or if he was no more than the physical medium of communication between Allah and humankind? And when I say medium, I mean nothing more than a mere mouthpiece. A conduit, if you will. Maybe, he didn't know, understand, or approve of the revelation. Is this possible?"

The students are engaged now. Gabby can tell by monitoring their eyes, most of which are glued upon her. They are beginning to sense the pain expressed by devout Muslims in Iran.

"If you think this is a problem only for Muslims, think again. How many of the traditional Hebrew prophets, such as Amos and Jeremiah, volunteered to mouth the words of the Hebrew god, Yahweh? Did Jeremiah? Or Amos? How about Jonah, perhaps the most famous of the prophetic renegades? You recall the hapless fellow who fled on a ship to Tarshish to escape from delivering a prophetic message to the people of Ninevah, then the capital of Assyria, now in the modern state of Syria. Remember, he was swallowed by a gigantic fish, then later vomited him back on a beach near Jaffa in Israel. Or how about the most celebrated prophet in Israel,. a fellow by the name of Moses? Take my word for it, Moses did not want to be the prophet of Yahweh. He was co-opted into the job. Now perhaps you can understand why problems with prophecy are so dangerous for a fundamentalist faith, whether it be Muslim, Jewish, or Christian."

The class is silent. She is shooting questions at them like machine gun bullets. Each requires time to think. They expect her to provide answers, but she doesn't. Instead she replies with sets of questions.

"You will soon see how Maimonides tackles the thorny problem of prophecy. The dilemma of prophecy is how a spiritual, non-corporeal deity can possibly communicate with human beings who are anchored in the world of matter. God, who is Mind, communicates with people, who are Body, by means of Prophets. Now you already know about these special folks. Most of them are possessed. They're not into the trade of prophecy because they like it. They're what we call *Reluctant Prophets*. God possesses them and uses their tongues and vocal cords to form the communication that people like you and me can understand."

There is a mood of bewilderment now. The students apparently had never given much thought to the subject. But what she says makes sense.

"What you read of Maimonides might make you think about people in our times who present themselves as prophets. A few are judged authentic to the practitioners of particular faiths, such as Joseph Smith to the Mormons, or Elijah Muhammed to the Black Muslims. Others enjoy a shorter shelf life, such as Jim Jones of Jonesville in South America or, more recently, David Koresh of Waco, Texas. Maimonides gives you tools to evaluate the credentials of these prophets and determine the likelihood of their endurance through the ages."

Hands rise throughout the hall. The subject touches sensitivities, releasing a flood of ideas. Answering requires spontaneous thinking and before long the students demand to participate not only in the questions, but the answers. The session is so animated that no one demands a break. When the second hour ends, few students are prepared to leave until forced by students arriving for another class at 8:15 p.m.

IN THE PLAZA OUTSIDE THE INTERCULTURAL CENTER, Morgan Zentner waits until the cluster of students thins around Gabby. When she can catch her eye, she breaks through the screen of bodies.

"We meet again," Gabby greets with an outstretched hand.

"Attending classes makes me feel like a young coed. It's a lie, of course, but we're allowed some fantasies, don't you think? How about a cup of coffee or tea in Georgetown?"

The invitation surprises her since everybody knows she is supporting Noah in his legal defense. The tension of lecturing before such a large group has exhausted her and she needs a rest. "I haven't eaten since lunch. If we can drink coffee in a place where they serve food, you're on. I'm not too particular in that department. Broiled river stones or grilled pasture grass will do."

"How about an Afghan restaurant where they have wonderful minted tea, kabobs, and pita?"

"Sounds divine, so long as they also serve beer."

SINCE THE RESTAURANT IS ONLY A HOP, SKIP, AND A jump from the campus, Gabby and Morgan walk to a trendy Afghan bistro at the foot of Wisconsin Avenue near M Street. Morgan's coiffure strikes Gabby as something one might see in a style magazine at a beauty salon. Her eyes do not fit the hair. They are dull and withdrawn behind dry reddish lids. Crow's feet trace a delicate filigree in the skin around them.

Once seated along the restaurant banquette, a waiter brings a plate of flat oval-shaped Afghan bread and a bowl of yogurt and honey for dipping.

A good start, Gabby thinks to herself before apologizing. "I wasn't hungry before the class. Guess I was nervous. Didn't know what to expect. But now that it's over I could eat a cow—a kosher cow, of course." She immediately judges Morgan as the type of Washington woman who pushes her food around a plate talking in educated ways about culinary fineries but, in fact, eating as little as possible. You don't maintain a figure like hers by overeating.

"You deserve a good meal after that *tour de force*." Morgan fondles the flat pita, rotating a small wedge in her fingers. She pulls the dish of yogurt close for dipping, but doesn't get around to dunking.

"This assignment caused me considerable anxiety. Teaching a college course isn't like a confirmation class at OS. Besides, who in her right mind could follow Seth Greer to the lectern? My bet is that at least half the class will drop out by next week. The students were disappointed with the substitution."

"There's always attrition at the beginning of the semester. They'd drop out if you were Albert Einstein. You kept them engaged the entire session. Don't be surprised. The majority will return."

Exhaustion possesses Gabby. A few swallows of beer, which the waiter was thoughtful enough to bring before the other food, restores some of her strength. "Will you return, Morgan?" She looks directly at the woman across from her.

"Of course."

"Why, of course? You told me you intended to audit only a few lectures."

"Because the subject intrigues me."

The waiter returns with extra-large menus displaying a very limited selection of Afghan dishes. Morgan's eyes rove up and down searching for something appealing. She claims to have eaten before the class and is looking for something light. Everything is either too much, too fattening, or too spicy. She finally decides on nothing more than Afghan tea, heavily spiced and heavily sugared. Gabby chooses a side order of spinach in clotted yogurt and another side order of ground garbanzo beans in olive oil and garlic, a variation of hummus.

"As I recall, you're working on a book with Seth Greer, aren't you? Lurianic Kabbalah, if my memory serves well," Gabby asks once the formalities of ordering are finished.

"Don't get me started on that subject," Morgan huffs, while cupping a warm pewter tea goblet in her fingers.

"If you want to know, Seth's disappearance has caused me a good deal of *tzoris*, too," Gabby chuckles. "I would have been home this evening if he hadn't thrown in the towel. I wish he had stayed to fight it out with his accusers. It wasn't like him to turn tail and run. What do people say? Shit happens. People make mistakes. Think of the boredom if people didn't fall from grace now and then. I went to a Billy Graham session last winter. A real eye-opener. You know who introduced him on the pulpit?"

"Mother Teresa, perhaps?"

Gabby dunks Afghan bread into the yogurt and swirls it around the plate, sponging the upper rim until clean."Nope. Chuck Colson from the Watergate coverup. When he stands up he doesn't have to say one word. Everybody knows he's a fallen man. A guy like Colson doesn't have to convince you he's a sinner delivered from damnation. The American public convicted him years ago. So when he claims his faith in Jesus saved him, it's convincing as hell. Then Graham confesses how he lusts for everything wearing a skirt. He too is spared ruination by his faith. What I came to understand is how much these people yearn for salvation. They truly believe in the power of redemption, but you can't have it until you've fallen first. Maybe that's why evangelical preachers often have lurid affairs."

"An insightful observation," Morgan comments. "Seth Greer was working through a similar idea with the Lurianic Kabbalah. He devotes an entire chapter to the indwelling of the Divine Presence in the form of the *Shechinah* and shows how it's linked with the concept of *tzim-zum*, the contraction of spiritual entities. Two chapters deal with spiritual deliverance. To the Kabbalist it's a two-step process. Redemption follows sin like a rainbow follows a storm. Ironic that in order to trigger a first-class redemption, one must stage a first-class fall!"

"Do you think Seth was describing his own fall? That he planned to sin in order to be delivered?"

"I've thought about it. Of course, you must have known him better than I."

Gabby's spinach and hummus arrives, along with an additional plate of warm breads. This time, Morgan shows interest and rips off a hunk of pita.

"I've begun to appreciate the complexity of Rabbi Greer's personality," Gabby pursues. "Like an iceberg, there's more of him below water than above."

Morgan appears less nervous now and her eyes begin to show animation. "He's left me with fragments of his book. I was hoping you'd know where he is. His manuscript has the makings of a big seller. I just don't have the expertise to finish it."

"Did he give you permission?"

"In a general way, yes. He delivered the manuscript and instructed me to do whatever was necessary to make it publishable."

"Well, if finding him is imperative, forget it. I haven't the slightest idea where he is and I promise you he doesn't communicate with me via psychic medium. Maybe I can help with the material."

Morgan withdraws again into her own thoughts, as though testing Gabby's idea. "Your course might be of help. According to the syllabus you're going to cover some of the same concepts. Seth's work is, of course, popular in nature. We'll see."

"Call on me. I might be able to direct you to articles or perhaps scholars in the field. So you believe Seth's book is publishable?"

"Absolutely, but not on Lurianic Kabbalah *per se*. People are interested in evil. And Seth shows how even good people manufacture it for their own purposes. I've already got two publishers interested. They see strong sales. I see a runaway best-seller."

"I'm dying to know how Seth treats the subject. His mind is so fertile. No doubt something controversial. Perhaps that's the sales pitch."

"He's not out to shock. This is actually a *How-To* book with practical suggestions."

"Can't wait to see it in print."

"Don't hold your breath. It's not ready. And I'm not qualified to whip it into shape."

"Even with my help?"

"Seth didn't tell you about this project for a reason. I hope I won't insult you, but I'm not sure you have the right personality for it."

A cup of strong tea served in a pewter goblet arrives for Gabby along with a refill for Morgan.

"No, you won't hurt my feelings, but you certainly have stirred my curiosity. Let me give his material a look-see."

"Wait a while. I'll know more about you after a few classes. In the meantime, Seth might return to surprise us."

Gabby thinks not, yet the remark surprises her. How would Morgan know what he might do?

Monday, August 22nd

Gabby is undressing after her early morning jog in preparation for a shower when her phone rings. Six-twenty a.m. is too early for anyone to be calling with routine business. A draft of cool morning air circulates through her condominium, causing perspiration on her shoulders and neck to evaporate. She shivers, lifting the receiver with apprehension.

Zoe's voice on the other end is somewhat muffled, as though she were trying not to wake a sleeper nearby, perhaps Clementine. "Sorry to disturb you, Gabby, but I know you're an early riser. What are you doing for lunch today?"

"Liturgy committee meeting with the Cantor."

"I hope it's a meeting you can break," Zoe responds. "I'm flying from La Guardia to our Washington office on the 8:30 Shuttle to meet with Noah. Should be there by 10:00. If it's at all possible, I'd like to see you. The staff will provide sandwiches. We've got troubles. How do you say it in Hebrew? *Tzoris*?"

"Let me hear what it is, then I'll let you know whether it's *tzoris* or just common run-of-the-mill trouble."

"Police in Queens located the kids who jumped me..."

"That's good news, not *tzoris*," Gabby interrupts before Zoe can conclude her thought.

"Wrong, friend. Bad news. Real bad news. I was working at my office late last night. Got a call from a lawyer by the name of Manny Fortuna. A personal injury vulture. Don't know him personally but a colleague does. Sleazy and unscrupulous. Claims he represents the kids who mauled us in Queens, one named Jose Piedro and the other, Reginald Casey Masters. Says he's got a case against us for assault and battery, not the other way around."

The magnitude of Zoe's disclosure registers slowly upon Gabby, who is chilled. There is nothing in reach of the phone to cover her nakedness. "Just wait a second. Are you telling me this lawyer thinks we're at fault? Let me get this straight. His clients rape *you* and he's claiming we assaulted *them*? That's outrageous!"

"Calm down for a second and don't jump to conclusions. Fortuna knows exactly what happened or, at least, he should because he can read our police record. He's on a fishing expedition."

Blood rushes to Gabby's head at the same time it seems to abandon her abdomen, giving her a sinking feeling. "Have the police made arrests?"

"Both kids are sixteen. Probably sixteen and a half, or three-quarters, but not yet seventeen. In the eyes of the law they're minors. That means they'll probably be remanded to the Juvenile Court."

"They fled the scene! Why run away if they were the victims and we, the assailants? The police have proof we tried to get an ambulance for them."

"Fortuna claims we threatened his clients. When we went for the police, they didn't know where we were going. They were frightened we'd return to cause greater injury. So they fled. Later, they discussed going to the police themselves, but concluded that nobody would believe them."

"Nobody will." Gabby leaned over to flick off wool threads from the carpet that hang to·her ankle. "I can't believe anyone will take this seriously. We're not alley brawlers. There's no motive."

"Maybe so, but it's more complicated than that. Remember the guy who entered the alley after us, the one who threatened to tell the police we jumped those kids?"

"Of course. A maggot who came for no other reason than to feed on the carcass of whatever died. Twenty bucks was probably the largest bill he'd seen in years."

Zoe is abrupt, becoming impatient. "The police located him. Or, I suspect, Fortuna did. He now claims that you bribed him with the twenty and that he's prepared to testify he saw us attack the youths."

"I can't believe I'm hearing this!" Gabby shouts. "Will the law believe this shit?"

Zoe is a model of composure under pressure. "Listen, friend. I can't argue with you now if I'm going catch the 8:30 plane. I know this must sound terrible, but perversion of truth is nothing new to our profession. We see this sort of thing all the time. Often worse. My firm has experience dealing with creeps like Fortuna. Their bark is worse than their bite. But we'll need to map out a strategy together. The firm has ways to fight back. By the time we're finished with Mr. Fortuna, he won't think much of his scheme to fleece us."

"Is that what it's about? Money?"

"Listen, Gabby, I've got to take Clementine to school then dash to La Guardia."

"Is it about money, Zoe? Tell me straight."

"Absolutely. If we can contain it to a monetary sum, that will be a victory. But it could spread to something else."

"What? What else? Tell me before you go."

"Could be dangerous. See you at twelve at our offices, 13th Street at New York Avenue. Eighth Floor. If you can't make it, call me there. The telephone number is on my card." She hangs up without a formal goodbye.

Gabby stands at the phone no longer shivering. Her brain produces ideas faster than they can be absorbed. When she finally makes it to the shower, her confusion succumbs to anger.

How dare those punks twist the truth! How dare Manny Fortuna pervert the law!

ONLY ON MORNINGS WHEN GABBY ATTENDS TALMUD *shiurim* classes with rabbinical colleagues does she arrive at Ohav Shalom after Chuck Browner. Still, this morning she is troubled and even dressing is a chore. The ignition of her Volvo floods and it is necessary to wait a full six minutes for fuel to drain from the carburetor. Traffic to the synagogue is inordinately heavy. When she finally arrives at her office, Chuck is waiting with a stack of phone messages.

There is an inquisitive, expectant look on his face as he blocks her route to the study. "You're famous, my good lady. Two calls from the Washington bureau of *The New York Times*. One, a Thorton Deal and the other, a Ms. Deborah Miller. They want to interview you this afternoon. What's this all about? Is the President going to appoint you to his cabinet?"

"If I had time to tell you, which I don't, you wouldn't believe me." She barks her impatience.

"Then maybe you'll talk with Betsy Hammel from *The Washington Post*. She says you know her from the National Coalition of Women. She's waiting at her home to talk with you. Wants me to call her back as soon as you arrive."

"Well, Betsy's going to have a long day in her kitchen because I'm not talking to anybody just now."

Chuck is accustomed to being left in the dark and is certain that sooner or later he'll understand the sudden publicity. Meanwhile, Gabby closes her study door with unusual vigor, almost a slam, and drops into her desk chair speculating how the synagogue doesn't need another scandal. The members have enough to sort out without reading headlines, like *Woman Rabbi Beats the Shit Out of Punks in Queens*. Certainly this is not the kind of rabbi they have in mind for the senior post at their synagogue. She can imagine the rumor mill churning into action and concludes she must alert President Doris Silbert what to expect.

Through her study walls she can hear Chuck's phone ringing in the outer office. Probably more journalists looking for a story. "Please get Doris Silbert on the phone for me," she instructs him through the intercom. "Try at her office first."

A few minutes later, he informs her that Doris Silbert is out of town and won't be back until the weekend.

"Then get Eph Rothman. His secretary's name is Dorothy. Tell her to break in on any of his meetings."

Gabby sits back to ponder the blackness ahead. She is inclined to take the pessimist side of issues and feels the need for a shot of optimism which she fails to conjure up. An urge to call Tim in New York causes her to place her hand on the phone and begin dialing, but she abandons the call before finishing. It will be hard facing this ordeal without his wisdom and wit. Time to stand on her own feet. The sooner she weans herself from him the better.

"Eph is out until noon," Chuck reports. "Dorothy promised he'll call as soon as he returns after lunch."

"Jesus, I forgot," Gabby says. "Please get word to Cantor Blass that I won't be able to attend the Liturgy Committee lunch today. Tell him it's an emergency. Then I'll give you the phone number of Greenwald, Molletz, Steiner, and Mavenhouse where I'll be midday."

"Lawyers defending Noah Zentner, right?" Chuck inquires.

"Right," she says, leaving him to draw what conclusions he might.

RATHER THAN PARK DOWNTOWN, GABBY ORDERS A taxi to take her to the Washington offices of Greenwald, Molletz. From the elevator, she enters a luxurious reception area, paneled in polished mahogany. Sculpted leather chairs with telephones on every table line the walls. Two receptionists in beige uniforms and ear sets handle the phones. When Gabby asks for Ms. Mountolive, both women smile warmly as though she were the firm's best client. Shortly after she deposits herself in one of the posh leather chairs, Zoe comes to greet her. She expects a very professional handshake but receives a warm hug.

"When it happened, I sort of pitied those punks on the street," she whispers close to Gabby's ear as they walk along the corridor, "but now I hate them. I'm not sorry I hit so hard. Too bad I didn't prevent him from running away. This wouldn't have happened if we hadn't gone for help."

In a conference room secretaries have set out sandwiches stuffed with various meats, poultry, and tuna on rye and wheat bread. Potato chips in small individual packages are distributed at each place setting and nearby are bottles of cold drinks accompanied by a bucket of ice. Three Greenwald, Molletz, attorneys are present, an impressive display of legal power on such short notice. Gabby's sour mood worsens. Not only is she embroiled in litigation threatening her rabbinical career, but the cost of paying for a defense is likely to deplete her savings.

"Godfrey Quanis is the firm's guru on criminal offenses." Zoe introduces a swarthy, balding male in his early fifties with a wide smile revealing elegant white teeth, too white not to have benefited from dental bleaching. "And you already know my assistant from New York, Andrea Delagnes."

Gabby turns to shake hands with Andrea. Midway through her forties, Andrea's face is powdered and painted to cover premature wrinkles. Gabby notes what she had overlooked in New York, the telltale signs of plastic surgery, a tuck of the chin and eyelids drawn so that the eyes appear implanted in their sockets. The last member of the team is Norman Kwan, whom Gabby also recalls from the meeting in Jonathan Zentner's New York condominium, the specialist on technical issues and investigation. His presence in Washington underscores the seriousness of the case.

In the process of choosing sandwiches and drinks, the participants make introductory small talk, then settle down around a polished wood conference table. Zoe sits to Gabby's left, with her colleagues taking up positions on the opposite side of the table. They assemble yellow legal-size tablets for notes, making it clear that lunch is to be a working session.

Zoe speaks directly to Gabby in a voice that is not designed to reach across the table. "You may be worried about the legal costs for these fine lawyers. Don't be. Our firm picks up all legal expenses when a partner requires assistance. Company policy so that our partners won't be intimidated. Each year we set aside a reserve for emergencies such as this. Sometimes we're forced to go to outside law firms for help, but with our wide pool of expertise that usually isn't necessary. Individual attorneys seated here get paid for their services just as they would for outside clients. Fees for their work come from the reserve fund."

"That may be true for you," Gabby says, "but I'm not a member of this firm."

"But you came to assist me in the alley. If you hadn't, I'd have been raped. If there are any additional charges attributable directly to you, I'm picking up the tab."

"You've got enough expenses as a single parent."

"I'm certain your congregation doesn't pay you half what you're worth, especially since you're pulling Rabbi Greer's cart as well as your own. Legal fees are an unwanted and undeserved expense."

"I have the police report you and Rabbi Lewyn made after the Queens incident." Norm Kwan addresses Zoe while distributing photocopies to his right and left. The document is two pages of closely printed text. He slides two additional copies over the table in Zoe's direction.

"Says at the end that the police dispatcher sent an ambulance from Rescue Squad 17 in Queens and made contact with Patrolmen Daniel Kelly and Stanley Veracruz. I understand that the two of you returned to the area but upon advice from the police did not reenter the alley, identified as Segelman Street, until Patrolmen Veracruz and Kelly showed up, which wasn't more than seven minutes."

"About ten to twelve minutes after the telephone call," Gabby offers.

"How do you know that, Rabbi?" Godfrey Quanis asks.

"I work all day in tiny segments of time. In order not to keep others waiting, I've learned to be conscious of every minute. I can usually estimate time without looking at my watch."

"Without glancing at your watch can you tell us what time it is now?" Andrea Delagnes asks. "No cheating."

"Sure. I'd say it's 12:18, give or take two minutes."

They look at their wrist watches to check. 12:19 p.m. The lawyers look at each other in wonder. Gabby passes an initial test for credibility.

Andrea Delagnes says, "Manny Fortuna claims he will soon produce medical records to show that Reginald Masters received a concussion from a blow struck by Rabbi Lewyn and has not recovered full hearing. He may never. Constant ringing in the inner ear. Jose Piedro is suffering from speech loss and insomnia. He is currently under the care of a psychiatrist."

"We'll have to deal with the medical issues in due course," Quanis says, "but for the moment I just want to get the structure of our case straight. When the police arrive on Parsons Avenue and enter Segalman Street, neither Reginald Masters nor Jose Piedro is there. The presumption is that they fled to avoid arrest. Is that true, Zoe? Rabbi Lewyn?"

They both nod.

"But you showed the police blood stains on the pavement? Right?"

"I found blood on the rubber bumper of the loading dock," Gabby interjects. "And someone discovered blood on cobblestones where I floored the first kid."

"Did the police take samples?"

Zoe says, "No. I think they were miffed at us for letting the kids run away. They blamed us for being naive. How could we think they'd stay put?"

There is a ring on the conference room phone which Andrea Delagnes answers. She whispers into the receiver so as not to disrupt conversations around her. Eventually, the interchange ends. "Sorry," she interrupts, pointing the receiver in Gabby's direction. "For you, Rabbi Lewyn. A man by the name of Ephraim Rothman. Said you asked him to call you here."

Gabby is on her feet in an instant, working her way around the table to take the receiver. She asks, "Can I take this in another room?"

Zoe comes to her side, squiring her through the door to a phone in an adjacent conference room. She lifts the receiver and directs the receptionist to transfer the call, then leaves Gabby to speak in private.

It takes a moment to unravel the phone cord and operate a strange telephone system, but Gabby eventually succeeds. "You there, Eph?"

"I hope this is good news, Gabby," he replies. "I could use some today."

"If you enjoy synagogue scandals, then what I have to tell you fits into your perfect day. Tell me, what the worse thing Ohav Sholom could experience now?"

"For Seth Greer to materialize with a harem full of Middle Eastern damsels."

"Close. Now I'm in trouble. You probably know the congregation exiled me last weekend. Went to see a friend in New York and we played tennis at a club in Queens..." Gabby chronicles the events and Ephraim Rothman listens. He requires answers to a couple of questions which demonstrate how fast he integrates information. She tells him about the lawyers from Greenwald, Molletz.

"I need you to inform the congregation's Board as soon as possible. I don't want them to learn about this from the newspapers."

"Is that a possibility?"

"Damn right it is. I'm being bombarded with inquires from the media. Zoe Mountolive and I are great copy. I had hoped that after visiting the police in Queens that would be the end of it."

"Apparently not. Gabby, now you listen to me. Don't worry about what our members will think. In the end, they'll stand by you and accept your rendition of the events. They'll never believe a couple of street hoods."

"I wish I could be as optimistic."

"You're paid to worry about things; I'm paid to fix them when broken. But I have to chuckle a bit, anyway. I'm trying to imagine you swinging your racket. It's not my first image of you, Gabby. That's for certain. I'll see that the Board members learn right away. Give me through the afternoon before you let hyenas from the press start munching."

As soon as they hang up, Gabby moves immediately to rejoin the others. She catches the tail end of Zoe's explanation.

"...because we thought they were more injured than they were and couldn't move. I thought to myself if we can't get an ambulance, they might die there. Imagine how surprised I was to find them gone. The police took Polaroids and appeared to make detailed notes in their report book."

"Haven't seen either of the photos," Kwan says. "The police won't offer anything you don't demand. If I know what to ask for, they have to cooperate. Incidentally," he looks directly at Zoe, "put your tennis rackets in a safe place. Don't wipe anything off them. We may have to compare what's on them with blood from those punks. Same with your clothes. You know what you were wearing that day?"

"Damn it," Zoe intones. "I threw my shorts out along with the underpants. I didn't want them around to remind me. It never occurred to me that I would be charged with assault, rather than those delinquents."

"That's not very professional," Quanis accuses with a biting snarl of superiority.

"Screw you, Jeff," Zoe barks. "You weren't raped in the gutter."

"I'm sorry, Zoe, but I thought you said they didn't get inside your jeans."

"Not with their peckers, if that's what you have in mind. With their fingers."

"Yes, of course. Now that doesn't apply to you, does it, Rabbi?"

"No, sir. I arrived when Zoe was on her back, against the loading dock. I called for the kids to leave her alone and when they told me to bugger off, I came in swinging with the only weapon I had."

"Well then, let's touch on the most difficult part of what happened. In the police report, Rabbi Lewyn, you said a man followed you from Parsons Avenue and that after the encounter he approached and threatened to tell the police *you* initiated the violence."

"That's right," Gabby says. "He called it *malicious battery*, as if he already had some experience with the law in such matters."

"Manny Fortuna claims his name is Cecil Thorner. Handyman who works when he can get employment, which apparently isn't often."

He asked for money, yes?" Quanis continues his fact-finding.

"I told him to forget it," Zoe adds. "I didn't survive a rape to be extorted by a street bum."

"We said we were going to the Sport Club for help."

"Fortuna says you threatened to hit Thorner with your rackets."

"I told him if he interfered with our getting an ambulance we'd flatten him. Yes, that's what I said."

"But you gave him twenty dollars?"

"I did," Gabby reports.

"And was it you who established that twenty dollars would persuade him not to stop you?"

"No. I think he suggested that sum."

"That's good," Kwan says. "And your reason for disagreeing with Zoe on this?"

"Twenty dollars seemed a small sum to get rid of a trouble-maker. I was worried about having seriously wounded those delinquents."

"Fortuna claims you bribed a potential witness. He was down and out. Though twenty bucks might not seem much to you, it's a significant sum for an unemployed handyman. That's witness tampering."

"At the time I didn't think of him as a witness. Since he didn't want to testify for us, he looked like a common thug out for a buck."

"But you needed to remove him in order to rush off for help, isn't that true?"

Gabby has to think about that for some time. "Yes, I guess it is."

"You don't sound convinced. Rabbi, it won't sound convincing to a judge if it isn't true."

"He was an obstacle. There were two youngsters bleeding on the concrete and he wouldn't let us get help. I didn't have time to think of the long-term implications. It was either clobber him with my racket or pay him off. I certainly didn't give him money to silence his testimony."

"Thorner would probably have been satisfied with the twenty had not our friend, Fortuna, enticed him with greater rewards," Quanis says. "I think we'll be able to undermine his argument about the payoff. Fortuna knows he's skating on thin ice with Thorner." He turns to address Zoe. "How do you want to handle the publicity side of this case?"

"Thought about that on the plane down here," Zoe says. "Best to have our own press conference first, to contain adverse publicity. Probably better to tell our side rather than react to false accusations from Mr. Fortuna and Company."

"What do you think, Rabbi Lewyn?" Quanis asks.

"Zoe has more experience in these matter than I. Perversion of truth scares me."

"I'll put something together along with Zoe," Delagnes interjects. "But before we release anything, I'll want Rabbi Lewyn to see it. Our stories must be consistent, like a symphony with all the instruments playing different roles but blending with each other. The worst thing is to let the press rip us apart with differing stories. For the time being, Rabbi, I'd like you to refer all inquires from the media to me. Don't let the press bully you. They'll use every trick including the right of the public to know. First Amendment and all that bullshit. Be tough. We'll back you up."

"Nothing I'd like better," Gabby replies, wondering if she should wear a wig and camouflage her face with rouge.

WHEN THE MEETING BREAKS, GABBY GRABS A PHONE to let Chuck know she'll be returning to the synagogue by taxi. When he finally answers his voice is tart, reflecting annoyance with her for sneaking out of the synagogue without telling him. The stream of callers from the media is irritating. "Those kids were stupid to mess with you," he says. "Never underestimate Rabbi Gabby."

She is irked. "How'd you hear about that?"

"Story's on the afternoon news. One of the gals in the accounting office listens throughout the day to talk shows. At the news interval they mentioned a story about a female rabbi and an unidentified lawyer beating up two kids in Queens."

"We didn't beat up anybody. They damn near raped my friend. Pure, unadulterated self-defense."

"I certainly hope so, Rabbi Gabby. And by the way, I've got a five-inch stack of phone calls for you. The Cantor insists on touching base with you before the afternoon's over about the Gerstenfeld Bar Mitzvah this Saturday. Tad Gerstenfeld's mother called about the luncheon afterward, then his stepmother called about dealing with his real mother. The dad called, too, trying to find out what the two women were squabbling about. A family circus. And also, Noah Zentner called. Did you know his father had an operation yesterday at Johns Hopkins in Baltimore?"

"No. But he's been diagnosed with cancer of the prostate. Last I heard he was considering a prostatectomy. Hopkins is famous for that procedure. When did Noah call?"

"About 1:15. Said his father would appreciate a visit if you could make time in your schedule."

"What's my schedule book look like this afternoon at OS?" Gabby inquires.

"A battlefield. I've already postponed fiances Cathy Norbeck and Alan Kliven. There are three people waiting to hear from me as soon as you return."

"Tell them I'm not coming back today. Medical emergency in Baltimore."

"Is it really?" Chuck mocks with an uplift in his voice as he toys with her.

"Maybe not. But I don't know much about medicine, do I?"

"You know enough to be downright dangerous. I see you looking up *Medline* on the Web. You never go to a hospital without understanding the disease in question."

"There is no profit in praying to heal diseases that can't be healed. That wouldn't be very responsible, would it?"

"Well, Dr. Lewyn, how do you plan to get to Hopkins without your car? It's on the lot outside."

She hadn't considered that, but a solution pops into mind. "I'll take the MARC train from Union Station. If I'm not mistaken, the old Penn Station in Baltimore isn't far from Johns Hopkins Hospital."

"Hold on. Am I missing something here?" Chuck interrupts. "You don't need to go running to Baltimore this instant."

Gabby is impressed how he comprehends her moods. "True, my little keeper, but I need time to think. Just had a very unsettling meeting in the office of my new lawyers. I could use quiet time on a train. OS can do without its racket-swinging street brawler for a few hours. Have you seen Harold yet? My bet is he's stomping the corridors, waiting to pounce on me. I'm not exactly eager to enter the lion's den."

"Not a word."

"Good. I'll call from Baltimore, if you're still in the office. Put important messages into my voice mail and I'll pick them up tonight when I get home."

Chapter Nine

August 22nd

In August, the countryside between Washington, D.C. and Baltimore is luxuriously green from thick forests of laurels and sycamore, punctuated by suburban sprawl and an unsightly jungle of shacks and discarded debris flanking a matrix of Amtrak rails. On the interurban MARC commuter train, Gabby grapples first with her anger, then her pity. Unexpected trouble in Queens has probably doomed her chances at Ohav Shalom. While members might have been sympathetic with her candidacy before the Queens incident, they certainly won't be now. Those who question her behavior will favor a less controversial successor for Seth Greer. It is no longer necessary to be concerned with her unmarried status, lack of children, or scholarly deficiencies.

From Penn Station, she takes a taxi to Johns Hopkins Hospital on Broadway and Monument Street in a blue-collar residential district that has seen better days. The hospital complex is Gothic in architecture, a *grande dame* of urban hospitals from a previous era when Hopkins had few rivals for teaching and medical innovation. Gabby arrives a few minutes after 5:00 and, upon consulting two receptionists in the lobby, finally locates Jonathan Zentner's private room on the fourth floor, East, designated as the cancer wing. Recently refurbished, it is painted in dazzling whites and yellows with a battery of fluorescent lights providing a cheerful, outdoor ambience.

When she enters Jonathan's room, he is alone, half-propped up in bed, looking emaciated although clean shaven, his gray hair combed without a lock out of place along the sides of his narrow crown. Reading glasses sit low on his nose and there is a small book propped against the feeding stand, but in a position impossible to read. She notes that he has dozed off, letting the book slip from his fingers. A urinary catheter runs from under the sheets to a plastic bag hanging from the stainless steel bed frame. An Orioles game flickers on the overhead TV screen, but the sound is turned off. She quickly rejects the idea of waking him and is happy to sit on the only chair in the room and watch a pitcher wind up and hurl balls at Toronto Bluejays batters.

She is embarrassed to find Jonathan has awakened and is observing her watch the game.

"You like baseball, Rabbi?" he articulates in slow, soft words.

"Not as much as basketball, but you have to admire the split-second timing. To hit a ball thrown as fast as it is, you have to begin your swing the instant it leaves the pitcher's fingers. And you, Mr. Zentner? Are you a fan?"

"Nothing so formal, but I like to watch a game or two. Takes my mind off my worries."

"I thought Noah does the worrying for you," she snaps back, immediately chagrined by her tone of voice.

"No, Rabbi. Noah's as good as they come. Bright and hard-working. But these days, I can't place full confidence in him. He's made a colossal error in judgment."

"If you're referring to the Chesapeake incident, he's the first to acknowledge that. I didn't come to talk about Noah. I came to visit you."

"Well, I'm appreciative, though I can't say I believe God will lift a finger to prevent cancer in my prostate from spreading."

"Nor I," Gabby inserts the moment he pauses. "If you think I came to invoke God's intercession, I didn't."

He smiles meekly at the very moment a woman four years junior to Gabby brushes through the open door from the corridor. She wears wrinkled blue operating room scrubs pulled tight around her waist with a cloth sash. Her ruddy hair is pulled back tight into a bun behind her head and secured with a bone barrette. No makeup, yet her features are elegant, causing Gabby to imagine what she might look like fancied up for a formal dinner party. As she breezes to the bed, her eyes fall immediately on the urine pouch hanging from the bedstand.

"Good, good," she exclaims before noticing Gabby seated in the corner, partially hidden by the bed. "Oh, I'm sorry," she says in a crisp, self-confident voice, "I'm Dr. Shapyro, surgeon in training with Dr. Durango on his prostate service."

"Pleased to meet you. I'm Rabbi Lewyn." Gabby rises from the chair and extends a hand out to shake.

Jonathan Zentner's face grimaces in pain as he struggles for a higher position in the bed. The arrival of a female urologist triggers an expression of confusion. "I was under the impression Durango would come to see me today. I don't understand."

If there is offense she takes pains to conceal it. "Dr. Durango is giving a lecture in Philadelphia this evening and couldn't make medical rounds. I assisted him in the operating room, so I have a pretty good idea what we did yesterday. I see that you're able to pass water. A good indication the urethra isn't blocked. The more urine you can pass, the better. The idea is to return your bladder to full functioning, which means filling and emptying. Has the nurse checked the catheter in your penis?"

There is an uncomfortable hesitation about speaking of such matters in the presence of two women. During this hiatus, Dr. Shapyro steps around Gabby to a ledge with a box of latex gloves and extracts two quickly. From another box she removes a new catheter wrapped in a paper pouch. "Did you notice if the nurses changed it?"

"No," he laughs with a series of short uncomfortable hoots. "If a lady was fiddling with my plumbing, I'd know it, wouldn't I?"

"Well, we'll make a change now. You'll feel better with a fresh tube anyway," Shapyro says as she looks at Gabby. "Rabbi, if you don't mind stepping into the corridor for just a tick. This shouldn't take more than a few moments."

Eight minutes later, Deborah Shapyro emerges from the room and pauses to chat in the hospital corridor.

"I take it he's all right?" Gabby questions.

"Men don't jump around after a surgical assault on the prostate. The mass was large, but we're hopeful."

"I'm sure Mr. Zentner gets excellent care," Gabby states with conviction. "I've read about Dr. Durango's procedure."

Shapyro seems surprised. "Where? We employ quite innovative techniques."

"*Medline* on the World Wide Web."

"You read *Medline*? First time I've heard of a rabbi reading medical articles."

"Professional secret. I fear making a fool of myself so, before visiting my congregants in a hospital, I read about their diseases. I learned that from my mentor. People today want more than prayers, if you know what I mean."

"You make me feel guilty."

"How's that?"

"When I go to the synagogue, which isn't very often, I don't take the time to look up Judaism on the World Wide Web. Consequently, I don't understand what's happening. If I followed your model, I guess I wouldn't feel like such an outsider."

Gabby has a way of making others feel comfortable. "Well, Dr. Shapyro, you have enough to occupy your mind. The world needs people who focus on diseases. Not everybody has to be fluent in Judaism."

"I'll keep that in mind when I'm derelict," she smiles back with the unspoken acknowledgment of another woman operating successfully in a professional arena. "Thanks, Rabbi, for coming to see our patient."

JONATHAN ZENTNER'S EYES ARE CLOSED WHEN GABby returns to his room. He half-opens his right eye to confirm who it is, then mutters, "Well now, every day there's a new experience. First, I have surgeons cut out parts of my prostate, now I have a pretty woman doctor stuffing a catheter in my privates."

"You find women working in urology threatening, do you?"

His cheeks expand and curl into a smile. "Hadn't given it much thought until now. Only, if I can be frank with you, Rabbi, in my earlier days if a handsome woman like that handled me, I would have gotten pretty excited. Shows you the aging process, doesn't it?"

She finds his candor ingratiating. "Well, Mr. Zentner, let's hope your vigor will return soon. You know the story about Moses. It says at the end of Deuteronomy that at the age of 120 he didn't die of old age. In fact, the Bible states that his strengths and powers were intact at the end and, the commentator Rashi adds, these powers refer to his sexual prowess. So you see, if Moses didn't lose it at 120, there's hope for younger men."

The conversation awakens Jonathan. "That might not be such a blessing. We don't need *alte cockers* like me siring more children at advanced ages. The world's already overpopulated. Men should retire from making children at an early age like women."

Gabby does not like to think about biological clocks, her own ticking away at breathtaking speed. She changes the subject. "Seth Greer often spoke about you with the highest regard."

"I must tell you, Rabbi, that these days I've been thinking a lot about my son and Seth. I think your colleague led Noah into trouble. Set a bad example. The fastest way for a man to lose fortune and honor is through lust. And by the way, just before you arrived, I thought I saw my son's lawyer, Zoe Mountolive, on television. I was dozing and the sound was turned off, so I'm not certain. She was with another woman at a press conference."

"It wasn't about Noah," she says, suddenly aware that Zoe and Andrea Delagnes must have decided to go public before Manny Fortuna. "It appears that Zoe Mountolive and I have gotten ourselves into a pickle, parallel but not identical to Noah's problem. Zoe and I were playing tennis in Queens and she was attacked in an alley by two juvenile delinquents. I came to her defense swinging my tennis racket and hurt her assailant pretty badly. Turns out those creeps were only sixteen. They're now claiming we attacked them."

A troop of seven medical students, five young men and two young women, led by the attending urologist, a thin, sinewy fellow with tousled black hair, march into the room. No knocks. No announcements. No request for permission. The attending physician introduces himself and his students. "Feeling okay, Mr. Zentner?" he asks, stroking his hand along the urinary catheter under the sheet. His students cluster behind him, some fanning out around Gabby. Jonathan greets the intruders with a stern scowl. There is a price for being treated in a university hospital, where patients are sometimes treated as guinea pigs.

"As well as can be expected."

The urologist turns to his students. "Dr. Durango's procedure ties off the seminal ducts before he removes the tumor. Then he reconnects after malignant material is removed. *New England Journal*, the May 1995 issue, reports good results. The *AMA Journal* questions his findings, November of last year, I think." To Jonathan he says, "I'd like to show these students how Dr. Durango closes the incision in order to go back in, if necessary. Have any objections to that?"

Jonathan Zentner's fiery eyes scan the arc of students. He had already exposed himself to enough indignity for one day with Dr. Shapyro. "Absolutely," he snaps back. "I've got my rabbi here at the moment and I don't need to expose my genitals for the sake of science."

"We'll take a raincheck then," the physician says, looking right and left to his disciples, who appear more bored than disappointed.

When the students leave, Gabby moves around the bed to her original position. "Hopkins is a busy place. Guess it's good for the training of new doctors, but it must take a toll on the patients."

He answers by tightening his lips and moving his head slowly in a vertical motion, causing a long pause in the conversation. "Rabbi, I'm glad you came this afternoon. Oddly enough, I'm not particularly worried by my cancer. It will do what it must do, and my doctors will try stopping it. I'm really worried about Noah. This rape charge is draining him emotionally. He tells me you've been attentive and how he enjoys talking to you. Thinks you're a very special person."

"I'm gratified to hear that."

"He thinks of you as his rabbi now. Everybody needs a rabbi in one form or another. If you're good for him, you're probably good for me too."

"That makes me feel very good. I'm giving everything I've got."

"In these tough times, Noah needs a friend. Somebody who won't be quick to judge him."

"Guilt or innocence is not my call," she says.

"Noah made a mistake with that Waller woman, but it wasn't out of the blue. He's too discreet to talk about things in his marriage which led to his indiscretion."

"He's told me how bad he feels about cheating on his wife."

Jonathan Zentner rolls to his side and painfully hauls himself higher in the bed, dragging the catheter under the covers. "Rabbi, he cheated on Morgan only after his marriage was dead. That's the story he won't tell. Morgan sabotaged the marriage, not Noah."

"Perhaps I should let him tell me this," Gabby steps back, reticent to have a parent introduce a personal matter concerning his child.

"He won't. Noah protects Morgan and makes excuses for her. Finds it easier to take blame himself rather than put it where it rightfully belongs. I'm more objective."

"Then let it remain with him. If he wants to say something, he will."

"He won't. If you ask him, he'll deflect. That's his nature."

"Then he doesn't want to reveal it."

"If you knew his part of the story, you wouldn't have problems testifying for his defense."

"Then it's up to his lawyers and him. Please understand I will not compromise someone's marital privacy. What happened between Morgan and Noah is not my business."

When Jonathan observes that Gabby possesses a strong will, conversation lulls, then stops. He is accustomed to having people satisfy his wishes and Gabby is adamant in her refusal. She introduces a new subject which he lets fall without sufficient interest to fuel further discourse. When his eyes close down into a disengaged doze, she knows it is time to leave.

She hangs a leather handbag on her shoulder and moves silently toward the door, only to be stopped short as Noah marches in. They cannot negotiate the narrow passage simultaneously and both halt midway, uncertain what to do next.

"Your father's resting," Gabby says as she twists past him and steps into the corridor. Noah glances toward the bed, then quickly reverses his direction and meets her outside.

"He's not really asleep." She cracks a devilish smile which has the effect of mitigating the surprise of their meeting. "The truth is your dad's perturbed with me and is pretending I'm not there."

"I don't see why he should be cross with you, especially since you have come all the way from Washington to see him."

"I'm headed back now. If I'm not mistaken we have an appointment at Ohav tomorrow."

He places a hand on her forearm, preventing her from going. "Please wait; I'd like to talk with you before you leave. Just let me tell Old Irascible I'm here, then I'll come right out."

Less than two minutes later, Noah rushes into the corridor and finds Gabby with a picture-filled movie magazine seated in a waiting area catty-corner from his father's room. "He wouldn't tell me why he's ticked. He's like that some days. Clams up and won't speak. Stubborn as they come."

"Well," she reaches to shake his hand goodbye, "maybe we'll talk more about this tomorrow. It's been an extremely long day and I must run."

He laughs. "Really. I can imagine you saying that to someone, then literally putting on running shoes for a jog. It's a great line."

"But in this case, it doesn't work. I'm taking the MARC back to D.C. to get my car at Ohav Shalom."

"Now wait a second, Rabbi Gabby. You're not taking the train when I have a perfectly serviceable car to drive you home. Have you eaten dinner yet?"

"No. But that's not unusual. The more meals I miss, the trimmer I stay."

"To a point, of course, and it looks to me as though you're pushing the envelope and getting mighty thin. If you'll go with me, I know a great Italian restaurant on Albemarle Street in Little Italy. Then I'll whisk you back to D.C."

"What about your father? You've come to see him."

He glances back in the direction of his father's bed. "He can do without my attentions for the evening. Between you and me, I think he'd rather I take you out for dinner. He thinks you're a good influence on me."

"A common misconception about rabbis. I guess Seth did his duty to disabuse the stereotype."

"From what I heard on the radio driving here, you're about to make a contribution to the image of rabbis, at least female rabbis with tennis rackets."

"I knew my escapade with Zoe would hit the news, but I had hoped for a few days of respite."

"No rest for the famous." He cocks his eyebrows for effect.

The thought of traveling home on a commuter train suddenly depresses Gabby. "I'll take you up on that invitation for dinner in Little Italy. I hope they have strong Chianti."

"Can you give me five minutes with Grumpy inside?"

"As long as I don't have to face him again. He's got his problems and I've got mine."

Noah plants both hands on Gabby's upper arms and presses with apparent delight. "A done deal. All the Chianti you can drink and still remain respectable."

MAMMA CELLINA'S IS AN OLD-FASHIONED ITALIAN restaurant, dark with red-checkered tablecloths and candles stuck in squat wine bottles wrapped in hemp and covered by melted candle wax. It enjoys a clientele of faithful locals who enjoy Southern Italian cuisine, which means tomato sauce on just about everything from pizza to chicken *cacciatore*. True to her habit of ordering vegetable dishes, Gabby chooses eggplant Parmesan with marinated bluefish for an appetizer. Noah selects angel hair pasta with an assortment of Chesapeake shellfish and minestrone soup for a starter. He knows Italian wines and orders a white Lacryma Christi from Atriplada, which the waiter doesn't have but suggests a younger vintage from the same region.

"You seem more relaxed than the last time we ate together. Do you have a better feeling about the trial?" Gabby asks midway through their entrees.

"If I appear relaxed it's not because of the trial. That's not going well at all, despite what my attorneys say. You have a calming influence upon me. It's a special gift. I can't describe it, but I'm sure others have commented, haven't they?"

She has to think about that for a long moment. People are often assessing her personality and it is difficult to know what is sincere and what isn't. She doesn't believe it necessary to answer his question. "I have a favor to ask, if it's not an imposition."

He lifts his chin, glowing softly from the flickering light of the candle.

"I'm exhausted," she says. "Mentally drained, as the expression goes. A walk usually helps recharge my batteries. Will you walk with me around the Inner Harbor? I adore lights on the water and the sound of waves lapping against ship hulls. I'll understand if you need to head home immediately."

He rocks back against the banquette seat and places his hands on the back of his head. A ranging smile enlarges his lips. "I can't think of anything I'd rather do with the rest of the night, Rabbi."

"If we're going to walk, just call me Gabby."

Noah's mood is elevated and he laughs aloud. "Of course, Gabby. And you can tell me what's happening with your legal problems. From what I hear on the news, we're both entangled in the law. How about this for a television lead: *Alleged Rapist and Alleged Child Abuser Stroll at Inner Harbor? Tune in on the seven o'clock news."*

A gust of air escapes her lips as she musters a laugh. "That isn't funny. Or least it shouldn't be."

AFTER DARK, BALTIMORE'S INNER HARBOR IS A TOY-land of lights originating from the piers, boats, and assortment of restaurants and shops lining the embankment. Centerpiece in this port is the historic ship-of-the-line, *Constellation*, a square-rigged relic from the Civil War. Painted black with horizontal masts, she reminds the visitor of Baltimore's importance as a port to the mid-Atlantic states, midway between New York and Charleston. In modernizing the harbor, city planners have provided public walkways linking piers and amusements, all with lighting made to look old so that visitors feel they are perambulating through an earlier maritime era.

Gabby and Noah stroll along the western perimeter of the National Aquarium which juts into the bay. She is enjoying the smell of decaying marine life in the water mixed with the fragrance of oil from the boats, along with the sounds of halyards tapping against aluminum masts on berthed sailing vessels. Outboard motors pushing small water taxis around the harbor hum in the distance. As the couple ambles along, from time to time their shoulders gently bump.

"Why was my father so disturbed when I arrived at the hospital?" he asks. "Dad thinks very highly of you; you must have said something that irritated him, which isn't very difficult to do these days. He gets more irritable every year. Normally he's a charmer. But on occasion, somebody will say something that annoys him. He devours you with his eyes, trying to intimidate. If he isn't successful in getting what he wants, conversation closes down."

"He wanted to tell me about you and Morgan."

"Perhaps he thinks you won't help at the trial if you believe I wronged Morgan."

"You've already admitted that you did. He intimated it was Morgan, not you, who sabotaged your marriage. That's not my business and I told him so."

Noah lets her observation trail off. His eyes are set on the channel where the lights of a ferry move across the harbor. Her eyes move from the water to him, settling on the squared jaw and strong neck, and she is glad he isn't watching her.

"My father doesn't get it." He suddenly turns to catch her looking at him, and there is another pause while each digests the fact that they are alone. "I've tried explaining to him that Morgan didn't torpedo the marriage."

Gabby knows she shouldn't ask, but is driven by curiosity, a sort of rabbinic prerogative which a colleague once described as *rabbinical voyeurism*. "You told me how you two ceased talking to one another."

He stops to admire the alluring shape of her head silhouetted against the concrete wall of the Aquarium. "Something was dragging her away from me. I can't tell what it was, but there was something tugging from a different direction."

"And you're sure it wasn't another man?" Gabby probes.

"Of course, I suspected that. But she denied it. I believed her. Whatever went wrong between us, she never lied. Still, something drained her energy, both physically and emotionally."

"Do you blame yourself for that?"

"To an extent," he whispers, his voice communicating pain. "My therapist has been working on that with me. Some of us have guilt written on our nameplates from birth. Comedians make fun of this, as if it were invented by Jewish mothers. What happened on the Chesapeake aboard *Dame Cynthia* was a symptom of our breakdown. It was a wakeup call."

They walk on to the end of docking area, then turn ninety degrees to follow the pier west. Noah's pain affects Gabby in an unusual way, triggering a humorous reaction. She begins chuckling, "Well, it looks like both of us may share the same fate. Zoe and I might join you in the slammer."

"I don't understand. If you permit me to laugh like you, then I'd love to laugh. But your situation is flat-out preposterous. No District Attorney will take seriously such flagrant twisting of the facts."

"Big lies seem harder to deflate than small ones."

"Tell me about it," he sighs.

Ahead, four large teenage boys in dark, sloppy clothes approach in a tight formation. Their presence ahead signals potential danger. Four youths in an isolated location could cause trouble. Noah glances over his shoulder to judge the practicality of retreating to the Aquarium entrance. Sixty yards. If they sprint they might make it. On the other hand, there's no telling how fast the kids might be. The water is on one side and the Aquarium on the other. An instant later, Gabby perceives the same threat, closes the distance and seizes his arm for protection. Two teenagers fan out and call to one another, as though preparing to outflank them.

"Damn it," Gabby swears in a low voice. "Where the hell's my tennis racket when I need it?"

Her humor elicits additional lightness from him. "Can you swim? Delinquents don't like water."

"Neither do I," she banters, squeezing hard on his arm with inordinately strong fingers.

"I may need my arms free," he explains. "Consider the water option quick because I don't know if I can handle all four. They look tough. I'm not going into the drink without you."

With his hand grasping hers, he pulls her in the direction of the water to increase the distance from the approaching youths. One is fat and uncoordinated, another slightly lame in the hip. The two flanking them turn to rejoin their cohorts. The moment they are within talking range, Noah demands, "What's on your minds, fellows?"

"That's a nice squeeze," the fat one says.

"You appreciate pretty ladies, I see." Noah inches slightly in front of Gabby.

"A racket, a racket," she snorts, "my kingdom for a racket."

"What the hell's she talking about?" the lame kid asks Noah.

"It's a famous quote from *Richard III*. You guys know who Shakespeare was?"

A tall black youth says, "Yeah, I heard of him. He was a big time scientist, I think."

"Not exactly," Noah responds. "Look him up at school."

"You a teacher of something, Mister?" the fat one retorts.

Noah jabs an index finger towards him. "No. Just a reader of good books. *Richard III*. Shakespeare. The greatest writer of the English language."

"Yeah, yeah..." the lame one says as the four youngsters resume their swaggering movement past.

Noah hauls Gabby further away from the retreating youths. One hundred feet more and she halts.

"Are you all right?" he asks, turning to face her.

Her figure silhouetted against lights shimmering on the water reminds him of a bronze figurine in a fountain. Her breathing is heavy and her eyes, which are fixed on him, appear distant. The hand he holds is no longer warm and inviting, but shakes with a nervous quiver that seems to envelop her body. A delayed nervous reaction sends her limbs into uncontrollable spasms. "I'm sorry," she mutters. "I shake when I'm afraid. I do okay for a while, then shake like Jello. It must be a reaction to what happened in Queens. Those kids scared the hell out of me. There's no reason to be so frightened."

"It's all right now, Gabby. The boys are far away now. They're just kids out for the night. Adults are always suspicious of young men in isolated places. I can understand why you're so edgy. I would be too."

Then in an effort to stop her shaking, he wraps his arms around her waist and draws her to his chest. It is warm and comforting. Her head sinks into the bed of his armpit and she can feel his hand stroking the crown of her head.

It takes several minutes for the shaking to subside and, when it does, she lifts her head under his chin and whispers, "You've just learned a secret I would love to hide. Some women cry when frightened. I shake. Embarrassing as hell, but now you know."

He releases her from the embrace. "Don't be embarrassed before me. Ever. If the truth be known, I was a little worried myself." He stops to survey their position on the dock. "Let's go somewhere where there's more light and some people."

They move away at a brisk pace and are surprised to find that their hands are still locked together.

"This isn't good," she finally says, pulling away. "If I'm going to help you at the trial, it wouldn't look right for it to appear there was something between us. You understand that, don't you?"

"Once a rabbi, always a rabbi."

Gabby's mind switches to Tim Matternly and her painful loss. Her relationship, sick as it was, was also wonderful. Suddenly, there is a sense that someday a man like Noah might replace him. Certainly not Noah but someone like him. The next relationship must be open to the world. Never again will she accept a secret alliance.

ONCE BACK IN THE DISTRICT OF COLUMBIA, NOAH drives her to her car in the parking lot of Congregation Ohav Shalom. Rather than dropping her off, he gets out and walks around his car to wait as she fumbles with a key. The door of her Volvo is between them and, when she looks up to say goodnight, his eyes are firmly fixed on her. And as she folds herself into the driver's seat, he moves around the open door and plants a kiss on her cheek.

Noah's headlights tail behind until she has safely steered her car into the street. She tells herself a simple kiss can mean many things to many people. Her left hand rises to her cheek. It remains there to trap moisture from his lips.

For Gabby, the day has been long, yet exhilarating. She knows that tomorrow she will pay a price for leaving the synagogue early and traveling to Baltimore. But the excursion provided her with a surprise she could never have anticipated. In bed that evening, she recites in Hebrew a portion of the *Kiriat Shema*, the prayer said after sundown by pious Jews. Since she was a little girl and her mother would put her sister, Terry, and her to bed, prayers had ushered her to sleep. As a child she would improvise petitions to the Almighty, but over time ran out of things to request and became dependent on Jewish liturgy, switching from English to Hebrew. No matter what her motivation she always felt that she slept in God's care.

Her eyes close in the darkness and she is surprised to find her finger once again on her cheek, feeling for traces of Noah's kiss. A tingle between her legs confuses her. Since the breakup with Timothy the dark places in her pelvis have been dead.

"Oh God," she murmurs in the darkness. "Don't do this to me, God! I'm warning You, dammit. I don't need this kind of *tzsoris*! You understand?"

Several minutes later she falls into the deep sleep that has eluded her since Tim Matternly walked out of the Pierre Hotel.

August 24th

Gabby decides to take her early morning jog before daring to open *The Washington Post* and read the Queens story. If Noah and Jonathan Zentner had heard about what happened on

National Public Radio, newspapers wouldn't be long to follow. Poor Chuck was probably inundated with phone calls from journalists seeking either to write a new story or corroborate details of ones already in progress. She is glad Zoe's colleagues in New York are handling the public relations and is determined not to speak without first conferring with them.

The thought of not going in to work this morning has definite appeal. Plead sickness and head for the beach like many people do when they don't want to face the work day. Given her druthers, she'd really like to drive to the Eastern Shore, take a long walk on the National Seashore at Assateague, smell the Atlantic surf and watch seagulls cavort in the air. There's new dimension to her fantasy for now she imagines Noah holding her hand as she walks. This is, of course, quite foolish and foolishness isn't in her nature.

Her usual morning run brings her back to reality. Jogging frees the endorphins in her brain and refreshes her.

When she returns to her condo, a young reporter is seated on her front steps, looking as though she has just gotten out of bed without a shower. Rebellious dusty blond hair in need of a blow dryer is pulled behind her skull and fastened with black hairpins. Her blouse is rumpled and shows a least two brown stains on the collar.

"Rabbi Lewyn," she stands and offers a hand to shake, "Melony Fry from the *Times* in New York. Sorry about this early morning intrusion, but reporters are always interrupting people. It's a sort of license, you know. Would you be willing to talk with me a little?"

Gabby is perturbed by this invasion of privacy yet feels no personal animosity toward the young woman who is probably trying to carve a professional niche for herself. She works with her key at the front door lock. "Sorry, Miss Fry, but my lawyers have forbidden me to talk with the press."

"Then we'll speak off the record. Guarantee nothing will go into our paper without you first approving. That's a guarantee."

The offer has some appeal since Gabby wants people to know what really happened in Queens and there's no way for this to occur without cooperation from the press. "What kind of guarantee have you in mind?" she snaps.

"My pledge. The word of Melony Fry."

Gabby's smile is patronizing. "I would imagine, Miss Fry, that yours is a very good word to believe, but I have my doubts about the reliability of your paper and I note you're not offering the paper's guarantee. I'm no student of business, but I've read that when people in commerce make a guarantee there is usually a sum of money pledged to cover the damage."

"I don't follow," the young woman says, sweeping back locks of hair that have fallen in front of her eyes..

"Money, Miss Fry. If *The New York Times* wants to put a hefty sum of money in escrow if it violates your pledge, well then, I'll consider talking with you."

"What kind of money have you in mind?"

Gabby feels playful. "Well, since you're certain your paper's word is good, I'd say a figure of $50,000 would do."

"That's a lot, Rabbi. I doubt the *Times* would offer that kind of dough for a story like this."

"It's only a guarantee. The paper loses this sum only if it breaks its pledge and I'm assured by a very reputable person that won't happen."

She thinks about the proposition for a long moment and frowns.

Gabby opens the front door and pivots to smile back. "Well, you see, this wasn't a wild goose chase after all. You've got something to talk over with your boss. By the way, are you based here in Washington?"

She nods, looking confused.

"Come back when you're prepared to back up your guarantee, Miss Fry. I'm certain you'd write a good story," she says as she closes the door and marches into the kitchen.

Just as she thought. The phone machine, which she had avoided when she came in late the previous evening, is loaded with unanswered messages. The register chronicles twenty-two left by family, friends, colleagues, and reporters. Voice-mail messages at the office are probably triple that number. She acknowledges that there's an exhausting side to fame.

THE DRIVE TO OHAV SHALOM PROVIDES A SLIVER OF time to listen to the purloined tapes from Harold Farb's office. Tape One from the original four seems to deal with the renewal of a medical insurance plan for Temple employees. Cost to the synagogue keeps going up, benefits for the employees keep going down, and the staff keeps getting more irritated. An insurance broker who once served on the congregational Board has provided OS with a series of alternatives—all more costly and less satisfactory than what was enjoyed in past years.

Harold Farb referees the debate as Gabby fast-forwards through the tape. More discussions about personnel salaries, in particular Chuck Browner's. Gabby is inclined to listen, but time is precious and she needs to maneuver in heavy traffic. She fast-forwards through a second tape, also concerned with synagogue business, all interesting, but nothing about Seth. Discussions on the third tape are animated and vociferous. Few of the speakers wait their turn to voice opinions. President Doris Silbert has lost control. Voices cascade upon one another, giving the impression that everyone is talking and nobody listening. The subject is definitely Seth Greer. It is difficult to distinguish individual opinions which are salted with heavy emotion. If Seth has any friends present, they are silent. Gabby listens intently for mention of the accusers' names. The first to come up is the pseudonym, Michelle Tickleman, who claims Seth had sex with her during an office visit after hours. Rabbi Greer took advantage of her emotional condition. To Gabby, that didn't sound like the Seth Greer she knew, yet she was disappointed that the Board had already begun utilizing the accuser's pseudonym, even for private discussion among themselves. How prescient.

In a rush to discover something concrete, she feeds a fresh tape into the deck and randomly fast-forwards, stopping only long enough to hear the name of a second accuser, Dorothy Kogent-Weiner. Damn—again a pseudonym, with a story how Seth screwed her in pews of the small, polished rosewood chapel used for Friday evening services. Once again there is initial acquiescence on the woman's part, then resentment. A discussion ensues about how much Seth misused his rabbinical position to woo unsuspecting women, a violation of everybody's professional and ethical code. By the time Gabby pulls into the OS parking lot, she has a better understanding of what her colleague is purported to have done, but not to whom he did it.

Chuck Browner arrives at the office an hour earlier than usual and greets her with the Cheshire-cat smile of a bored man suddenly resuscitated by a subject of interest. "Well, well, well," he stretches out both hands to accept a double-shake. "You never cease to surprise me, Rabbi Gabby. I always knew you were a great jock, but a pugilist extraordinaire is something new. Rabbi, *sushi* chef and now prizefighter, what a resumé!"

"Gimme a break, Chuck," she says, brushing past him. "I'm in no mood at this moment. Have I a million messages?"

"A wheelbarrow full. And I've arranged for a press conference this morning at 10:00."

"You did what?" She halts, staring with wonder at him. "Let any of those reporters in here and you'll be waiting tables at Dupont Circle. You understand me, Charles Maximillian Browner?"

"Just kidding. Zoe Mountolive phoned a few minutes ago. Wants you to call her at her apartment in New York. The number's written down here. And members of the Board want to have a meeting with you tomorrow evening. In a restaurant. Urgent, they said. You set a time."

She dumps herself in her desk chair and bangs her elbows down on the desktop strewn with papers and monographs. She was never a neat individual and the surge of things to do has only increased the mess. "Good news if it's a four-star restaurant. Two stars means I'm cooked. They'll fry me over Queens," she says. "Looks like I'll be waiting tables with you at Dupont Circle. We can apply for jobs together."

He stands at the door, his hands on the door frame. "Somehow that doesn't convince me. You always land on your feet. That's a talent, you know. Some people have it, others don't."

"Well, let's start this wonderful day by telling the Board members I'll be available seven o'clock tomorrow evening. Wherever they want to meet. Then see if you can reach Zoe Mountolive and patch me in." She watches as Chuck steps back to close the door. "Wait, friend. I've got one last question for you. I'm picking up some vibrations. Do you enjoy seeing me squirm?"

While Chuck is a complex individual, he is also open and readable, seldom dissembling. "*Squirm* isn't quite the right term. Nothing can be as boring as synagogue routine. I love you, Rabbi Gabby, because for you nothing is ever routine. You ride the waves. It's all part of life's game. It's a good ride, now isn't it?"

She smiles widely with appreciation. "Well now, Chuck, I can always count on you to be observant and wise. Thanks for noticing. And is it a good ride? But that depends on what link of the roller coaster you're riding, now doesn't it? One thing's for sure; it goes up and down. For the moment I'm going down."

"And when you get off?"

"Then I guess I'll have to say, yes, it's been a damn good ride."

Chuck's grin widens. "That reminds me, you also had a call from Noah Zentner. To confirm the appointment with you tomorrow at 2:00. A bit early in the morning for a confirmation."

When he closes the door she feels her blood pressure rise, then wonders if Chuck's smile is as omniscient as she thinks. Mention of Noah's call arrests the sinking feeling in her stomach. The roller-coaster descent starts to level off.

Chuck tries to reach Zoe by phone at her New York apartment, then at her office, concluding she must be en route to midtown. A half-hour later, he announces success. Zoe is on the line.

"So shit hit the fan, didn't it?" Gabby opens. "I thought your people were going to control the press. We're getting a drubbing."

"No alternative," Zoe interrupts. "One thing you learn in this business is that events build their own momentum. You can't afford to chase. Godfrey and Andrea decided to move quickly and get the first licks in before Manny Fortuna marshals his allies in the streets."

"He can do that?" Gabby sounds dubious.

"Listen, Gabby, by the law we've got a damn strong case. Did everything right except leave the scene. Fortuna's got a weak case, but strong human appeal. Instead of a professional woman raped in a Queens alley, he's got two vigilantes beating up underprivileged juveniles. That's bound to capture public sentiment."

"Sorry, this isn't a routine morning and I'm a little touchy. How are you feeling, Zoe?"

"For a woman who almost got raped and now is falsely accused, not too bad. My eyes still water too much and I can't walk the street without wondering who is going to jump me next."

"I know exactly how you feel. Last night, a few innocent kids sent me into a near panic. If you're going to put yourself into the dating market, that isn't going to help."

"Don't feel very appealing these days. Let's go into the meat market together. I'm going to need support."

Gabby doesn't answer that immediately. "I'd love to, but doubling is not the way to go. In dating, it's every woman for herself. Besides, with your looks, you'd steal all my prospects. What's our next step with Fortuna?"

"We're trying to convince the police not to take the case before the District Attorney. For the time being, don't talk about what happened. It will only confuse matters."

"I must talk to my congregation. Members have a right to hear my side of the story."

"I understand," Zoe says. "Just tell the facts. No accusations against Mr. Fortuna; no targeting the kids. Count on whatever you say leaking; that's a given."

"I can't imagine this advancing my career. It's hard enough for Jews to accept women as rabbis, let alone ladies who defend themselves on the streets. We challenged the popular perception."

"I'd rather other women did the groundbreaking. I'll be in D.C. on Friday. Thought I'd stay in town until Sunday to participate in the pro-choice demonstration on the Mall. No idea how you feel about abortion, but you're welcome to join me."

"Are you kidding, pal? Got to be there, Zoe. I'm scheduled to give the opening invocation. Me and some female Presbyterian minister I don't know. Already made plans to attend with Emma Greer, the separated wife of my old boss. When I'm finished with the invocation, you can join us. We'll be in the VIP Staging Area. I'll get you a pass."

"That might not be a good idea. You know, of course, who just got herself a major spot on the program?"

"It's only a short walk from the White House for the First Lady. Don't tell me she's going to take the political plunge and support a woman's right to choose."

"If only she had the guts. But it's someone who can cause us heartache—Eli Waller. She'll probably be in the VIP area and it wouldn't be proper for us to meet. There's talk in New York she's going to make a run for President of the National Coalition for Women. Her speech will be entirely political."

A surge of misgiving stalls Gabby. "That can't do Noah any good."

"You got the big picture."

"Want to stay at my condo for the weekend, Zoe? It isn't the Hay-Adams, but it's serviceable."

"Can I turn down a sister in crime?" she replies with barely a second thought.

EPHRAIM ROTHMAN CALLS AT 9:30 A.M. AS GABBY knew he would. His voice is resonant and friendly.

"I'm calling to give you a heads-up on the dinner scheduled with Board members," he says. "There's been debate about the congregation's official response to the news about you. We all agreed that nothing should be done until we have a thorough and frank discussion. Nobody believes this guy Manny Fortuna, but we want to hear your version. This ad hoc committee will recommend an official response to the full Board."

"My lawyers have forbidden me to talk with the press. I'd love to tell my story—all the gory details. However, the attorneys fear the press will exploit small discrepancies in differing renditions. You understand, of course?"

"Absolutely, but if you want to stay in the running for Seth's job, it's important to be forthright."

"Will you be there, Eph?"

"I hadn't planned on it, but now I think it's important."

Before putting a question to him, she pauses. "I'd like that. Sounds as if I need to prove myself once again. Can I count on your support?"

He chuckles with nervousness for he doesn't do well with direct questions. "Well, naturally. But remember, I'm not the chairperson."

FOR LUNCH, GABBY HAS CHUCK ORDER COTTAGE cheese and fruit salad from a local delicatessen and set it on the low table before her sofa. From the bookshelf, tucked amid books of every size and shape and barely distinguishable, she removes two spiral-bound appointment books taken from the desk of Seth Greer's secretary, Margaret Sayer, the day after his resignation. The sooner they can be secreted back to Harold Farb's office the better.

A random search reveals only routine appointments running through each day. During the last two years of his tenure at Ohav Shalom, Rabbi Greer was extremely active, packing his daytime schedule from 8:30 each morning until after 5:30, when Margaret Sayer left for the day. It was not unusual for him to interview people at the rate of two per hour, taking off only for lunch and reserving the hours between 2:00 and 3:30 for reading and writing of sermons.

Gabby recognizes many names but certainly not all of the people who came to see him and, with those she knows, she can surmise the nature of their discussions: Board members seeking his counsel, families planning life-cycle ceremonies from *brises* to funerals, community leaders from the District of Columbia seeking his support, occasionally Congressmen and Congresswomen and a Senator, or members of the Cabinet and their deputies, a slew of civil servants working in federal agencies from the Departments of State and Agriculture to the Pentagon. In addition, he had ongoing responsibilities with the rabbinical associations and the Jewish Welfare Federation. Each activity requires a slice of his time and energy. His calendar appears positively exhausting.

To make sense of his appointments and link any of the hundreds of names with the pseudonyms Amanda Caen, Dorothy Kogent-Weiner, Elizabeth Silversmith, and Michelle Tickleman seems impossible. The multitude of names is confusing. Nowhere to begin. Nowhere to hang a hat. And nowhere to end. She sits back with a plastic bowl of pineapple, melon, and blackberries in her lap and runs the situation through her mind. Concentration is difficult when her attention constantly slips away to ponder the mess in Queens. It requires supreme effort to focus on the matter at hand for she is determined to have Chuck return the appointment books at the earliest moment.

After eating several spoonfuls of cottage cheese, she hunkers down to work and from midway into the second volume she randomly selects Tuesday, March sixteenth, to review. Routine appointments in the morning and a religious school faculty conference which she probably attended but doesn't remember. More appointments occur until Seth's midafternoon study break. This had been his private time Gabby knew not to invade.

When she has consumed her lunch, she rises to clear the

paper and plastic from the table and deposit them in her wastebasket, then paces back and forth, convinced that she will not identify Seth's accusers from his appointment books. She is about to plunge back into a sea of names when a novel thought strikes her. Random inspection will lead only to random observation. She needs a more scientific approach, one which will divide the people Seth sees into groups, then redivide them into even smaller groups. For that she'll need to create a spreadsheet on her computer.

The very process of formatting the spreadsheet stimulates a significant deduction. At the outset, she can dismiss the men Seth sees. The list suddenly shrinks. On her sheet she establishes a column to record the age of the women he saw. Since no one accused him of statutory rape or child molestation, she conjectures that his women were at least eighteen years old. She doubts he would have had sexual interest in women far past menopause nor would they him, which excludes women over fifty-five years. The spreadsheet gives structure to her reasoning.

The next thought proves seminal for it stands to reason that secrecy is paramount. Chances are he would schedule appointments for women he planned to seduce after 6:00 p.m. She breaks a horizontal row on the sheet into time sequences, starting 5:00 p.m. until 7:30 p.m.

From memory of events during the ordeal, she is able to select the month of January when one or more of his seductions occurred. The next step is write into the appropriate columns the names of individuals he saw after 5:00 p.m., excluding Fridays when he was occupied with *Erev Shabbat* services. Knowing what to look for makes the task easy. Gabby's mind is now sweeping ahead as she methodically enters names, recognizing some. After completing the third week of January in this manner, she is startled by the result. While Seth met with men every day, he had reserved the late hours exclusively for women. Throughout the month of January no males met with him at the end of the day!

Filling in the ages of the women proves more problematic. If Gabby does not know them personally, she has no way of discerning their ages. Two names occur three times. Four names, twice. These she jots down for Chuck to research from the congregation's roster. Though she has failed to identify a single one of Seth's women, Gabby nevertheless feels she has made progress. Her lunch hour ends on an optimistic note.

NOT SO OPTIMISTIC IS HER DINNER WITH MEMBERS of the Board at Kinkead's Restaurant on Pennsylvania Avenue. Doris Silbert has passed chairing of this meeting to Ohav Shalom's President-elect, T. Zachary Shugoll, who awaits Gabby in a corner booth selected for its privacy, along with Stephen Blau of the Rabbinical Search Committee, Zelda Lyon, a past Trustee known for her strident criticism of the rabbinical staff, and Ephraim Rothman.

When Gabby arrives they are sipping cocktails, indicating that preliminary discussions have already occurred. The gentlemen politely stand to greet her in the tight space of the booth. Zelda Lyon stretches forth both hands to shake, followed by a disingenuous hug. While she is settling herself, the others welcome with introductory small talk, remarking how important it is for her to order a cocktail and catch up with their drinking. Comments circulate about the excellent review restaurant critic Phyllis Richman gave Kinkead's in the weekend edition of the *Post*. Others remark about friends who have recommended the chef's unusual preparation of fish from local Chesapeake waters. Gabby is only vaguely amused and even less stimulated by the elaborate menu or the waiter's dull recitation of how the evening's specials are prepared. If ever she felt less like eating rich food, it is now.

"We want you to feel relaxed, Gabby." Zachary Shugoll abruptly turns from banter toward the subject of the evening. "We're not here to criticize or censure you."

Gabby chuckles and looks at the one person certain to be critical, Zelda Lyon. "Oh yes, I'm sure you won't throw me to the lions."

The others quickly absorb the sarcasm with muted laughter.

"We want to hear your side of the story," Zack continues. "You see, Gabby, we've been asked to prepare a letter for our members. In ticklish matters such as this, they look to us for an official explanation, if that doesn't sound too pedantic. Everybody reads the papers. And you can't get away from television coverage. We're bombarded with inquiries. It seems bizarre that people can't make up their own minds. The reality of this situation is they're waiting for an authoritative statement from the Board. I suspect the media will use it for their own purposes, but that's not our concern at the moment."

"I'm prepared to make that statement myself," Gabby inserts when Zack hesitates.

Stephen Blau says, "That will be helpful but unfortunately doesn't preclude a pronouncement from the congregation's officers. What we want you to know at the very outset is that we all support you. That should go without saying. For a woman to be attacked on the street is nothing short of appalling. I don't believe there's a single member of the congregation who doesn't feel terrible about what you've had to endure."

A waiter arrives with menus. There is no better time to order so everyone agrees to interrupt the discussion to accommodate this necessity. What impresses Gabby is that no one hesitates over the wide variety of menu choices. These are people accustomed to making decisions and navigating through sophisticated restaurant menus doesn't stymie them. They ask the waiter questions about the offerings, as much to test his knowledge as to illustrate their expertise.

Gabby would have preferred to meet around a conference table or in somebody's living room. She waits until the others have ordered, then reluctantly chooses a green salad with Sicilian olive oil and balsamic vinegar dressing and a local delicacy, bluefish from the Chesapeake, broiled simply, without garnish. The waiter suggests ways in which the chef might embellish this fish without adding calories, but Gabby remains stolid—a simple broil without additional culinary additions. Unable to change her mind, the waiter diverts his attention to others and suggests a fruity California Chardonnay which nobody seems to want.

As soon as he leaves, Zelda Lyon turns her head to regard Gabby with stern eyes. "Rabbi, before we make a statement to the congregation, we need to know if you have anything to add or subtract from the press coverage. Most of us have a pretty good picture of what happened. At this point, is there something we should know that we don't?"

Gabby notes Zelda's lack of warmth yet tries to avert subtle intimidation. "It's rather simple and pedestrian, from our point of view, the same we reported immediately to the police in Queens. My friend Zoe Mountolive was being molested perhaps raped by two youths, depending upon your definition of rape. I came to her rescue using what defense I had at my disposal, which happened to be a tennis racket. I hit one kid pretty hard—harder than I should. But then one can't always contain the degree of rage once it breaks out. And let me point out it was not Zoe or myself who initiated this violence. We were justified responding to it. Pure self-defense."

"We have some individuals in the congregation who abhor violence in any form," Zelda responds.

"Then let rapists ravage them in the alleys of Queens." Gabby's patience is tested. "That isn't good common sense, and it isn't Jewish. By not defending themselves against the Nazis, our people were almost wiped off the face of the earth."

"Let's say they hope to avoid such circumstances." Shugoll enters the discussion. "I believe one hundred percent of the women in our community commend you for what you did. For too long women have waited for men to help them in this department and they received little more than lip service. But there's another issue —whether it's appropriate for the spiritual leader of a leading congregation to take the law into her own hands."

"So rabbis are not permitted the right of self-defense?" Gabby takes umbrage.

"Of course they are," Ephraim states energetically. In conversations he normally waits patiently to add succinct and pithy summations. Knowing his style, Gabby is surprised to see him enter so early. "But this situation is new for Ohav Shalom. Our members cherish a different image of their rabbi, rightly or wrongly. I don't have to tell you how Seth Greer tarnished that conception. This situation in Queens is taxing. We need to do everything possible to restore and preserve the image of our rabbi."

Gabby feels like contracting into herself but sits stiff in her seat, her back ramrod straight. "Have I further tarnished that image, Eph?"

He exhales with discomfort. "We're not sure."

"And had I done nothing to help my friend? What then? What kind of a rabbi would people think I am? A windbag, incapable of taking action. Is that what Jews want from their rabbis? What in our faith precludes them for doing something other than praying and talking?"

Ephraim looks to his left at Zachary Shugoll for support and receives none. "If you ask my opinion, Gabby, most of us haven't given that much thought until now. What you did in Queens forces us to confront the issue. Some will think you a hero. Others, I'm afraid, will use it to anchor criticism of you and your colleagues."

"Well said," interrupts Steve Blau, "and that's why the Board must make a statement. In the end, every member will come to his own conclusion."

A bevy of waiters and busboys circles with trays containing the dinner's first course. It's clear to everyone that until food is served they ought to back off from the subject. There is some confusion over Shugoll's salad, which he claims was ordered without the blue cheese liberally scattered over the top. The waiter checks his order book and discovers he did not make a mistake, nor did the sous-chef. Nevertheless, he offers to have the chef prepare a new salad. In an effort to save time, Shugoll accepts what is in front of him and immediately begins removing clusters of the cheese with a fork.

Once everybody has commenced eating, Steve Blau asks, "Rabbi, there are those who say you reacted with excessive force. How would you respond to that accusation?"

"At the time, I didn't know my strength. If I had to do it all over again, I wouldn't have swung so hard. But I was alarmed and responded impulsively. No innocent people were hurt. Only delinquents who caused bodily injury to Zoe Mountolive."

"Bodily injury?" Zelda Lyon voices her skepticism. "I've seen Ms. Mountolive on television a couple of times and she didn't appear to be suffering any bodily harm. But maybe you know something I don't."

"Those creeps were in the act of raping her," Gabby shoots back.

"Have the police corroborated such charges?"

"No. They stopped their investigation and remanded the case to juvenile authorities."

"Perhaps they were just playing."

"You've got to be kidding. I was there. It certainly wasn't playing."

"Then possibly you acted rashly. I mean not in defense of Ms.

Mountolive but with, let's say, uncontrolled anger."

Gabby thinks about that for several seconds to be certain she understands the question thoroughly and concludes that she has already answered it. "The police have charged neither Zoe nor me with using excessive force. And yes, Zelda, I was angry. I faced a real emergency. Not a rehearsal. Not a psychodrama, but a real rape. I was not trained to handle such things. Not at the university and certainly not at rabbinical school. I did the first thing that came to mind and swung the only instrument I had in my possession likely to get those rapists to stop. I'm only human, you know."

Ephraim knows that the questioning sounds too much like legal interrogation and injects, "Gabby, if I were Zoe Mountolive, I'd consider myself very fortunate to have a friend like you. I know some women would have run off in search of the police, but by the time they were likely to arrive, the rape would be completed. The perpetrators would have disappeared. To my mind, you took a courageous course of action. Anything less was bound to fail."

"I hope we're not going to put that in our letter to the congregation," Zelda says, peeved at being interrupted. "I don't think we want to condone vigilantism when we have authorized the police to deter criminals."

Gabby's sense of exasperation sharpens her voice. "In a perfect world, no one would quarrel with that, Zelda. But Zoe Mountolive and I were on the street, struggling with evil people."

"Evil?" Zack Shugoll interjects. "They are adolescent boys with too much testosterone. Just minors."

Gabby snaps, "We call them juvenile delinquents where I come from. I can't imagine a single family at Ohav excusing this criminal behavior because the perpetrators happened to be sixteen years and eleven months old. I learned a lesson in Queens: there's a big difference between talking from the pulpit and surviving on the street. If I had been asked about a similar situation which occurred in some distant city, I would probably say the defenders overreacted. But being there myself is something quite different."

Waiters hover about to remove empty plates from the first course. The minute Ephraim puts down his fork, an obsequious waiter with a bald head and handlebar mustache snatches it from over his left shoulder. Free from the necessity of using a fork, he frames his thinking with his hands, cupping them as though holding a glass sphere. "The issue as I see it, Gabby, is not so much your rush to a defense. Everybody here knows my feeling that you had every right to help your friend. And you did a damn good job, too. Heroes are made of such stuff. But there will be questions how you handled the potential witness. Mr. Cecil Thorner, I believe is his name. People will ask why you gave him money."

Gabby senses her patience waning further and, for a moment, she questions why she should be answering these questions at all. "Eph, I already told the police why I gave that jerk, excuse me, now I must call him by his full name, Cecil Thorner, Mister Cecil Thorner, if you will, twenty dollars. It was another quick decision. Thorner—and I didn't know his name then—was loitering on the street when I first noticed him. He followed me from Parsons Avenue into the alley, I think to panhandle for money. What he found was something he couldn't resist, an opportunity for more than a few coins. He showed up just as we floored the kids, claiming we beat them up and threatening to report us to the police. At the moment, I was more interested in getting an ambulance than the police. Thorner blocked my way. He suggested we give him twenty dollars to disappear from the scene. I didn't want to argue with him, so I quickly accepted. It was convenient and I had a recollection of having two twenty-dollar bills in my pocketbook. He snatched the bill. Zoe and I went for help."

"So it wasn't exactly a bribe," Ephraim declares.

"I never thought of it as one. Just a way of eliminating Thorner from the scene so we could get help. To call it an obstruction of justice or a bribe is obscene."

Two waiters approach the booth, one transporting a portable serving stand, the other a tray with five entrées covered by stainless steel warmers. A busboy descends on the table like a vulture, scooping plates and silverware from the diners. No further discussion can take place during the exchange of dishes. Gabby keeps her salad and pushes it aside to make room for the bluefish, sizzling from a high-temperature broiling oven and, despite her orders to the contrary, garnished with green onions.

When the diners are resettled, Steve Blau lifts his fork and points it in Gabby's direction, unaware how rude this appears. He sighs, then opens his lips in a wry expression of pain. "Bad time for this to hit the congregation, Rabbi. What with Seth Greer's resignation and everything..."

"I didn't choose the time these delinquents tried to rape my friend. What happened with Rabbi Greer and me is mere coincidence, nothing more. I shouldn't be blamed for the coincidence of two events, any more than for what I did to help a friend."

"In your perfect world, Rabbi, we agree," Blau continues. "But we're dealing with perception as well as fact. And public perception is a fickle thing. Different expectations for rabbis."

"I'm learning fast." Gabby makes an effort with her fork to cut the bluefish and release steam captured inside the flesh. She thinks of the hot fish as a metaphor for her own feeling. Ready to explode. The thought of resigning from Ohav Shalom races through her brain and stays around just long enough to be rejected. She's a fighter not a quitter, as those kids on the street in Queens learned to their disadvantage.

The others are finishing their entrees when Zack Shugoll notices how little Gabby has eaten. That she has failed to consume anything he attributes to the multitude of questions answered, not a lack of appetite or desire. "I think we've exhausted our rabbi," he says, cutting the interrogation short, "and prevented her from eating the meal we promised. Besides, I believe we now understand her views, which should be sufficient to draft something for our congregants."

"Should we mention something about the pro-choice march on the Mall?" Zelda Lyon asks, her tone provocative. "We've learned that Rabbi Lewyn is planning to address the demonstrators this Sunday. There are bound to be those who do not want our congregation associated with this march though, of course, she has every right to express her private sentiments."

Gabby does not like the new direction and pounds the table gently with her fist. "Thanks for your support, Zelda. I assure you I have no desire to imply that pro-choice is a position endorsed by Ohav Shalom. And before you jump to conclusions, let's set the record straight. I'm not addressing the demonstration, though I admit being miffed that I wasn't invited to. I've got a lot to say on the subject, but apparently other women have more credibility. A three-minute invocation is all the time I've been given. Other clergy will share the honor. There will be a female minister of the Presbyterian faith. Maybe also a Catholic layperson, if we're lucky to find a rebel."

"Won't your very presence send a message?" Zelda pursues.

"God, I hope so."

"I think we can leave the rally until later," Zachary interrupts before a new brush fire breaks out. "Gabby must be tired; time to let her eat."

To Gabby's mind, Zack is correct about one thing: she is exhausted mentally. Inside, she feels a deep isolation. What should be perfectly clear requires endless explanation. A straightforward confrontation in Queens becomes the subject of tedious analysis, each person taking a different perspective. The obvious becomes obfuscated.

She knows those at dinner want to talk about what they have heard and perhaps begin drafting a memorandum. Before dessert arrives, fatigue provides her an excuse for leaving. For once, the others appear sympathetic, understanding that it's been a long and tense day.

Kind words are exchanged, empty expressions about which she has become cynical. People say one thing in her presence and another behind her back. Standing on Pennsylvania Avenue waiting for the parking attendant to fetch her car, she wonders whether she wants Seth Greer's job after all. Her attention is distracted when the Volvo rolls into view and a handsome, dark-haired college boy jumps out and opens the driver's door. She slips him two dollars, which he accepts with a flirtatious smile. En route home, it occurs to her that no one has smiled at her like that for some time. Her thoughts transfer to Noah.

WHEN CHUCK MAXIMILLIAN BROWNER SHOWS UP FOR work the next morning at 9:25, he appears hung over and somber.

"What's wrong, Charles?" she inquires.

"You don't want to hear, Rabbi."

"*Tzoris* is my métier. If nobody had problems, they wouldn't pay me to help them out of jams. You know I'm good for a little ventilation."

"Meat market problems. Lover issues. I told you, Rabbi, you don't want to hear. And frankly, if I want to keep my job, which

I do, I'd better not tell you." He trots to his desk and a moment later returns to her study with a notebook.

"Found the ages of the women you asked me to look up on the synagogue roster," he says while ripping the top page from the tablet and passing it over the desk.

To refresh her memory, she rereads the names of frequent visitors to Seth Greer's study after 5:00 p.m. Chuck has written in pencil the dates of birth and the calculated ages of these visitors. What impresses her immediately is that no one seems to be younger than forty-six, but none are older than fifty-three. That fact requires a review for confirmation. She rolls this around in her mind while Chuck watches from across her desk, awaiting further instructions. None come. He tries guessing her thoughts and comes to the conclusion that she is more or less inscrutable.

"Is there something I've missed?" He invades her musing.

Suddenly aware of his presence, she corrects her position in the chair, then threads the fingers of one hand into those of the other, resting her elbows on the arm of her chair. "The fog is beginning to clear, Chuck," she declares.

"It might help if you let me know where you're headed."

"Seems our elusive friend, Rabbi Greer, made a habit of seeing a special group of people after hours. What's conspicuous is who isn't on this list rather than who is. Apparently, he stopped seeing men in the late afternoon. Also absent from the list are women younger than forty-six years of age and older than fifty-three."

"Middle-aged women seek more counseling than younger women."

"Young women are busy keeping families together. Middle-aged women accumulate aches and pains and need attention. But answer this question for me, young man. What happens to men in their early forties?"

"They add weight around the midsection, their hair thins, their libido wanes, and their careers flatten out."

"I mean psychologically."

"They usually go through a mid-life crisis. Question everything. What they're doing. Who they're sleeping with. What they want to do with the rest of their miserable lives."

"And women in their forties?"

He shrugs his shoulders.

"Nothing comparable until a decade later when they reach menopause. For women, life changes in their early fifties. The crisis they skipped in their forties they discover when their ovaries stop doing their job. Psychologists make millions off menopause, to say nothing of the doctors and the pharmaceutical industry. Some women say they dry up, inside and out. I've got a hunch that the women who came to see Rabbi Greer after hours were menopausal."

"Good theory, but where does it take you?"

"Don't know until I learn more about the individuals."

"Is that possible?"

"We'll see. Tell you a little secret, Chuck, if you promise not to repeat it."

"Cross my heart...if that isn't heretical in a synagogue."

"Rabbis can ask personal questions nobody else can." A naughty grin pokes dimples into her cheeks.

When playful Gabby stirs a yearning within Chuck. It occurs to him that in her presence the hurt which normally gnaws inside him seems mollified. Her strength transfers.

"It isn't holiness one wants from the clergy—but hope."

Chapter Ten

August 31st

A rabbi's work comes to a climax each weekend with the celebration of Sabbath rites and family life-cycle ceremonies. Sunday afternoons are the only hours free for rest and recreation. And yet in the spring and summer even these precious hours are filled with duties. Most brides want to be married at this time of year and, in order to accommodate the assembly of family and friends from out of town, weekends are preferred. Jewish law and tradition prohibit weddings on the Sabbath, which leaves Sunday for most nuptials. Though Gabby's followers do not like to think of her conducting multiple ceremonies on the same day, they seldom consider the logistics. Demand for the limited number of peak-season Sundays compels her to schedule more than one wedding per day. She enjoys officiating at such ceremonies, though they play havoc with plans for weekend recreation. Not only will a ceremony preclude going out of town, but it also requires her to stand by for many hours in advance.

By the time she arrives at the Four Seasons Hotel to conduct the wedding of Ellen Lazaraus and Douglas Weil, she is enervated from a previous ceremony in Potomac, Maryland, twenty miles to the north. As soon as she enters the Four Seasons, she checks the banquet room for unexpected problems. Next, it is necessary to confer with the musicians regarding the order of the wedding service. An agreement is rapidly made with the photographer concerning the use of flash during the ceremony. When arrangements have been concluded at the wedding site, she seeks out the groom and his best man to gather witnesses for signing the traditional Jewish *ketubah*, and preparation of the marriage license for registration with the District of Columbia. During these preliminaries, people crack jokes, none off-color but none very entertaining. Wedding ceremonies spawn nervous reactions.

Gabby's last stop before returning to the *chupah* is to talk with the bride, separated, by custom, on a different floor from her soon-to-be husband. The clock races toward the four o'clock ceremony, only eleven minutes away.

The bridesmaids, dressed in sky blue silk with simple lines, are clustered around the bride who is lying on the king-size bed, her head hanging over the side. Her mother, Madeleine Lazaraus, has her fingers clamped against Ellen's nostrils to stop the blood flowing from her nose. Nothing serious. Last minute jitters play mischievous games. After months of intense planning, nerves become frazzled, bladders incontinent, and nasal passages dry. The bride's sister-in-law emerges from the bathroom with a damp towel. Her attendants have lost their composure, but Mrs. Lazaraus appears to be handling the event as an everyday occurrence.

When Gabby presents herself, Ellen's eyes peer upward in an expression of sheer terror. According to a prearranged schedule, in the banquet room below ushers have begun seating members of the family and the musicians have started playing their introductory repertoire. The groom is waiting to enter the *chupah* but the rabbi is standing over her. Nothing could be worse than to face her new husband and family with blood cascading over her lips like Yosemite Falls.

Gabby glances at her wristwatch to calculate how much this disrupts events downstairs. She can easily get caught up in nervous activity but dares not. Her calm is essential to keep others from losing composure. She elects not to reprimand bridesmaids for aggravating the bleeding by placing Ellen's head below her heart.

"Let's get Ellen's head high so blood must flow against gravity, not with it." Her voice is soft but reassuring.

A muffled cry of despair slips from Ellen's lips through her mother's fingers. "My gown!"

"She can't sit up in her wedding dress, Rabbi," one of the attendants states.

"Then let's get it off," Gabby instructs.

"She already has spots on her bodice."

"Nothing cold water won't remove. We must get her head high."

"There isn't time, Rabbi," Mrs. Lazaraus says. "We've only got a few minutes."

"I'll make time for this. Leave it to me. We'll postpone the ceremony a little. As soon as Ellen's out of her dress, I'll go downstairs to explain the delay."

"Sounds terrible." Ellen shakes her head, momentarily freeing her nose from her mother's grasp.

"Happens every day. Nothing unusual," Gabby fibs a little. "Never seen a wedding yet in which something untoward didn't occur. A nosebleed is the least serious. We'll have to get the witness signatures on the *ketubah* later. Within forty-five minutes you will be a married woman, Ellen. And that's a rabbi's promise."

"I should be as sure as you," the mother snorts while the other women begin unzipping the elaborate gown. They must work around Mrs. Lazaraus who is still holding her daughter's nose.

"Listen carefully, everyone," Gabby says in a firm, confident voice. "I'm going to the banquet room and tell Douglas, then the families. The musicians will repeat their repertoire." She turns to the matron of honor. "I'm sorry I didn't catch your name."

"Sally. Sally Kerner-Strom."

"Sally, in approximately twelve minutes I'm going to telephone on the house phone. Answer and tell me exactly what's happening here. Ellen, you're going to spend a lifetime with Doug so a few minutes more or less now doesn't matter. No need to hurry."

"People will think something bad has happened," Ellen utters through her mother's fingers.

"Not when I explain. There isn't a single person here who hasn't had a nosebleed, and don't they always come at the wrong time? You can't have a wedding without a bride so she arrives when she's ready, not before. Sally, we'll be talking soon. Mrs. Lazaraus, I'd be very proud to have a wonderful mother like you. Ellen, the next time we meet will be under the *chupah*." Gabby signals with both thumbs up, a gesture she feels might be interpreted as more appropriate for a sports coach than a rabbi, yet it conveys the intended encouragement.

GABBY DRAWS DOUG WEIL AND HIS BEST MAN FROM a group of friends and explains why a short delay is required. "Did you know that Ellen's a nose-bleeder?" she teases with a smile that spreads beneath the tip of her nose.

"News to me." Doug manages his concern.

"Your first insight on marriage's endless learning curve. There will be many more to come. Ellen's got a small bleed at the moment. Just nerves. Now if you'll excuse me, I want to chat with the musicians and the guests. Everybody will be speculating if I don't get to them first."

In front of the groom's party, Gabby strips the jacket from her black suit and reveals a white blouse. She then climbs into a black clerical robe, fastening it down the front with clip buttons. Her heavy rabbinical *tallit* fits snugly behind her neck and trails along the front, providing a contrast in black and white. While many rabbis prefer white or brightly colored skullcaps to symbolize the purity of marriage, she uses a simple black yarmulke. From this moment forth, nobody will fail to recognize her clerical status.

The musicians agree to prolong their introductory medley, then repeat what they have already played. Gabby paces to the *chupah*, does an about-face and clasps her hands in front of the *tallit*. "Ladies and Gentlemen." Her voice penetrates cello strains of Brahms Opus 81. The music softens, then dies altogether. Slowly the guests stop talking and turn to look for the bride. "I am Rabbi Gabrielle Lewyn of Congregation Ohav Shalom and I will be officiating this afternoon. We're going to have a short delay." Her voice seldom requires artificial amplification. "Nothing serious. Ellen is upstairs and extremely eager to become Mrs. Douglas Weil. Unfortunately, her nose has put up a little resistance. With all the comings and goings of this happy event, she's developed a slight nosebleed. We thought it wise to solve the problem in her room, so she could enjoy the ceremony. It shouldn't be more than a few minutes. While we're waiting I have a question to ask and nobody has to respond if he or she doesn't want to. With a show of hands, how many married people here had nosebleeds on their wedding day?"

The question catches everyone by surprise but diffuses anxieties. Nervous chuckling spreads through the rows of guests. Two hands shoot into air, followed tentatively by two more. Chuckles mature into full laughs.

Gabby moves from the *chupah* and circles the banquet room in the direction of a house telephone. She walks with deliberate slowness to instill confidence. This gives a middle-aged woman an opportunity to offer a hand to shake. Gabby recognizes the face from among her congregants but cannot put a name to it. Her skin is clear without freckles or blemishes and her figure is frail like a slender porcelain statue. "Rabbi Lewyn, I'm Eleanor Weissborg and have been wanting to speak with you."

Gabby stirs the name through a mental archive and comes up blank.

"From Ohav Shalom. I've known Rabbi Greer for many years. Had many discussions with him. I'm delighted you've taken over."

That Eleanor Weissborg mentions Seth Greer triggers Gabby's memory. Her name was often in Seth's appointment books. She is a congregant who would visit him after five in the afternoon when the staff had left for the day. "Fact is, Eleanor, I've been wanting to call you. I'm trying to follow up with people who saw Rabbi Greer. My secretary's provided a list. As you can see, I've got duties to perform at the moment, but I'd love to talk with you at the reception. Is that possible?" Her hand pulls back.

Eleanor Weissborg is equally accommodating, "Why, of course. Don't let me hold you up. We'll talk after the ceremony."

While Gabby waits for Sally Kerner-Strom to pick up the phone in Ellen's room, she recycles Eleanor Weissborg's remark about having discussions with Seth Greer. Sally answers with news that the bleeding is now under control. It will take another ten minutes to redress the bride. Gabby establishes a new time for the ceremony to begin.

When it does, twenty-seven minutes later, Gabby positions the bride and groom in front of her under the *chupah*, facing one another. They hold each other's hands, gazing expectantly in the eyes of their chosen mates. After introductory Hebrew blessings, she solicits from them private words, first from Douglas whose voice cracks with emotion, then Ellen, who sniffles as if wary that blood will again flow from her nostril. To Gabby's mind, there is no more intimate moment of bonding than this. A couple speaks of their loves and their dreams, followed by a Hebrew declaration that binds them as husband and wife. *Haray aat mekudeshet li...*

After the recitation of seven wedding blessings, the couple crushes a wine glass under their feet, symbolically recognizing that while they stand on the summit of their happiness, other lives are in travail and pain. There are kisses and well-wishes. Amid a shower of *mazel tovs*, the newlyweds retreat through the central aisle to receive their families and friends. Gabby waits until those near the *chupah* have left, then carefully slips aside to remove her ceremonial garments. For the moment, her job is done. Rejoicing belongs to others. She habitually resists sadness that follows each of her wedding ceremonies: Always a rabbi but never a bride.

Eleanor Weissborg is waiting as Gabby moves along the aisle. "Your ceremony was beautiful, Rabbi." She tilts her head and nods slightly. "Very touching. I've been to a lot of weddings; this was the best. Personal and thoughtful. I must confess that until now I've had a rather low opinion of rabbis. Seth Greer didn't elevate it much."

Gabby finds herself suddenly jumping from one rabbinic role into another. "But you thought enough of rabbis to see Rabbi Greer on several occasions, didn't you?"

"I did."

"That's why I wanted to call you," Gabby adds. "He left quite suddenly. I wondered if there was a rabbinic matter that was left in the air. If so, could I help?"

Her eyes drop but suddenly rise to meet Gabby's. "I was depressed about a lot of things. Change of life was only the tip of my iceberg. Rabbi Greer had a reputation for counseling women. I thought he might help me. I'm afraid he made matters worse. After listening to your service this afternoon, I know you would have been better. Women understand these things."

"I'm not menopausal yet," Gabby grins, "and when I am, there's no guarantee I'll be any better prepared than you. I also have moments of depression. Do you have children? I should know this, but I'm afraid I don't."

"Three. All out of the nest. Along with their father. The moment I finished rearing his family he found a younger chicken."

"Sorry to hear it. I can see why you were depressed. When the time is right, I'd love to know what Rabbi Greer did wrong so I won't repeat his mistake. Still interested in seeing me?"

She considers this for an extended moment. "The thought never occurred to me until this afternoon. I was deeply moved by your ceremony. You're a compassionate woman. Yes, I'd like to talk with you."

"I warn you in advance I'm no expert on menopause."

"That doesn't matter. You could say I've passed through that station. This might sound odd, but something constructive came from my affair with Seth Greer. It made me very angry. But with good professional counseling, I came to understand I wasn't really angry at him. The real target was myself and my gullibility. Now that he's gone, I'm truly sorry about what's happened. He was only partly to blame."

This disclosure confirms Gabby's hunch about Seth. At least now she has a hook on which to hang a theory.

During the wedding reception it is impossible to probe further. Everyone wants to talk with the rabbi and Eleanor Weissborg is circled by acquaintances. They agree to talk more in the near future.

THAT EVENING, GABBY SCREWS UP HER COURAGE and lifts the telephone receiver, dialing a number she knows by heart. It rings four times until interrupted by an answering machine. A familiar voice, still crystal clear and dancing like the notes of a clarinet at the top register of an orchestra. "Tim Matternly's palace. By now you know I'm not at home, but after the beautiful music, leave a message and I'll get back to you." What follows is Tim singing a few bars from Gilbert and Sullivan's *Iolanthe* hopelessly off-key. He never could carry a melody. A beep interrupts his tortured rendition.

"Tim, Gabby. Always enjoy G and S," she responds. "Since you don't phone me these days, I called to find out how you're doing. Love to speak with you. Lots of things happening in the Nation's Capital. Good, bad, and utterly confusing. I'll give you an update on my race to hell. Also need to remind you, if you're planning to get married in a garish Presbyterian Church, I still expect an invitation. Fail to invite me and I'll use my influence with the powers above to put a hex on you. Don't write your old friend Gabby out of your life just yet."

For dinner, Gabby munches on celery stuffed with humus, to which she took a liking during a year's postgraduate rabbinical study in Jerusalem. Not much of a meal, but events swirling around her have continued to steal her appetite. Nor is she looking forward to the evening; it is time to begin writing *Rosh Hashanah* and *Yom Kippur* sermons, only a month away. She knows this year will be different from the past when sermons were shared equally with Seth Greer. In his absence, her load is double. Due to the seating limitations of the sanctuary, Ohav Shalom schedules two services for each major convocation, *Erev Rosh Hashanah* and *Rosh Hashanah* day, as well as *Erev Yom Kippur* (*Kol Nidre*) and the day-long *Yom Kippur* worship. Mirroring the liturgy and choir selections, she plans to deliver the same sermon at the early and late services for each holiday. Zealots who attend both services will have to forgive the repetition.

A telephone call to Doris Silbert confirms that Ohav Shalom will be interviewing a candidate for Seth's position the weekend of September 9th. She tells Doris of her plans to be at the Delaware beach town of Rehoboth, on the Delmarva Peninsula. Nearby are beaches for walking, the perfect place to inspire holiday sermons.

Zoe Mountolive calls that evening to say hello. "So how's my partner in crime holding up?" she asks during preliminary small talk.

"So busy I haven't got time to take my pulse. Late summer to a rabbi is like early April to a tax accountant. Hell on Earth. All our educational programs are starting up right after the High Holidays. With Rabbi Greer gone, I've got to pick up the pieces. Twice as many sermons to write."

"Shame you didn't get any summer vacation," Zoe adds with her normal empathy.

"Can't get off the treadmill. I don't know what I'd do if your firm wasn't handling our legal problems. Guess you called me with a progress report."

At the other end, Zoe fumbles with the phone receiver, passing it from one tired ear to the other. "Not really. There isn't much to tell at this point. The police are still investigating. Very slowly, I might add. That shows there isn't much enthusiasm. When Manny Fortuna finally realizes that Greenwald, Molletz isn't going to offer a cushy settlement and he'll have to try his case in court, he'll lose zeal for his clients. His time is better spent on a more lucrative case."

"You think money is driving him?"

"Personal injury lawyers are gutter vermin. But we can't afford to be blasé about the righteousness of our position. Overconfidence buries many a good case."

"What can I do to help?"

"From what you say, you're so busy taking care of other people you haven't a moment for yourself. That's why you need good legal representation. May need you in Queens to talk with the police or the District Attorney. If the D.A.'s office believes there's a case, they'll take it to the grand jury. That's usually a rubber stamp for a trial. We'll fight every step."

"I hope it doesn't go to court until after the Jewish holidays."

"Many judicial officials in New York are Jewish. The judiciary manages to hiccup around their holidays. Delays are routine."

"And Clementine? How is she?"

"Impossible, like the rest of her pubescent friends. At this age, she's 102 pounds of wild hormones. One day she's mad at me; the other at her father."

"Are matters settling down with Peter?"

"Absolutely not. They get worse every day. And I get more unreasonable and irritable. I'm most upset at having once fallen in love with this creep. I simply can't imagine how foolish I was."

"We all grow at different speeds. And in different directions. When I see marriages break up, it's helpful to remind myself that most mammals don't mate for life. Most animals just go bump in the night frequently enough to produce offspring, then separate. Females care for the children. Males find another female with whom to go bump in the night again. Sometimes I believe people are bucking Nature. When their marriages break down, they feel they've failed. That doesn't compute."

"You always have a novel viewpoint that makes me feel good. And I'm not the only one you have that effect upon."

"I wish I could believe that."

"Noah talks about you every time we speak. You've made quite an impression on him. It's starting to sound a bit personal. Could be dangerous."

"Nothing to worry about." Gabby is pleased with what she hears but communicates no evidence of it to Zoe.

"I hope so. You won't be much of a witness if a jury learns that there's something going on between you. Your testimony must be objective and professional. Mix romance into it and I might as well be putting a touchy-feely psychiatrist on the stand. Could hurt Noah. Understand?"

Gabby does not answer immediately, then in weaker voice says, "Yes, of course. Understood."

Sunday, September 4

The crowd (estimated by the pro-choice organizers at 830,000, but by the District of Columbia Police at slightly more than 500,000) fills the rectangular Mall, from the Capitol west to 23rd Street at the Lincoln Memorial. The speakers' platform is constructed in front of the Eastern Reflecting Pool, with the familiar majestic white dome of the Capitol as backdrop, leaving no doubt that those assembled this Sunday noon want to make an impression on Congress. Concurrent with this march in Washington, more modest demonstrations are organized throughout the nation. Eleven national and regional feminist organizations have allied in an effort to show how they feel about freedom of reproductive choice. In 1,017 towns across the country, groups of like-minded people are standing at village intersections and before federal courts and city halls. Some rallies number in the thousands, but more commonly in the hundreds.

In Piel, Wyoming, with a population of forty-eight, a lone woman in her mid-thirties stands at the junction of Ranch and First Street beside a placard with the single word CHOICE. She has stood vigil since 8:00 that morning. Her chin is lifted in the late-morning sun, her eyes trying to catch the attention of an occasional driver. Passengers in a dusty station wagon returning from Sunday prayers at New Baptist Church jeer through open windows. "Janice," they call out, "You people are murderers. For the love of God, get off your dung heap. We got enough preachers in this town."

"Homer!" she cries back, well after the station wagon has passed along the dusty street, "you're a goddamn jerk. If the oversexed boys of this town would stop knocking up their neighbors' teenage girls, this wouldn't be necessary."

In some larger towns, there are speeches; in others, just signs stating, PRO-CHOICE, FUNDAMENTAL FREEDOM FOR AMERICANS. Let elected officials take note. Vote whores that they are, they must acknowledge the will of their constituents, over fifty percent of whom are women.

On the Washington Mall, Gabby's invocation follows the Episcopal Reverend Claudia P. Brown and Mary Louise Riley, a vicar from the rebellious community calling itself Catholics for Choice. Gabby feels reticent about associating God's name with the pro-choice message since she believes the propriety or impropriety of abortion is not a Divine verdict.

For the theme of her invocation, she selects passages from Leviticus dealing not with abortion, but with bodily hygiene. She ends with a Hebrew blessing, extolling God's compassion for fellow sisters of the earth. It is a good invocation, but is barely heard by a restless crowd waving placards and not yet ready to settle down. And why should people listen? Gabby asks herself. Crusaders repeat their mantras ad nauseam. From prominent speakers assembled behind her on the platform they will hear nothing new.

She tries to be ruthlessly honest about the limited service she is providing. Her invocation, at the very beginning of the program, is designed more as a Call-to-Order than a divine petition. So little do the march organizers think of the three clergywomen that they fail to provide seats for them on the platform. They are expected to step up to the microphone, deliver their prayers (hopefully short and sweet), and immediately retire. Once Mary Louise Riley is finished, an organizer shepherds the trio down a wooden stairway to a security area. A young female volunteer in a yellow T-shirt with *pro-choice* stenciled on the chest in maroon letters, offers Pepsi in paper cups.

It is here that Gabby becomes aware how many police guards are on duty. Every event produces a counter-event. Anti-abortion advocates will not permit their adversaries to convey a message to Congress without a measured response. While the pro-life demonstrators are outnumbered, they benefit from being better organized. Their folks forego crowds on the spacious lawns, preferring to broadcast their message at strategic locations, near Metro stations, television scaffolding, crosswalks, and conspicuously in front of the speakers' platform. Placards reading STOP CRIMES AGAINST HUMANITY, professionally lettered and mounted on twelve-foot high poles, ensure that television cameras will be forced to capture the pro-life message.

As previously agreed, Zoe Mountolive is waiting outside the security fence. "You did a great job," she says with a semi-hug, planting her cheek against Gabby's.

"Glad somebody listened," she replies, searching for Emma Greer, who also agreed to rendezvous nearby. "I've never spoken to a half-million people before. From the lectern they look like ants. Weird feeling to have your voice amplified so much. A million ears and none but yours heard my prayer."

"How about women from your congregation and their spouses and children? They're probably proud as hell at having their rabbi speak. Maybe few on the Mall heard you, but people throughout the nation saw you on TV. They'll ask, who is that attractive female rabbi? Tomorrow morning, a thousand Gentile men will want to convert. Your telephone will be ringing off the hook with guys asking for a date."

"From your mouth to God's ear. I should be so lucky," she says as she wonders if Tim Matternly will see her. Or perhaps Noah Zentner.

"Guess who just entered the security area looking like she stepped off a Hollywood set and, would you believe it, carrying a laptop computer? A phalanx of courtiers trailed her."

"Eli Waller? The Wicked Witch of St. Michaels? First time I've heard of someone toting a laptop to a march. Must be an important woman, or at least she wants others to believe she is."

"She'll be my witness soon. When she sweats her makeup won't look so picture-perfect."

Emma Greer plows through the bodies along the police cordon, unable to find Gabby. They are not far from each other but screened by people on the move. Gabby chides herself for not having designated a more specific place to rendezvous, but at the time they agreed to meet she knew of no fixed reference point. When their paths eventually cross, Emma throws her arms around her in a welcoming hug, a gesture that tension over her husband's indiscretions is past. They are now sisters in a common cause.

"Your prayer was marvelous," she says while untangling her arms. "Not a disingenuous word; not an insincere thought. Generally, I find invocations a big bore. Ministers tack clichés and platitudes together with nothing but commas. Nobody listens because the drivel is demeaning. Your words were thoughtful, as always."

"I'm flattered." Gabby is taken by surprise. "I didn't think anybody was listening."

Turning to Zoe who is waiting behind Gabby for an introduction, Emma says, "You must be Zoe Mountolive. Heard about you. At a cocktail party someone said that among Greenwald, Molletz's lawyers, you're the best man they've got. I hope that doesn't offend you."

"Who, me?" Zoe blurts. "That's a compliment. Folks obsessed with political correctness don't get to laugh much. In my book, laughing beats correctness any day."

"I like you already," Emma says as she turns with the couple. They must weave a path through a crowd near the speaker's platform where Zoe might inadvertently make contact with Eli

Waller. Better to move toward the Reflecting Pool where they can hear the program from a distance. Emma has a pair of binoculars.

Pro-life demonstrators are loud and confrontational, engaging demonstrators in debate wherever they can. Gabby overhears one argument and is impressed by the adversary's debating techniques. Unlike the pro-choice women who shout until their vocal cords fail, they rely on visual messages to convey information. They come equipped with computer-generated presentation boards to illustrate with pictures and graphs. If it is true we remember more of what we see than what we hear, the anti-abortion devotees are better teachers.

Between introductory speakers on the platform, an all-female Bavarian oompah band pumps lively, rhythmic music over the loud speakers. The lawns are damp from an early morning shower and most people stand, though well-prepared folks bring tarpaulins and blankets.

Eventually, Zoe and Emma lay claim to a tiny patch of open space to view six giant projection screens flanking the speaker's platform. The familiar face of Democratic Senator Joanne Mills from California, a ripple of double chins descending from her pudgy jowls, is depicted on all six screens simultaneously. The camera angle exaggerates defects in her skin. Nobody surrounding Gabby seems to notice that only a few minutes before her face was also enlarged to gargantuan proportions.

The senator's presence at the microphone triggers angry heckling from pro-life factions. Coordinated chanting erupts from the Mall near Constitution Avenue. "NO MORE MURDER. LIFE IS SACRED. NO MORE MURDER." An orchestra of drums accompanies these jeers with a martial beat. Senator Mills, confident in the capabilities of the amplification equipment, pounds the lectern and shouts her message. Volume overloads the loud speaker system, muffling her words. An athletic man in sweat clothes standing near Zoe mutters, "It's time to put her out of her misery."

Zoe is thinking much the same and laughs.

By its applause the crowd encourages the senator to stop, though she misinterprets the clapping as an appeal to continue. The more folks clap the more she gesticulates. The band must begin an Alpine march in order to persuade her to relinquish the microphone.

Zoe looks for the athlete who addressed her and discovers him in a cluster of women. Two have infants in backpacks.

"Well, you got your wish." She makes contact with him. "They finally retired her."

Attentions are drawn back to the dais where Maria Bellcava, chairperson of the sponsoring Coalition for Choice, takes the microphone to introduce the next speaker. Emma, who is looking through her binoculars, reports that Eli Waller has stepped forward, still clutching her laptop computer.

"Many of you are familiar with Eli Waller from television." Bellcava half-pivots to acknowledge Eli's presence a foot behind her. "You know her as a leading financial analyst on Wall Street. What you perhaps don't know is how she's helped invest funds for the National Association for Women, the National Coalition of Women, the Population Council, and the National Women's Health Organization. She's on the Executive Committee of the National Association of Women and is a candidate for its presidency. Of course, Eli Waller's name is currently in the press over a different matter. Few of our sisters are bold enough to fight back when molested. Those who do are heroes. They make it easier for other women to seek protection that the law guarantees. At great personal cost, Eli is showing us the way. Today she is a beacon of light illuminating the darkness of the past. It's my honor to introduce her. Ladies and Gentlemen, Eli Waller."

Applause begins modestly at first, then as Eli inches toward the lectern, spreads from the front to the rear. Her face on the multiple screens is immediately familiar: large penetrating eyes and sculpted lips without lipstick. Her image makes instant rapport with the crowd. She does not rush to speak, but instead appears to be fidgeting with something on an adjacent table. Off-mike, she makes remarks to a technician, then fusses more at her side.

"Jesus," remarks Zoe. "This is all I need. They're grooming her into the patron saint of feminism. I might as well be putting Mother Teresa in the witness box. If Eli is beatified, you know what that makes me? Father Torquemada, the High Commissioner of the Spanish Inquisition."

"Sisters, Brothers, Lovers of Freedom." Eli's voice resonates over the loudspeakers, commanding attention. She pauses, then begins in measured phrases without gestures. "Our cause needs no histrionics. I am reminded of a notation on the sermon of a noted theologian from New York. Beside his typewritten sermon one Sunday, he had penciled in the margin the following words, 'Wave hands, gesticulate wildly, raise voice, bang the pulpit... Logic weak.'"

It takes a few seconds for the vast audience to appreciate the humor. Zoe pivots around to find the man in the sweatsuit fishing through the contents of a duffle bag on the lawn. Meanwhile, chuckling breaks out in concentric circles, infecting row after row of listeners. Eli lets it disseminate until most of the audience is laughing, then raises her left hand in salute. "Friends, we will tolerate no backpeddling on Roe *versus* Wade. The Supreme Court has already ruled in favor of a woman's right to choose. Let Congress take no action to alter this. We, the Women of Choice, are neither for nor against abortion. Some of us favor it and some do not. That's a matter of individual choice that cannot be legislated away. It is inalienable."

Cheers ring out from the rear and are answered by placards waving in front. She takes the opportunity to lift the laptop computer and place it before her on the lectern. She punches a few keys, triggering a computerized caricature of crocodiles with dueling sabers labeled CHOICE and NO CHOICE. Another key stroke changes the picture of the same crocodiles, this time no longer dueling but shaking hands. Now the names are PRO-LIFE and PRO-LIFE. "Both sides are pro-life," she interprets. "But make no mistake. Both camps are not for freedom of choice."

A quick tapping on the laptop keyboard and the projection screens broadcast the words, NO...DON'T.

Zoe is distracted by a hissing noise behind her. The man in sweat clothes, a cohort, and the two mothers with infants in backpacks are fumbling with something. From her position it is impossible to see what. The thought of a bomb rushes through her mind. A gap opens when one of the mothers steps aside. On the ground there is a 14-inch gas tank, its valve hissing. The man in sweats and one mother are inflating what appears to be a large balloon.

"No. Do not underestimate the determination of our NO CHOICE adversaries." Eli's words correspond with words flashing on the screens. "They are zealots who believe in the correctness of their cause with the same conviction that we do. They believe with unshakable faith that they speak in the best interests of society—only they play dirty pool. They want the government to suspend our rights as women, to limit our freedoms, and to dictate our reproductive choices. But we are not bamboozled. And we vow not to let the nation be bamboozled either!"

Applause spreads with electric rapidity. Women are yelling, "Tell 'em, Eli! Tell 'em..."

When Zoe's attention returns to those behind her, their purpose dawns upon her. The balloon they are inflating is not egg-shaped, but sculpted to the form of a fetus with a premature head, spine, and genitals. It enlarges to approximately six feet in height with a three-foot girth. A mother tethers it to the ground. Are they fellow pro-choice advocates, or the enemy? What do they hope to accomplish with this balloon?

The screens around Eli Waller now convey the words, "DO...DO..."

A loud bang from far in the rear startles the crowd. On first impression, it sounds like a bomb or a shot from an assassin's rifle. People strain to observe someone on the platform catch a bullet and drop onto the stage. But there is no bullet. Nor, as best anyone can discern, a bomb. From what transpires next, they become aware that the bang was a signal shot. From forty locations on the Mall, life-size balloons in the form of human fetuses ascend into the air. A concentrated cluster of ten rises directly in front of the speaker's platform. Simultaneously, pro-life enthusiasts howl their mantra, "MURDERED BABIES FLY TO HEAVEN, MURDERED BABIES FLY TO HEAVEN," as a flight of airborne fetuses waft heavenward. Television cameras once targeted on Eli Waller now scan this impressive sight.

Eli's speech is interrupted by heckling. She knows there is no purpose to outshouting her adversaries, even with the benefit of a good sound system. Instead, she leans over and taps something onto the keyboard of her laptop. By the time the balloons rise above the platform level, the capital letter "C" is repeated three times on the projection screens. While she cannot be heard over pro-life chanting, she can communicate by the written word. Pro-choice zealots expect a response.

Beside the first "C," she fills in the word

CORNY

Pro-choice folks applaud. She got it right. Balloons in the form of human fetuses are nothing but cheap, publicity-seeking corn.

Beside the second "C," she fills in the word

CUNNING

Yes, this trick is cunning, designed to disrupt the rally. This stratagem shouldn't fool many for long.

Beside the third "C" comes the word

CHILDISH

True enough. Balloons are the toys of children and those who play with them act like children.

The chanters are stunned by the immediacy of Eli's response. Their mantra falters. Laughter eclipses the recitation. Once the balloons reach an altitude above the crowd and are driven southeast over Anacostia, the chanting dies altogether. For all its energy and planning, the balloon stunt dies shortly after birth. Television cameras leave the balloons and pan the audience for reactions. VIPs on the platform are clapping for victory. Eli Waller doesn't try to speak over the noise. Three words beginning with "C," chosen in the heat of the moment, have won the day.

When Eli finally steps away from the microphone, the rally gives her a hearty ovation. In a theater the audience would have stood, but since the majority of demonstrators were already on their feet that gesture would have been insignificant. Instead, the clapping continues until she returns to the lectern for a second farewell.

Pro-life advocates are dumbfounded. The event they had rehearsed and executed so effectively backfires. Bad timing. The result would have been entirely different had not their enemies controlled the projection screens.

After Eli, the remainder of the rally is an anticlimax. There is not much more for subsequent speakers to say. The audience is restless. Embarrassment stuns pro-life advocates. District of Columbia police now target agitators, threatening to arrest any who disrupt the rally further.

Emma Greer leaves the Mall early in order to beat the crowd to the Metro at the Smithsonian Station. A quarter-hour later, Zoe and Gabby move in the direction of Gabby's car, parked at Zoe's nearby law firm. Folks around them talk of a successful demonstration, telegramming several feminist messages to Congress. Victory over anti-abortion forces is an additional reward. Eli's name is on everybody's lips. She had begun as a television celebrity and, in the course of a single speech, had emerged as a spokesperson for women's causes.

The pair walk but do not talk. Both are lost in thought, pondering the implications of Eli's success. On 13th Street moving north, Gabby plants an arm around Zoe's waist. "It's bad for Noah, isn't it?"

There is a tug-of-war inside Zoe between her professional and personal self. The former is objective and optimistic, the latter subject to wide swings of emotion. "A disaster. How can I undermine testimony of a saint?"

"The trial's a ways off. You'll find a way."

Zoe sighs, more from exhaustion than resignation. "I hope I will."

"I pray Noah wasn't watching," Gabby adds.

"I instructed him to spy out Eli. Thought it might trigger a lost memory to trade on."

"I'm still torn about what I should do. One side of me says it's my duty to help him. The other says don't be a fool and go down with a sinking ship."

In front of Greenwald, Molletz's office building on New York Avenue, Zoe says, "I have a responsibility to Noah and he needs you. But I don't want to see you hurt."

Gabby gives her a squeeze on the upper arm. "There's a heart behind the lawyer's armor. I appreciate your sensitivity. Just do a good job for him. Somehow I'll work things out for myself."

Chapter Eleven

September 16th

Congregation officers tried to hide from Gabby the identity of the second auditioner for Seth Greer's position. But secrets are hard to contain in a synagogue's leaking conduits and she learns the candidate is Rabbi Norman Abramowitz, Ph.D., Senior Rabbi of Congregation Emanuel in Atlanta, a scholarly contributor to numerous Jewish periodicals and one of the most dynamic public speakers in the American rabbinate. From the moment she sat in Seth Greer's empty chair and dreamed about succeeding him, she has been determined to be ruled by political wisdom. An immediate promotion to the senior position had been her best chance. When that didn't happen the odds against her had increased. In a lengthy competition there are too many qualified, ambitious, and talented competitors. The entrance of Norm Abramowitz, holding a doctorate degree from Duke University in bio-ethics, spells doom. For large metropolitan congregations in need of a rabbi, it is a buyer's market.

Sooner or later, she'd have to consider serving under a new boss. Resignation of her junior post is an open possibility. But that would require finding a new position. Not a pleasant thought, especially when there is so much else on her plate. It is easier to handle the daily routine than think of making a career move. Until the charges against her for assault and battery in Queens are resolved, no congregation would seriously give her the time of day.

Noah Zentner is early for his two o'clock appointment at Ohav Shalom. Gabby has been glancing at her watch throughout the morning in anticipation, still she waits a few extra minutes before asking Chuck Browner to send him into her study. Her heartbeat increases. His innocent kiss the night they spent in Baltimore stirs emotion she both fears and welcomes. Noah has breached a defense perimeter between professionalism and friendship, and she doesn't know how to be both a rabbi and a friend at the same time. He has slipped into her private space and, more important, she has done little to stop him. Professional wisdom cautions against letting this man close. Rabbis can afford to be no more intimate with their congregants than physicians with their patients or attorneys with their clients. About that her mind is absolutely clear, yet her instincts tug in the opposite direction.

He is dressed in a navy-blue blazer with a beige Italian shirt and a brightly flowered Liberty necktie, knotted neatly at the collar. It is the last pattern and color one would expect on a condemned man. There is a welcoming smile on his lips, though she spots inflammation around the eyes. Suffering is not something she accepts in others without assuming a small fraction for herself. Her own eyes often moisten when people close to her are crying. She attempts to mask this reaction by reaching across her desk in a formal handshake. Her natural inclination is to sit informally with him on the sofa, but she drops back into her chair, allowing her desk to separate them.

"Eventful time," she opens. "I know you've been through hell, Noah."

His hands fly up to cup his cheeks, permitting long fingers to range down his neck. "I won't deny it. Saw you on television at the rally yesterday. We're all proud of you. You were much better than the other angry windbags. Elisheva is a different matter."

"I'd hoped you didn't see her in action."

"They almost crowned her Queen of Feminism. If I had shown up on the Mall her minions would have hanged me from the nearest tree."

Gabby struggles for something optimistic to say and comes up flat, therefore remains silent, just staring at him.

"Got to tell you, Gabby, I'm losing hope a jury will believe me. Guess I could live with that, but what hurts is silence from my friends. I'm a gregarious guy. But these days my phone doesn't ring. Okay, I say to myself, you'll have to initiate contacts. Some old, old friends call back at odd hours when they know I won't be at the office. They call my apartment during the day when I'm not at home. Many just don't bother. I know what's on their minds. They probably don't believe I raped Elisheva, but they are too politically correct to say so in public. Best just to remain silent and let the jury make the call. If I'm declared innocent, they'll be back. If I lose, they'll never visit me in the slammer."

"I'm sorry; it must seem like a nightmare," she responds, knowing enough about people in the community to confirm his evaluation. Washingtonians enjoy association with winners. Once their associates are perceived as losers they quickly shift loyalties to new prospects.

"That's why seeing you is important to me. I feel quite alone these days. I've asked myself if your kindness is because you're a rabbi, or because you're just a kind person."

This gives her the opening she needs to steer conversation into safer territory. A hearty chuckle precedes her words. "I don't know anyone who is intrinsically kind. My observation is that it's a learned trait. You sort of want to be kind, then practice it over and over until it becomes routine. Being sympathetic is in the rabbi's job description. Nasty or self-serving rabbis don't last very long. Still, I hope there's a decent human being beneath my skin."

"Things are going to get worse, not better. Support for Elisheva is growing. I feel convicted before the jury hears my side of the story."

Gabby laces her fingers into a fist. "Zoe won't let that happen. Her team is too good at what it does."

He lapses into momentary silence, withdrawn into somber thoughts.

"Plans for the weekend?" she says, drawing him back into conversation.

"Weekdays are bad enough; the weekends horrible. Of course, it would be a great weekend if you'd agree to have dinner with me, someplace far away like Middleburg or maybe Frederick where we won't be spotted."

Her initial response sticks in her throat. Why of course she'd love to have dinner with him in some quiet, out-of-the-way place. But what emerges is a more cautious answer. "I'd like to, Noah, but you probably remember Seth went away to write his holiday sermons a few weeks before *Rosh Hashanah*. I've decided to follow his example and this is a perfect time since the congregation is auditioning a candidate for Seth's job. Going to the beach at Rehoboth, then back on Tuesday. God, how I need inspiration! Already written a story for a *Yom Kippur* sermon, but besides that, nothing. Flat nothing."

"Folks will want you to talk about Seth. It's on everybody's mind. Or about me and my troubles."

Caution prevents her from saying what first pops to mind. "I can't speak about you in public. If I testify, the prosecution would make mincemeat of me."

"What about Seth? You've kept inordinately quiet until now."

"We'll see."

He crosses his legs, uncrosses them, and squirms in his chair, toying with an idea he wants to launch but hesitates with uncertainty. After a moment, he throws caution to the wind, saying boldly, "Gabby, let me come to Rehoboth. We could jog together. Or just walk. I know you like both. Nothing would make me feel better than to walk on the shore with you. A calmness comes over me when we talk."

"You know the original name of Rehoboth comes from the Bible," she declares with a didactic uplift of her forefinger. "From Genesis. It means *the wide place*. Chaim Weizmann founded his scientific research institute at Rehovot, Israel. A center for Israeli citrus growing once, but these days I think it's mostly a residential suburb of Tel Aviv."

"I know a good seafood restaurant at Bethany. It specializes in crab, but they also serve a variety of Atlantic fish."

"Last time we tried taking a stroll in Baltimore I lost my composure and fell into a shaking fit."

"That's nothing to be ashamed of. After what happened in Queens, it was an understandable reaction. If you like, we can rent a sailboat. Sailing comes almost as naturally to me as running."

"And how am I going to write my sermons if you interrupt my concentration? I'm telling you as straight as I can. As we speak I've only got one sermon in the can. Besides that, no ideas, no notes, and no themes. I've got to use this weekend for inspiration. The way my schedule is filling up for the next few weeks, there isn't going to be another opportunity."

Noah plunges into silence. The gleam in his eyes disappears and for a moment he turns his head to hide disappointment. "Then have dinners with me, Gabby. You've got to eat. Nobody likes to eat alone in a restaurant. Let me take you to dinner each night. Eat with me, then go back to your work. I promise not to intrude more."

The idea is attractive, but she doesn't wish to let him know how much. "Which night? The candidate for Seth's post is supposed to be here *Erev Shabbat*, which means I've got to skedaddle out before he arrives. Driving to the beach about two o'clock on Friday afternoon."

"How about Friday, Saturday, and Sunday evenings? I'll get a hotel room near the beach and spend the daytime doing paperwork. Might take a jog or two."

"How about Saturday night, Noah? Take me to your fish restaurant in Bethany."

"Agreed on one condition. That you leave Sunday night open. If your work is progressing well, then we can eat together Sunday, too. The decision is up to you. I promise not to be hurt if you're too busy. Agreed?"

Both Gabby's palms strike the desktop with a crack. "Bargaining is in your blood."

"I just need to know where you're staying. I'll come get you Saturday evening, say about six-thirty. Everything's easy at the beach, so dress casually."

She hesitates, fearing a dozen things at once and for a moment is paralyzed. Too much caution. Why can't she react like other women and enjoy a man who invites her to dinner? Does she have to be reserved just because she's a rabbi? Can't she spread her wings and let her spirits soar once in a while?

She opens her electronic organizer and manipulates the stylus. A moment later she has the name and phone number of the Gull's Haven Bed and Breakfast transcribed for him onto a piece of note paper.

At the door to her office, he tries to grasp her arm in a gesture of affection, but she steps back and extends her hand formally. He takes it and holds on far longer than necessary. She should pull back but doesn't. Chuck Browner, whose eyes are fixed on the open doorway, notices their hands together.

As soon as Noah is down the hallway, Chuck stops and studies Gabby with penetrating eyes. It doesn't bother her that she is unable to hide things from him. He never exploits her vulnerabilities.

REHOBOTH BEACH, DELAWARE, SITS ON A PROMONTORY of land that juts into the Atlantic at the mouth of the Delaware River. A narrow spit connects it to a string of sandy white beaches, summer playground for yuppie beachcombers from the mid-Atlantic states. Gull's Haven Bed and Breakfast, operated by a gay couple with a taste for antebellum furniture, is situated on the shore of Rehoboth Bay, adjacent to the Delaware Seashore State Park. It is a quiet hideaway catering to overnighters who shun gaudy seaside motels flanking the boardwalk. Gabby installs herself in a room decorated with candles in glass flutes, antique oak furniture, and a four-poster bed with a cheerfully patterned and colored bedspread. A cedar writing table from the early 1930s is a perfect workstation for her Toshiba laptop. One window commands a view of Rehoboth Bay.

After changing from her synagogue clothes into shorts, a T-shirt, and sneakers, she drives north, stops at a roadside general store and buys a can of Miller Lite. From there, she parks on the shoulder of the road and sets out to walk a sandy beach of feldspar, quartz, and igneous minerals. Afternoon sunbathers have long since abandoned the shore, leaving behind a field of plastic soda bottles and fast-food wrappers. Gone too are the lifeguards who man stations near designated surfing and bathing areas. Further south where the sand gives way to rock, large billboards warn beachcombers against swimming in waters known for their dangerous undertows.

Drinking beer at sunset is a favorite pastime. A jetty, constructed from boulders bulldozed into a hundred-foot long sea wall, provides a fine platform on which to watch gulls flying to their evening rookeries, some moving north and others in the opposite direction. She sits with her back resting against the foundation of a billboard with bold red letters: WARNING DANGEROUS UNDERTOW. It partially screens the setting sun which casts a pale, grayish hue over the ocean. Afternoon sea breeze has slackened and turbulence of the waves is at a minimum. Her eyes rest on a cove of calm water, sheltered from gentle swells by a granite outcrop. The depth and color of this pool inspire her to move onto a flat rock beside it. Were she to ignore the undertow and enter the inviting water for a swim, this would be the place. She is not wearing a swimsuit and has no intention of wrestling potentially dangerous currents. A prudent compromise comes to mind. She takes off her shoes and dangles her feet in the refreshing salt water. Next, she introduces her hands to the wrist, inviting a cooling sensation to pulse through her limbs. As twilight turns into night the smell of the ocean is pungent, damp, and sweet. Sabbath peace now rests upon the beach like a comforting blanket. It is here that she drinks her can of beer, allowing the liquid to tickle down her throat.

For her *Shabbat* meal, she later buys a cup of low-fat lemon yogurt, three oversized high-fat chocolate-chip cookies, and a can of Diet Coke. Back at her room in the Gull's Haven, she heats the ends of two candles and attaches them to a paper plate, then from the bathroom retrieves a glass for her Coke. Observing *Shabbat* rituals sometimes requires ingenuity. She repeats the blessing over the *Shabbat* candles and lights them, drawing their light into her eyes with open fingers. Next, she apologizes to God for substituting Coke for kosher wine and recites a *b'racha* for God's bounty. Having made the first concession, it is easy to substitute the chocolate chip cookies for the traditional *challah*. The candles produce a faint warmth against her cheeks.

Having concluded a few *Shabbat* rituals, she must face her laptop computer and begin jotting down sermon ideas. Her computer screen fills with notes in outline form. They wouldn't mean much to others, but they provide her a measure of security. She doesn't really know where she's going with these sermons, yet but now has some sense of direction. It is already decided what to do on *Yom Kippur* morning—a few touches to her story titled *Redemption* and it is ready to go.

After eleven, her eyes begin to water from fatigue. From the veranda, she views the quiet inlet water of Rehoboth Bay. Above, the sky is blanketed with starlight dominated by a three-quarter full gibbous moon. Insects chirp from the shore of a shallow lagoon below her window.

Her sleep that evening is sound but awakened in the early hours of the morning by thoughts of her story *Redemption*. She sits up and turns on the light. Water is still lapping on the small beach under her window, but at this late hour insects have settled into their world of silence. She opens the laptop and boots up, then double-clicks with the mouse on a file labeled STORY. A title followed by text materializes on the screen.

Redemption
By Rabbi Gabrielle Lewyn
For Delivery on *Yom Kippur* Morning. Ohav Shalom.

I... owe... my...life... to Heraclitus. You, friends at Ohav Shalom, may say to yourselves, so what? I can hear some of you mutter, who cares? And when you get off your pedestals, you'll probably confess you don't know who Heraclitus is in the first place. My hero, Heraclitus, was a philosopher who lived and wrote before Socrates in the Golden Age of Greece. He taught that the universe is in constant flux, such that no man can step into the same river twice, for each time his toe touches the water, the river is born anew.

Now you ask, how could such a philosopher save my life? The answer is complex and I must draw upon your indulgence. You see, I am not the person I was once. I could not be that person who, so to say, inhabited the body which, some fifty years ago, housed my soul. Like the river into which my savior Heraclitus wades, I, too, am made anew. And thank God for that!

Let me introduce myself. My name is H. Henry Watt, spelled with two Ts. Everybody drops the initial of my given name.

In an earlier portion of my life, a long time ago now, I was known as *Oberleutnant* Erich Steinmatz.

My occupation before retirement: Mechanical Engineer.

My occupation as a young man: *Oberleutnant, Waffen SS. Einsatzgruppen*, Special Services, Army of the Third German Reich.

You must understand that I was fortunate or, perhaps, smart. For when the Wehrmacht began losing the war, I made preparations. I could have been captured, tried, and certainly convicted of heinous crimes against humanity. Had I been arraigned at the end of the war justice would have prevailed and I would not be here this morning. But fortunately in my case, justice was on holiday.

Let me ask a question, and please answer only to yourselves. Had you been young and patriotic and gullible and willing to follow the leaders of your nation, and had you mistakenly believed you were functioning for your own people's welfare, and had you also committed shameful crimes against Jews, then managed by virtue of your wits to elude Allied authorities hunting down war criminals —would you have *voluntarily* turned yourself in and faced being hanged?

Now turn to the person seated next to you, look him or her straight in the eyes and say, "Why of course I would." That person will look back and see if not a fool then certainly a liar.

So ask me, "Henry Watt, did you know about the butchery in Eastern Europe?"

I'll answer that on one condition, that you put that question to the *Oberleutnant* Steinmatz, not to the civilian Henry Watt. Like the river into which Heraclitus dipped his toe, Henry Watt is reborn. Erich Steinmatz is long since gone.

If you accept my condition I can tell you about Steinmatz. Of course he knew about the savagery.

"And you participated in it?" you demand.

I beg your pardon. Not me. The man before you did nothing and condoned nothing. Steinmatz, on the other hand, had a villainous history. In Poland, he helped organize deportation from scores of Jewish villages. Many he deported died en route to the East. Others worked on the roads and died from cold, hunger, or disease.

In Hungary, he established temporary internment camps.

In Czechoslovakia, ahhh, Czechoslovakia—there he participated in far lesser crimes. His job was to collect Torah scrolls and other holy books from Jews sent to the death camps. After all, they had no further use for them.

High-ranking officers in the SS planned to sell them and pocket the proceeds. Josef Goebbels had a different idea—to put these scrolls in a museum dedicated to the people his *Oberleutnant* Erich Steinmatz was determined to liquidate. Before its construction they dubbed it *The Museum of an Extinct People*.

Once the war was lost, Steinmatz decided to refashion his life and perhaps to restore something of value to the world he desecrated.

On this day of *Yom Kippur*, Jews read from the Book of Deuteronomy, which challenges them to choose life and live. You see, I know your Torah because I study it. I listen to it weekly as it is read in synagogues all over the United States.

By this time, you are incredulous. Why would a man guilty of the worst crimes in history listen to the sacred Torah?

Once again, you have forgotten. I am not Steinmatz.

I know what you're thinking. This man before us is weaseling out of criminal responsibility. We know casuistry when we hear it. First, he deifies Heraclitus, then excuses his sins by distancing himself from them. He claims to be trans-formed only because anti-Semitism is now thoroughly dis-credited.

I am not here to trick you. I agree that Steinmatz is guilty. His memory is shameful. I have the power to transform myself, but I cannot blot out the memory. I drag it like an iron ball chained to my leg. I may rationalize, but still feel the need for punishment.

We both detest Steinmatz. But Henry Watt is another matter. I cannot expect you to admire him, though I believe him to be a gentleman who makes weekly contrition for the foul deeds of his ghost.

I visit synagogues every week, here in the States, in Canada, and in Great Britain. But not just any synagogues. Carefully selected ones. They're usually small congregations, relatively remote. And with young families.

Can you guess how I make this selection?

I have a list from the Westminster Synagogue in London, whose rabbi purchased a cache of Czech Torahs in 1947 —the very same scrolls originally stolen by Erich Steinmatz in 1944. The Museum of an Extinct People was never built. The Torahs outlived the Nazis who stole them. They were eventually distributed to infant congregations so that Jewish life outside Israel might be reborn from the ashes of extinction.

Now that I'm retired I have time for travel. I go to these synagogues and listen to the *Baal Korah* or the rabbi read from these scrolls. It's best to hear a young man or woman stand up to read his Bar or her Bat Mitzvah portions from one of the Steinmatz Torahs. When young Jews read from these precious scrolls they punish Erich Steinmatz and his cohorts. The Nazis are dead and disdained, while the people they tried to destroy are alive and respected. Steinmatz and his puny band of tin soldiers had planned that no young Jews would ever read these Torahs again. But now they do.

What must a man like Steinmatz think when he hears your youth read a Galician scroll from the whirlwind of the Holocaust? Your children stand tall with the symbol of Jewish continuity, forging bonds with Abraham, Moses, Maimonides, Judah ha-Levi. They honor and love their parents.

Erich Steinmatz's children, in contrast, have a past they are ashamed to recall. They have parents, but none they can respect. Their nation is moored in disgrace and will be for decades to come.

Your Holy Book states that the sins of the parents descend upon their children. I promise you, they do.

And that is why I come to Ohav Shalom this morning. Your congregation is on my list. Your children make music when they read from that small holocaust scroll. Number sixty-three on the Westminster list. For Erich Steinmatz their young voices burn and scratch. For Henry Watt they gather the angels of heaven.

And where there is music, forgiveness is not distant.

I know there are some who think this punishment too lenient. They would have both me and Steinmatz imprisoned or executed. Though their vengeance is justified, they will not receive satisfaction.

Your young testify to Steinmatz's transgression and foolishness.

Perhaps you now understand why I need Heraclitus. I must believe that as the river changes so does the man. Only in a physical sense am I the same person who once drew innocent Jewish blood. I cannot restore life or property. The psychological statute of limitations has elapsed. There was a period when the man and his deeds were one. After so many years that is no longer true.

Penance renews me.

Is this not promised by the Almighty on *Yom Kippur*? Is not a man who makes contrition welcome at the portals of Heaven? Is it not written in your Holy Book that any man may redress his sins and remold himself?

You teach that on *Yom Kippur* a man or woman may examine his deeds and repent. Atonement unifies him with God. Is he who steps into the river not cleansed by it? Is that river not renewed day by day, minute by minute?

Let me pose one last question. Are the Gates of Forgiveness open to the petty sinner and closed to the gross sinner?

In your tradition, the Gates of Divine Pardon remain open until sundown on this Holy Day.

Will your god refuse forgiveness to Henry Watt, and, if so, how about to a human being as sinful as Erich Steinmatz?

End

Gabby remains silent before her computer, her eyes downcast on the table where the remains of her simple *Shabbat* candles rest in a heap of unconsumed white wax. The anomalies of forgiveness weigh upon her. Bizarre as it is, she envies Henry Watt who nurtures confidence in the river of Heraclitus. Wouldn't her congregants enjoy cleansing themselves in the river and stepping out on the other side reborn? And isn't the key to being forgiven the ability to forgive?

By the time she has scribbled down more notes, it is 4:30 in the morning. A deep, satisfying fatigue settles in. She is once again asleep, this time without dreaming.

MORNING SUNLIGHT STREAMING THROUGH THE thin curtains into her room awakens her at 9:10. Before breakfast, she recites the morning *Shema* from the *Shabbat* liturgy and follows it with seven blessings of the *Amidah*. Her obligation completed in the shortest time, she finds her mind ranging over thoughts from the early hours of the morning. The Hebrew concept of *Teshuvah*, Return to the Maker, obsesses her. There is a natural inclination to resist Henry Watt's pleas for forgiveness. Yet there is also a need to bury grievances and begin afresh.

After breakfast, she has difficulty concentrating on her sermons. She finds herself glancing at her watch and wishing away the hours until Noah's arrival. Lack of sleep makes her groggy. A nap might be in order but that indulgence she will not grant. As a substitute she plans an easy jog on the beach.

IN LATE AFTERNOON, SHE SHOWERS AND PREPARES herself for Noah's arrival. Her upper eyelids receive extra eyeshadow. A modest tinge of lipstick colors her lips. His instructions were to dress casually and that translates into freshly pressed khaki shorts which show the flatness of her stomach and expose her thighs and calves. They are a bit tight, but these days it is fashionable to display the form of one's rump if not fleshy, which hers certainly isn't. A white tennis blouse provides an attractive profile.

When Noah arrives on the half-hour as scheduled, he comments on her appearance. She is glad he notices. He has let his beard grow and wears a pair of tinted glasses as disguise. Photographs that appear in the media show him clean-shaven, usually in a business suit and tie.

THE TERRAPIN RESTAURANT IN BETHANY CATERS TO vacationers during the warm weather season and a crowd of local drinkers and smokers after Labor Day. Clusters of young people stand at the bar sipping ale from frosted steins. There is a familiarity among the patrons who carry on conversations from the bar to the tables, adding decibels to the noisy atmosphere.

Their presence in a such a public place unnerves Gabby, who worries they will be noticed in each other's company. She confesses, "I try not to worry about everything, but it's in the genes. A leopard can't change its spots, can it?"

"I like your spots just where they are," he replies. "Don't change a single one. And don't let any man attempt to. Worrying doesn't bother me. I've got a few of those genes myself. You heard the story of the *nebbish* who is walking on Dissengoff Street in Tel Aviv with one shoulder slumped. His friend asks him what's wrong with it. 'Nothing really,' he replies, 'but that's just where everybody pounds my shoulder telling me not to worry.'"

She issues a compulsory laugh. On first blush the joke isn't funny, but upon reflection, it grows. She's glad Noah can find mirth in the unpleasant events around him. That's worth encouraging, even though she isn't by nature very funny.

"And are you feeling like that Israeli *nebbish*?" she asks.

"Absolutely. Only my problem is more serious than a bad shoulder. Bad luck, bad timing, and bad choice of women to hit on."

"No quarrel with that." There is a mellow, nonjudgmental ring in her voice as she trains her eyes on his. "From what I know about you, Noah, what you did on the Chesapeake seems out of character. You might not want to talk about this, but I'm curious. Were you drinking?"

His head jerks upward in a sudden jolt. "I do want to talk about it. I think you're somebody who wants to understand. Yes, I was drinking. Everybody was. It was damnably hot. Beer and wine. No booze. But I wasn't drunk. I thought about making that case to the jury, but nobody aboard would substantiate it. They know I'm a one-perhaps-two beer man. Because of the heat, that afternoon and evening I consumed three in total. Getting *shicker* isn't my *shtick*. Everybody knows I wasn't intoxicated. Nor was anybody else."

The disclosure is followed by a long silence, broken when Gabby asks, "What was it about Eli that attracted you?"

"I'm embarrassed to tell you, just about nothing. Absolutely nothing more than male lust for conquest. Despite what she claims, she initiated the sex, not me. Her word is gold and mine isn't. Had I my wits about me, I would have rejected her advances. Clearly, I didn't. The irony is I knew she wasn't the least bit interested in me. We were almost strangers. She wanted Pyramid's business. My father has long been an advocate of securitizing our debt and taking Pyramid public. For him, it was not a matter of what to do but how to do it. Elisheva's firm is impressive. Their people are pros who have been successful in the past. Going public is okay for my dad because he'll take his money and retire. But I'll have to manage a public company and become accountable to the shareholders and the stock market. Control freaks like me don't do well in large corporations. Chances are the shareholders will throw me out in a year or two. Elisheva knew I was her main resistance at Pyramid. The account meant millions. Perhaps a million to her personally. She was using sex to get me on board."

"Why didn't you say no?"

He pauses to phrase a response and she reads the pain on his face. "How many red-blooded males would reject someone like her? She's a contemporary Helen of Troy and just as dangerous."

"Sex and danger seem to go hand in glove. Anger and sex are also close companions. I don't see you as an average male on the hunt."

"I'm not. But there were troubles with Morgan. Troubles over money, family and, yes, sex."

"The usual trio. From the outside, you guys looked like an ideal couple. Appearances deceive, don't they?"

A college-age redheaded waitress working her way through a summer on the beach deposits two Molson Goldens and two heavy frosted glasses on their table and, in haste to deliver additional drinks from her tray, moves off without pouring. Gabby is quick to pour the first beer into Noah's glass. "Morgan is so attractive. I would have thought..."

"Assumptions often prove wrong. Most of my mistakes occur because I've made a bad assumption along the line. When people decide to marry they have only rudimentary knowledge of their mates. Morgan caught me by surprise. On the surface she's an attractive, intelligent, rather charming individual. But below, she's haunted by a dark, troubled spirit. Many of her hours are spent in meditation—twice during the day and again for an extended period at night. I could have tolerated her special interests, but not when we made love, if that's what one would call it. It took me a long time to understand that she was trying to couple with some universal spirit. She wanted to make love with God, not with me. Maybe you understand these things because you're a rabbi. Morgan had little or no use for me in bed, except to help her fuse with a deity."

Gabby is intrigued. "She shared her aims with you?"

"Not at first. But you'd have to be blind not to pick up the signals. You know she edits for Seth. She was obsessed with his ideas. On the one hand, she's very practical and planned to make a bundle publishing his works for popular consumption. But on the other, she's a dreamer, consumed by weird ideas. When we talked, which wasn't often, she'd tell how big the market is for religious books. Seth's ideas were more than potentially good copy. They were a crusade. She saw him as a modern-day prophet and herself as a contemporary Mary Baker Eddy, packaging his ideas."

Gabby had long suspected Seth's mysticism, but never any pretensions to prophecy. Yes, he dabbled in Kaballah, but no, he didn't live the life of a recluse or ascetic. She knew of his collaboration with Morgan on the mystic doctrine of *Tzimzum*, spiritual contraction, but never believed it had significant commercial potential. "You don't have to go into the personal details," she says.

"I don't mind. The story is so bizarre no one is likely to understand it but you," Noah insists. "Morgan dropped out of conjugal life with me. I think the last time she used my name in bed was a week after our wedding. From then on she found other names. Not of other men, but incantations, names from the Kabbalah. Some were acronyms. At first, it was kind of cute and chummy. I tolerated it as a passing religious fad. But over time I came to understand she wasn't making love to me at all. She looked at me as a facilitator, not a lover. I knew people do this kind of thing through prayer, but sex was something new. My amusement turned to bitterness."

Gabby is incredulous and for several seconds doesn't have a response. "That must have hurt a lot."

"More than you can know. It's one thing to be jilted for another fellow, quite another for God. Unfair competition, don't you think?"

The waitress finally gets around to bringing menus. Noah runs his eyes down one side without pausing to read closely. Gabby does likewise.

"Hungry?" he asks.

"Not particularly. You've stolen my appetite. I simply don't understand."

"No appetite myself. How about taking a walk and coming back later?"

That's precisely what she wants. They delay long enough to slosh down what is left of their beers. The waitress is too busy to take an order for dinner and when she returns, she finds her customers have gone, leaving behind a twenty-dollar bill for the drinks and tip.

After parking Noah's car, they head to the beach, leaving their shoes behind to walk barefoot on the sand. The sea is black and the surf is up. The first stars of the evening begin to poke through a broken bank of wind swept clouds. Venus, the sun planet, is the most luminous spot above them. Gabby remarks that the moon she saw the previous evening will soon rise from the horizon.

Their feet spike holes in the soft sand near the receding surf. Not a word passes between them. Gabby wrestles with what he has told her, searching through her understanding of the Kabbalah for references to sexual union with the deity. She knows there is a strong association between fertility and religious experience. Statues of ancient gods often depict enlarged or exaggerated genitalia. In biblical times their forefathers were obsessed with the need to reproduce and, knowing little of reproductive physiology, they tended to deify forces which led to offspring. Sexual union between male and female imitates divine creation. She supposes it requires only a small mental jump to bypass one father to have intercourse with another.

They head south along the beach, facing a warm sea breeze saturated with the ocean salts. Noah's hand slips over hers and gently squeezes. Instinct tells her to pull away. He is probably going to prison. An eight-year romance with Tim went nowhere and at her age she cannot afford another dead-end affair. Women in their thirties are smart but foolish. Fear of spending their lives alone and childless propels them into unhealthy relationships. Noah has the attributes of a fine man but one without a future. Instead of withdrawing her hand, her fingers fold tightly into his, though not without a measure of self-pity. Where might she meet eligible men if not through her profession? At the Tuesday Evening Tennis Club? Or in a saloon watching demolition derbies on a TV set mounted over the bar?

"Did you talk with Seth about Morgan's obsession?" she asks Noah, diverting attention from her conflict.

He is momentarily distracted and does not answer until she repeats the question. "Of course. Said he was interested in the metaphysics of having sex with God. Quoted several references from the Kaballah. Not the mystic thought I've read about, but the fringes, you understand. Esoteric experiences. He mentioned a splinter group in the wake of Shabbati Zwi. Seventeenth century, I think. Cited a sect called Domneh in Turkey or Syria that practiced sex as a nexus with God. Never heard of such people before."

"They're almost off the radar screen, a mere fringe group that eventually died out. Did he give any practical advice?"

Noah chuckles. "Seth? You know him. He's not the type to give advice. Thinks it's in bad taste. Believes with a passion that people shouldn't tell others what to do. To him, folks learn not by advice, but from trial and error."

"Sounds like the Seth Greer who trained me. He let me fall on my face more than I like to admit. When I screwed up he just wrote it off as an educational expense. One of the few people in this world who truly believe in the proposition live and let live. Lots of people say they do, but you know they don't. Seth does. Once he told me the biggest failure of modern parents is when they won't let their children stumble."

"I guess he was right; still, I was in trouble and wanted insight he refused to give."

"Hard to imagine he couldn't offer you anything more substantial than a reference to outcasts of the Domneh sect."

"He made jokes. Can you believe it? Jokes!"

"His recipe for difficult subjects. I'd love to possess his armor."

Neither Gabby nor Noah notices that waves pounding the beach have suddenly grown. They are lost in conversation and do not pay attention to their cyclical nature. Every sixth or seventh wave seems to overwhelm the previous emissaries. As a medium-sized one assaults the shore, they are forced to scamper through the sand to higher ground. Their hands clamp together for support and when they have beaten the wave up the beach, they laugh. When their laughter recedes they are not looking at the ocean, but at each other. For a few moments there is nothing to say. Their proximity speaks words they do not wish to share.

"I've wanted to ask a question, Gabby, but I'm afraid of the answer so I've postponed."

"Ask. I promise not to take offense."

"Don't know exactly how to put this."

"Put it any way you want. Why stand on formality?"

"Are you involved with another man?"

She pushes back, jerks her head to regard the ocean, then jerks it back to look at him. "You know how to put it direct, don't you?"

"And you promised not to be offended."

"I had a relationship until quite recently," she says. "But I'm a free agent these days." She expects him to say something but he doesn't. Eventually, she asks, "Starting to feel hungry?"

He ignores the change of subject. "You know what I wish? I wish like hell that I could be in your life. I know it's impossible. Especially now. But if I had only possessed the good sense to look at you as somebody other than Seth's junior colleague, I wouldn't be in this pickle. Of course, I was as blind then as I was on the *Dame Cynthia*. We'd be a great team, you know. We're both interested in sports. Hell, I could even learn to like demolition derbies."

She kisses him affectionately twice on the neck but carefully stays away from his lips. Next, she gives him a full-body squeeze, feeling the curvature of his body against hers. "I'd like that too, Noah. Very much. But I won't let it happen, at least not now. I can't afford it. You can't either. But I want you to know I'm flattered. Now let's continue walking. There's a jetty a ways down the beach where we can sit." She turns, throws her hand forward for him to catch, then drags him towards the water's edge. A desire to stretch her legs and run suddenly possesses her. Without warning, she plunges forth, leaving him behind. In an instant, he bolts after her. When he catches up, she accelerates into a sprint. They find themselves racing in soft sand, plowing through a film of surging surf. They are hurling themselves along the shore, running with everything they have and screaming encouragement to each other. Their lungs are gasping for air to fuel the race.

Eventually, Noah seizes Gabby's arm to slow her. She resists but slowly decelerates until they resume a walking pace through shallow water. When they arrive at the jetty discovered the previous night, she climbs onto the concrete and heads along the flat surface, past the warning sign. Pebbles transported by sea waves to the jetty cut into her toes, forcing her to creep forward. At the eddying pool, she crouches amid weathered rocks preparing to dangle her feet into the water. Both are still winded from the race.

"Not afraid of sharks?" he asks while assuming a position beside her.

"Should I be?" she asks, unfastening her grandmother's wristwatch and cautiously placing in on a flat rock nearby. "I learned a trick of immersing my wrists into the water. It cools one off without getting the whole body wet."

"How about man-eating eels? Not afraid of them either?"

She is repositioning herself to immerse her hands in the water when her elbow taps the wristwatch. It slides horizontally until hitting another rock, then drops into a dark crevice out of sight.

"Shit!" she barks, scrambling into position above the hole. Moonlight fails to penetrate the darkness below. "It was my grandmother's. She gave it to my mother when she left Germany. My most valuable possession!"

Noah crouches over the opening and peers into the darkness.

"I hope you were joking about eels," she says when it becomes clear she must plunge her arm into the crevice to grope for the watch with her fingers. Below are barnacles and slippery tidal vegetation, but no watch. After a few minutes, she withdraws. Noah's long arms are no more successful.

Her head falls on his shoulder and her arms wrap around him. Moisture from tears transfer to his neck. "I'm so careless."

"You're human like the rest of us. And it isn't lost yet. We can come back in the early morning. We're bound to see it in the sunlight."

"What about the tide?"

"It's flooding now. By early morning it will be ebbing. If it's not in the water now, it will probably be okay. Does it work?"

"You bet it does. I've spent a king's ransom with a watchmaker in New York."

They make additional efforts to retrieve the watch and fail. When Noah turns to Gabby he finds her standing on the highest point of the jetty, shaking. He steps close to hold her against his body and kisses her on the temple, just below the hairline.

"You already know I shake when afraid. I also tremble when upset."

He is slow to respond. Eventually he says, "Well, you can shake with me any old time you want."

GABBY'S SLEEP THAT NIGHT AT GULL'S HAVEN IS FITful. She falls asleep, awakens, dozes, and awakens again. Thoughts about the loss of her grandmother's watch will not grant her rest. En route back from the bathroom, she passes before the window and gazes over the lagoon now bathed in bright moonlight. It occurs to her that armed with a flashlight she might return to the jetty and search for the watch before significant tidal action. Most hotel rooms on the Delaware coast are equipped with flashlights in the event of power blackout. She doesn't recall seeing one but eventually discovers a rubber-handled flashlight on the closet shelf. Fortunately its batteries are fresh enough to provide a modest beam.

At two o'clock in the morning, the concave disk of the moon is high overhead, casting a pale luminescence on the water. The moon provides enough light to navigate the deserted beach. She is impressed how sounds of the ocean change after sundown. Gone are the squawking gulls and the grind of motorboats. The lapping of waves on the shore fills the silence.

The air is thick with humidity, fanned by a warm breeze from the ocean. Her body is damp with a mixture of moist air and perspiration. Earlier in the evening she and Noah ran in bare feet; now she is better equipped in sneakers.

Rocks supporting the jetty appear different in the moonlight. It's imperative to identify the rock on which she originally laid the wristwatch, then the crevice into which it fell. None of the surroundings are immediately familiar. Perhaps her memory is playing tricks. She taxes her recollection. Sweat builds on the nape of her neck and she is aware that she's trembling. Nothing can be achieved in a state of panic. To succeed she must be calm and methodical. But how is that possible when sweat streams down her brow and her muscles quiver?

She kneels to inspect a crevice where the watch might have dropped. The flashlight beam penetrates beyond her arm's reach into the cavity. That's promising, for she can inspect almost everything above the water line. The tiny grotto below cannot possibly house what she's looking for. To fall there the watch would have to leap several feet from where she and Noah crouched. A second grotto produces nothing, as does a third and fourth. As she acknowledges the loss, her mood plummets. Time to drown her sorrow in sleep at Gull's Haven. She stands upright and begins climbing back to the level surface above, but stops to consider a final inspection and make absolutely certain nothing has been overlooked. The thought of not seeing the treasured watch on her wrist drives her to renew the search.

In the second fissure her beam produces a reflecting glitter. She leans into the grotto for a better look and discovers the gold buckle strap of her watch. No wonder she missed it on earlier inspections. Her eyes were searching for a rather large sextagonal wristwatch, not a small, golden buckle. The watch itself had slipped out of sight, buried in a bed of seaweed. She scrapes her shins while maneuvering into the cavern to snatch it. Her heart pounds as her fingertips extend downward. There will be a single opportunity. If she is unable to transfer it from her fingertips to her palm, the watch is likely to fall into water below and be lost forever. A slight wiggle puts her torso into an improved position. She has difficulty focusing the flashlight beam on the right spot. Her arm sinks as deep as possible into the cavity. Fingers tremble as they cautiously touch the buckle then gently urge it upward. "Careful now. Careful...," she instructs herself, "slowly...very slow..." The watch snags momentarily on a cluster of barnacles then slips free. With great care she circles her thumb around the strap and lifts it into the bed of her palm.

Her hand is trembling when she brings the timepiece before her eyes for inspection. She is certain it will now have to be returned to her watchmaker for repair. Being old, it is neither waterproof nor water resistant and is usually stopped by a minute trace of moisture. That the mechanism is still ticking despite the moisture and humidity she interprets as nothing short of a miracle.

She sits down to control her nerves and realizes that she is drenched with sweat. Though she did not come prepared for a swim, water in the tranquil backwash suddenly looks inviting. Her figure is complemented by a bikini, though her sense of dignity would never let herself be seen in one. There are no jokes about women rabbis in bikinis simply because no one has imagined that possibility. When swimming in public she wears a one-piece suit so conservative it covers her hips and thighs. Unfortunately, she has left her one-piece at the Gull's Haven. For a moment, she studies the sign above her with large block letters: UNDERTOW.

When her nervous shaking slows, she is enveloped by a sense of well-being. As a reward, she decides on a quick dip into the protected backwash. What danger of undertow could there be if she swims very close to the jetty? It is 2:37 a.m.; the beach is dark and deserted. What creature needs a bathing suit when God created men and women without clothes? She strips all her clothing and advances cautiously into the water.

It is not true that she is more buoyant without a swimsuit but she does experience an exhilarating freedom. The current is negligible, providing confidence that there is nothing to fear from an undertow. Her strokes are well-grooved and powerful, propelling her away from the jetty into open water. Moonlight reflects off the water surface with a surrealistic glow. Within a few seconds she can no longer tell whether she is a few feet or many fathoms from land. The sound of waves pounding the beach provide her rough bearings. Time to turn back.

Cool, salty water elevates her spirits. She splashes in child-like play, rolling onto her back and exposing her breasts to the Man in the Moon. Is he aroused? Or does he consider her display indecent? She laughs and awkwardly swallows sea water, coughing until it can clear the breathing tubes. She vows not to make the same mistake again and returns to her play, kicking her feet above the surface and watching the splash rejoin the water. Next, hands fly over her head in a classic backstroke. Never has swimming been so free and pleasurable.

Mindful of the warning against undertows, she avoids moving

into deeper water and heads back in the direction of the jetty. She has never been one to believe in subsurface currents hauling unwary swimmers to their deaths. But unpredictable tidal action is quite another thing.

While she makes a right turn toward the beach, a flash of light catches the corner of her eye. At first she believes it is on the beach proper but soon determines it to be on the water. It does not repeat itself for several seconds, then appears to circle and disappear. On the third occasion, she sees a cone of light scanning the water. It originates from the jetty, which means that someone is near her clothing and valuables. Maybe beach people or homeless vagabonds or perhaps just kids up to no good. The thought of having another conflict with juvenile delinquents is most unappealing. Though she is at a disadvantage without her clothes, she. paddles closer.

In the moonlight it is possible to discern the figure of a man. During her approach, no further light shines from the jetty, then suddenly it appears as though the possessor were inspecting the rocks. The beam flashes in front of the large UNDERTOW warning. It is only a few feet from her belongings. Suddenly, the beam scans the water again.

"Gabby? GABBY? Are you out there? It's Noah. Talk to me, honey. Where are you? The current's dangerous. Talk to me, honey!" The light swings around in a loop and crosses the water. She sees it move along the jetty as he seems to be running to give greater scope to his search. "Talk to me, honey!"

She calls from the water, relieved that her grandmother's watch will remain in her possession, yet aware that she is naked and in no condition to leave the water. "Come in Rangoon! Come in Rangoon! Father Neptune here."

The flashlight streaks over the water in the direction of her voice. "You all right? I saw your clothes. The undertow's treacherous."

"Don't worry. Never had such a good time. What the hell you're doing here at this hour?"

"Looking for your watch. I wanted to surprise you in the morning. Brought this flashlight from the motel, but I'm confused as to where it fell. "

"Already found it, Noah. It's in the sock stuffed into my sneakers. Thanks for your thoughtfulness. You're an angel."

"I'd rather be a hero. How's the water?"

"Wet and wonderful. Want to come in?"

"No swimsuit."

"I'm in my birthday suit. If you're not shy, try skinny-dipping."

This is the last thing Noah expects. It's good he had few expectations because if he had planned to swim at this place and at this hour, he would have brought a suit.

And that wouldn't have been half as much fun as skinny-dipping with Gabrielle Lewyn.

September 21st

Eleanor Weissborg called Chuck Browner, asking that Rabbi Lewyn meet with her in the Ohav Shalom chapel, not in the rabbinical study. It is an easy request to honor and gives Gabby a chance to stretch her legs. She is surprised Eleanor should carry through with the pledge given at Ellen and Douglas Weil's wedding and phone for an appointment. People make social promises at life-cycle events, never fully intending to fulfill them. But Eleanor had called the next day.

The rich rust color of the carpet merges almost perfectly with the chapel's polished rosewood walls, offset with stained glass. Large wrought-iron chandeliers hang from the domed ceiling. Recessed spotlights shine through them, casting the shadow of a seven-candle candelabra on the carpet. The chapel is open daily for prayer meditation, but few congregants avail themselves of the opportunity.

Gabby pauses in the small foyer, gazing into the sanctuary. The lights are dimmed to conserve electricity. The pews are empty except for Eleanor's solitary figure huddling in the third row on the left side, folded into itself. Her head is low into the breastbone, but her shoulders ramrod stiff. The carpet absorbs the sound of Gabby's feet as she approaches, fearful of interrupting her privacy. So silently does she approach that only when she drops into the pew does Eleanor take notice.

Initiating conversation is not Gabby's style. She is inclined to wait for the other person to speak first. The long interval of silence is broken by Eleanor's sniffles. Gabby notes that occasionally Eleanor's hand will rise to her cheeks. When she spots a crumpled handkerchief she understands that Eleanor has been drying tears. All the more important not to interrupt.

For a moment, she closes her own eyes and lets herself mentally replay what happened with Noah at the beach. When Tim walked out on her, she believed it would be impossible to replicate her feelings for him. A broken heart upset the hormonal balance of chemicals in her body. "Humpty-Dumpty had a great fall," she had repeated as though a mantra, thinking how her emotional caring for someone could never be restored. But to her utter amazement, she has begun to feel healing inside. When she and Noah emerged naked from the ocean she discovered an erotic impulse in her loins. It had been weeks since her body had felt any secretion of the hormone oxytocin. Her appetitie improved immediately. The thought of telling Tim about Noah cannot be dismissed. She wants him to know that her wounded heart is beginning to heal. But calling him is unwise. The upcoming trial makes absolutely taboo any mention of a nonprofessional friendship with Noah.

"This is a special place," Gabby breaks her rule of thumb and finally whispers to Eleanor. "I can almost feel the divine presence here."

"The *Shechinah*." Eleanor draws her eyes onto Gabby. "The indwelling presence of God. That's what Seth Greer called it. He said it was possible for one to *feel* the *Shechinah.*"

"He didn't make a joke of it, did he?'

"Absolutely not. I wanted to talk with you here rather than in your study. I sat in this pew for a special reason. It was right at this spot that Seth Greer and I made love three times. And they were good, too. The best in some ways; the worst in others. Memories now haunt me."

"It's over and past, Eleanor," Gabby says, still in a whisper. "I expect you're not the same woman today you were then. Mistakes were made. Rabbi Greer taught me that we grow from our errors, not our successes. In love and war, the vanquished always learn more than the victors."

"It's not that simple, Rabbi Lewyn. I want to tell you because I can't tell anyone else, certainly not my children or friends. The kids hardly know Rabbi Greer and they're into a different mindset. If I told them, they'd only yawn and change the subject. My women friends would offer saccharine. I think you can understand what others can't or don't care to."

"I can try," Gabby smiles, nodding her head.

"I don't believe having sex is a sin. God made us sexual creatures. If He didn't want us to screw once in a while, He shouldn't have given us urges to do it. But what I did went beyond normal sex, even with a married man. I don't believe I ruined Rabbi Greer's marriage. Everyone in the congregation knew it was in deep trouble well before I started seeing him. I might have contributed to its demise, but not alone. We all know there were other women involved. But I did something far worse. I helped ruin his career. And that's not something he can easily rebuild."

A host of comforting responses come to Gabby's mind, but providing comfort at such a moment is not helpful. Eleanor's remorse will not be healed by adding a soothing balm. "What makes you think you scuttled his career?" she eventually asks.

"When I learned he was screwing other women, I thought he had taken advantage of me. I was as furious as a wife with a cheating husband. I lashed out. My letter to the congregational Board implied that Seth had seduced me for his own enjoyment. It didn't say this in so many words but strongly suggested it. And I knew the Board would jump to that conclusion, even if I didn't spell it out."

"But you did have sex with him, didn't you?"

Eleanor rotates in the pew so that the stained glass windows crown her head like a diadem. "Yes. But he didn't seduce me in the normal way. I came to him for help. Menopause, you will learn soon enough, is the pits. I felt myself drying up, both inside and out. Loss of estrogen was destroying my zest for just about everything, including sex. Depression was the worst."

"And was he helpful?"

Eleanor must think about the question before answering. "Yes, I think he was. But only indirectly. He'd be proud of the progress I've made since he's gone. You understand, don't you?"

"No, Eleanor, I'm afraid I don't. How could he help you with depression?"

"He taught me it was both hormonal and psychological. He possessed a great understanding of medicine, you know. But the other part was more important. My depression was caused by an egocentric, inward mind-focus. He urged me to identify with wonderful things outside of myself—air, water, people, ideas, books, art. And God, too."

"Easy for him to say," Gabby adds, not sounding critical.

Eleanor's voice drops into a low whisper. "That's what I said to him. I could jump out of my own skin under a single condition—that I had at least one person to believe in and love me. And he replied, he did. I complained about being alone and drying up. He recommended I embrace God as a friend. It was me, not him, who suggested making love with God. He didn't think much of the idea, but I did. The notion intrigued me. My mind was so befuddled it didn't take much to convince me that sleeping with him in some holy place like this very chapel was as close to God as I was going to get."

Gabby slides toward Eleanor on the pillowed seat and takes her hand in hers. She wants to exhale and vent her frustration but doesn't. "Substituting a clergyman for God is an old, tired practice," she says. "Women seem most susceptible to it, perhaps because our language speaks of God in the male gender. Rabbi Greer should have known better."

"Perhaps, but everybody has the wrong idea about his involvement. People infer that he had a great time screwing a lonely divorcee like me. It wasn't like that at all."

"He didn't enjoy it?"

"Don't know what he felt, but I know he didn't have an orgasm, if that's what you mean."

"And did you?"

"That's what's so bizarre. I did. And on the third and last occasion, I had double orgasms. Never did that in all my younger days, even when I caught my ex-husband cheating on me and I reacted by cheating back on him with a member of our golf club."

"Are you angry with Rabbi Greer?"

"I *was* angry but no longer. Today, I'm disgusted for acting like an adolescent girl. When I learned he was sharing his therapy with other women, I lost control. I wanted to monopolize him and couldn't. The temporary high I experienced turned into gloom. It was only when I came to realize that I had no claim to him or other things around me that I started to feel better."

"Did he teach you about the *Shechinah*?"

"Yes."

"And did you bond with God during sex?"

"No. But what I felt was perhaps more important. Seth turned me inside out. I stopped trying to get in touch with my inner self, whatever that was, and started getting in touch with others."

Gabby mulls over the psychic sequence. The foggy picture of her colleague is beginning to come into focus. She had never thought he would commit adultery with a congregant to satisfy his own lust. Despite his ailing marriage to Emma, his ego wasn't sick enough to bed women for his own pleasure.

"This is private, Rabbi," Eleanor says, squeezing the hand that has held hers for most of the conversation.

"Of course. First, because whatever people tell me of their lives remains absolutely confidential and, secondly, because nobody would believe me even if I told them."

Eleanor laughs for the first time. "Would you do me a favor? When you communicate with Seth Greer, tell him I'm much better now. Tell him for me how sorry I am about what happened with the congregation. My letter to the Board was unconscionable."

Gabby sighs. "Sorry, Eleanor. I don't know where he is and haven't communicated with him since the day he resigned. If we happen to make contact, I'll be happy to relay your message, but it isn't very likely."

"Maybe God will tell him how I feel and what's happened."

"Maybe He will," Gabby says while leaning forward to pull

herself up from the pew.

"It's a relief to have told someone." Eleanor moves to her feet after Gabby. "It's so hard to get out of my mind."

"You're welcome to come and talk whenever you want."

"I think you understand this confusing situation."

They walk down the aisle together. "To a degree, yes."

"Do you blame me?"

"In part. The other part belongs to Rabbi Greer."

Eleanor stops at the door. "Thank you for listening, Rabbi Lewyn. If it's all right with you, I want to go back and sit awhile in the pew."

"Good idea, Eleanor. Call me when you're ready."

September 22nd

Gabby receives an urgent call from Zoe on Monday morning. There will be a meeting between Greenwald, Molletz, lawyers and the District Attorney for Queens the next day. Zoe asks that Gabby be available in Manhattan should the D.A.'s office have questions. It is customary for attorneys but not defendants to meet with the District Attorney's staff, so the two of them will wait outside. It is unlikely that specific questions will be asked of them, but it is best to be prepared if necessary. Their legal counsel is determined to see that the case doesn't go before the Grand Jury where the prosecution usually has the upper hand.

"Worried?" Gabby asks on the phone.

"Of course. This case has many subtle twists and turns. Politics, not the law, often govern such situations. On one hand, the D.A.'s office must show sensitivity to blue-collar, disadvantaged families in Queens. Such people don't like yuppies getting away with things for which the law prosecutes them. On the other hand, inane charges like those against us must be a royal pain in the ass."

"What about our case against those two kids?"

"They're juveniles in the eyes of the law and that's a different jurisdiction. Our lawyers will be responding only to the charges made against us."

"Sounds like a lose-lose situation."

"D.A.s are usually smart lawyers. They know the score. Sharks like Manny Fortuna are in their faces every day. They've got to figure out how to block them without perverting the law. No sense going before the Grand Jury with a case they can't win in court. My guess is they'll offer to reduce the offense to a misdemeanor."

"That's outrageous. What about getting women's organizations to help fight back?"

"Not yet. We don't want to come out swinging until we know if the D.A.'s our enemy. See you in New York."

GABBY MUST CATCH THE 7:30 A.M. DELTA SHUTTLE to La Guardia which means she must rise at 5:15. No jog this morning. She arrives twenty minutes late, after a dash from La Guardia into Manhattan to find Zoe in the District Attorney's waiting room. Godfrey Quanis, Andrea Delagnes, and Norman Kwan have already passed to inner offices through a door guarded by an armed marshal.

Zoe greets with a hug, pushes away to study Gabby's features. She notes a glimmer in her eyes and flushed, healthy coloring in her cheeks.

"Something's right in your life," she observes. "Expected you to be deep in the blues, but I detect a different condition. Did they appoint you Senior Rabbi at Ohav Shalom?"

"Absolutely not. With assault charges hanging over my head they're not likely to appoint me Dog Catcher."

"Then the President's called and asked you to lunch at the White House."

"I've turned him down so many times he no longer bothers. There's just no chemistry between us, I'm afraid," she says, dismissing the Chief Executive with a theatrical fling of the right hand.

They sit opposite one another at the corner of a graffitied steel desk. Zoe debriefs her about proceeding with their legal counsel inside.

"Any progress in Noah's case?" Gabby asks after a long pause.

Zoe is reluctant to reveal much, but she trusts Gabby to have

Noah's interests at heart and suspects there's more between the two of them than Gabby reveals. Woman's intuition. Perhaps that's why Gabby is looking so chipper. Sooner or later, one of them will disclose something.

"Making good progress," she half-whispers. "Nobody's a better investigator than Norm Kwan. He's been trying to establish Eli Waller's habit of trading sex for business. Seems the lovely, talented, and attractive partner at The Hawthorne Group has a pattern of spreading her legs for the right customers."

"You mean she seduced Noah?"

"Yes, but I can't prove it and proof is what governs a trial."

Gabby ponders the implications and is puzzled. If Eli seduced Noah for Pyramid Development's business, why didn't she follow through? It doesn't make sense to seduce somebody, then charge him with rape. She asks Zoe, "Why would she change her mind?"

"We're working on that. Still in the theoretical stage. But it helps to make a case that Eli isn't Caesar's Wife. Nobody likes to see a professional woman drop her underpants and roll on her back to get ahead. It gives additional credence to Noah's contention that sex between them was consensual, not forced." Zoe pauses, thinking that she has revealed more than she should about strategy, even to one she trusts. She fails to make a proper transition when introducing a new subject.

"Spoke with Noah last night. He's keeps asking me about your character testimony. I've been holding him off. But when he's got a bug in his cap, he's a bulldog. He needs you in court but doesn't want you to sacrifice yourself. Uses the expression about the futility of throwing good money after bad. He wants me to find another character witness and is providing a list of associates and friends. Professional people of good standing. Due to the publicity I expect most will turn me down."

Gabby slips her chair back along the tile floor with an unpleasant screech. She stands up suddenly to stretch muscles in her thighs.

"Neither Noah nor I want you to screw up your career for what might be minimal advantage. In fact, the way things are lining up, your testimony might not be needed at all. I'm going to take Noah's advice and look for other witnesses."

"You don't need me any more?" Gabby is nonplussed, relieved, and speechless at the same time. What she does not express is a feeling that Noah has a strong hand in this. Is he making it easier for them to have an affair? Is he preventing her from perjuring herself under oath? An urge swells to explain her feelings for Noah. A counter-caution nullifies it.

Zoe is nervous about what is transpiring between her colleagues and the District Attorney, yet she maintains enough composure to read the confusion on Gabby's face. Conversation suddenly loses it direction and begins to meander from one topic to another. The chatter mitigates Zoe's nervousness and, as long as it is not about Noah, Gabby feels comfortable.

IT IS NOT THE FATE OF THE GREENWALD, MOLLETZ team to speak directly with District Attorney Anthony Timolocus. They are delegated to meet with an assistant D.A. for Queens. Raymond Ladzinsky is approximately thirty-seven, about the same age as the attorneys facing him. He is a new generation lawyer with a Hewlett Packard computer on his desk displaying cute but distracting screensavers. Jet-black hair dashes over balding patches above his forehead, but there's a wild flush of compensating growth around the ears. When the Greenwald, Molletz, trio enters his office, he reaches out to shake hands but does not leave the confined space of his desk.

"Greenwald, Molletz does nice work." He pastes a manufactured smile on his lips. "Prosecution would get more convictions in New York were it not for a few good law firms, such as Greenwald..."

A high stacks of legal files which appear ready to topple over hide part of Ladzinsky from view. One is open on the doodle-stained blotter in front of him. Rather than engage in introductory banter, he elects to turn immediately to the case in point. "I'm aware that your partner, Zoe Mountolive, is not just the defendant here, but the lead lawyer in the Zentner rape case. See her on TV a lot. The challenge for me and my colleagues in this office is to keep both cases absolutely separate. You're aware of how Manny Fortuna is building public support for his young clients?"

"We hope you're not going to take this media campaign seriously," opens Quanis. "Fortuna gives the legal profession a bad name."

"We try to stay out of the sewer, Mr. Quanis, but everybody knows the office of the District Attorney isn't deaf to community sensibilities. You have every right to take your story to the press, too."

"You know that's impossible." Quanis is impatient. "Zoe Mountolive heads arguably the most celebrated rape case of the last decade. Her client cannot afford to have his counsel dragged before the public."

Ladzinsky adjusts glasses that are crooked on the bridge of his nose. To correct the way the frame rests on his ears, he bends the temples. The correction makes the imbalance worse. "I agree with you there," he says.

Andrea Delagnes enters the interchange. "It must have occurred to you, Mr. Ladzinsky, that our clients, two successful professional women, have absolutely no reason to attack kids on the street. And if they had some diabolical motive, why would they report it immediately to the police as the record clearly shows and then call for medical assistance?"

Ladzinsky eases against the spring back of his chair and rotates the stub of an old-fashioned wood pencil between his fingers. "We're considering that. Fortuna argues that it's a question of stereotyping. Two rather scruffy looking kids make their way through Segelman Street to Parsons Avenue. Two females armed with tennis rackets going to their parked car immediately assume they are in danger and go on the attack. A stretch of the imagination, but not inconceivable either. We see Caucasians overreacting to disadvantaged kids on the street all the time. White people often pack weapons in shoulder holsters and handbags."

"Our client's charge of rape against Reginald Masters and Jose Piecho is far more probable," Delagnes says. "Can't get a peep from Juvenile Court on the status of our charges."

"That's because there have been meetings between our department and the J Court. It's really their call, not ours. A judgment came down yesterday. Faxed here last night. J Court released Jose Piecho and Reginald Masters on three grounds. First, this is their first offense. Second, whether they attempted a rape or not, no actual rape happened because your client maintains that there was no sexual penetration. Third, and probably most important, the court has judged that their injuries are sufficient punishment."

"Outrageous!" Delagnes trumpets.

"Maybe, but the truth is nobody wants to send physically injured kids to an institution and have the state pick up their medical bills. We don't know the long-term ramifications of their wounds, but they could have lifelong problems and cost the taxpayers millions. The court put Masters and Piecho on probation."

"Great. That sends a message loud and clear to seventeen-year-old kids. Cause all the mischief you want, then don't do it any more."

"Once again, Ms. Delagnes, I don't disagree," says Ladzinsky, "but that doesn't solve what to do with your clients. We've taken a good look at the medical reports on Piecho and Masters and it appears your clients exceeded the boundaries of self-defense. Excessive force is not difficult for a jury to understand, especially when one side is armed and the other isn't."

"You calling tennis rackets 'arms'?" Norm Kwan is curt and challenging.

"Well, maybe not a firearm or a dagger, but capable of the injuries the kids sustained. They weren't hurt by a racket accidentally falling on their toes. The police report shows your clients used them for clubs. Cecil Thorner claims to have witnessed this."

"He was in no position to know whether the force of the blows was excessive or not," Quanis speaks.

"If we put him on the stand that will be your challenge during cross, Mr. Quanis."

"Have you looked into his credentials?"

"We have. He's not going to win an award for Citizen of the Year. But he has good eyes and was present on Segelman Street at the right time. One can't preselect one's witnesses, can one?

We're still wrestling with the accusation that Rabbi Lewyn bribed him as a potential witness. She did, after all, give him twenty bucks."

Kwan says, "You know damn well the sequence of events. Cecil Thorner, an unemployed fix-it man, seizes the moment. Does he go to help the kids? No. Does he seek out the police or an ambulance? No. Does he commiserate with a woman who's just been sexually assaulted? No. Instead he attempts to extort money, not from the kids who probably haven't got any, but from the women who play tennis at the North Queens Sport Club. Rabbi Lewyn offers twenty to shut him up so they can get emergency help. Twenty bucks is more than he ever expected. The rabbi never intended this as a bribe. Thorner actually shows up as witness only after Manny Fortuna found him. He didn't trot down to the Precinct Station or stick around to talk with the police. In fact, he disappeared with Masters and Piecho, along with his twenty-dollar loot."

Ladzinsky's hands rise to massage the back of his neck. His eyes drop to the legal file open on his desk and he appears to be reading from notes scribbled into the margin. Eventually, he says, "You know, going against Greenwald, Molletz on this case isn't my first choice. The State has better things to do than pursue issues of excessive force. Bribing a witness with twenty bucks is small potatoes. But community sentiments, thanks to Mr. Fortuna, are strong. If we drop it, there's going to be a hue and cry out there. An unemployed lawyer by the name of Ray Ladzinsky might show up at Greenwald, Molletz looking for a job."

Godfrey Quanis relishes being blunt but deadly to the point. "How much does Fortuna want to make his accusations go away, Mr. Ladzinsky?"

"That's not for me to say. You'll have to approach him."

"He'll probably want his legal fees. And something for medical expenses and damages. Could be expensive."

"The State doesn't take a position on this, Mr. Quanis."

"But would the State have a different attitude if we came to an arrangement out of court?"

Ladzinsky inhales noisily and pretends to scan an outline of the case open on his blotter. His hand paws at his chin in a gesture of internal decision. Or is he just being dramatic?

"Godfrey, if those kids got something for their injuries, I believe the State would be favorably inclined. I might add that your clients would avoid further publicity at a time when they must have other things on their minds."

"Will Fortuna wait until after a criminal trial to put the screws to my clients?"

"He might if we had a stronger case. But the way I see it, we've got a long way to win this despite public opinion. I'm not suggesting we haven't got a case. I think we do. But so do your clients. Manny Fortuna will probably take his money and run. We all know he's no crusader for juvenile rights. Besides, if I'm not wrong, he'll be back here in a month or two with a new case. He works his niche, if you know what I mean."

GABBY FLIES BACK TO WASHINGTON THAT AFTERnoon buoyed by her attorneys' confidence the case will not be tendered to a Grand Jury. What they fail to say is that they will soon be on the phone with Manny Fortuna's secretary. A flurry of documents will zap through fax machines. A deal will be struck.

Forty-eight hours later, Zoe calls with good news. Assault and battery charges against them have been dropped. They can put the entire incident behind them once and for all.

It is toward the end of the conversation that Zoe drops her bombshell. Twenty-one thousand dollars did the trick. Paid for out of the same Greenwald, Molletz reserve fund that covered their attorney fees. Since there will be no trial, what will be saved in legal fees will go toward the settlement. A trial would be far more costly. This is all just pocket money compared to the fees generated by defending Noah Zentner. It is to Noah's advantage to be rid of this distracting nuisance.

Gabby is furious. Her faith in the justice of American law is utterly shattered. If the righteous must pay off the wicked, then she should share half the penalty. Zoe will hear nothing of this. Gabby came to her aid on Segelman Street. Why should she have to pay legal fees and settlement charges for being a Good

Samaritan?

There are strong words between Gabby and Zoe. Neither is able to change the other's opinion. A friendship teeters on the rocks.

Chapter Twelve

September 12th

Substituting for the funniest lecturer on campus, certainly the funniest rabbi in the mid-Atlantic states, isn't easy. To Gabby's credit, she does not try to compete with Seth's ghost. Instead she ratchets up the pace of her lectures at Georgetown University, challenging the students on several intellectual levels. Her principle of active engagement works. She burdens them with essays, class preparations, and required readings. Special reference books for her course are on reserve in the University Library. Had students failed to perceive they had something to learn from her, they would have rebelled and transferred out. It is most gratifying to her that, of the original sixty-six students, only thirteen have left the class. Among the faithful remains Morgan Zentner. After what Noah had disclosed about her infatuation with mystic ideas spawned in medieval times, Gabby is not entirely surprised.

"I've reconsidered what we spoke about a few weeks ago." She catches Gabby at the end of a gab session in the Student Union. Paper cups, soda cans, and plastic fast food wrappers are everywhere. Morgan's manicured beauty is gone. Her hair is pulled tight behind her ears in an improvised ponytail, secured by a simple rubber band. Several locks have escaped and fallen over her right ear and she makes no attempt to retrieve them. There is a squirrel-like nervousness in her movements. "It's critical I get help with Seth's manuscript. Don't know where to turn. Is your invitation still open?"

Gabby is surprised by the about-face. At the Afghan restaurant Morgan was protective about any attempt to review Seth's material. "Why the urgency? The High Holidays are looming. My schedule is madness through mid-October."

"I'm holding a time bomb. Seth's book is a gold mine. A similar manuscript is now circulating through publishing houses in New York. Not identical, mind you, but similar. The longer Seth's work languishes, the higher the risk that a competitive book will beat it to the market. First one to the bookstands often saturates the demand. Forget quality. In the publishing world, timing is everything."

Gabby is eager to peer into Seth Greer's inventive mind and believes this manuscript might provide just such a glimpse. "I'll do what I can," she tells Morgan, "only not until after the holidays."

"I live on California Street in Kalorama. You must be traveling home in that general direction. I'll give you a portion of the manuscript now. When there's a moment, take a look."

Excuses course through Gabby's brain. She doesn't want to enter Noah's home or ex-home. Nor does she seek familiarity with his soon-to-be ex-wife. There is also the question of disclosure. Can she enter Morgan's home in good faith and not reveal that she's developed a crush on her husband? "I'm exhausted tonight," she taps Morgan on the sleeve and fibs. "Bring the manuscript to class next week. I'll get to it as soon as I can."

"You don't understand, Gabby. The competing book is already in auction. Time is of the essence. Besides, I need to explain a few details about organization of the material. It's impossible to talk with your student admirers hovering around. It won't take but a few minutes, then you can scan the manuscript as soon as you have free time, if that isn't an oxymoron."

In the end, Gabby's caution is overruled by her curiosity. She follows Morgan home in her own vehicle.

THE ZENTNER HOUSE IS SET BACK FROM A STREET dotted with residences inhabited by diplomatic emissaries to Washington. Outdoor lighting illuminates its red masonry and pitched slate roof. Extensive landscaping screens most of the windows from the street. Morgan collects mail from the mailbox and, without sorting through it, dumps the pile of envelopes on a teak credenza in the foyer. Her slender presence seems dwarfed by the cavernous entrance.

After accepting a Diet Pepsi from a near-empty refrigerator, Gabby follows Morgan upstairs to her home office. It strikes her odd to locate a study amid a warren of bedrooms on the second floor, but Morgan's explanation makes sense. She suffers from Seasonal Affective Disorder and large box elder and maple trees surrounding the house block sunlight from filtering down to the ground floor. Gabby can sympathize with this seasonal depression because she often finds herself sullen and moody when deprived of intense light.

Passing through the bedroom en route to Morgan's office is unpleasant. Gabby does not like entering the private bedrooms of married couples where secrets are made, kept, and often broken. Her eyes scrupulously avoid everything connected to Noah's former intimacies. A glass door at the far end leads into a spacious office constructed above what, in days before the advent of air-conditioning, was a screened-in sun porch. Glass on three sides usurps all space normally dedicated to photos, degrees, and awards. A wraparound desk flanks the windows, dominated by a large seventeen-inch computer monitor. Several neat piles of books and manuscripts rise like stalagmites from the carpeted floor.

As they enter, the phone is ringing. Morgan snatches the receiver too late. Either this ring is the last in a series or the caller changed his mind and hung up.

She rummages through two piles of manila folders and soon extracts four which she stacks into a bundle. "Three chapters in each folio," she declares. "I like to make a hard copy from my word processor. Old fashioned, I guess. It's dangerous to lose the feel of a real book. I intend to give Seth's work a special cover and jacket. Something seductively mysterious, if that's possible."

She explains the structure of the proposed book and hands the pile to Gabby who recoils at the sheer volume, far more than she originally anticipated. Her eyes fall upon the title on the top folder: *Divine Synapse*.

When the phone rings a second time, Morgan is quicker to answer. Gabby seizes this interlude to fumble through the top file. After several moments her eyes shift from the manuscript to Morgan, her face dominated by a painful expression. Occasionally, she whispers a short phrase and glances over to assess whether Gabby is listening. At one point she apologizes, "I'm sorry, Gabby. I'm very sorry," then goes back to the caller.

To provide privacy, Gabby steps from the office into the bedroom, taking Seth's manuscript with her. Her folly confronts her immediately. This is precisely where she doesn't want to be...or is it? Once she is in Noah's old bedroom, curiosity about his failed marriage overwhelms her.

A quick survey provides a confusing impression. What first appeared to be a bed is really carefully stacked silk pillows without a bed frame. Two bedstands delineate a sleeping area connected by a sturdy wooden headboard with an array of symbols chiseled into it. She steps alongside to examine them and immediately recognizes an image from sixteenth-century Kabbalism in which divine virtues are anthropomorphized as regions of the human anatomy. Carved into the headboard is the skeleton of the male body, with appendages extended to their maximum. Various points on this figure are marked in Hebrew as stations of the Heavenly Spheres, beginning at the head with the *Kether Elyon*, the supreme crown of God. The human chest is the physical center for the primordial idea of God's dual personality, consisting of *Hochmah*, Divine Wisdom, and *Binah*, Divine Intelligence. One arm symbolizes the attribute of God's Mercy, *Hesed*, and the other God's Justice, *Din*. Centered at the genital region is *Rahamim*, the attribute reconciling Compassion and Justice. Though seen reproduced in numerous texts on Jewish mysticism, Gabby has never witnessed this symbol employed in someone's home, let alone bedroom. To her mind, neither Hellenic nor Hebraic thinkers managed to do anything more profound than name the Heavenly Spheres. No authority in modern astronomy or psychology would give this hierarchy of heavenly virtues the time of day.

An aroma of incense seems trapped in the surrounding air. Matches and unburned incense rest on a bedstand. On a shelf beneath them Gabby identifies a battery-operated vibrating phallus. That might startle some, but she knows that, in the privacy of their homes, single women are often avid masturbators. During the six months when Tim traveled in Asia, she indulged herself. While the sensation was pleasurable enough, her anxieties proved too severe to make this a permanent habit. Tim's return to New York made it easy to stop the practice.

Gabby's imagination is fired up but produces little—until it dawns upon her that the absence of a bed is intentional. Morgan's pillows are not randomly stacked. They are arranged in the shape of an altar, drawing the eyes upward toward a modern chandelier with tiny halogen lamps. Thin, almost invisible electric lines tether it to the ceiling.

She is surprised to note an elaborate design in azure and cardinal red painted on the ceiling near the chandelier. To examine it fully one must stand beside the pillows and crane one's neck. She expects to find the form of an animal or a mythological figure, but instead discovers an inscription in ornate Hebrew calligraphy: *EL SHADAI*.

These letters spell out the name of an early deity among the aboriginal Semites. In some early tribal practices, when Semites lived in a polytheistic world where individual gods were attached to specific geographic regions, this deity became known to the ancients as the God of Eternal Procreation. *EL SHADAI* is most likely a fertility god, one of many worshiped during the era of the Hebrew Patriarchs.

Gabby is pondering the presence of this puzzling symbol when the door to the office opens.

Morgan is suddenly silhouetted by high intensity lamps behind her. The phone is no longer at her ear. There is a cold, disapproving expression on her face.

Nothing is said between them until they are back in the study. Gabby breaks the strained silence with a biting question. "Morgan, did you sleep with Seth? If I am to understand his manuscript, I must know."

She is silent. Her lips curl inward and, for an instant, her attractive features appear to decay into themselves. "Seth helped me ascend toward God. He taught me about the Indwelling Presence. He led me across the gap of earthly existence to the God-head. You probably think I'm nuts, but he taught me to transcend myself. I reached a point where only a small bridge separated me from the Deity. I was very, very close. But I never quite made it across the divide. It might have happened if Seth had not left."

Gabby's eyes narrow as she tries to comprehend Morgan's thinking. "Did you sleep with him?" she demands a second time.

"Read his thoughts on *Divine Synapse*, Rabbi. Read carefully. I was absolutely certain he could trigger a nexus with the Almighty. I was preparing to break through the Mind-Body barrier. I came so damn close. Really close. All I needed was a holy man of Seth's nature to catapult me across. Unfortunately, he got in trouble and wasn't available to shepherd me the final distance."

"So you slept with him? Or he with you?"

Gabby's questions ring with the bite of interrogation. Morgan barks back, "No, I didn't. Not because I didn't want to or didn't try, but he refused. Not once but several times. I tried to seduce him. We spoke about the most intimate sexual things, but he refused to sleep with me."

"Why? If he's the author of *Divine Synapse*, why wouldn't he want to leap across the barrier himself?"

"It had nothing to do with his theories. Nothing to do with his manuscript. He wouldn't make love to me because I'm Noah's wife. He felt closer to Noah than me. It's that simple."

A question possesses Gabby. She knows it is impertinent to ask, yet cannot resist. Rabbinical prerogative is her only excuse. "Why couldn't Noah help you?"

Her expression softens and her volume eases. "Noah? You've got to be kidding! I tried introducing him to the spirituality of sex. I wasted my breath. He's too physical for such things and not interested in spiritual matters. I've got to give him credit for trying, but not for succeeding. Noah is a carnal animal, not an ethereal lovemaker. Spirituality just isn't in his nature. "

Feeling guilty for having trespassed on the privacy between husband and wife, Gabby returns to an earlier subject. "So you're not one of Seth's women?"

"I knew he was experimenting with other women. He couldn't hide that. He was active as hell but wouldn't touch me."

Gabby laughs a mock laugh.

"What's so funny?"

"Private humor."

"I've just spilled my guts out to you. Why hold back from me?"

The question gives one pause for thought. Her feelings for Noah will remain hidden, but what happened or didn't happen with Seth Greer is another matter. "Because Seth didn't lay a finger on me either. It bothers me when I think of all the women he screwed. How does the expression go? 'What am I, chopped liver?' I can't help wondering what the hell they had that I didn't. Apparently, our friend Seth was quite discriminating. He didn't want either of us."

THE NEXT MORNING GABBY CALLS CHUCK INTO HER study with a host of chores for the day.

"How current is the congregational mailing list for our kids at college?" she asks.

"About as accurate as the Federal Roster for Social Security. People in the know say half the beneficiaries are deceased. Uncle Sam is supporting an army of dead people. We try updating the list of college kids every two years. "

"See if you can get me the latest address and phone number of Rabbi Greer's son, Jeremy. He's at U.C.-Berkeley. A junior or senior this year, studying environmental sciences. If he's not on the list, call the University Registrar and say it's an emergency. Use my name and title. If you don't have success, I'll get in touch with Hillel on the campus."

"Love to know what you're cooking up this time, Rabbi Gabby. I suppose it would be too much for me to ask."

She manufactures a mischievous expression and cocks her head in the manner of girls twenty years her junior. "Why, not at all. Just ask."

"Well, what have you in mind?"

"Oh nothing. Nothing at all. Thought I'd call to say hello."

"Don't bullshit an old bullshitter, friend."

She turns Chuck's request over in her mind and concludes that for his loyalty he deserves her confidence. "I need Rabbi Greer's address. Jeremy and Seth are as close as any father and son. Can't imagine Seth isn't in contact with him. Not sure about his sister, Marge, who I'm told is angry with the way her father treated her mother. I don't blame her. If I were the daughter, I'd be pissed, too. Jeremy's a different story. Try our college list first, then the University Registrar."

By late in the afternoon, Chuck knocks on the door to Gabby's study. When she asks him to step inside, he flashes a yellow Post-it in the air.

"You got the number, didn't you?" Gabby looks up from papers on her desk.

"Nope. Struck out with the list and the Registrar. So I got the name and phone number of the Hillel Director at Berkeley. Rabbi Esther Spears. Know her?"

She runs the name through her excellent memory and comes up blank. "Must be a recent graduate from the seminary. Thanks for your help. If it were up to me, I'd double your salary. I'll give Esther Spears a call this afternoon."

Gabby has good luck with Rabbi Spears who produces the number early the next morning. But her luck runs sour when she dials it. Jeremy Greer's phone in California rings and rings without an answering machine on the other end. Nothing to do but try every few hours, hoping to eventually catch him.

THAT EVENING GABBY GOES HOME TWO HOURS early to fulfill a family ritual. It was the custom when she grew up that seven days before the Jewish New Year her parents would decorate their home in Los Angeles. Flowers here and holiday fruits there, a silver candelabra along with historical souvenirs. Her mother used to say that an animal marks its passage through life by peeing at wayside markers. Jews should also mark life's journey but in a different way. Festive decorations in the home register passage through the years. Central to the Lewyn tradition are tapestries strung below the ceiling from hooks embedded in the picture molding. On them elaborate Hebrew letters in vermilion and yellow slash in all directions from a central point, as though the earth's core were erupting with calligraphy. For years Gabby attempted to make sense of these letters without success and ultimately concluded that the artist conveyed only impressions, not concepts.

She continues to display her mother's tapestries in the living and bedrooms of her own condo. The ritual hanging elicits tearful memories. One would expect such feelings to fade with time, but they do not. On the same day, her sister in Cleveland will display the silver candelabra and other family keepsakes.

It is an hour and a half later before she notices there is a message on the phone machine from Noah.

I want to see you, honey. Name the time and place. Call on my cellular phone as soon as you get this. N...

Her heart flutters. The term of endearment *honey* flushes a dash of the neurotransmitter dopamine in the brain. It is warm and inspirational and, during this season, she feels a desperate need to be close to somebody. As a rabbi, people naturally feel friendly toward her, but not close. Friendships are one-sided. People reveal themselves, but she cannot reciprocate. A professional wall prevents mutual intimacy. Friendships can never be more than partial commitments. The word *honey* sounds wonderful. This endearment rolls like a snare drum. She thinks that this is the evening she has been taking cooking lessons for. Why not try a recipe on Noah? But as usual, counter-reservations prevail. Her mental high disappears as fast as it emerges.

When she finally reaches him on his mobile cellular there has been another change of mind and she must admit to herself that she is daffy. His voice is so friendly and familiar that her resolve to maintain distance dissolves. Instead she says, "I could make stir-fried something if you want to come over."

No need to repeat the invitation. He is enthusiastic. "Let me pick up Chinese food. No pork. No beef. Vegetables, noodles, rice, and more vegetables. Vegetables for hors d'oeuvres, vegetables for dessert. Tea, no caffeine."

"Just bring yourself and stop ribbing me. I've been taking cooking lessons. Give me a chance. You owe me at least one effort before we head for the restaurants."

"Let me bring beer."

"Good idea."

GABBY PLACES A SERIES OF CALLS TO BERKELEY, California, and fails to make contact. She begins chopping celery, mushrooms, green peppers, broccoli, garlic, and onions for the stir-fry, then places rice in an electric rice cooker and adds the appropriate amount of water. How many times had she watched Tim orchestrate such dinners? When the chopping is finished she moves silverware, yellow placemats, and navy blue cloth napkins to the dining room table. Not uncharacteristically, reservations about entertaining Noah gnaw at her from inside and she decides to forgo candles.

She continues to debate the wisdom of her invitation until he appears at the front door. He kisses her on the cheek and she does not pull away. He cannot do more since his hands hold a bag with three six-packs of beer. How much did he think they might drink at one dinner? There is a chipper, energized look on his face, happier than she has seen him since his troubles began.

Observing the tapestries overhead, he asks, "What have we here, an Arab harem?"

"A family tradition. When I was growing up, we decorated our home before the holidays. Makes us feel festive. These tapestries are from my mother. When they're up, I feel her arms hugging me. Silly, isn't it? And how are you today?"

"Not silly at all. And yes, I'm feeling a bit more confident. We can now show that Elisheva marketed her body along with her business, so her claim of rape isn't as credible. Zoe believes my case is strong enough to convince at least one juror."

They move into the kitchen where he stands beside her, asking to be of help in preparing the meal. She likes bumping against his shoulders and backside as she moves from a butcher-block island to the sink and back to the island. Her Chinese wok simmers with canola oil and she is ready to add chopped ingredients, but at the last moment remembers Jeremy Greer.

"Noah, I must place a long-distance call before we sit down. Have a beer and make yourself comfortable. Move around if you wish. If I can't get through I'll be back in a tick. If I'm lucky, it will take a little longer. Then I promise no more interruptions, that is if my beeper doesn't go off."

She doesn't want him to know she's trying to contact Jeremy, who once looked upon him as an uncle. Jeremy has reason to be confused if not disappointed in Noah. She closes the bedroom door and sits on the bed beneath more of her mother's tapestry. A canopy of splashing Hebrew calligraphy smiles down at her. By now, the Berkeley phone number is engraved in her memory. She expects to hear the phone ring endlessly at the other end, but to her surprise the ringing stops and a voice greets with a distant hello.

"I'm looking for Jeremy Greer," she begins.

"This is he."

"Jeremy, Gabby Lewyn in Washington. I'm calling to wish you Good *Yom Tov* and...," she pauses long enough to register her discomfort with the next thought, "to ask a personal favor."

"Rabbi Lewyn?" Jeremy was always formal and deferential with respect to officers of the congregation. "I'm not sure there's anything I can do for you."

"Hear me out first, Jeremy. Your dad and I were close professional colleagues and very good friends. He was my teacher and a rabbi reveres a teacher more than anyone on the earth. You know how well we worked together, yes?"

There is prolonged silence on the other end. Jeremy finally answers without enthusiasm. "Well, I guess so."

"I see your mother from time to time," she adds, changing the subject. "We marched together at the pro-choice rally on the Mall. She's one great lady. We're restoring our friendship."

"She told me about it, Rabbi Lewyn. I'm glad you stay in touch. Most people in the community haven't. It's like she's got an infectious disease."

"I'm not making excuses, but people just don't know what to say. The easiest thing is to say nothing. We all take the easy route when uncomfortable. Your mother's done me a great service. Everybody thinks I slept with your father. It never happened. She told me she didn't share that view. Her confidence means a lot to me."

"The thought had crossed my mind, too, Rabbi. But I'm glad to hear you deny it. We've known each other a long time and I don't think you'd lie to me. Would you?"

"I won't. A solemn pledge."

"I am planning to fly home for the holidays. Marge will come down from Frederick. Mom wants us to escort her to services at Ohav. We haven't been back since the trouble. It's going to be tough for all of us."

Tears moisten Gabby's eyes and she is glad no one sees them. She fights emotion. Her voice is deeper, under strain. "That's very courageous. You, your sister, and your mother are doing the right thing. And if this rabbi has anything to say about it, it won't be as painful as you anticipate. But I must warn you, folks expect me to say something about your father. Originally, I had thought I wouldn't. Everything that needed to be said was said. *Ad nauseam*. My thoughts were no more insightful than anyone else's. But very recently I've changed my mind. At the time things broke I didn't understand your father's motivation. I didn't say anything, but I was furious with him for making a mockery of our profession. Recently, I have learned the complexities of his situation and now I intend to place new facts on the record."

"Can you tell me what you're going to say so we won't be embarrassed?"

She pauses, trying to accommodate. "Not at the moment, Jeremy. I'm still formulating my thoughts. But I can tell you now, things were not as they appeared. Your father is not the man people gossip about. He challenged me to find out for myself what happened. I understand now. People know only the superficial facts. The jury never got the full story. The rush to judgment is a tragedy."

"Will you embarrass us? My mother can't take any more abuse."

"Absolutely not. You have my word. In fact, there's reason to be proud of your father. He is a remarkable man. That's not to say I always agree with his judgment. He made a series of bad choices. But I respect him and, between you and me, I wish like hell he was still at Ohav. We were a great team. It will never be better."

"I appreciate that, Rabbi. I'm certain my father would, too."

"Which brings me to the favor I need. I must get in touch with him. But no one knows where he is. Not his friends or his colleagues. He seems to have dropped off the face of the earth. Tell me where he is. I promise I won't divulge it to a single person."

Again, a long hiatus at the other end.

"Jeremy? Talk to me, please," she pleads.

"Why are you asking me?"

"Because you and your father are extraordinarily close. When you're together, the world around you seems to disappear. You jabber at one another as if no one else in the world exists. I know your father. He couldn't walk out of your life. I know you're in touch. I feel it, Jeremy. Tell me, please."

He doesn't deny it. That confirms Gabby's speculation. Finally, he says, "I'll be in Washington next week. We'll be at your services on *Yom Tov*. Let me think about this for a while."

"I haven't got much time, but next week would work. I'm swamped with preparations. It will be good seeing you at Ohav. It's your home."

"We'll see, Rabbi. Don't tell my mother about this conversation. Or my sister. We made a pact not to talk about my father. It's better that way, although they suspect I'm in contact with him."

"You have my promise. See you *Erev Rosh Hashanah*."

GABBY IS SO LOST IN THOUGHT THAT FOR A FEW MOMENTS she has forgotten about Noah, who is near the living room bookshelf, browsing through a volume of Immanuel Kant's *Critique of Pure Reason*. He replaces it among other volumes after she enters. "Everything okay?"

"Oh, yes," she says while stepping close to him. Her mind is still on the conversation with Jeremy Greer and gives no thought to an innocent kiss she plants on his cheek. In that instant, the mystery of Seth Greer's behavior begins to gel in her mind. And an instant later, clouds surrounding Noah's rape open. She steps away from Noah, turning to the side. The insight makes her tremble.

"What is it, honey?" he says, reclosing the distance between them.

She cannot speak.

He places his arms around her torso and draws her into his chest, firmly enough to contain the shaking. A kiss lands just in front of her ear. "Tell me, what's going on?"

"Just hold me, Noah," she whispers. "Just hold me."

His embrace tightens and her breathing slows. The smell of her hair and the warmth of her breath wafting upward cause his spirits to soar. "You feel so good to me," he whispers near her ear.

"You also feel wonderful."

Chapter Thirteen

October 1st

Gabby is embarrassed. In his Post-it note Seth Greer challenged her to solve a mystery and, in the swirl of events, she has overlooked the most obvious clue—the Hebrew Bible he had left behind. She had brought it back to her office and placed in her bookshelf then, when necessary, referred to her own annotated copy. Why should she use Seth's when she possessed an identical version of her own, complete with personal tabs and notes cribbed into the margins? But what she observes at Morgan Zentner's home stimulates fresh speculation. Forgetting to examine Seth's Bible is just dumb oversight.

His volume of the Masoretic text is a heavy tome of 1,400 pages printed on high-quality paper and with crisp Hebrew lettering and diacritical marks for scholarly reference and liturgical chanting. In keeping with the principle of never altering their eighth-century version of the text, the Masoretic scribes score voluminous notes on the bottom of each page but leave the sacred words to speak for themselves, even when there are obvious spelling and syntax errors. Seth Greer maintains the tradition. He had a penchant for highlighting favorite verses with a fluorescent yellow marker.

Gabby falls back into a gaming mode. She could thumb through his Bible and note the verses he marked. But it is more challenging to guess what might attract his attention and turn immediately to check her intuition. She synchronizes her thinking to mimic his and turns to a verse she feels he might have highlighted. The most obvious comes at the very end of Deuteronomy in the eulogy for the deceased Moses. What is curious here is that Moses predicts his death. With little regard for modesty, he declares that after him there will be no prophet in Israel as great as himself. She emits a howl of victory to find

Seth's yellow marking exactly where expected: "...no other prophet [than Moses] has known God face to face." Additionally, there is a red line under the Hebrew verb *yedao, has known*. It is the same verb used in the Bible to describe conjugal unions between the Patriarchs and Matriarchs of Israel: Abraham and Sarah, Isaac and Rebecca. Biblical scholars have often noted that physical bonding between husband and wife is depicted by the same term as the man's most intimate and immediate knowledge of God.

She is less successful guessing what else might have attracted him and it is necessary to thumb through the volume, hunting for yellow markings. Passages dealing with the Tabernacle that passed along with the Children of Israel as they wandered in the wilderness before crossing the Jordan River intrigue him. Other noteworthy verses deal with the *sanctum sanctorum*, the Holy of Holies of the First Temple. Gabby quickly discerns a thread linking these highlighted passages. Seth seems to bypass the familiar psalms, prayers, and incantations, favoring verses which tell how humans touch the divine presence at a specific location. He is drawn to events in which biblical figures transcend the gap between the corporeal and spiritual and make physical contact with God.

Her speculation momentarily returns to the Hebrew verb *yedao*. The fact that this verb is used to describe both sexual and intellectual communication stirs her imagination. Does he really believe that the gap separating God and men can be bridged through sex? Her attention eventually turns to something less speculative—the approaching High Holidays.

NORMALLY, *ROSH HASHANAH* IS A SEASON OF GOOD will and celebration, but this year the mood at Ohav Shalom is sullen. Congregants return to the sanctuary to fulfill their yearly obligation to worship, but Seth Greer's behavior has severely shaken their faith in Judaism. The sense of betrayal and anger experienced three months before is subsiding and in its place there is general confusion. After Seth, Gabby's congregants are now ambivalent about rabbinic leadership. The moral bedrock of Judaism personified in the authority of a rabbi, the scholar/saint and successor to the high priests of yesteryear, has turned to shifting mud. It will take years to rebuild the lost trust.

Rosh Hashanah is the first time since Seth Greer's resignation that the entire congregation has come together and it is the first major holiday in which Gabby is officiating without a Senior Rabbi. She is acutely aware that many members regard her as a mere apprentice. The air is filled with tension. Rabbi Lewyn is on trial. Only a near-perfect performance on the pulpit will sustain her candidacy for the senior post. Humor might lighten the atmosphere, but she is no comedian. Common sense tells her not to compete with her predecessor.

Along with Cantor Irwin Blass, Past-President Doris Silbert and the newly elected President T. Zachary Shugoll, she sits on the pulpit gazing out at the members. The sanctuary is filled to capacity during the first service. It will be equally packed during the second. Visitors without assigned seats are forced to stand at the rear. Where are the Greers?

Behind the lectern her fingers quiver over the text and her knees knock. She is haunted by fear of breaking out in a fit of nervous shaking, yet her voice is faithful and does not betray inner anxiety.

While she knows that her congregants expect her to speak about Rabbi Greer, she approaches the subject obliquely. No expressions of condemnation or outrage; no petitions for pity. On the evening of *Rosh Hashanah* when the sun has set and a sober, pious mood settles on the congregation, she speaks about the need for renewal of spirit and how rabbinical authorities regard the concept of *Teshuvah*, or Return to one's Maker. The Jewish New Year encourages a sense of optimism and rebirth. At the turning of a season when one year begins to fold into another, vows and resolutions come naturally.

During the following morning's service, with bright sunlight emblazoning the stained glass windows of the sanctuary, she offers a lecture. Her theme is the challenge to Zionism in a world where Jews are no longer fleeing for their lives and the Jewish state is a respected member of the United Nations. In her view, Fortress Israel, sanctuary for oppressed and destitute Jews, can afford to make compromises with moderate Arab neighbors. To frame every issue of the Jewish state in terms of life and death is an anachronism. When thousands are killed or maimed in traffic accidents each year on treacherous Israeli roads, why should the loss of a Jew to Arab terrorism hold hostage Israel's foreign policy?

She monitors the attention of her congregants by watching their eyes. While she knows many do not agree with her views, she has attracted their attention. Critics will be quick to express themselves.

During the congregational reception on *Rosh Hashanah* afternoon, members express wishes for health during the New Year. Voices reverberate in the social hall, making sustained conversation difficult. The mood is cordial though Gabby senses disappointment in her unwillingness to confront questions of Seth Greer's betrayal. The compliments received on her sermons are perfunctory. Stalwart allies like Ephraim Rothman and his family are nowhere to be seen.

En route to her condo after the reception, Gabby comes to the conclusion that her evening sermon on *Teshuvah* was too conventional, the sermon on Israel too controversial. In the end, though she might have made some significant points from the pulpit, she had failed to tap her congregants' sensitivities. Opportunities lost. Failure is not easy to swallow.

Noah, who has purposely stayed away from Ohav Shalom, arrives secretly at Gabby's condo to find her crestfallen, lacking her usual vivacity. Her mood compounds mounting tension over his own upcoming trial. Jury selection begins in Baltimore in two days. The press has forced him from his Watergate apartment into hiding at the condo of a family friend near Reston, Virginia. The moment he is spotted anywhere, photographers with large black cameras and video equipment materialize around him. He would love to make a comment or two, but Zoe Mountolive has forbidden it. One cannot view television without talk-show commentators, lawyers, consultants, and journalists analyzing the Zentner Assault Case. No one refers to it as the Eli Waller Case, though pictures of her at feminist events are constantly on the screen. Prosecutors Sidney Hines and Sylvia Junqueira are also lionized, but in their professional capacities they provide only censored information. Both shun the talk programs. People speculate about the book and movie contracts they will sign after the trial.

Noah and Gabby sit on living room couches facing each other and sipping Scotch in crystal tumblers. Dinner he has brought from a neighborhood Italian restaurant is kept warm in her microwave oven. While glad for his company, Gabby is mentally and physically enervated. Her voice is spent. Whisky medicates her throat, made raw from overuse.

"My father said services were as beautiful as the rabbi who conducted them," he says. "Sorry I couldn't be there, honey. It's a sad day when a Jew can't attend his synagogue on *Rosh Hashanah*."

She likes to be called *honey* and gives him a sympathetic smile. "Absolutely. This is not the kind of celebrity any of us want. I would have liked you to come, but then you would have made me more nervous than I was. Standing on the *bimah* is a lonely experience. I knew people wanted me to talk about Seth, but it wasn't right. *Rosh Hashanah* speaks to the renewal of the spirit, not sewer gossip."

"You've kept your views even from me. Seth was important to both of us and yet we've hardly spoken about him. That's got to mean something, though I don't know what."

She closes her eyes and yawns, a common physical reaction to mental fatigue. "When preparing my sermons at Rehoboth I didn't understand Seth. I know more now. But I still need a few more days to put it all into perspective."

"So you'll speak on *Kol Nidre* or *Yom Kippur*?"

"Not during the services. I don't want to interfere with the mood for worship. It's my job to preserve the sanctity of prayer, no matter what. Talk of Seth would only detract from the mood. Besides, members may not like what I have to say. If all goes well, I'll say something on *Yom Kippur* afternoon at the discussion session between *Yizkor* and *Nilah*. Those who want to disagree can do so from the floor. Plenty will. If this costs me my job, so be it."

"Love to be there. Wouldn't want to draw a regiment of journalists on the congregation in the middle of *Yom Kippur*. I'm ordered to Baltimore tomorrow. From then on, they'll hide me in one place or another."

"Will you tell me where?"

"At the moment, I don't know. If I can find a phone that isn't bugged, there's nobody in the world I'd rather talk with."

Her eyes rise to encompass him, then she forces them away while thinking to herself, *I love talking to you too, Noah*. What she actually says is, "From what you say, I'm afraid this will be our last evening together."

He is on his feet suddenly and steps around the coffee table to kiss her forehead. His lips linger on the skin just below her widow's peak until she reaches up to run fingers like a comb through thick brown hair along his ears. An instant later her lips touch his closed eyelids, smothering them with warmth. Oxytocins flood their bodies, stimulating the mysterious attraction of touch. An internal resistance causes Gabby to pull back.

"How about something to eat?" she whispers near his ear. "The longer the pasta stays in the microwave, the less it will taste Italian and the more like shoe leather. I've barely eaten in two days."

His head jerks up and his back snaps to a vertical position. "Not only our last evening, but our last meal together. Maybe I can persuade you to come to Baltimore and share a meal or two with me in secret."

She unfolds her legs and an instant later joins him on her feet. "Love to, Noah. But after *Sukkot* I'm going away for a week or so. You'll be in the middle of the trial. I'll be back well before it's over."

"May I ask where you're going?"

"Not sure yet. I need a rest."

He is once again close to her, enveloping her torso with his arms and kissing her lips lightly. She answers his caress by wrapping her arms around him and rubbing her fingers into the small of his back. Eventually, they fetch spinach-stuffed ravioli from the microwave.

SHE HAS SET OUT CANDLES AND AN EXPENSIVE CALIfornia Cabernet Sauvignon. The ravioli suffers from reheating in the microwave. Blackberry tarts with a custard cream and small demitasses of strong Italian coffee end the meal. Conversation which was brisk and lively at the outset trails off into a sad silence. Communication is through expression alone. They cannot escape the realization that the present feeling between them will be short-lived and perhaps never duplicated. The second cup of coffee finds them staring through the candlelight at each other as if to emboss a vision of the other on their memories. Gabby pushes back her chair.

She steps behind him and combs his hair with her fingers. When he cranes his neck to look up, her lips touch upon his and linger for several moments.

"Will you make love with me, Noah?" she whispers close to his ear.

The petition startles him and he has trouble with an immediate response.

"Do you want to?" She fills the silence.

"Yes. Very much. But it isn't fair. If the trial goes bad, we won't be able to repeat it. I don't want a one-night stand with you, honey. You've become too precious to me."

"Let's do it then for memory's sake, for something wonderful to remember."

"It will be wonderful while it lasts but miserable after. A broken heart will be a bitter memory in prison."

"I'll give you license to break mine in return," she says, while encouraging him onto his feet where she presses her body into the folds of his arms and kisses his lips.

IN HER BEDROOM SHE UNBUTTONS HIS SHIRT WITH exceeding care, moving from his waist to his collar. Her movement is slow and cautious. His parted shirt exposes an expanse of flesh which needs to be touched, explored, and later kissed, including the dark disks of his nipples. He is far less adroit in unfastening her blouse, with its extra small buttons and hidden clasps. Passion disguises what is physically awkward for both. Arousal eclipses all other sensation. Nothing is rushed. They wander along a rising crest of desire, at each stage admitting the other into closer intimacy. Their bodies commingle as though aware that the memory of this union must last a long time.

Atop her bed, Gabby separates herself from him by pressing at his chest. "Stop for a moment, Noah," she says. "I've got a request. When you come inside me, I need to be on top. I know you'll find some deep symbolism in this, but it's not what you think."

He hadn't gotten around to thinking about symbolism. "Sure, honey. Tell me why."

"Whatever happens between us, I don't want any suggestion that you raped me. I never want you to think you seduced me into something I didn't want to do. If ever there is sex by consent, this is it. You can't rape someone who's on top, can you? We do this together, Noah." She rolls him sideways on his ribs and untangles her legs from his, then climbs onto him. A moment later her thighs straddle his hips. From time to time she rocks forward to kiss his lips, then leans back to feel him pressing against her cervix. His eyes gaze up at her, then wander beyond to rest on the calligraphy of her holiday tapestry hanging from the ceiling. A jungle of Hebrew letters merges and explodes from the center, enlarging beyond themselves to fill the room. The calligraphy momentarily transports him into a distant world he has known before.

Simultaneously, a hormonal transformation occurs inside Gabby, sending electric impulses to her limbs and torso. Her breathing shortens and her groans of pleasure increase. She is repeating in a lover's mantra, "Noah…Noah…Noah…"

His name rescues him from the distraction. To the woman above him he repeats her name, "*EL SHADAI…EL SHADAI…EL SHADAI.*"

Mention of the divine name rather than her own triggers a spontaneous physical response in Gabby's pelvis. Her brain is suddenly receptive to a host of *shut-down* neurotransmitters which flood hormones into her bloodstream immediately interrupting her orgasm. As though dashing cold water on a fire, the heat turns off in an instant. Her vagina contracts, closing down the path of penetration. Within a brief second, all bodily systems seem to reverse. The high becomes low, the hot cold, the drive to join in union becomes a desire to expel. For a few moments Noah is unaware of Gabby's shift and continues to thrust upward.

At the first opportunity, she rolls off him and onto the bedspread.

"Honey, honey…" A terrorized look glazes his eyes as he reaches to pull her back.

"What did you say to me?" she barks.

"When? What are you talking about?" There is utter confusion in his voice.

"What did you just call me? Tell me again what you said?"

"What I usually call you—honey, I guess. I'm not sure what I said."

"No recollection at all?"

"Honey, did I hurt you? Did I do something I shouldn't have?"

Gabby moves from the bed to stand up, her bronze body glistening with perspiration. The eruption of anger within begins to subside. One instinct tells her to put clothes on; the other to remain naked before him as a proud lover. "You called me something, Noah. Three times in succession you mentioned a name. I can't believe you don't remember. Tell me what you called me."

He throws his legs over the bedside and plants his feet on the carpet but does not rise. How could he turn her off so dramatically? What did he do to alter the feelings they shared? His eyes fall to her toes and remain there. Shame and bewilderment rule him.

She becomes aware of his state and steps forward, taking his hand in hers then dropping down to sit on the bed beside him. "You called out *EL SHADAI* three times," she says. "Do you know what that name is?"

He does and he doesn't. He has heard it in the synagogue but his mind is foggy about details and he is still confused.

"It's the divine name of God. *Shadai* is usually engraved on mezuzahs. Combined with the name of God, *El*, it refers to God's creative personality. Ancient people were in awe of fertility because they didn't understand the physiology of reproduction and reproduction was central to the continuity of their lives. *EL SHADAI* was probably the Hebrew equivalent of fertility gods in other cultures."

He squeezes her hand to restore their bond. "I didn't know that. How could I utter a name I didn't even know? That doesn't make sense. You must have heard something different. Maybe my words got jumbled. Or I said something that sounded like *EL SHADAI*."

Her arm reaches around him to grasp his shoulder and tug him closer. The gesture of forgiveness stimulates affection. He kisses her cheek in gratitude. There is no thought of rekindling sex.

"I don't think so," she eventually mumbles.

"Don't think what?"

"That you said something I misunderstood. Does this bedroom remind you of anything?"

"Not especially. Only that it's yours and I love being here with you. On your bed. Touching you. Kissing you."

"Look up and tell me what you see."

"Your mother's tapestry. Hebrew letters flying over the ceiling."

"Do they remind you of letters you've seen before?"

"Hebrew isn't my specialty. I leave that to you rabbis."

"Look at the two just above us. There's an *aleph* and a *lamed*. Two letters of God's name *El*. I know you've seen this before. Tell me where. Think hard. I know you have."

The strange turn of events scrambles his brain and he is unable to make an association.

Gabby angles her torso to scrutinize him. "I told you Morgan has been coming to my class at Georgetown. She asked me to look at Seth's manuscripts about divine synapse, so we stopped off at your home. We were in her office when a call came in and I slipped into your bedroom to give her privacy. It's unlike any sleeping quarters I've seen. Looks like a shrine. The ceiling's painted with something special, Noah. Tell me, what's painted there?"

"Hebrew letters like these here!" he declares, sensing where Gabby's leading.

"And exactly what letters?"

"Not sure. But I think there was an *aleph*. It's a great letter for calligraphy. "

"It says *EL SHADAI*, Noah." Her animation is gone and she is didactic now. "Did you repeat the divine name when you made love to her?"

He has to think about that for some time. "I'm not sure."

"You don't have any recollection?"

"None for certain. I don't remember much about having sex with Morgan. That's odd, but true. I can only recall how I didn't like it because it was always filled with her spiritual mumbo-jumbo."

She ponders that before standing up. "Let's get some clothes on and take a walk outside. It's dark. I don't think anybody will recognize you."

"Sorry for my faux pas. I hope we can begin again."

A few minutes later, they are out on the street, hand in hand, breathing the humid evening air deeply into their lungs. "Not to worry." She kisses him on the cheek, then nibbles playfully at his ear. "Funny," she says. "You can't understand what you don't first conceptualize...and I'm just beginning to conceptualize now."

October 8th

Tracking down Zoe Mountolive in Baltimore challenges Chuck Browner's sleuthing abilities. Due to publicity about her client, the law offices of Greenwald, Molletz, both in the District of Columbia and New York City, refuse to disclose her whereabouts. Gabby leaves messages in Washington and New York but doesn't expect a reply. Now that the trial has begun she assumes Zoe is inundated with work and far too occupied for phone calls, even from friends. Nothing from Noah either. He promised to call but said he would not leave messages that a moderately skilled telecommunications hack might steal. An appeal to Jonathan Zentner at Pyramid Development is her last chance, though she knows he will be spending most of his time at the Circuit Court in Baltimore. Give a busy man something to do and he will usually get it done. It is no surprise that five hours later he calls her study at Ohav Shlom and leaves a private phone number at the Marriott Inner Harbor Hotel.

No, Jonathan Zentner doesn't know where Zoe is staying, but yes, he can get a message to her. About Gabby's inquiry into Noah's spirits he is more willing to engage. "You've made these past months bearable for him, Rabbi. Before he went to see you, he was depressed. Thought the world was conspiring against him. His initial shock turned to anger, then withdrawal. Your friendship has heartened him. Though he is still pessimistic, he wants to fight. Says he's got something to fight for now. We're biased, of course, but we think he's going to win, no matter what the odds. I'm deeply grateful to you, Rabbi."

"Glad I've been helpful, Mr. Zentner," she says, wondering how much Noah has confided about their relationship. "Zoe Mountolive knows me well. It's imperative I talk with her for just a few minutes. Can you ask her to call me—at the office or home?"

"I'll do what I can, Rabbi Lewyn. Look forward to seeing you on *Yom Kippur*. The court's already announced a recess for the day. You were great on *Rosh Hashanah*. A lot of people must have told you that. Ohav would be loony not to appoint you Senior

Rabbi, but then congregations have been known to shoot themselves in the foot before."

"Tell me about it, Mr. Zentner. How'd you like to work for an organization like that?"

"I wouldn't. And I couldn't. Hats off to your patience."

TWO DAYS BEFORE *YOM KIPPUR* THERE IS NOTHING significant on television but commentary about the Zentner trial. Jury selection in Baltimore stimulates fresh media coverage. Facts of the case are reviewed and repeated, chopped up and dissected by panels of experts. Views on Noah's guilt or innocence polarize. People make allusions to celebrated criminal trials of the past, naming the Kennedy rape case in Florida and, of course, the O.J. Simpson murder trial. As two camps form along gender lines, the trial kindles interest in the prevalence of date and marital rape. Women are on the warpath. They seek revenge against violent, sex-crazed men.

Despite hurricane winds in Baltimore, Zoe finds time to answer Gabby's call.

"You all right?" Gabby asks as soon as she hears her voice.

"Exhausted, but I seem to thrive on adversity. There is nothing more exhilarating than a running trial. Sisters in the movement think I'm a black-hearted heathen for my role in this. Eli Waller and Sylvia Junqueira get star billing. Sylvia's on the cover of every women's magazine. There's talk she will run for Lieutenant Governor of Maryland when it's over. Eli Waller is America's favorite feminist. How did your holiday services go?"

"Not over yet. Tomorrow evening is *Kol Nidre*. *Rosh Hashanah* went moderately well."

"Any word about your appointment?"

"Everything's on hold. Hard for a rabbi to tell whether she's succeeding. Folks lie to me. But that's not why I called. Zoe, I've got to talk to you about Noah. Fifteen minutes, no more. I've learned something you might be able to use in his defense."

Zoe releases a low grunt. "Can you tell me on the phone? Or at least give me a hint?"

"I'll drive up to Baltimore. If I tell you on the phone, you'll think I've lost my marbles. I know now what happened on the Chesapeake. I understand it or at least think I do. It's not like anybody thinks. The media has spent millions trying to understand this case and they've got it all wrong. You must listen to me."

There is a prolonged silence on the other end of the phone. "Your mind is as good as anybody's I know, Gabby. If you say I must listen, then I must listen. My team has a block of suites at the DoubleTree Hotel, fourteenth floor. We have security guards on the corridor twenty-four hours a day. When do you want to come?"

"Tonight, if possible. I've got *Kol Nidre* worship tomorrow."

"For dinner?"

"No, after dinner. Say, at nine."

"Tell the reception desk to ring Greenwald, Molletz, then identify yourself. I'll leave a message to expect you. And Gabby, if I forgot to tell you, Happy New Year."

Tears suddenly well up in Gabby's eyes. Pressure of the holiday season, being in love with one's hormones out of balance, and the trial itself—all drive her emotions to the skin. She is glad Zoe cannot see moisture on her cheeks. She wants to tell her thanks for the good wishes, but that's not what escapes from her lips. Emotions govern her vocal cords and she actually says something quite different. "Zoe, save Noah, will you?"

Without losing a beat, the lawyer replies in an omniscient, confident tone. "Why, of course, Gabby. We'll do everything that's humanly possible."

FAR LONGER THAN THE FIFTEEN MINUTES GABBY HAD promised by phone, the nine o'clock meeting with Zoe stretches toward midnight. For Zoe to understand what happened aboard the *Dame Cynthia*, Gabby must reveal the extent of her affair with Noah and the fact that they had made love together in her condominium. Zoe listens and take notes, refusing to speculate without consultation with her advisors. In the end, Gabby is as relieved as Zoe is grateful. The defense team must take it from there.

The afternoon before *Kol Nidre*, Gabby leaves the synagogue early to go home, review her sermons, and grab a bite to eat in anticipation of the twenty-four hour fast ahead. Lack of food is seldom a terrible deprivation, but the lack of water is. Biblically ordained fasts may serve God's intentions, but little thought was given to rabbis who must talk all day long without moisture in their throats. By the time the concluding *Nilah* service arrives in late afternoon, one's voice is shot. It usually takes three days for Gabby's vocal cords to recover. A single, prohibited glass of water at midday might alleviate this misery. Too bad she can't modify the proscription and avail herself of one.

Before sundown, she eats cottage cheese and sliced peaches with blueberries, along with a double-thick slice of seven-grain bread. Habit would have her turn on television for company, but at this hour there is nothing on but children programs and Noah's trial. On one hand, she wants to know what's transpiring; on another, she's frightened. An advertisement for Dodge cars is the first image to form on her TV screen. Her second channel opens with a view of the Baltimore courtroom in which clusters of lawyers, reporters, and court officers are standing around talking. A camera focuses upon Judge Lucien D. Weil, hunched over his bench in a black judicial robe, conducting an off-the-record pow-wow with two lawyers, one a woman who, from the camera angle, looks like Andrea Delagnes. Zoe Mountolive is absent from the picture frame. From time to time commentators speak about the composition of a jury. A criminal attorney by the name of B. Blane Anjou provides statistics that illustrate how emotion-packed cases such as this are won and lost with jury selection.

To Gabby the legal process is mysterious and somewhat depressing. She has a sense that justice will not be served, though she knows the system is designed to protect the innocent. The camera suddenly pans to a corner of the courtroom and rests momentarily upon Zoe, dressed in a gray suit with the collar of a white blouse covering her lapel. She is in a heated discussion with two men, one grossly overweight and the other, extremely thin. Though not on microphone, it is clear she is holding her own in the argument. Never has she seemed so radiant.

AT OHAV SHALOM, NOAH ZENTNER'S TRIAL LINGERS like a storm cloud over *Yom Kippur* worship. Though preliminaries to the trial produce nothing unexpected, television coverage during the afternoon galvanizes interest. Gabby's challenge is to direct this morbid fascination to the sanctity of the holiday. During the traditional chanting of *Kol Nidre* at the beginning of the liturgy, the congregation stands in humility before its Maker. But as soon as people sit, attention wanders. Her sermon deals with the dangers of moral outrage in a world of political correctness and hypersensitivity. To date, it is her most intellectual and erudite effort at social commentary. Greetings after services are warm and appreciative, but few comment directly upon the content of her sermon. Were they bored? Confused? Or both?

When it is time to deliver the sermon the following morning, congregants settle into their seats, uncertain what to expect. Will Rabbi Lewyn finally speak about Seth Greer? Or will she avoid controversy as she has done before? Gabby studies the congregation from the pulpit, then dramatically slips the yarmulke from her head and drops her *tallit* from her shoulders. She hangs it from the arms of the pulpit in full view. Expectation grows in the long silence. Her introductory words drift upward and seem to hang among the large incandescent chandeliers overhead. The story she worked on on the weekend with Noah at Rehoboth Beach, titled *Redemption*, begins on a theatrical note. Her delivery is slow at first, building momentum.

> I... owe... my...life... to Heraclitus. You, friends at Ohav Shalom, may say to yourselves, so what? I can hear some of you mutter, who cares? And when you get off your pedestals, you'll probably confess you don't know who Heraclitus is in the first place.
>
> My hero Heraclitus was a philosopher who lived and wrote before Socrates in the Golden Age of Greece and taught that the Universe is in constant flux, such that no man can step into the same river twice, for each time his toe touches the water, the river is born anew.

When *Redemption* ends, there is silence in the congregation. People are stunned and need time to digest its implications. Gabby knows that will occur during the question-and-answer session scheduled to begin immediately after the service. Since worship continues throughout *Yom Kippur* afternoon, there is no formal conclusion to the morning prayers. Services for this morning end abruptly with no further songs or announcements.

Normally at this time on *Yom Kippur*, the sanctuary empties as parents gather their children for the afternoon. Those interested to talk with the rabbi trickle back to participate in a dialogue. But this day is different. Virtually no congregants rise to leave. Rather they sit immobilized in their pews, some whispering, some meditating, others glancing from side to side to judge the reactions of their neighbors.

Gabby descends seven stairs to the well of the sanctuary where a radio microphone she wears under her clerical robe will amplify her remarks. To her satisfaction, the Greer family is in the fourth row, sitting silently together. Jeremy's eyes burn with betrayal. On the phone to California she had promised to speak out in defense of his father. She never actually promised that in so many words, but the implication was strong. No such defense has yet occurred. Marge and Emma Greer, who know nothing of this conversation, have their eyes lowered to their laps, where Gabby surmises, they have been throughout the worship.

Standing before her congregants, Gabby smiles warmly and raises her arms in petition. "Well, friends, I've inflicted myself upon you long enough. It's said of sermons that if you haven't struck oil in twelve minutes, then stop boring." Light, nervous laughter ripples through the pews but fades. "It's your turn to talk."

This is not what anyone expects and no one has prepared a comment. Though more than six hundred seats are filled, there is no immediate response.

"Rabbi Lewyn," a voice eventually calls from the rear. Folks turn to see a graying man with heavy spectacles and a well-trimmed beard on his feet. "Is the point of your story about H. Henry Watt that we should forgive Nazis? And if so, should we then consider something much closer to the heart of this congregation and forgive Rabbi Greer? You spoke on *Rosh Hashanah* about the need to forgive if, in fact, we ourselves hope to be forgiven by God. Then last night you talked about the dangers of righteous sensibilities. But doesn't this draw us onto the horns of dilemma? If you can forgive a man like Henry Watt, then is there no standard of deportment which is simply unacceptable? Would you have us forgive Adolf Eichmann himself? That's hypothetical, but closer to home, if we're asked to forgive Rabbi Greer, who knows what sexual conduct will follow? We appreciate the gentleness of your heart. But shouldn't Judaism stand for something lofty? Can it survive if its standards are lowered to accept sinners with warm compassion?"

"All Nazis weren't the same," says an elderly woman with a heavy German accent a dozen rows in front of Gabby. "I survived in Berlin during the war and saw this with my own eyes. Most Nazis were butchers, but a few in the Gestapo were men with education who knew anti-Semitism was wrong. Your story, Rabbi, speaks to that gradation among people. It is very human. Very touching. Very refreshing. People are different. Even villains."

David Sigmond, a thoughtful, scholarly stalwart of the congregation, hauls himself to his feet and asks, "Can you now tell us, Rabbi, your thoughts on Rabbi Greer? You have an insider's perspective. Have we all missed something? How could a man of his stature do something as pathetic as this?"

She adjusts the microphone on the lapel inside her gown, then lifts her chin and nods affirmatively. "I can speak now. Friends, I purposely didn't during the services in order to maintain the sanctity of our worship. What I have to say is controversial. I felt it wrong to damage the holiness of these Days of Awe by discussing a local scandal. But now that the liturgy is mostly completed I can say something. This is outside our prayers. David, you just asked if we had all missed something in this affair with Rabbi Greer. The answer is yes. Emphatically we have. I missed it just like the rest of you. And only recently have I come to understand something hitherto concealed to me."

A murmur of approval travels laterally through the pews, then rocks back along the rows. Bodies become erect. Attention rivets on the rabbi. Gabby's delivery is measured in slow, rhythmic phrases, as though she were delivering a sermon. There are no notes for her to read, yet she does not stammer or search for words:

While thinking about these holidays, friends, I made a pilgrim
age to the Vietnam Memorial, on the Mall in Washington
I walked beside the black marble wall inscribed with
50,000 names of the fallen

For those of us who experienced the anger and frustration of that
period in American history
nothing has healed the nation's war wounds like

this touching Memorial
It tells a story—sad and unpleasant as it is
but it tells an honest story, without embellishment
without phony patriotism
without pompous expression of heroism
It says what we all know is true
that more than 50,000 men died on that battlefield
and when they died it didn't matter if they were
generals, combat infantry, medics, or pilots
They were just red-blooded people like us

The stark, unadulterated truth of this monument has helped
heal our pain
No less than the near-perfect words of a lanky
young President from Illinois at a bloody
battle town called Gettysburg, over a century
before.

Ohav Shalom is wounded by the scandal and resignation of
Rabbi Seth Greer
Its wounds are still open and sore
Sensitivities have been trampled
Faiths questioned
Cherished notions about rabbis shattered

As the Vietnam Memorial heals a national wound
So, I pray, may the truth about Seth Greer.
For three months now I have held my peace
It was important for the Associate Rabbi to keep her nose to
the grindstone and fulfill numerous rabbinical duties
Despite Rabbi Greer and the media, our life here must go on
So I dedicated myself to the life of this congregation
It was a good thing, too.
Because had I rushed to judgment
Had I offered my opinions at that time
Had I condemned or defended Rabbi Greer's actions
Had I pontificated then
I would have been wrong
Dead wrong

The best thing I've done for Ohav Sholom is to keep my trap shut
And, as you all know, that's a trap that doesn't usually stay shut long

(Nervous chuckling ripples through the congregation. Gabby waits patiently for it to settle down.)

We all know what Rabbi Greer did—the facts are undisputed
But until now, we didn't know *why* he did it
You may not accept what I have to share with you
But I hope you'll agree with me that
Your rabbi, a man once loved and much respected, is not the scoundrel many believe

You know that four women came forth with accusations of inappropriate sexual relationships
You probably don't know that all four were going through what we euphemistically call the *change of Life*
and were undergoing involuntary hormonal changes to their bodies
Each was depressed
desperately in need of spiritual rejuvenation, physical tenderness and a renewal of self-confidence

You know that Rabbi Greer possessed a rare talent for counseling those in trouble and over the years had developed
considerable skill at helping women
His appointment books
document countless sessions with women battling
the physical and psychological effects of aging
You probably don't know that he worked with his four accusers for many months *before* any sexual contact was made

You may know that Rabbi Greer was working on a scholarly book about
Lurianic Kabbalish, a sixteenth-century Jewish school of mystic thought

You probably don't know that he took a special interest in the
coupling of Man with God
an act he called in his manuscripts
Divine Synapse

This is a difficult notion to fathom in a modern context, but
suffice it to say that a small, rather isolated school of mystic
thinkers experimented with the concept of
using sexual intercourse as a pathway to unite with God

Today, most of us think this is a silly notion and we're skeptical,
yet for all our skepticism, the notion doesn't die, but
comes back to revisit us throughout the centuries
The idea of bonding with God through sex
dies hard

In an unpublished manuscript about Lurianic Kabbalah he
describes the physiological states in which males and fe-
males rise along a sexual
curve until reaching orgasm
At the very peak of this experience they
depart from their bodies and jump, like
an electric current
over the divide between
the Earthly and the Divine

Please do not misunderstand me
I do not advocate or underwrite this use of sex
I'm only trying to describe it, so you will understand
Rabbi Greer's frame of mind when he committed his
transgressions

A Midrashic tale is told about four venerable rabbis, led by
Elisha ben Abuya
who delve into deep mystical speculation
Together these four colleagues enter a *pardes*, or garden
of mystical ideas, exploring notions few scholars
were hitherto prepared to entertain
In the modern lingo of space
exploration, they were

And like Mephistopheles who descends into Hell
They probe deep into mystical
and arcane secrets of Life and Death

In the end, only Rabbi Akiba returned to normal life unscathed
One scholar went mad
Another died an unexplained death
The leader converted to Christianity

From this tale rabbis later conclude
that mystic speculation and practice are unhealthy
Only the highly trained and mentally strong should
ponder secrets of the underworld.

I'm afraid Rabbi Greer followed his predecessors into this
speculative garden
By now you appreciate how he lives dangerously
Far more dangerously than suits my tastes

The women with whom he slept were desperate
to restore lost youth
and rekindle sexual attractiveness

As all of us know, this is no easy task for unmarried women
who are past their prime
Lovers are scarce
Time is short
Desperation is compelling
The body is often uncooperative

Rabbi Greer did not initiate or seduce those who accused him
But he did respond to their solicitations

He has been an observer of Christian Evangelism and has long
noted how divine deliverance is usually prefaced by a fall
into sin
In other words, a person cannot be saved until he is
first lost

We have sufficient examples of Christian evangelists who
seem to dive into hell in order to seek redemption from
their Savior

Rabbi Greer raped no one
Women who experimented with *Divine* (or perhaps
orgasmic) *Synapse* did so with their eyes open
It was only when sex failed to restore their youth
that they turned on the person who offered them
help
What do we say? *They shot the messenger*

His accusers were fully mature women who must bear some
responsibility for what occurred

It is important to consider that Rabbi Greer did not do this for
his own gratification
I cannot prove it, but I believe he achieved no erotic
pleasure
He was merely a conduit for *Divine Synapse*

I ask a simple question.
Had he succeeded in helping the desperate, would he have
been judged a knave?

It is because he failed and because *Divine Synapse*, if it occurs
at all, does not happen
at the moment of orgasm
that we have reason to be upset with him

Now, another question
Did Seth Greer exploit his rabbinic position?
And this I will answer without hesitation
Yes, he did. People place trust in a rabbi

Throughout his years at Ohav Shalom
he showed himself extremely trustworthy
But in these acts he offended sensibilities
and embarrassed the women who came for
help

Now please let me conclude by saying something very personal about him
First, Seth Greer was my teacher whom I deeply respect
Second, because I was his apprentice, we spent many hours together
We were often at rabbinical meetings in distant hotels
We had occasion to eat many meals together

There have been persistent rumors about an affair between us
You could make a case that we had ample opportunity to establish a sexual relationship
But it never happened
Never
NEVER

NEVER once did Rabbi Greer engage in an illicit act with me
Nor did he hint, suggest, or intimate that we might become lovers
His behavior with me was beyond suspicion
an absolute model of gentlemanly deportment

And from that admission you will kindly note that Rabbi Gabrielle Lewyn has never experienced *Divine Synapse*!

There is laughter in the sanctuary.

Gabby steps back to signal she is finished. Nothing further need be said.

After a long pause, a few questions trickle forth. They are honest queries, neither baiting nor interrogative in nature or tone. She answers with simple declarations. Her voice is failing now for want of liquid. Her dry throat is on fire. She hacks. The congregation is sensitive to that and does not wish to make her suffer. Most congregants just want to sit in silence and think about what she has said. Clearly, they would like to reconstitute their fallen hero. But the pain is too great and Seth Greer's foolishness too egregious.

When the session ends in preparation for *Yizkor*, the service of memorial for deceased members of the congregation, Jeremy

Greer works his way toward Gabby and plants an arm on her shoulder. She is in discussion with two adolescents who are groping to understand the notion of *Divine Synapse*. Sexuality is exploding in their bodies and they are fascinated with the possibilities. She fears these youngsters might draw the wrong conclusions and is attempting to play down Seth Greer's exploits.

"This is for you, Rabbi Gabby," Jeremy interrupts with a soft voice, while handing her a sealed envelope. "Thank you very much. My father always loved you. Now I understand why. My mother is too emotional to speak, but she asked me to convey her gratitude. When the dust settles, she'll call you." As their eyes meet she notes his tears.

The envelope disappears into a skirt pocket under her clerical robe. Without looking she knows what is inside.

Chapter Fourteen

Bizarre sex is newsworthy. Kinky sex among the clergy is a show-stopper. Gabby's statement at the question-and-answer session about Rabbi Greer on *Yom Kippur* afternoon leaks beyond the congregation to revive interest from the media. Rabbi Greer's merging of sex and Kaballah is guaranteed to attract readers and viewers. Phone calls from journalists seeking interviews with Rabbi Lewyn, including the CBS and ABC networks, inundate Chuck Browner. A suspicious battery of cars and communication vans with broadcasting antenna are parked across the street from Ohav Shalom twenty-four hours a day. To this siege are added legitimate calls from congregants who want to discuss with the rabbi what she said and particularly what she meant by it.

Yom Kippur services ends with the synagogue in a state of shock. Worshippers go home to break the fast in silence and it is only after they have time to decompress that sensitivities rise to the surface. Families debate the issues and there is plenty to argue about. If Gabrielle Lewyn is correct in accounting for Rabbi Greer's unseemly behavior, then a host of questions arise about situational ethics, extramarital sex, sexual fidelity, and professional standards. Congregants talk not only to themselves but also to their friends and professional associates across the nation, their kids in college, their high school buddies, their grandchildren. Radio and television talk-show hosts pounce on the subject. Geraldo and Dr. Ruth increase their programming, interviewing psychologists and professors of religion with specialties in mysticism. Gabby knows she's in trouble, but then these days trouble seems to be her middle name. For a long while she has considered her candidacy for the senior rabbinical post dead. Now even tenure in her current associate position seems problematic.

She places a call to Ohav's newly-elected president Zachary Shugoll at his telecommunications consulting office at Tysons

Corner, Virginia, and, when he doesn't return her call, places a second call. The fifty-two-year-old Shugoll responds late in the afternoon. Contrary to her expectations, he is friendly and communicative. He thrives on controversy in business and is energized by it in the congregation. His presidency at Ohav Shalom is likened to that of President Lincoln, who found himself in a conflagration from his first day in office. It seems natural to extend his talents as a consensus builder in the telecommunications industry to congregational politics.

"I need some time off," Gabby tells him after the preliminary small talk about being inaugurated into office on a raging battlefield. "You can imagine the pressures. Since Seth Greer's resignation, I've been on a treadmill almost twenty-four hours a day without a holiday. Weekends are work days. Work days are work days."

"Whatever else people might think about you, Rabbi, there isn't a soul in the congregation who thinks you've slighted your responsibilities. I'm not against a well-earned vacation to recharge the batteries. Everybody needs some R&R and you certainly deserve it. If you go, are we covered for rabbinical emergencies?"

"I won't leave until after *Simchat Torah*. I've already spoken with Cantor Blass about covering at services. Reuben's the unsung hero of our *shul*. Diligent and unassuming. Cheerful at all times. It's easy to overlook the work of a cantor. Reuben Blass gives the word *mensch* a new standard."

"Nice to hear you say it. I'll take note of your views. And yes, we recognize your need for time off. I'll have my secretary inform the rest of the Board. How much time?"

"A week. Can't take more while Noah Zentner is on trial. I'm no longer scheduled to be a witness, but his attorneys have asked me to be available just in case."

"May I ask where you're going?"

"You might, indeed, but I'm not telling. Don't know if you have seen the corps of reporters outside the synagogue. There's another battalion outside my condo. Staying with a friend to beat the crowds. Nobody knows where I'm going. Let's say I'll just drop off the face of the earth for seven days, then I'll reappear to face the music."

"Don't like it, but I understand."

She expresses her gratitude and is about to hang up when he says, "Gabby, before you go, I want to say something personal. I haven't had the opportunity to get to know you yet. I was close to Seth. He bar-mitzvahed my son and bat-mitzvahed my daughter and officiated at Danny's wedding. I was mortified when he left. But we're surviving this sordid affair thanks to you. The calm leadership you've shown is a contributing factor. Still, you've become a lightning rod for debate. Your critics are loud and vociferous. But you also have strong supporters. Perhaps more friends than you believe."

"Why, I thank you, Zack." She is genuinely touched by his choice of the word *friends*. She never doubted it, though the president's comment makes her feel better.

GABBY KNOWS HOW TO COPE. IN ORDER TO ENTER her condo without reporters descending upon her, she is forced to enter through the garage and mount two sets of odorous and clammy fire stairs. She can bear just about anything to be back in the familiarity of her own home—blinds down, curtains pulled. A neighbor has left a pile of mail outside her door which she assumes nosy reporters have sifted through.

Flyers, catalogues, and throwaway mail usually dominate the pile. But today, the number of first-class letters eclipses the junk. There are thirty-three letters from people who know they cannot contact her by phone. A New York return address catches her eye: 135 Mercer Street, Apartment 406—Tim Matternly's.

She rips the envelope to extract a handwritten note. Tim's handwriting is bold but not well-controlled. His "e"s look like "i"s and his "m"s like "n"s.

Dear Gabby:

Never a dull moment with you, is there? I follow your exploits in the papers and on TV. Should have married you to keep you out of trouble. Kidding aside, I'm behind you all the way. Hold tight. Don't let the bastards get to you. And always ask, now what would Tim do in my situation? Then do the absolute opposite and you're bound to succeed.

You could say that Sally and I are now a unit, though there is no talk of a permanent arrangement. She's no Gabby Lewyn, but then I couldn't have kept up with you anyway. The love Sally and I experience is measured and steady, not wild and passionate. Maybe that's best at *our ages. And yes, fear not, you will receive an invitation to the church wedding, if and when it occurs. I'm still prepared to bet $1000 that you'll beat me to the altar. It would be the happiest money spent in my entire life.*

Love, Tim

Gabby rereads the letter, then for a short moment presses it against her bosom. Tim's support means a lot. He always makes her feel important. While he is distancing himself from her, it is good to know he's still a friend. If necessary she could hop a shuttle flight to New York and seek his counsel. It isn't necessary, but it's nice to know he's there for her.

ON CHANNEL 45, THE LEGAL CHANNEL, PROCEEDINGS in Baltimore have concluded but commentators are dissecting the day's activities. Since TV stations are not permitted to broadcast jury selection, their programming is flat. Just talking heads on the boob tube. Experts speak about the composition of juries and lawyers seeking jurors sympathetic to their client's position. Both prosecution and defense use all their peremptory challenges with the effect of slowing down the final selection. From the slow progress of the court, Gabby feels secure she may escape from Washington for a week without missing much. In five working days the court may not even complete the selection.

THE FOLLOWING DAY CHUCK BROWNER ANNOUNCES that Noah Zentner is holding on the phone.

"Like a rat in a hole," Noah answers her query about how he's feeling. "Can't move out of hiding. Fortunately, there's an exercise room with weights and a treadmill here. Nothing to do all day but run and do sit-ups. Physically I'm in great shape. My moods are something else. How are you, honey?"

"Holding up, I suppose. Worried. Wish I could be there to hold your hand. Zoe will make things right, but she won't be affectionate. Besides, you want a mean grizzly bear to represent you. I'm going away. Out of town for a week. But I'll be with you in spirit. Along with whatever prayers I can muster."

"Where, honey? I need to know where you are."

"Can't do that, Noah. But I will say what I'm doing."

"Scuba diving off Guadalupe. Rock climbing in Argentina?"

"Nope. I'm going to see Seth."

"You know where he is?" Noah's voice is a mixture of surprise and uncertainty.

"Yes, but I can't share the location. I'm under oath not to tell anyone."

A long hiatus occurs while Noah attempts to patch together his thoughts into a coherent sentence. "Well, well, when you see him, say hello for me. Give him my best, please."

"A promise. I have to be back at the congregation on October 23rd. If you need me, leave messages with Chuck Browner. He's one of the few I trust these days. And do me a favor, Noah. Tell Zoe that I've gone, but will return on the 22nd. She can also leave messages with Chuck."

"You got it, honey. A big hug from me."

"Ditto..." She doesn't want to hang up until Noah must cut the conversation short.

"Gotta go," he says and a moment later the phone goes dead.

"Bye, love," she replies into the inactive receiver. Her uncensored response surprises her. She remains on her bed by the phone wondering about the motivation that prompted it. Noah Zentner, who may go to prison for raping another woman, is now a significant part of her life.

THE ADDRESS JEREMY GREER GAVE GABBY FOR HIS father turns out to be in Haifa. No surprise on this score because many speculated he would turn up in Israel, a natural place for a Hebrew-speaking Jew to flee. The note said he didn't know exactly where his father was living, but letters addressed to a nightclub called Moadon Baccus always managed to reach him. And when he left phone messages there, his father had always returned the call.

Gabby completed a year's rabbinical training in Israel and has accompanied two Jewish Welfare Federation missions to the Jewish homeland. For this, her fourth visit, she arrives in early morning at Ben-Gurion Airport on the outskirts of Tel Aviv and takes a limousine north to the Dan Hotel on the western summit of Mt. Carmel overlooking Haifa Bay. The nonstop flight from Kennedy Airport has exhausted her and she needs some industrial strength sleep to combat jet lag. Yet adrenaline pitches into her bloodstream and prevents her from sleeping. After a sweet

Turkish coffee at a sidewalk cafe, she descends through winding commercial streets to seek out Moadon Baccus. The city sparkles in the midday sun. Port cities are usually cosmopolitan and Haifa is no exception. Everywhere it radiates with prosperity and she recalls words of the Israeli author A.B. Jehoshua that Haifa, unlike Tel Aviv and Jerusalem, was spared Arab terrorism. Somehow in this cauldron of commerce Jews and Arabs have found a formula for peaceful coexistence.

Jerusalem, not Haifa or Tel Aviv, is the city of choice for most American Jews. Perhaps the port of Haifa appeals to Seth's contrarian spirit. Or maybe his spirit is freer in a city unencumbered by Jerusalem's religious fundamentalism or Tel Aviv's rampant materialism.

Moadon Baccus is located on a narrow winding alley called *Rehov Aleph Daled Gordon*, sandwiched between ugly buildings from the prewar British Mandate era. Neon lights and blue bunting dress its undistinguished facade. A glass billboard displays glossy theatrical photographs of current entertainers. Top billing is given to a Yemenite vocalist by the name of Yael Barkani, a high-cheeked beauty with large, deep-set Semitic eyes accentuated by azure eyeshadow and full, sensuous lips—every male's fantasy of what a modern Israeli woman should look like. Gabby notes that unlike herself this beauty never had to bother with plastic surgery on her nose.

In second billing is a promotional photo of someone familiar. She is amused but not surprised to see Seth Greer in a open-collared shirt, his hair stylishly tousled and much longer than in his previous life. The photograph captures a wry, provocative smile, balanced by a light emanating from his forehead like the horns on Michelangelo's statue of Moses. Below him in block letters are the Hebrew words *Comedia Hitulit*, Satirical Comedy, then his name. In the world of comedy Seth Greer has become Set Gaon.

His versatility of mind and inventiveness of spirit never cease to amaze her. His energy is magical. Some say he is a *Luftmensch*, a man who lives not on the ground but in rarefied currents of air, like a frigate bird in the Arctic who glides through uplifting air drafts with little need or desire to alight on land. Others claim he is a Renaissance man with an unbridled imagination. In this photographic image, she sees a wild and untamable spirit. She knows differently. Like Tim, Seth is fundamentally a morose man who medicates his wounds with laughter. Humor is his beacon in the dark night of human suffering. How fitting that he should become a stand-up comedian. Congregations employed him to tell jokes from the pulpit. Now he does it from a stage.

It is approximately noon and Moadon Baccus doesn't open for dinner and entertainment until 8:30 p.m. After planning to catch his act that evening, she climbs up Mt. Carmel toward the Dan Hotel to collapse in bed.

WHEN SHE ARRIVES AT THE NIGHTCLUB IN EARLY evening, the thought of going backstage crosses her mind and is promptly dismissed. Her unexpected presence in Haifa might upset Seth's routine. Besides, she is eager to see him in his new role untainted by memory of his past. This decision requires her to take a side table where she orders *mizrachi* food, *salat yerakot* of tomatoes and cucumbers, humus and grilled chicken with lemon. During her meal, a trio of kibbutz singers croon nostalgic ballads from the 1950s to prepare the audience for the star attraction. Gabby finds her foot tapping the beat on an imaginary bass drum. The rhythm is lively and contagious. Though still suffering from jet lag, the energy of these entertainers inspires her.

Yael Barkani is every bit as beautiful as her photo and possesses a deep resonating voice to match. Tall and flat-chested, she wears a skintight black leotard and a paper-thin white blouse. No bra. The dark disks of her nipples occasionally appear behind the translucent material. Her songs are spirited renditions of melodies from Middle Eastern countries which, unlike Western ballads, seem to go on and on without resolution. The nasality of her voice diminishes as it rises into high octaves. Only after an extended medley does it occur to Gabby that the zither, drums, and flute are being played by Arabs, not Jews. Music brings together former enemies.

Yael Barkani finishes her act to loud applause, takes several half-bows in appreciation, smiles to reveal a mouth of teeth no less perfect than her facial features, bows again, smiles, then raises her arms for quiet. Her native Sabra accent is quick and crisp, pasting together subjects and predicates without pause. Gabby, whose conversational Hebrew is good enough to carry on a simple conversation but not good enough for a heated debate, understands her introduction.

oleh hadash, recent immigrant
m'amerika, from America
adam hituli b'ivrit, very satirical man in Hebrew
adam letzani b'anglit, a hilarious man in English
bilti muvan b'aravit, an unintelligible man in Arabic
rosh memshalah shelanu b'moadon Baccus...the Prime Minister of Club Baccus
Rabotay v'gevirotay, takiru Set Gaon...Ladies and Gentlemen, meet
Set Gaon!

Gabby's heart pounds with anticipation. Before Seth shows up on the stage, her mouth is open and she finds herself giggling. He has her on a laughing roll as he bounds toward the stage and pops into the spotlight. Folks clustered around nearby tables stop eating. They put down wine glasses and lean forward. Clearly, he is not someone who has yet to prove himself before a skeptical audience.

He looks healthy and trim. His hair, salted with silver, is long, floating down past his ears in a rather sexy, unkempt way. His flowered shirt is casually unbuttoned, revealing a hirsute chest.

With opens hands he signals to his minions. "*Todah rabah, lachem*, please...I see you've all been enjoying a meal at Moadon Baccus. And most of you are finished by now...therefore *rabotay, nevarech*, Gentlemen, let us say the traditional blessing over the meal..." The irony of a comedian calling for prayers of the devout after dinner is obviously a joke. This is not the type of meal for blessings. Nor is this audience pious. And the non-kosher Moadon Baccus certainly isn't the right place to do it. His preposterous suggestion causes the audience to laugh eagerly. They love poking fun at Israel's Orthodox community.

"Know what the blessing over lobster is?" he asks rhetorically, hammering the Orthodox custom of reciting different blessings over various items of food. In their wildest dreams, observant Jews had never conceived of blessing food which is outlawed in the Bible.

"*Ha-motzi sheretz min ha-yam*... Blessed is the Almighty who brings forth creeping, forbidden creatures from the sea."

His Hebrew is peppered with biblical expressions, a sign of education. His accent is unabashedly American with no attempt to mimic the speed or rhythm of native-born Israelis. That doesn't surprise Gabby, who never witnessed him trying to be more than he was. She follows most but not all of his jokes which focus upon political squabbling in the capital. With a copy of *Yediot Ahronot*, the evening newspaper, in his hand, he begins with a shaggy dog story, then a dozen one-liners to take advantage of the momentum. His audience follows with increasing pleasure. First, he takes on the Likud Party, then the Labor Party. Laughter from one joke collides with laughter of another; no one knows exactly which gag he is reacting to. With the aid of a radio microphone, he dodges and feints into the audience to badger the diners, then moves back on stage. Like many good comedians he enjoys his own material, laughing freely but never so hard as to obscure a good punch line. The fact that Gabby cannot understand all the Hebrew is insignificant. It feels good to let go and no one can make her laugh as freely as Seth Greer. For a moment, she feels the old times at Ohav Shalom returning with Rabbi Seth Greer on the pulpit. But she also senses him transcending his past.

He has her laughing so hard air cannot escape from her lungs, causing her ribs to ache. Her cheeks hurt from over-extension. To relieve the pain she must stop howling which, for the moment, she is unable to do.

Like most comedians Seth chides the hypocrisy of the politicians whose acts and words seem to bear no relationship to each other. Politicians are windbags and voting for them only provides encouragement. Seth's puns, the bedrock of Israeli humor, are subtle and erudite. He's so quick that one must not only hear the pun but know how the word is spelled. Stretching for laughter is not necessary: it follows him. His act goes fast. He leaves his audience howling with approval, comes back with a rapid series of one-liners. A bow ends the routine, followed by thanks to his audience for helping him have so much fun. The Arab trio assists his departure with a peppy tune from Jordan.

Gabby jots a note on a paper napkin and asks her waiter to see that it gets into Seth's hands as soon as possible. That requires the help of a ten-shekel note. She orders Turkish coffee with chelm, a Middle Eastern spice from the cardamom family, and is sipping it when Seth approaches from the rear. The first clue to his proximity is a kiss on her left cheek. She stands to meet him. His arms hold her from him, studying her like a bride under the bridal canopy. A strong bear hug follows.

"*Shalom lach*, you look wonderful, Gab," he exclaims, genuinely overjoyed to see her. "Jeremy telephoned to say he had given you my address. I expected a letter. Not a visit. And certainly not so soon!"

"Since you left, I've been on a merry-go-round. Needed to take time off from Ohav for a few days. But most of all I wanted to talk with you. Can we?"

"Absolutely," he trumpets with enthusiasm. "By all means, Gab, let's talk. As long as you want."

"Where?"

"Let's start here," he suggests. "Got another show at eleven. I hope you'll stay a few days in Haifa. I must show you around. It isn't Washington, but then it isn't Tel Aviv either."

After they take seats and Seth orders a brandy for her and a Goldstar beer for himself, she says, "You look better than I anticipated. And you're funnier on stage than on the pulpit. More natural, more spontaneous. My cheeks hurt from laughing. My ribs are sore. You obviously enjoy what you're doing."

"Easy work. Never thought I could make a living telling jokes, but seem to be doing all right. I hope to bring the act home some day. Maybe a few people in the States will come to see it. I've already written the billing: *Sex Rabbi on Stage—Is This A Joke Or Something?*"

"More than a few admirers I believe."

"Jeremy told me what you said on *Yom Kippur.* Quintessential Gabby. I knew you'd figure it out."

"Why didn't you tell me?"

"Embarrassment, I guess. What I did wasn't what people would call a successful experiment. Pretty damn stupid actually."

"All experiments don't have to succeed. Isn't that what Karl Popper wrote about science? Experiments that fail are just as important as those that succeed. Did I get it right, Seth? It was *divine synapse* you were seeking, wasn't it?"

"Close. A few details wrong, but you hit the target. How'd you figure out that I wasn't just a dirty old man?"

"I knew that from the beginning. We've been too close for too many years. Emma convinced me. We've become friends, closer today than in the past. She told me something you never would. Or could. We were at a funeral, walking between graves. It was the most unlikely place to talk about sex, but our conversation fell upon your relationship and what went wrong. I assumed that when things between you two went afoul sex did as well. She told me things too intimate for my ears, things about physical intimacy in the bedroom between husband and wife. But she had a purpose. She went out of her way to praise you as a lover. Said you were a giving partner. Never selfish. You wouldn't expect that from a dirty old man. Unselfish bedfellows are usually giving people. Selfish folk climax first and don't care what their partners experience. I hope this doesn't embarrass you."

"I'm an expert at living with embarrassment."

"Eleanor Weissborg corroborated Emma's experience. By the way, she asked me to send her apologies. She's quite remorseful about blaming you for her troubles. Whatever you did seems to have helped her through the bad patches."

He smiles, sipping his beer and keeping his lips on the edge of the glass. "Glad to hear it. Well now, Little Friend, it sounds as if you've managed to rack up some experience between the bedsheets as well."

Her eyes dance with youth, a look that always endeared her to him. "I've had my share of lovers. Not as many as you, of course."

"You've been keeping secrets from me, Little Friend."

"No more than you've kept from me."

"Thanks for defending me at Ohav. It was political suicide, you know."

"We'll see soon enough, but the fact is I don't really care any longer. I told the congregation the truth. Had to cut through all the garbage said about you. About time somebody said something truthful there. If umbrage is taken, then it might not be the place for me to work. Hell, I might become a comedian in Jerusalem. You could teach me the jokes."

Music begins over the club's speaker system in preparation for more live entertainment and it is necessary for them to raise their voices. He slides his chair sideways to be closer to her.

"I came to ask you a few questions still open in my mind. If you don't feel you want to answer then don't. I know only a portion of what went on between you and those women, you understand."

"How can I turn down a friend who stood up in my defense?"

She does not jump into the interrogation, but pauses to find the right words. When they don't come, she abandons all artifice. "Seth, did you screw Morgan Zentner? Of all your disciples she seems the most eager. She's a lusty woman with a passion for mysticism. Her bedroom looks like a sex shrine. Pedestals, mystic symbolism, incense, pillows galore. I wouldn't be surprised if there's a symbol for *divine synapse* tattooed at the entrance to her *pupik*. She must have been all over you."

He puckers his lips in momentary contemplation. "She was. Repeatedly. You won't believe me when I say I turned her down. It wasn't easy, I can tell you. Tough to reject a woman as gorgeous as she. Can you imagine how flattering it is to be propositioned by a Venus? Morgan could stir the carnal instincts of a tortoise. But the truth is, Gab, I resisted. One of the hardest things I've ever done. Never got to see that tattoo on her *pupik*."

"Why?"

"You're looking too deep." He shoots his eyes up to meet hers. "You're good on tough stuff, but then err on what should be obvious. Noah is one of my closest friends. The idea of screwing my friend's wife didn't appeal. I knew my job and career were in jeopardy. Jobs can be replaced; old and trusted friends can't. When it comes down to it, my friendship with Noah was more important than a tumble in the hay with Helen of Troy. Did a lot of stupid things, Gab. More than I'm proud of. But screwing my friend's wife wasn't one of them."

"Actually, Morgan doesn't exactly fit the profile. She's a bit wacky but not desperate or menopausal like the others. That is the profile, isn't it?"

"Women at wit's end. I never sought them out. Each one approached me. We did a lot more than screw, you know. I talked with them for endless hours. They complained about the lack of libido. Worse, about the lack of lovers. It was only when talking seemed to go nowhere that I entertained the idea of orgasmic rejuvenation. I had deep reservations, but I was prepared to experiment. I felt an orgasm or two wouldn't do them any harm and might help them rebuild lost self-esteem. *Divine synapse* wasn't a joke. Though my experiment with *divine synapse* was a bust, something good came from it. These women were living ghosts who learned there's still life between their legs. What they needed most was someone to take interest in them. It turns out a good, old-fashioned tumble under the sheets is a better antidote against aging than bonding with God."

Gabby feels so comfortable with Seth's response that she throws caution to the wind. "Did you ejaculate?"

"Are you kidding?" He is blunt. "It was supposed to be their synapse, not mine. I was only a conduit. Any fellow who could muster a reasonable erection could have done the job. Maybe even a vaginal vibrator."

"So you withheld?"

"I was far too skeptical about the mechanics to attempt synapse myself. Never felt the need for it. Besides, I knew that if I allowed myself to climax it would change everything."

"If you understood from the outset that it wouldn't work, why were you so foolish?"

He does not answer, but instead leans back against his chair, looking directly at her, then letting his eyes wander around the nightclub. The stage is brightly illuminated. He knows musicians will soon begin their gig with a medley of loud, spirited songs. She lets the silence between them linger. Arab musicians play Israeli folk music on an accordion, electric guitar, and clarinet. She doesn't want to lose the train of thought and repeats the question. "Why, Seth? That's why I came here to see you. That the only thing I don't understand."

"You know it, Gab. You're not looking in the right place. Put on your sleuth's hat. Roll the possibilities in your mind. Then think of all the time you and I spent together."

"I have. And that's why I don't understand why you'd do such a self-destructive stunt."

"Do I have to spell it out for you, Little Friend? I did a stupid thing to prevent doing a wicked thing. The bloody truth is I screwed those women in order to keep my dirty mitts off you. You're the only one I wanted to make love with. And not to achieve *divine synapse* either. In my fantasies about getting you into bed, there was no place for God. From the first day you came to interview for a position at Ohav, I watched you grow and mature. How I resisted falling in love! It took all the skill I had. I should have gotten a big medal for resisting. If a man has to sin, cheat on his wife, and shame his children, if he has to fall from grace, he should do it with someone who appeals to him. When things went sour with Emma, I wanted you in the worst way. It became an obsession. The only way I could keep my hands off you was to keep them busy with other women. I concocted this ridiculous scheme to divert my attention. That part of the experiment worked, didn't it?"

"You never put a finger on me. When I learned about those other women, I felt left out. But you were always a gentleman."

"Not a gentleman, but a fool. In my madness I was prepared to throw away a career. But I couldn't nor wouldn't endanger yours, too. Nothing would have been worse than that, Gab. You're too good a rabbi. Actually, you're far better at it than I ever was."

"You're a lot funnier."

"A gift from God. Nothing acquired by my own merits. But your professional craft is learned and practiced."

"Are your feelings the same about me now? Here in Haifa?"

A gush of air exits his lips which he replaces immediately with a gusty intake. "If I thought I could get away with it, I'd grab you this very second. But it won't work. You know it, and so do I. The minute you return to Washington my heart will break. Besides, every man needs a goddess to worship. Just because I'm no longer practicing as a rabbi doesn't mean you shouldn't. You work hard at the job. There's no one better. No, my Gabby. That wicked I am not. Better just to let me rejoice at your wedding. I'd be a very happy man to officiate at that *simcha*."

Aaron Snitzer, stage manager at Moadon Baccus, breaks into the conversation and addresses Seth in Hebrew. No excuses for the interruption. No attempt to meet Gabby. "Yael is up next, Seth. I want you behind stage. Makes me feel more comfortable. Just in case she needs to cut her act short."

Seth puts a hand on Gabby's shoulder and squeezes. "So you know my soul now. I hope you're not insulted."

"I'm flattered beyond words. You'll always be my mentor. You did me a great favor. What better rabbi in the world to train under? There's no one in the world I'd rather have officiate at my wedding."

He stands, still holding her hand. "Before I go, tell me what favor I did for you."

"Had you made a pass at me, I probably would have succumbed. There were times when I secretly hoped you would. Until recently there was a man in my life. A clandestine romance in New York. A wonderful man who has everything I ever wanted with one exception: he's a Presbyterian minister who loves his Christian savior as much as I love the God of Abraham. Our romance was doomed from the start. I'll tell you about it after your show."

He is startled. "What? A competitor? God dammit, Gab, who's telling jokes now?"

The table is empty before she can marshal a reply.

The beautiful Yael Barkani is again in the spotlight. Her beauty dazzles everybody. Gabby is warmed inside by the thought of Seth's love. Maybe she loved him, too. Maybe she still does.

SEEING SETH REPEAT HIS COMIC ROUTINE THAT evening, she is able to appreciate his versatility. While the core of his act remains the same, he improvises generously, matching his humor with a new audience.

After the last performance, they climb Mt. Carmel to the Dan Hotel, sit on the now vacant verandah overlooking lights of the port. Conversation is easy and fluid. Their personal histories and interests overlap. Rather than conflict, their manners of thought complement each other. What they have never formally acknowledged is now apparent. They are very good friends.

When she suggests that he might return to his rabbinical career and they'd find a new congregation in a new community to serve together, he laughs off the idea.

"Been there, done that," he utters. No retrogressive steps. She understands. He is living testimony to the fact that people can constantly create their lives anew.

HE SPENDS HIS FREE TIME SQUIRING HER ON A touring escapade around northern Israel. In between dashes from this vista to that archeological site, they sit in cafes and resume an old pastime, challenging each other with intellectual games. Pasta in Israel isn't worthy of the name, so they make a concession to *mizrachi* foods, yogurt and eggplant-based dishes spiced with pine nuts and exotic oriental seasonings. Desert doves, split down the middle, marinated in olive oil and garlic, then broiled on charcoal fires Arab-style, are an instant favorite. Noah is the topic of much discussion. They watch the trial on CNN television. *The Jerusalem Post,* which caters to English-speaking readers, provides extensive coverage.

Gabby withholds her relationship with Noah. She is able to maintain the secret until the third day when further secrecy seems unfair. Besides, it becomes clear that Seth has not misread expressions on her face. He possesses an uncanny instinct for such things.

"There's more to this than meets the eye," she finally blurts.

"Usually is. No, let me guess. You've already dropped a dozen not-so-subtle clues. Dusted the path quite liberally with them. Noah is separated, lonely, devastated by the swirl of events around him. He needs help, someone to lift his spirits for his fight in the deadly corridors of Chancery. At his family's congregation there's an extremely attractive, athletic rabbi with sensitivity and kindness. She's single, heterosexual and plays a respectable game of tennis."

"Do you want me to go into details?" She is coquettish. Dimples ripple her cheeks.

"You already have. It's in the sparkle of your eyes, Little Lady."

"And do you approve of an affair between Noah and me?"

"He's my friend, Gab. You're my friend, Gab. Don't pray much these days, but I'm praying now that his lawyers get him off. I wouldn't like to see either of you in love if he's going to prison."

SETH'S LIMITED FINANCES DO NOT PERMIT HIM TO own a car, yet he takes a shared taxi with her to Ben-Gurion Airport on the evening of her departure. The parting is upbeat;

both individuals are determined not to show sadness. Seth makes jokes. Bad ones which he knows aren't working.

As they sit in the waiting lounge before Gabby enters Security and Customs, he falls silent.

"I'll keep you posted by e-mail," she promises.

"I'm beating my brains now to say something witty. Nothing comes."

She stands and leans over him, gently kissing his forehead, then combs her hand through his salt-and-pepper-colored hair. "No need, friend. Just keep 'em laughing at Baccus. That's all that counts."

"A big, big hug for Noah when you see him."

"If I can get that close. He's under twenty-four-hour guard in a secret place. Planning to go to the trial in Baltimore if his lawyers will let me."

The airport loudspeaker bristles alive. A female voice in Hebrew, then in English, and lastly in Arabic, announces Gabby's El Al flight to New York and the need for passengers to pass through Israeli security checks.

"I'm real glad you came, Gab," he says just outside the security gate.

"I am, too, Seth. There's something special between us."

"Could make a joke about that, but it's too precious. *Niseah tovah*," he says in Hebrew. "Have a safe journey."

"*Shalom, Rav Set Nechemya Gaon*." She recites his full name and title in Hebrew, pausing after each word as if setting it for a memorial in the air. Before tears flood her eyes, she passes into the security zone.

Chapter Fifteen

Jet lag drags at Gabby, causing fatigue and listlessness. Countless demands await at the synagogue and there isn't time for a full night's sleep, even if she were in the mood to enjoy one. Fortunately, Chuck Browner has her work backlog well organized: interviews with prospective new members, meetings with the religious school faculty, rehearsals with Cantor Blass, visits to four sick congregants, all in different hospitals (of course!), invocations at benefit dinners for the Jewish Welfare Federation and the Washington Ecumenical Conference. A whirlwind of details. What catches her attention in the stack of phone messages is one from Zoe Mountolive in Baltimore, asking for a return call at the earliest convenience. A surge of acid floods her stomach. This is not good news. Zoe should be occupied with more important matters. A special telephone number is provided with a code to breach the security cordon around the Zentner legal team.

When telephone contact is finally made, Zoe sounds as fatigued as Gabby feels. The trial, as Gabby has been able to discern from the Legal Channel on television, is set to begin with a sequestered jury. Names and identities of jurors are kept from the public, but their gender and ethnic composition are not. Seven women and five men, along with four alternates, three women and one man. Of the sitting jury four members are black, two Asian, and six Caucasian, two of whom are reported to be Jewish. Four of the sitting twelve hold full-time jobs. Three are housewives. Two on welfare. The rest support themselves with part-time employment. Lawyers interviewed on television question whether Noah Zentner is really being judged by his peers. Whether justice can be done by people who neither read newspapers nor watch television news is yet to be determined.

"You're a celebrity, Gabby." Zoe's voice is raspy. "Read about you in *The Washington Post* the day you left town. Your explanation of Rabbi Greer's sexual exploits was ingenious. Missed your profession. Should have been a sex detective. You convinced me to take Morgan Zentner's mystic practices seriously. It may be necessary to introduce the subject into this trial. Hope not, but I need to be prepared. Would you reconsider appearing on the witness stand?"

"I'd prefer not, but am willing if necessary. Is it?"

"Not as a character witness but..."—there is a distinguishable pause before Zoe continues—"maybe as an expert witness."

"Nothing I know is pertinent to the court."

"How about Jewish mysticism? The Kabbalah? You're teaching a course in Medieval Jewish Thought at Georgetown University, aren't you?"

Gabby almost snorts her frustration. "That, above all, should disqualify me. If the truth be known, I'm only one chapter ahead of my students in the readings. There are at least a dozen scholars in and around Baltimore who know more about the subject than I."

"True," Zoe cuts her off, "but none who understand how medieval mysticism operates in a modern context. With modern Jews, not medieval mystics. Anyway, we haven't crossed that bridge yet. Counter-culture experience is a can of worms. To introduce the subject might backfire on Noah. Still, I'd like you to stand in reserve, just in case."

"Andrea Delagnes said she's getting me a seat in court on Thursday. Will that screw up things?"

One of Zoe's staff asks a question on the other end of the line. She excuses herself and places her palm over the phone speaker to reply. A minute later she returns with an apology. "Sorry about that, Gabby. I'd rather you didn't appear in the courtroom. Your picture was everywhere in the media. People know you, especially the press. Don't want to stimulate unnecessary speculation about your relationship with Noah. Watch the trial on television."

"If I testify, will my friendship with Noah come out?"

"I'd be surprised if it didn't. But I would hope to control the manner in which it becomes public. Things will get nasty. Wouldn't want you exposed to a broadside from the prosecution. Or hand the press a juicy story it isn't entitled to. Unless we establish up front your personal relationship with Noah, the prosecution will undermine your testimony. Control is the key."

"I think Noah expects me there for moral support. Hard to stay away. How is he?"

"Holding up. But trials grind away at the accused. He's putting on a cheerful face. This is just the first step to hell."

Changing abruptly to a more comfortable subject, Gabby inserts, "And Clementine, how's she doing without her mother?"

"Staying with her father in Manhattan. When Peter isn't poisoning her mind against me he's stuffing her body with junk food. By the time I get her back home she'll probably hate me, look like a zeppelin, and have a face full of acne."

"Don't worry about it. You can fool adults every day of the year, but not kids. They figure out the truth about their parents. If Peter threatens her loyalty to you, Clemmy will revolt. Mark my words. I've seen it more than once."

"You always make me feel good, Gabby. I'll remember what you said when I get depressed. Is there anything you'd like me to tell Noah tomorrow?"

Gabby has to ponder that. There are a zillion things she'd like to tell him. About Seth Greer. About her trip to Israel. About her confidence he'll be found innocent. But nothing seems appropriate. Words shoot from her mouth before she can harness them. "Send him my love, Zoe."

"Well now, Rabbi Lewyn, that's something I'm absolutely certain he will cherish. You mean a lot to him. I'll be in touch. Or one of my staff." The telephone goes dead, then emits a familiar dial tone.

AT THE CIRCUIT COURT HOUSE IN BALTIMORE, ELIsheva Waller attracts television cameras like a topless bather on an Atlantic beach. There are long moments in the preliminary proceedings during which nothing appears to happen in court and cameras must provide viewers with something to hold their attention. The program director has the option to use pretty-girl frames to fill moments of slack. Eli is every director's dream face. Alluring dark eyes and a sensuous mouth. A slim neck below a gentle, rounded jaw. Strong white teeth convey an impression of a woman in excellent health. Her skin requires little by way of cosmetic enhancement. Short hair hugs the skull, not a wisp out of place. She wears a dark, professional suit with striped blouse, simple gold earrings, but no necklace. From time to time, she dons a pair of reading glasses to peruse legal documents. Waller is photogenic and she knows it.

Sylvia Junqueira possesses little of Eli's beauty, but knows how to exploit her endowments. A professional hair stylist has sculpted her jet-black hair. From time to time, a flick of her fingers returns an untamable strand behind her ears. In interviews with the press she vehemently denies using theatrical make-up despite thick facial powder that corresponds with the hue and composition used by studio cosmeticians to cut glare.

The press interprets the trial on multiple levels. Philosophical ambiguities over the legal definition of rape and sexual harassment are best explained in a human context. Eli, Sylvia, and Zoe, three professional women navigating a sea once sailed only by men, spawn a host of human interest stories. Their faces are ubiquitous: on TV screens, specialty magazine covers, and newspapers. Three different personalities are compared and contrasted.

PROSECUTOR SIDNEY JEFFERSON HINES OPENS THE trial with a recital of the People of Maryland's charges against Noah Zentner. During his forty-five minute oration his eyes fail to fall upon the stack of yellow legal notes before him. To look down would break eye contact with the jury. One by one each juror comes under his scrutiny as though this were his final summation and he expected an immediate verdict. Confident eyes convey a message: listen to me, follow my thinking, trust me. The prosecution wouldn't be going through this exercise if there wasn't strong evidence of the defendant's guilt.

At times Sidney's hands open as if trying to contain in his palms the simple facts of the case. "We all know that many women are sexually attacked in private." His view sweeps along the front row of jurors, then lifts to the second and continues in the opposite direction. "Usually they are alone with their tormentors. No witnesses. No corroboration. To convict a rapist under such circumstance it often comes down to a case of credibility. Do you believe the man who claims he didn't do it or the woman who claims he did? Not so in the People's case against Mr. Noah Zentner. Here we have credible witnesses to the crime.

Not a single witness, but four different witnesses. You will learn from them that they distinctly heard the victim, Eli Waller, protest against this assault. What they will tell you are the very words from her lips. Not one witness who might, in some way, have misheard or misunderstood, but four, each confirming testimony of the other.

"Now, ladies and gentlemen, Mr. Zentner's defense will soon argue that what happened aboard the *Dame Cynthia* on the Chesapeake Bay on the night of July fourth was an act of mutual consent. His lawyers will claim that Ms. Waller willingly participated in this sexual act and that it's no crime for mutually consenting adults to have sex. Our case will prove the contrary: that Ms. Waller was blatantly and maliciously violated against her will." For the first time, Sidney Hines moves his eyes horizontally from the jury to the Judge, as if to catch him in the act of napping, which he isn't.

The alert expression on the sunburned face of Judge Lucien Donald Weil, a sitting judge on the Circuit Court of Maryland for eight years, conveys the kinetic energy of a cheetah stalking breakfast on the African savanna. His nose is puffed and enlarged, and his silvery hair extremely full. Sixty-two years of age have failed to bald his scalp. One might assume from his reddish hue, protruding veins, and puffy nose that he is a drinking man and that assumption would correspond with the facts, though no one suggests that alcohol interferes with his judicial duties or that he sits on the bench in any condition less than absolute sobriety. A series of lectures he delivers at local Rotary and Chamber of Commerce lunches on Mandatory Sentencing Laws establishes him as a tough-minded, conscientious judge. Criminal lawyers in Baltimore City laud Chief Administrative Judge Raymond Lyman for selecting him to sit at the Zentner trial. Junqueira has tried one case of aggravated assault before him and won. Mountolive, who became a member of the Maryland Bar when serving a clerkship for an appellate judge in Washington, has no history in his court. Her associates in the District of Columbia office of Greenwald, Molletz are reasonably satisfied with his competence, though they warn that his penchant for publicity makes him unpredictable.

In her first appearance before the jury, Sylvia Junqueira decides to recast the Chesapeake outing on July fourth through questions put to Arlene Houston-Gephardt, Director of Finance for Eli's firm, The Hawthorne Group. Since Houston-Gephardt almost lost her life that night aboard the skipjack she attracts natural sympathy. The jury learns from her about the swim in the Chesapeake and how close she came to drowning.

Junqueira leans over the speaker's stand and asks, "Can you, Ms. Houston-Gephardt, describe what happened *after* you were rescued from the water?"

Her memories of the horrible incident are clouded, a fact which causes her to struggle for a point of entry. "At first, there were cheers. It was still pitch dark but somebody was passing around a bottle of rum to celebrate. Someone pulled my head back and poured rum into my mouth. I gagged. People were relating their own experiences in the water. We felt we had cheated death. Despite the humidity and heat, I was shivering."

"With that rum circulating around, was anybody drunk? Or tipsy?"

"Not that I was aware of. The bottle moved from mouth to mouth. A mere gulp or two and it passed to another. No one drank enough to be affected. I remember how it burned my throat."

"And how was it that you came to sit near the ventilation hatch over the cabin?"

"I didn't at first. I had originally entered the water to empty my bladder, but I was so frightened I completely forgot. Once safely aboard I almost exploded. So I had to make my way to the head in the cabin below."

"Did you see Ms. Waller there?"

"No, it was even darker in the cabin than on the deck, if that is possible. As far as I knew the cabin was empty. The air was stale and acrid. Heat was unbearable. Who would want to be there?"

"Can you tell us what you did when finished in the head?" Junqueira asks.

"I made my way back to the deck, then wove a path forward. Exhaustion suddenly overwhelmed me and I needed a place to sit. But it was dark and hard to move around. I kept bumping into people until I discovered a relatively flat surface above the cabin. Others were already there but I managed to find space. I didn't feel like talking."

"Is that how you came to sit by the open hatch to the cabin below?"

"Yes."

"Can you tell us how far you were from that hatch?"

"The sails were down and skipper was using a diesel engine to motor home. The engine is located below the cabin. You could hear it cranking through the hatch."

"Did you see Eli Waller go below?"

"No. I did not."

"Did you speak to her before she went below?"

"I can't remember talking with her after being rescued. Others congratulated me, but I don't think she did. On the other hand, I was in such a bad state I might not have remembered."

Junqueira moves to a new subject. "We've established that you were near the open hatch at the time contact between Mr. Zentner and Ms. Waller occurred below. Can you tell us what you heard from that hatch?"

"I heard people talking. Can't tell you what they said.There was considerable noise from the engine. Others were chattering beside me, so there was distraction. It was only when the screaming started that I paid full attention."

"What did you hear? Please be as specific as possible."

"I heard the words, NO, NO, NO, STOP. Then, STOP GOD DAMMIT."

"These words, NO, NO, NO, STOP...STOP, GOD DAMMIT. How is it you could distinguish these words above the engine noise and chattering of people around you?"

"They were much louder than normal conversation."

"Were they spoken or screamed?"

"Screamed."

"Can you tell us whether this was a male voice or a female voice?"

"Definitely female."

"How do you know that, Ms. Houston-Gephardt?"

"Because I recognized the voice."

"Is it possible that you have heard this female voice screaming before?"

"Yes, ma'am."

"Where and when, Ms. Houston-Gephardt?"

"At the office of the Hawthorne Group in New York City."

"Please tell us, who screams at The Hawthorne Group?"

"Eli Waller."

Chuckling breaks out in the courtroom.

"Does she scream often in the office?"

"Only when we're under pressure to get a project completed."

"Has she ever screamed at you, Ms. Houston-Gephardt?" Junqueira pursues.

"Yes, she has."

"And did her voice during these occasions sound like what you hear from the open hatch of the skipjack?"

"Yes, it did."

"And there's no doubt in your mind who said the words, 'NO, NO, NO, STOP...STOP GOD DAMMIT!'?"

"None."

DEFENSE COUNSEL MORTIMER STEEL'S DELIVERY during cross-examination of the witness is slower than Junqueira's, yet his voice is sharper, almost biting. "Ms. Houston-Gephardt, I'd like to ask you about events that occurred when you were rescued from the bay. Now you've told the court about your rescue, how you saw a flare light up the dark sky, then sputter out. Then, I believe, you heard a voice calling your name. Do you remember who called out to you?"

"Yes. It was Bill Pell. I was later told that he volunteered to call out my name because he is a tenor in a church choir and has a powerful, projecting voice."

"And when you heard your name, what did you do?"

"I answered with all the strength I could muster. It wasn't much. I was so frightened that I just didn't have enough voice to make contact."

"Did Bill Pell call out again?"

"Yes, once. But then there was nothing. I feared that they didn't hear me. And I couldn't see the sailboat because it was so dark."

"But you were rescued, weren't you?"

"Of course."

"By whom?"

"Two men dove off the *Dame Cynthia* to get me."

"Do you know who these men were?"

"Stephen MacNeille and Noah Zentner."

From the spectators in the courtroom, there is an audible gasp, followed by a flurry of whispers. Judge Weil is annoyed by the interruption but doesn't issue a reprimand. His disapproving glower is sufficient to mandatc silence throughout the court. Three jurors rearrange positions in their chairs; the remainder stare out into the courtroom expressionless.

"Let me get this straight," Steel continues. "Is one of the two individuals who helped save your life the same man who is here accused of raping Eli Waller?"

She nods until prodded by Steel to state a yes or no answer.

"Now let me draw upon your memory a bit more. You said that both Stephen MacNeille and Noah Zentner swam out to help. Did both support you in the water? Or guide you back to the boat?"

For a moment, Arlene Houston-Gephardt's eyes dart from her questioner to Eli Waller and then back. The movement is noted by Noah's defense team, a nuance they hoped would be noticed by the jurors. "No," she says. "Only Noah Zentner actually swam with me."

"Why? What happened to Stephen MacNeille?"

"He paddled to a position midway between us and the skipjack. Steve kept in voice contact with crewmen aboard *Dame Cynthia* who were maneuvering into position for a pickup."

"How did Noah Zentner help in the water?"

"He spoke to me in the dark. Said that the skipjack wasn't far away and that I would be safe. Told me to roll on my back and stretch my arms straight out in front and hold onto his shoulders. An old Boy Scout lifesaving technique. He paddled to the boat with me on the bottom. I didn't think it would work, but it did."

"Did he make any sexual advance while you were in the water?"

"No."

"Feel any of your private parts? Take advantage of your peril in any way?"

"No. Nothing like that."

"Any bumps under the water. Touching in private places?"

"No."

"And did he say anything to you once aboard *Dame Cynthia*?" Steel's tempo speeds up.

"Everybody was congratulating me. I can't remember exactly. I think he said I was great or something to that effect. I wanted to thank him for his help, but he disappeared in the dark and I lost the opportunity."

Steel stiffens behind the rostrum in a signal he has completed this line of questioning and wants to wrap up. "Ms. Houston-Gephardt, would you say that Mr. Zentner and Mr. MacNeille rendered you a vital service?"

"Yes, sir. Absolutely."

"And during this terrible episode that Mr. Zentner didn't take advantage of you in a sexual way?"

"That's true," she says.

"And did he make any suggestion afterward that you owed him a favor for his endeavor, whether sexual or otherwise?"

"Never."

"Thank you, Ms. Houston-Gephardt, you've been very helpful."

TWO DAYS LATER, ZOE MOUNTOLIVE'S QUESTIONING proves to be more strident when cross-examining the third witness for the government, Robert Crane, Financial Assistant and Records Keeper at The Hawthorne Group. Twenty-six years of age, Crane is fidgety in the witness box, uncertain where to plant his hands and focus his eyes. His lanky, post-adolescent presence does not instill confidence but his strong, assured baritone voice does.

After establishing how Crane came to be seated by the open hatch and overhear words from the cabin, Zoe asks, "Now, Mr. Crane, according to your testimony you heard the following words in a female voice state: NO, NO, NO, STOP, YOU SONNAVAH BITCH. Is that what you heard?"

"Yes, ma'am."

"You said this was a female voice. There were ten women aboard the *Dame Cynthia* during the Fourth of July sail. Can you identify which of the ten women you heard say NO, NO, STOP, YOU SONNAVAH BITCH?"

Robert Crane hesitates, shaking his head. "No, ma'am."

"But you're certain it was a female voice. Is that correct?"

"Yes."

"And you heard this female say STOP among other words?"

"Yes. No doubt about that."

"Ms. Houston-Gephardt has just testified that she heard other words in the cabin below but, due to noise of people speaking nearby could not distinguish their meaning. Did you hear other words?"

Robert Crane improves his position in the witness box. "Yes, ma'am."

"Before you tell us what you heard, would you tell the court when you heard them. Were these words before or after the NO, NO, NO, STOP, STOP, YOU SONNAVAH BITCH?"

"Before, I think."

"Please think again, Mr. Crane, because *when* you heard these words could be very important."

"Before. I'm sure of it because after the screaming I made my way aft to the ladder to help. So the words must have been before."

"Very well. Then could you tell us what words you heard?"

"Not precisely."

"Can you be precise about *who* said them?"

"Mr. Zentner."

"How do you know that?"

Because the voice was male and second, because it has a special clarity and ring."

"How did he utter these words? In a loud voice or a soft voice?"

"More like a shriek. As though he were expelling air from his lungs. He wasn't shouting and yet he wasn't just talking. Something in between."'

"Can you remember the sounds of the words even if you can't recall them exactly?"

"Yes, I can."

"Do you think they were English words?"

"I didn't recognize them, if that's what you mean. The one I remember sounded like the letter L in the alphabet. It was the sound EL."

"Any other sounds?"

"Something like SHA—something. Sounded strange to my ears."

"If I were to give you a sound which begins with SHA would you be able to identify it?"

"Maybe."

"You agree that the first part of the sound is SHA?"

"Yes."

"Could the last part be BAB?

"No, that's not it. Not the right syllable."

"How about LI?"

"No."

"MIEL?"

"No."

"Or perhaps DAI?" Zoe is matter-of-fact.

"Repeat that, please. That's closer to my memory."

"MIEL or DAI?"

Hard concentration contorts his expression. After a moment he selects, "DAI."

"Let's try both sounds together, Mr. Crane. SHA-DAI?"

"Tough to remember exactly. But I think that was close. Can't be sure, mind you. But it's close."

Zoe glances to Norman Kwan on her left. Eye signals pass between them until she looks back at Robert Crane. "So you're telling us that before Ms. Waller screamed for Mr. Zentner to stop whatever he was doing, he uttered the sounds, something in the nature of SHA-DAI?"

"Sounds right to me."

"But what about the sound you did remember? The sound EL? Does it come before or after the SHA-DAI?"

"Not sure."

"Well try SHA-DAI EL. Is that it?"

"No, I don't think so."

"Then try EL SHA-DAI. Is that it?"

He nods affirmatively.

"Please answer the question out loud, Mr. Crane."

"Yes, that's it."

"Then combined, the sounds are EL SHA-DAI? Is that what you heard?"

"Yes." He sounds more confident now.

"You're certain, are you?"

"Yes, ma'am."

"Thank you, Mr. Crane," Zoe says while turning from the podium to end the questioning. She masks her satisfaction with what the court record will later confirm. It is too early to reveal where this line of questioning leads. Let the prosecution guess.

There is relief in the court when Judge Weil declares a recess for the day. Jurors are dismissed to their hotel with admonition not to communicate about the trial with outsiders. Talk among themselves is restricted to subjects beyond the scope of the trial. The time will come to air their views of the proceedings, but that time has not yet arrived.

PROSECUTOR SIDNEY HINES MINIMIZES THE CHANCES his witnesses will inadvertently assist the defense by carefully rehearsing them in advance. Like Socrates among his Athenian peripatetics, he uses each answer as a springboard for another question. Karla West and Martha Low from the staff of Pyramid Development were also resting near the open hatch to the cabin at the time of the alleged rape. Karla remembers hearing Eli shout, NO, NO, GOD DAMMIT, STOP, STOP. Martha quotes, NO, NO, NO. PLEASE STOP. It was Karla who first heard the bang of the grinding winch thrust against the boat's bulkhead. Neither paid attention to what was uttered before the NO, NO. Yes, they were both aware of voices, but no, they didn't make the effort to discern whose they were.

Mortimer Steel cross-examines the witnesses by firing questions in rapid succession. His purpose is not to discredit their testimony but to derive a consistent picture of events aboard the skipjack prior to and after the alleged rape. For his questioning, he produces diagrams and charts to probe inconsistencies in what was heard and where the witnesses were stationed when they heard it. It is sufficient to demonstrate that the witnesses were not paying full attention to noises from the cabin. What one witness heard is substantially but not identically similar to what is heard by others.

Gil Brillenbourg, who directs the appraisal unit at The Hawthorne Group, thinks he recalls the sounds of lovemaking before the words, NO, NO, NO, STOP.

"I know this might be difficult, but can you approximate these sounds for us?" Steel entreats. "You know, the lovemaking sounds...or words. Just give us a flavor for what you heard. We don't wish to embarrass you."

Brillenbourg flushes. "It's not in my repertoire, sir. I can do a mean imitation of James Cagney, but not of lovemakers."

The response produces chuckles throughout the court, easing the tension.

"Was it like OOH, OOH, AAH, then heavy breathing and more AAHs?"

"Remotely."

"Did you hear additional words that were recognizable?"

"Not that I can think of."

"Well then, did you hear the sound EL?"

"Yes, I did. Twice."

"And how about SHA-DAI? Did you hear those sounds too?"

"I'm not certain of that. I heard something that began with SHA, but not the rest of it."

"And what came after the SHA?"

"Nothing for a while. Then, NO, NO, NO, STOP, STOP."

"So let me be certain I understand the sequence of what you heard, Mr. Brillenbourg," Steel recapitulates. "First, the sounds that may or may not be lovemaking, that is the OOHS and AAHs, then the EL SHA..., followed by an interval of time, then the words, NO, NO, NO, STOP, STOP. Is that correct?"

"Yes. That's it."

"And one last question, Mr. Brillenbourg. About the interval. Could you say how long it was?"

"Not long. A few seconds, maybe."

"Ten seconds, twenty? As long as this?" And here Steel dramatically puts a finger to his lips and holds for what feels like an extraordinary long silence. "How about now, Mr. Brillenbourg?"

"Yes, that's close."

Steel reads the face of his wristwatch aloud. "About twelve seconds, then."

"Yes, sir. Give or take three or four."

"Is this the proper sequence of events, Mr. Brillenbourg? One: you hear sounds that resemble those made by people having sex. Two: you hear the sounds EL and SHA... Three: approximately twelve seconds elapse, give or take three or four, then you hear the English words NO, NO, STOP, STOP. Is that correct, Mr. Brillenbourg?"

"Yes, with one small exception. You said there were two words STOP, STOP. I can only be sure of one."

"All right, we'll make note of that alteration. Thank you, Mr. Brillenbourg. Your testimony has been very helpful."

Chapter Sixteen

Years of fielding questions on television talk programs have honed Eli Waller's skill. Without circumlocution or guile she answers questions from the prosecution retelling her version of what occurred in the cabin of the *Dame Cynthia*, the same story she told police at Easton, Maryland, shortly after returning to St. Michaels.

Sylvia Junqueira carefully monitors the jury's reaction to the gory details of the assault. Emotion is ready to break out on several faces, though jurors struggle to remain expressionless. Small clues reveal the impact. Jurors squirm in their seats. Their fingers wipe their cheeks and necks. Their torsos remain ramrod straight but pushed back against the chairs as though wishing to distance themselves from this unpleasantness. Junqueira believes in Eli's ability to convey the shame, degradation, and humiliation women feel when sexually violated. People sense how painful it must be to talk about sexual matters in public, particularly before television cameras. The depth of her personal sacrifice makes Eli a commanding victim who will win her own case. The prosecution needs only to provide the opportunity.

After receiving a nod of approval from the Judge, Junqueira departs from the lectern and moves into the open space between the bench and the witness box. She knows the plaintiff's version of events by heart and is not obliged to remain with her notes.

"Ms. Waller, I'd like to focus now on what happened when others rushed into the cabin to rescue you."

"Objection!" Zoe cuts her off mid-sentence. "The motive of *rescue* has not been established."

"Sustained," Judge Weil responds. "Rephrase the question, Ms. Junquiera."

Sylvia doesn't miss a beat. "When others entered the cabin, what did Mr. Zentner do?"

"I'm afraid I cannot comment on that, Ms. Junqueira. You see, I had my own problems finding my underpants and shorts on the floorboards. I used the darkness to pull myself together and was so relieved to be free from him that I didn't pay attention to what he was doing."

"So you got clothes on—not that it would have mattered because it was so dark, but I can see why you wouldn't want to go around naked, just the same." There is amused chuckling in the court. The idea of being clothed only by darkness strikes some as bizarre. "When you were dressed, what did you do next?"

"Made my way after the others up the ladder to the deck."

"Did anybody ask you what had happened?"

"I heard Noah Zentner's voice. He was explaining how the wave toppled him onto the bunk and how glad he was nobody got hurt."

"How did that make you feel?"

"Like crying out that it was a lie because he failed to mention how he had forced himself on me."

"Why didn't you set the record straight?"

"Because I didn't want a confrontation. Noah Zentner is a popular man. His employees at Pyramid Development would never take my word against his. Besides, some of us had almost drowned. There wasn't one person aboard who didn't acknowledge how close we had been to a tragedy. While the skipjack was moving slowly to shore, nobody really believed we were entirely safe. Folks were still very tense. I made a decision to remain silent until we were safely on land. The thought of disclosing this matter to Captain Danberry crossed my mind. I was aware how maritime law states that the skipper of a vessel carries with him or her the authority of government and the responsibility to see that laws are obeyed. But at the moment Alex Danberry had his own problems, somewhat larger in scope than mine. He had to navigate his sailboat to harbor in the dark and he would eventually have to answer for the faulty electrical system and the near loss of life of a passenger. It was hardly the time to divert his attention."

"Did you decide to report the incident immediately, Ms. Waller?"

"No, Ms. Junqueira. That took additional deliberation on my part."

"When did you make that deliberation?"

"Most people aboard were clustered near and around the aft cockpit. I needed quiet to think, so I moved forward to the bow where I could get maximum breeze, which wasn't much."

"Can you tell how you came to your conclusion about reporting the crime?"

"It did not come immediately. Though I was mad as hell at Zentner I still had to consider the loss of business to The Hawthorne Group. Were I to press charges against him, my firm would lose a very large commission from Pyramid Development. It is axiomatic in my firm that no officer may permit his or her personal agenda to interfere with the company's income. To advance this kind of personal claim is tantamount to corporate treason. It was not in my interest or the interest of my firm to press charges."

"Then what possessed you to sacrifice such interest and report the rape to the Easton police?"

"That's what I debated on the bow. A very difficult decision, but in the end I told myself. this is a women's issue which is larger than Eli Waller. Thousands of American women are raped by strangers, lovers, and husbands. Infinitesimally small numbers are prepared to press their grievances in court. The result of timidity is that rapists escape punishment. And this has the effect of encouraging other men to commit similar sexual violence. It took about an hour for the *Dame Cynthia* to make St. Michaels. I had time to think about my dilemma. In the end, I felt obliged to go public."

There is a long silence after Eli ends her explanation. Junqueira has a keen sense of courtroom moods and she decides to let this testimony sink in. Whatever time it takes, let the jurors think about how much this woman had to lose by pressing charges. Let them consider not just the lucrative commissions her firm lost, but the humiliation. Personal sacrifice engenders credibility.

Throughout Eli's testimony, Zoe Mountolive's worries grow. She has underestimated Sylvia Junqueira's ability to make a victim into a martyr.

THE FOLLOWING DAY THE OPPORTUNITY TO CROSS-examine Eli arrives. Zoe must tread cautiously and not alienate jurors who are likely to believe Waller's version of the event. In order to confound this rendition she will have to approach each subject obliquely and plant seeds of doubt which will eventually grow into full disbelief.

"Ms. Waller," Zoe tilts her narrow reading glasses up to her forehead and gazes across to the witness box with affected innocence. "You have stated how after the alleged rape you went to the bow of the *Dame Cynthia* to take the air and gather your thoughts. Is that not so?"

Eli is wary. The District Attorney warned her about Zoe Mountolive's craft. She is said to be as stealthy as a leopard attacking its victim from its blind side, sinking incisors into the jugular before there is time to resist.

"That's correct," she sighs with theatrical fatigue.

"And you also said, if I understand correctly, that you were torn between the interests of The Hawthorne Group and the interests of women at large. You consider yourself as an example for other women, an encouragement to them. Is that correct?"

"More or less. Yes."

"And you were on the bow about an hour, is that right?"

"I didn't look at my watch. It was too dark to read the dial anyway. But from what the skipper told us before I went below, I estimate we had about an hour's sailing to St. Michaels. The *Dame Cynthia* had a small diesel engine that wasn't very powerful. The vessel was made for sailing, not motoring."

"Since you spoke with Captain Danberry *before* you went to the head, you must have an idea of how much time you spent below, including the time when Mr. Zentner is accused of attacking you? Isn't that right?"

"Not to the minute. But my profession makes me acutely aware of time intervals. It's not necessary to look at a watch to sense how many minutes have elapsed."

"Was your ability to judge time sequences impaired by physical pain from the alleged rape?"

"No. I don't believe it was."

"How about any mental anguish suffered from the alleged rape?"

The witness has to consider her previous testimony before answering, "No. No. It wasn't. When people attempt to misuse me I usually get mentally sharper."

"Then is it fair to conclude from what you've just said that you had at least an hour to consider charging Mr. Zentner with the crime of rape?"

"Yes."

"And that in coming to this decision you were in full control of your mental and emotional faculties?"

"Yes."

"Now during this deliberation, you thought first of your firm, then of countless victimized women who fail to come forward and fight their attackers in court. Were these the only two subjects of your thoughts at the time?"

"I'm not sure I understand your question," Eli replies, looking puzzled.

"Objection, Your Honor." Sidney Hines is half on his feet. "The question is vague."

"Sustained," the Judge says. "Simple, straightforward queries, please, Ms. Mountolive."

Zoe reacts with the swiftness of an alley cat. "Did you consider anything other than your firm's loss of revenue and women who are fearful of charging rapists in court?"

"I think that's the sum total."

"Are you certain you didn't consider anything else?"

"Quite."

"Ms. Waller, did you not consider the possibility of an unwanted pregnancy?"

"No."

"How about the transmission of HIV virus?"

"No. I guess I should have, but I didn't."

Zoe presses, "In such a situation, wouldn't you think it unusual to be so selfless, Ms. Waller?"

"I'm a principal in The Hawthorne Group. If it loses money, so do I," Eli snaps.

"True, but you haven't mentioned any personal interest advanced by pressing charges against Mr. Zentner. Did you consider any benefits to yourself in charging Mr. Zentner?"

Sylvia Junqueira snaps, "Objection. The question has been asked and answered!"

"Overruled. Asked, but not entirely answered, Ms. Junqueira. Please, Ms. Waller. Answer Ms. Mountolive's query."

"I can't discern any advancement achieved by wanting Mr. Zentner brought to justice."

"None, Ms. Waller? Really, none?"

"None."

There is a twang of angry impatience in Zoe's response. "Well, let me spell one out for the court. Do you have an idea how many times you appeared on television last year?"

"No, I don't keep track of my appearances. Many, I suppose."

"Do you employ the services of a publicist, Ms. Waller?"

Eli is momentarily stopped by the question, but loses not more than a beat before replying. "Yes."

"For what purpose?"

"To oversee my public appearances. Publicity is a necessary evil of our business. Large corporations want to do business with people they know about."

"Do you recall the name of this publicist?"

"Grand and Moravac."

"How many years have you retained the services of Grand and Moravak?"

"I'm not certain. About four."

"Do you know how many television appearances Grand and Moravak has book for you?"

"No. I'm afraid I don't keep track."

Zoe pulls down her reading glasses and glances over her notes, not rushing. "Grand and Moravak has a web page on which they advertise services rendered to successful clients. According to data on their page, they booked you for forty-one television appearances last year. This year, you've already made fifty-one and there are still months to go. Are these correct data?"

Eli shrugs her shoulders, then replies, "I honestly don't know."

"Do you have any reason to believe that Grand and Moravak is padding the numbers?"

She shakes her head. "No."

"And do you perceive such public appearances as beneficial to you or your career?"

The witness is aware of where such questioning might lead and is cautious. "I guess so, but it's hard to quantify."

"Has your exposure on television increased since the alleged rape in early July, Ms. Waller?"

"Yes."

"Has your income increased since that date?"

"A little, I believe."

"Could you put a number on what you mean by *a little*?"

"No. All such matters are handled by my accountant."

"Is what you state *a little* less than five hundred thousand dollars?"

"No. It is more than that. Partly because the firm got paid for work performed during the previous year and has nothing to do with any notoriety I might have received."

"Is it less than seven hundred and fifty thousand dollars?"

"No."

Zoe's gesture of palms up, fingers open commands attention. "That sounds like a lot of money to me, Ms. Waller. But for the moment, let's leave the subject of increased earnings. I'd like to ask if all this publicity has furthered any personal interests besides money?"

"I can't think of any."

"You are on the Executive Committee of the National Association of Women?"

"Yes, I am. And proud to be so."

"With good reason. And are you not currently a candidate for its presidency?"

"I am."

"Do you recall the deadline for candidates to submit their applications?"

"Not offhand. Sometime this past summer."

"According to minutes from the National Conference in San Francisco, August eighth, to be exact. Is that correct?"

"Yes, I guess so. It sounds right."

"Isn't that a little more than a month *after* your decision to press charges against Mr. Zentner?"

"Yes, but one has no relationship to the other."

"Let me understand this." Zoe is coy, playing the conventional role of the naive country lawyer. "A few minutes ago you told this court that on the evening of the alleged crime you pondered the example you might set for other raped women. You decided to sacrifice a healthy commission from Mr. Zentner's firm and carry the torch for raped women. Is that correct?"

"Yes. That's what I said."

"And in order to succeed as a role model for abused women, wouldn't that require favorable treatment from the press?"

"It would help."

"Did it help get you a speaking slot in the Right of Choice March in Washington?"

"That's hard to assess."

Zoe fishes a stack of papers for a manila file which she raises to shoulder level in full view of the jury. "Flyers published on June 1 by Women for Choice and Feminist Health Coalition for the March on Washington do not list you as a speaker. News about the alleged rape hit the papers and television on July 6th. The newsletter of July 27th from National Alliance of Feminist Organizations lists you as a featured speaker for the March. Didn't publicity about this case propel you into the national spotlight, Ms. Waller?"

"I was not on the planning committee."

"Can you tell us why you were invited at the eleventh hour?"

Eli knows she is being led into a trap and takes her time. "No."

"I am not questioning your credentials as a role model. Let me rephrase my earlier question, Ms. Waller. When you were on the bow of *Dame Cynthia* on the night of July Four and pondered the future, did the thought of becoming a crusader for women's rights enter your mind?"

Eli starts to answer, then pauses. Just an instant too long to be credible. "No, Ms. Mountolive. I thought of becoming a role model, not a crusader."

"And did you perceive any professional benefit from the notoriety?"

"No. It never crossed my mind."

Zoe smiles. She has succeeded to cast doubt about the woman's sainthood. There is a small crack in the feminist icon.

When a natural break arrives, Judge Weil asks the defense if it is prepared to interrupt its cross-examination and end the day's session. No objection is raised. When an appropriate moment occurs, he releases the jury and, due to a conflict in his schedule, calls a recess for an additional two days. Because a story has been circulating among network news that a day-old *New York Times* was discovered in a stairwell outside the jurors' hotel floor, the Judge warns all and sundry that his commitment to the First Amendment right of free speech and access to information does not extend to a sequestered jury. Any attempt to influence the jurors will be answered with stern punishment.

From Zoe's point of view, the postponement is welcome. It wouldn't be bad for her client if the jurors take extra time to think about Eli's character. The day's testimony has begun to tarnish her persona. Perhaps now a few jurors will question her motives.

AFTER HER RETURN FROM HAIFA, GABBY'S ROUTINE in the synagogue eventually stabilizes, yet there is a subtle change in her attitude toward it. Being with Seth Greer produced a sense of emancipation. His success in a new profession stimulates thoughts about changing careers. She understands the reasons why Ohav Shalom will not appoint her Senior Rabbi, yet no matter how rational she attempts to be she cannot shake the resentment. Rejection is never easy to absorb and, no matter how the Board sugar-coats the appointment of another rabbi, it is still a rejection.

Chuck Browner knows her mood and in his omniscient way counsels her to disengage from the congregation emotionally. Divert interest and attention to something or someone who can reciprocate. Ohav Shalom cannot. It is too institutionalized and, despite her apologia for Seth Greer on *Yom Kippur*, still wounded by his deceptions.

At the end of the day, Chuck drops into the chair opposite her desk without waiting to be invited. She is cleaning up messages on the blotter and he is studying the features of her face.

"You look sad, Rabbi Gabby," he almost whispers to attract her attention. "You haven't been the same since you've come back."

She lifts a squared chin which her jogging regime has kept exceptionally lean. "Now what makes you say that, Chuck? Fact is I feel quite rejuvenated. Despite the jet lag."

"Remember who you're talking to, Rabbi. I know when you're sad."

"Gay men think they possess extraordinary sensitivities into other people's feelings."

"We do. And you know it. And I'm telling you, you're sad and dejected."

"Well then, if you're so perceptive, tell me why."

"My guess is because of Noah Zentner. When I come into this study you close the doors on the entertainment console, but occasionally I can hear voices. You never used to watch television during the day. Now you've got it on whenever you're alone."

Gabby eases back into her chair and regards Chuck with uplifted eyebrows that make her forehead wrinkle. Her dimples deepen when tense. That he reads her so well is flattering. "Well now, Dr. Freud, what do you make of the trial so far?"

"You don't want to hear my opinion because it's painful."

"So what else is new these days, friend?"

"Looks lousy for Noah. Your friend Zoe Mountolive is clever, but fighting a losing battle. It comes down to Noah's word versus Waller's and you know who this jury will pick."

"Noah is not the kind of man to rape a woman. I felt that about Rabbi Greer, too, and history proved me right. There's nothing, absolutely nothing in Noah's character to suggest he would abuse someone like that."

"His lawyers haven't convinced me yet. And if they can't convince a pushover like me, they're not likely to win a jury."

"Is there something the defense could do?"

"Beats me. That's why I think Noah is cooked."

She doesn't answer but falls into deep thought. "I hate what you're saying, Chuck. Thanks for ending a terrible day with a terrible thought."

"Do you recall what I told you about getting appointed Senior Rabbi? I said you must be ruthlessly honest with yourself. I'm afraid Noah Zentner's managed to find himself on the wrong side of the feminist revolution. Innocent heads always fall during a revolution. Way of the world. You're fond of him, aren't you?"

"Yes." Gabby is terse.

"More than that, Rabbi Gabby? Attached, perhaps?"

"Yes."

"Well good." He stands to reach across the desk to grip her wrist with an affectionate squeeze. "Now most people would tell you to forget him. He's history. Not me. Just be realistic. I'm sure your feelings help him absorb the pain."

The phone on Gabby's desk rings. She excuses herself and lifts the receiver.

"Gabby, it's Emma Greer here. Been wanting to talk with you since *Yom Kippur*. Jeremy was ecstatic. Marge was in tears. It's brought the family back together. Released a burden from my heart. You put into words what I always felt about Seth. He's a bastard all right, but he wasn't governed by lust."

Gabby sighs. "Emma, I have things to talk about with you. Gotten swamped at the synagogue. And with the trial in Baltimore."

"Can you make it over for dinner on Thursday?"

Gabby takes a moment to search her electronic organizer and finds that a meeting at a local high school with adolescent girls has been postponed. The idea of being with Emma pleases her. "Yes, I think that would work."

"Good. Come directly from Ohav. I've got someone I'd love you to meet."

"And who might that be?"

"A new friend. We've been dating, if that's the right term for a broad like me. A widower from Richmond."

"Sounds wonderful, Emma. I'm looking forward to meeting him. Bet he's handsome and rich and kind and generous."

"All of the above," Emma says, excitedly, "but you forgot his most redeeming quality."

"What's that? I'm stumped."

"He's funny, Gabby. Hilariously funny."

Gabby chuckles aloud. "Not another comedian, Emma?"

"No, no. You've got it wrong. He's funny in a different way. No one-liners, no puns, like Seth. He's a joke teller. Got a repertoire you wouldn't believe. Haven't heard the same gag twice yet."

"You will, Emma. Just wait. A comedian recycles faster than he creates. I look forward to meeting Prince Laughter."

"Well then, Chuck." Gabby pats him on the back as they close down the office for the night. "Something good for a change. Sounds like the inimitable Emma Greer's got a boyfriend. If anybody deserves one she does."

WHEN THE TRIAL RESUMES ON MONDAY MORNING, people nervously await Judge Weil, whispering to themselves and speculating about what is likely to ensue. Television trial-watchers concur that so far the defense has approached its cross-examination cautiously, yet they predict fireworks to come. Since nobody actually saw the crime committed, the State's case lies with the credibility of its victim. Folks who know Eli Waller say that when cornered she is capable of becoming either a stubborn bulldog or a snarling pit bull terrier. Speculation is rampant.

Noah Zentner has been schooled to remain alert at all times, to focus his eyes on the witness and occasionally to scan across the front and rear rows of the jurors. If untrue things are said he may show no emotion, but quietly relate the falsehoods to his attorneys. His suit is dark gray with a starched ivory Armani shirt fitted with a warm yellow-and-beige silk necktie. Zoe and Mort Steel encourage speculation whether or not he will take the stand in his own defense. While they do not commit themselves, the threat of an articulate man speaking for himself puts the prosecution on guard.

Eli appears exceptionally calm. When called, she marches in front of the jury to enter the witness box. One must be impressed by her figure. It is easy to imagine why a man would want to have sex with her, even to the point of violence. Light make-up and slightly colored lips enhance her beauty. Brunette hair with soft strands of golden highlights is neatly brushed down over the ears.

"Good morning, Ms. Waller." Zoe Mountolive pastes a false friendliness on her cheeks and grins but does not smile. "As you know, we're trying to understand exactly what transpired aboard the *Dame Cynthia* on the night of July Four. The prosecution has carefully elicited your testimony and drawn a picture of how and why you were temporarily in the skipjack's cabin rather than on its deck. I'd like to ask you a few questions about that. According to your testimony, you descended into the cabin in order to use the head, or in landlubber's parlance, the toilet. It was dark and unpleasant. Upon your way topside—in landlubber's parlance, upstairs—you encountered Mr. Zentner, or perhaps he encountered you. Does that fairly represent your position?"

"Yes, it does." Eli's lips open, slightly more on the right side than the left.

"Would you characterize the meeting between you and Mr. Zentner as a chance encounter? Two people below deck, ostensibly to use the head?"

"I cannot say that, Ms. Mountolive. I know why I went below. Not why Mr. Zentner did. Perhaps he followed me there."

Zoe cocks her head and nods. She wants the witness to question why she is taking one tack rather than another. "Did you tell anybody aboard you were going below?"

"Not to my knowledge."

"And it was dark, very dark, yes?"

"Yes."

"And you didn't talk to Mr. Zentner, did you?"

"No."

"Then perhaps you can explain how Mr. Zentner could have *followed* you below."

"I didn't say he did. Only that he might have."

"Did you invite him to meet you below?"

"I said I didn't speak with him."

"Could he have gone below for the same reason you did? To relieve himself?"

"Perhaps."

"We know that Ms. Houston-Gephardt went below to relieve herself. Do you have knowledge of any males besides Mr. Zentner who did?"

"No. I do not."

"Could it be that they took advantage of time in the water to urinate?"

"Objection," Sylvia Junqueira barks. "Defense counsel cannot speculate aloud and expect the witness to concur."

"Objection sustained," the bench rules.

"Well, let's see if we can get away from speculation." Zoe is unfazed by the censure. "After you emerged from the water, what did you do, Ms. Waller?"

"Dried myself with towels supplied by the crew. Took awhile to find my sandals in the dark. Shoes and sandals left on the deck got scattered during the excitement. Arlene was still in the water at the time and people were worried about her."

"Did you panic, Ms. Waller?"

"No. Somehow I believed we'd find her. I've trained myself not to worry about things that haven't yet happened. In my trade you can drive yourself crazy worrying about what-ifs."

"So you remained calm and, let us say, optimistic. Did you remain in the cockpit or move to another location aboard the vessel?"

"I think I just mixed with the others."

"Talk to anybody?"

"Yes. To several. Just a few words. No sustained conversations."

"To whom?"

"That I can't remember."

"Did you speak with Mr. Zentner?"

There is a faint pause, barely noticeable to any but experts. The pause might replay well on television, like a slow motion play on Monday Night Football. "No. I don't think so."

"Did you move forward to the bow during the hunt for Arlene Houston-Gephardt?"

"To midships. Not to the bow itself."

"Wasn't Bill Pell on the bow, yelling out Arlene's name?"

"Yes, he was."

"So, Ms. Waller, for the record let's pull this together. After you emerged from the water you spoke to several people, but definitely not to Noah Zentner. You remember none specifically and, according to previous testimony from others, none recall speaking with you. The one certain thing about this scenario is that Noah Zentner and you did not meet or talk. Is that correct?"

Waller nods assent. "Yes, Ms. Mountolive."

"Now let's jump ahead, just a few minutes. Arlene Houston-Gephardt is lost, then miraculously rescued. There is great relief and jubilation. To celebrate, a bottle of rum makes its way from mouth to mouth. In your earlier testimony, you stated that you congratulated her. Did you converse with anyone else?"

"Of course. But like before, there were no sustained conversations."

"None with Mr. Zentner?"

"No."

"First, the passengers hear the splash of two swimmers going out to fetch Arlene. Then, they hear Stephen MacNeille's voice from the water. A few minutes afterward, Noah Zentner brings Ms. Houston-Gephardt safely to the boat. You are a principal owner of The Hawthorne Group and Mr. Zentner is an owner of Pyramid. He has just accomplished a feat of considerable courage. Your firm is attempting to secure business from his. Yet you do not bother to congratulate him. Doesn't that seem a bit odd?"

"We must have been at different locations on the boat. Because of the dark it was difficult to move about. I thought there would be ample time later."

Zoe mops her brow with theatrical precision and her fingers come to rest on the temple of reading glasses which require adjustment. She appears to be chewing something behind closed lips.

"Now, Ms. Waller, you said that you were at midships. Do you think that Mr. Zentner could have been at midships, too, and you just didn't notice him?"

When she speaks, Eli has a manner of jogging her chin upward like an orchestra conductor lifting his baton to begin a musical bar. "Not that I know of. But it was dark; he might have been there."

"Could he have gone directly below to rendezvous with you?"

"Absolutely not. He came below *after* I went to the head."

"Does that also mean you had no physical contact with him? I mean by that a friendly hug, shake of the hand, pat on the shoulder, or perhaps a kiss."

"Absolutely not."

"Can we infer there was no contact between you and Mr. Zentner from the time swimmers went into the water until the alleged rape?"

"Yes. That's what happened."

"During the early portion of the voyage you and Mr. Zentner are friendly, at least professionally so. After the swim and near fatal ordeal in the water there is no further contact between you until, as you allege, he traps you in the cabin to have sex against your wishes."

"That would be a fair assessment, I believe."

"So you talk with him until such time as he performs a heroic deed in rescuing Ms. Houston-Gephardt. Then communication stops abruptly. Isn't that odd?"

"It's a mystery to me, Ms. Mountolive. I am a businesswoman, not a psychologist."

"A businesswomen, you say." Zoe is quick to pick up her suggestion. "Would you say you're an ambitious woman?"

She is equally fast to respond. "Absolutely! Ambition drives people in my trade. It's an essential ingredient for success."

"I understand you're considered a rainmaker at your firm, is that not so?"

"It is, and I'm proud of it."

"Could you explain to the court what it means to be a rainmaker in the world of finance?"

"One who brings new business to the firm."

"Like getting the account from Pyramid Development?"

"That would have been an example, yes."

"And how important would it have been to get Pyramid's business?"

"All business is important. Pyramid is a large developer. Fees would have been significant."

"How significant, Ms. Waller?"

"Approximately four or five million."

There is a gasp in the court which displeases the judge. By the time he pounds a small teakwood gavel with a silver ferrule, the audience is silent. "Sounds like a lot of rain to me, Ms. Waller," Zoe says. "What percentage ownership in Hawthorne do you have?"

"Twenty percent."

"My arithmetic says that's a million for yourself, less of course operating expenses. And there's always a reckoning with Uncle Sam, who isn't shy about demanding his cut. Approximately how much did Hawthorne invest in getting Pyramid's account?"

"Thirty-seven hundred dollars to charter the *Dame Cynthia* for the afternoon. Then salaries, accounting for a tremendous amount of preparation time analyzing the Pyramid portfolio, and travel expenses for the Hawthorne team. I hesitate to give an exact figure. Our accountants allocate expenses to a given job and usually provide quarterly totals to a partner for review. That's not my job."

"Would you say it is over a hundred thousand dollars?" Zoe pursues.

"With salaries included. Yes, I assume it must be."

"Would you call that an all-out effort on your firm's part?"

"Yes. We only chase business that we want. And we're prepared to spend to get it."

"You already testified that providing sexual favors to secure business was never your style. Without wishing to sound disrespectful, I'd like to ask you once more for the record, is that a true depiction of how you conduct your business?"

Sylvia Junqueira jumps to her feet. "Objection, Your Honor. Ms. Waller has already answered the question. Repetition is insulting and degrading!"

"Sustained," Judge Weil states. "Ms. Mountolive, the court already knows the answer to your question. Move on, please."

Zoe looks to her left and eyes Mort Steel, whispering to Norman Kwan. While fellow attorneys meticulously work out the legal ramifications of a defense, Kwan is given free rein to hunt down facts, operating as the firm's private detective. He slides a large stack of legal folders in Zoe's direction.

"Ms Waller." Zoe is soft, barely audible until she adjusts the volume of her voice. "Do you recall the electronics manufacturer, Pulse D?"

"Yes, I do."

"And was Pulse D a client of The Hawthorne Group?"

"Yes."

"A large one?"

"Quite significant. When it went public we underwrote its Initial Public Offering. Very successfully, I might add."

"And were you the..."—Zoe pauses for an instant to emphasis the word—"rainmaker in this transaction?"

"Yes."

"Since Pulse-D is now a public company, we learned from its Prospectus for the Stock Offering that Hawthorne received a fee of four and a half million for its services. Is that the correct number for the rain you made?"

"It was a substantial fee. Hawthorne earned every penny of it."

"And do you recall the Chief Financial Officer at Pulse D at the time?"

"Not offhand. I've got the files at my office."

"His name was Terrance William Baird. Does that refresh your memory?"

"Of course, I recognize the name now."

"And do you know what happened to Mr. Baird after his company went public?"

"He left Pulse D, I believe."

"Did he leave voluntarily? Or was he dismissed?"

Waller is slow to provide an answer and when she does her volume is diminished slightly. "Dismissed, I think."

"And was there a lawsuit over his dismissal?"

"Yes. It was settled out of court."

"And were you deposed in that case, Ms. Waller?"

Waller snaps with a crisp self-assuredness. "Yes."

"And was the case about mismanagement of company funds?"

"I don't recall the exact charges. But they were resolved in settlement."

"And to your knowledge was there a nondisclosure agreement as a part of this settlement?"

"Sorry, I don't know that."

Zoe looks to her left at Norman Kwan to receive a bound volume of legal papers. "Well, there wasn't any nondisclosure agreement. In fact, Pulse D had no legal problems sharing their records with the defense in this case. Pulse D fired Mr. Baird because of alleged fees paid to The Hawthorne Group. In the suit Mr. Baird contended that while the four and a half million dollar fee was large, it was justified. Pulse D responded by providing evidence that during the stock offering Mr. Baird was having a personal alliance with a Ms. Elisheva Waller, Senior Vice President at the underwriters, The Hawthorne Group. Did you have a sexual affair with Mr. Baird, Ms. Waller?"

Waller becomes stiff in her chair. The features of her face appear to harden. "The matter was grossly exaggerated. Mr. Baird and I had a few drinks together in public. That was the extent of it."

"Are you aware of how Mr. Baird's charges of unfair dismissal were resolved in this matter, Ms. Waller?"

"No. I am not. It was private. After my deposition I was no longer involved. My response to the allegations of a sexual liaison are answered in the deposition."

Zoe's eyes flash over the jury, a signal she wants the jurors to pay special attention to the answer. "Pulse D agreed to pay Mr. Baird his vested retirement benefits. No medical benefits, no legal fees, and no additional damages. Mr. Baird withdrew his lawsuit. Now, Ms. Waller, I'd like to repeat an earlier question because you might wish to reconsider your response. Did you ever have a sexual union with Mr. Baird?"

"There was a single moment when he tried to get chummy."

"Were the two of you alone in a place where sex could have happened?"

"We were in St. Louis staying in the same hotel, if that's what you mean."

A sprinkle of whispers breaks out in the courtroom. Zentner's defense attorneys have just crossed a line of civility to impugn the integrity of the victim. Whispers increase until everyone in the court is expressing opinions.

The Judge gavels for silence. The audience fails to respond. Judge Weil pounds into an oak platform. Eli Waller is stone, her expressionless face fixed as though a bronze statue. She does not blink.

Zoe hugs the lectern and her voice bellows over a continuing din from the audience. "Do you recall the name of Cecil Kornbloom from Aztec Materials in Harrisburg, Pennsylvania, Ms. Waller?"

This time Eli Waller is slower to answer, but she rallies with a powerful, "Yes. President of Aztec, I believe."

Zoe receives a thick legal folder from Norm Kwan and opens it on the lectern. "His wife left him just before retirement. Acrimonious, bitter divorce. There was a nasty court encounter over custody of the youngest daughter. Mrs. Kornbloom claims her husband had a sexual dalliance with you during the four months in which Hawthorne was restructuring Aztec's financing. Is that true, Ms. Waller?"

"In the course of our business together, Mr. Kornbloom and I became good friends. It was necessary to travel often to California together on business. We passed leisure time having dinners in each other's company. The relationship was not sexual."

"Was it responsible for breaking up Mr. Kornbloom's marriage?"

"That I cannot say."

"But you just said he was your friend, your good friend. Surely, he must have given you some explanation for the divorce. Did he say nothing to you about it?"

"That occurred largely after my firm had completed its business with Aztec. We have not stayed in touch."

"So after your fees were collected, you dropped him as a friend. Is that correct?"

"We both agreed it was better not to continue our friendship. The break was mutual. We are business people. Pragmatic, if you will. It was time to move on."

Norm Kwan is deliberate in passing another folder across the defense table in Zoe's direction. It travels over several pairs of hands, high enough for jurors to see. Zoe has her reading glasses low on the nose as she fingers through papers in it. "Oh yes. Yes. And here we have a Donald T. Seal, from MicroSequencing, Inc. which your firm helped go public three years ago. Do you recall him, Ms. Waller?"

"Yes."

"And how about James Matthew Johnson from Stelton & Jones in Kansas City?" Two more files move in Zoe's direction.

THE AFTERNOON IS LONG. JOURNALISTS ARE ELATED by the turn of events for now they have a lusty story to tell. Many new faces to hunt down and interview. However tarnished, Eli Waller remains aloof, almost regal. The defense has much to prove before its allegations are taken as fact. Having one or multiple affairs with other corporate officers doesn't prove she entered into a sexual alliance with Noah Zentner to procure Pyramid Development's business. But it does establish a pattern.

"You knocked her down a few pegs." Mort Steel congratulates Zoe and Norm Kwan as they leave the courtroom that evening. "Planted some doubts into the minds of the jury. The government's chief witness is no longer a vestal virgin. There have to be reservations about her integrity now. A national icon is no longer on the witness stand. Tomorrow you'll face an ambitious woman hot to make a deal."

"Norm." Zoe pats Kwan on the shoulder. "You're a genius. I never expected you to dig up this goddamn shit. You're a fucking garbage collector, but I love you anyway. Don't tell me how you did it. Your work is a godsend for Noah."

"Will you put him on the stand?" Kwan asks.

"Hope it won't be necessary. When the dust settles, the jury will understand we haven't proved our great rainmaker consented to sex with him. And just as important, we haven't proved she enticed him into sex to get the Pyramid account then, at the last moment, changed her mind. We can't do that without your showing what really happened in *Dame Cynthia's* cabin."

"Noah's story has a million holes in it." Steel is flat and unemotional. "I can't believe Junqueira won't exploit them. If

Waller and Zentner were just having a friendly *shtup* on a hot, sultry night, why holler what the witnesses heard? Why tell the police? We'll need a damn good reason why this rainmaker gave up a million dollar commission."

Zoe angles her head and grins. "Okay, I'm working on it now."

"Could have fooled me," Steel quips. "What have we missed?"

"Because you don't know exactly what happened between Noah and Ms. Rainmaker in the skipjack's cabin."

"I know what Noah's told us. Am I missing something?"

"Absolutely."

Steel and Kwan turn into a corridor leading from the courts to the parking lot where taxis are waiting to take them to seclusion at the DoubleTree Hotel. Kwan asks, "Is Noah holding back from us?"

"Don't think so," Zoe answers.

"I must have missed something, too. How can you possibly know what he doesn't?" Kwan comments.

"This isn't the place or the time to explain it, friends," Zoe says.

"That's just great." Steel sounds addled. "Where is the right place?"

"Okay, fellows." Zoe grasps their upper arms and hauls them close to her where her voice will not carry through the corridor. "Don't want to get personal, but I'm sure you guys have had some pretty great orgasms in your lives. Think what happens. Like a woman, you rise along a sort of peak and then explode with a climax. And it's at the very top of that peak where something extraordinary occurs. The mind sort of blacks out. The body is transfixed. It's only a second or two. But what happened to Noah during those seconds is the key to everything. Go back to the list of potential expert witnesses we supplied the prosecution. Buried near the bottom I listed a Dr. Stephanie Crower, a sexologist from Los Angeles. I've notified the prosecution we intend to call her to the stand."

Kwan exhales a deep breath. "Sounds like mumbo-jumbo to me. The last thing we need is a quack doctor from California."

"Dr. Stephanie Crower, author of *The Chemistry of Sex* and *Sex and the Hormones that Drive It*, is no quack. She's an M.D. who has studied the hormonal ingredients of sex. A modern-day Masters and Johnson but more sophisticated, equipped with new research tools. I intend to put her on the stand Thursday."

"Tell us more at tonight's debriefing." Kwan is intrigued, but skeptical. "This could backfire in court, you know."

"Absolutely."

"We made progress today," Steel adds. "Our Queen of Feminism has feet of clay."

"We're inching forward." Zoe pats them both on the shoulders, acknowledging their good work. "But we still have a long way to go."

LEONARD ROTHLY, BORN IN RICHMOND, VIRGINIA, IS plump with squared shoulders, a wide forehead trenched with wrinkles characteristic of Eastern Europe extraction, very thick reddish hair above his ears and very thin gray hair on the top of his head. He possesses a self-assured, open friendliness, pulling Gabby a few inches toward him in a powerful handshake, and almost enveloping her in his toothy smile. A master at tying a gag to a theme, he begins with his gags while Gabby is still removing her coat in the foyer of Emma's home. Before she has a cocktail in her hand, he has unleashed a salvo of jokes, bestowing upon his characters multiple voices and accents, creating and re-creating them as he goes. Because the voices change it isn't necessary to introduce each gag with *Did ya hear the one about?* It doesn't matter whether someone has heard the joke before. If the listener wags his head, a sign he has, Leonard will adroitly change directions to end with an unexpected punchline. With his talented embellishments even old stories sound fresh.

In response to a joke about a Jewish bachelor who calls his mother in Fort Lauderdale, Gabby belly-laughs so hard Scotch escapes the lip of her crystal glass and spills on her skirt. Leonard notices and quickly launches into another gag about a Jewish *noodnick* who spills soup on his lap in a Chinese restaurant. Her cheeks begin to ache, the same euphoric sensation experienced at Moadon Baccus in Haifa. "Laughter cleanses the soul," she tells herself, breathing hard to catch her breath.

Margarie Greer, Emma's and Seth's daughter, arrives from Frederick, Maryland, to join them for dinner. Since *Yom Kippur* she has failed to communicate with Gabby because her feelings have been so raw. Though she still blames her father for womanizing, she no longer suspects that Gabby was one his paramours or that in some undefined way she encouraged him. Her hug envelops Gabby with sincere warmth.

Emma makes a toast to Gabby with a glass of Chenin Blanc. "Scuttlebutt has it you've made the short list to succeed Seth. *Mazel Tov*. Now to beat out the others. How many are on the short list, Gabby?"

"According to rumor, three. The Search Committee has scheduled another interview with me, so things are heating up. To minimize gossip and pressure, follow-up meetings with the other candidates are out of town. Probably in their home cities. I suspect the Committee is going to do a little spying *in situ*."

"Know who they are?"

"No. I can only speculate."

"You sound surprised," Emma follows.

"I am," Gabby says. "I expected to be weeded out in the initial cut. This is either a terrible mistake or the heavy hands of a few loyal friends."

"You underestimate your allies. Surprising thing about loyalty. It creeps up when least expected. The truth is I don't think many people would like Ohav Sholom without Gabrielle Lewyn. And there's an easy way to ensure she won't get a better job elsewhere."

When the topic turns to Seth, Gabby becomes uncomfortable. Whether Emma or Margarie knows Seth's whereabouts or what he's doing is unclear. Unless they drop clues that they do, she is not going to volunteer information. Withholding from one's host is unpleasant. How odd to think that she probably knows more about Seth than his own family.

Emma rises from her chair to announce dinner. "I want to get started so we can watch the replay of the trial in Baltimore. It tears my heart out to see Noah. On our trips together, he and Morgan seemed like such a compatible couple. Mutually attentive to one another. He always tried to see that she was comfortable. Once we were camping together in British Columbia and there was a freak blizzard. He insisted she take his parka for additional warmth and damn near froze to death himself. There's no way in the world I'll believe he raped Eli Waller. Lots of stuff coming out now about how she conducts business. She certainly isn't my taste in feminists."

Throughout a fine dinner of striped bass baked with tomatoes, green peppers, and cilantro, Gabby's conversation is restrained. She feels compelled to withhold everything Zoe has told her about Noah's frame of mind. Even less will she talk about her visit with Seth in Haifa. Fortunately, Leonard Rothly's repertoire includes many fresh jokes about trial lawyers. Laughter has a way of deflecting serious discussion.

Before dessert, Emma rolls a TV cart into the family room. Margarie follows from the kitchen with a stainless steel coffee thermos and a plate piled with her mother's homemade oatmeal and raisin cookies, Gabby's favorites. The television screen displaying a panoply of courtroom figures immediately captures Leonard's attention. The engaging smile that usually captures his face disappears. He views the scene as though studying the movement of actors on a stage. Viewer and viewed unite. His jokes stop; this is serious business.

Gabby settles on the sofa, her eyes searching for Noah. The camera does not cooperate because it is trained on Zoe, who is examining a witness. She is in a smart dark suit with a long gold pin on the breast pocket. Her signature white blouse collar covers the lapel. A court reporter for the Legal Channel recounts the salient events of the day. The camera pans to a witness Gabby does not recognize. A caption running at the lower edge of the screen identifies her as Dr. Stephanie Crower, M.D., Sexologist. A second caption reads, "Expert Witness: Author, *Sex and the Hormones That Drive It*." Seated in the witness box is a trim, well-kept blond woman in her mid-forties. She wears designer glasses of considerable distinction and her narrow neck bears the shape of a significant skin-tuck by a skilled plastic surgeon.

"What's a sexologist?" Margarie inquires. "Sounds dirty. Do you know, Rabbi Gabby?"

"Someone who studies sex, I presume. You know, fertility, impotence, response."

"Sounds like a job manufactured in heaven," Leonard intones. "Where do I apply?"

"You're a dirty old man," Emma says.

"Old yes. Dirty, perhaps; a man, absolutely."

Dr. Crower is invited to stand and point to a display board with a laser pointer. On it there is a graph with a curve sloping upward, then falling precipitously. Along the *x*- and *y*-axes are integers.

"Can you explain in layperson's language, Dr. Crower," Zoe asks, "about the function of hormones in the sexual response?"

Crower is a professional who has given this explanation to lay audiences many times before. The words are on the tip of her tongue. "Think of men and women as engines, each with cylinders pumping different chemical hormones into the bloodstream. It is these hormones that fuel sexual response. We like to think of sex as driven by libido, love, and romance and, to some extent, it is. That's the stuff of the movies. Our culture governs romance and reproduction. But a level below these sentiments, human sexual responses are stimulated by the hormones secreted from various glands. Depending upon their age and physical condition, when potential sexual partners come together they are the sum total of the hormones they generate."

"Are you saying that sexual alliances are purely driven by hormones?"

Fearful of confusing or misrepresenting the known physiological facts, Dr. Crower pauses to choose her words carefully.

"No, Ms. Mountolive, I am not. What we know about sexuality in humans is that hormones are generators which trigger sexual stimulation and drive individuals to sexual alliances."

"If that is so, can you give us a thumbnail sketch of the hormones governing sexual response in a female?"

"In general terms, yes, but you must keep in mind that each individual secretes a different package of hormones at different times. If we monitor hormone secretions of women at different phases of sex, from arousal to climax, we find that hormonal mix differs from woman to woman. But not the *kind* of hormones. The overall formula is something like this. Dehydroepiandrosterone or DHEA makes a woman or perhaps a man feel the desire for sex. This is stimulated in a manner we don't fully understand by other hormones called pheromones. These are transmitted between individuals through the sense of smell. But smell is by no means the only ingredient. Touch promotes another important hormone, oxytocin. The feelings of sexual connection are powered by what is known as phenylethylamine or PEA. And then there are the more celebrated members of the sex team, so to speak, estrogen, testosterone, serotonin, dopamine, and progesterone, and two standbys, prolactin and vasopressin."

"Are they all pumping at the same time?" Zoe interjects.

"By no means. That would cause chaos. They don't even pull in the same direction at the same time. Some counteract or neutralize each other."

"Could you explain that in lay terms, please?"

"While estrogen and DHEA are driving a women into intimacy with a partner, vasopressin is stifling her indulgence. One is balancing out the other, so to speak."

Gabby fidgets in her seat. Zoe's line of questioning makes her uncomfortable. No woman likes to reduce her sexuality to a hormonal stew. Popular notions of romance as motivators for lovemaking die hard. If possible she would like to turn the TV down and discuss this with Margarie and Emma, but not with Leonard. But clearly they are fascinated by the physiology—particularly Emma, who during menopause has been wrestling with a loss of libido.

"Dr. Crower," Zoe dramatically removes her half-frame reading glasses and points with them at the graph on the display board, "would it then be accurate to say that during the petting period of sex, a woman's hormones are cranking up? And if so, is more than one type of hormone operating during this phase?"

"Absolutely."

"And would that also be true during the phase popularly known as foreplay?"

"Yes, Ms. Mountolive." Crower directs the laser light on the ascending line of her graph. "That's what I've tried to chart here. DHEA, estrogen and phenylethylamine are acting in concert. They are arousing a woman along an upward sweep."

"And in your professional opinion does that always lead to orgasm?"

Crower is more circumspect here. "Why, yes. I would say that it *leads* toward orgasm, but it doesn't always reach it."

"It doesn't always reach it." Zoe repeats the words slowly with great emphasis. "Do you mean to say that this upward pitch of arousal is sometimes interrupted and if so, by what? Do you have a physiological explanation for it?"

"Clinical studies have shown how the hormones I've just mentioned conspire, as it were, to create an orgasmic pitch. But they are offset and countered by other hormones that tell the body organs to slow down. We call these chemicals *inhibitors*. They tell the body to stop because this is not in the body's interest."

"Which hormones are inhibitors?"

"Vasopressin is the senior inhibitor. But it may be aided by another inhibitor serotonin."

"Let me see if I understand what you're saying, Dr. Crower. During the arousal and foreplay periods, a group of hormones and neurotransmitters work in concert driving a woman toward orgasm. But in some cases they may be opposed by a second set of hormones that puts the brakes on, if you will, and prevent orgasm. Is that a fair summation?"

"More or less."

"Why more? Why less, Dr. Crower?"

"Because this conflict of hormones is not always measurable. Obviously, we don't monitor each and every sexual contact when couples have intercourse. But when we do, we find each individual producing different hormones at different times. What you have just described, Ms. Mountolive, has been documented. Women rise precipitously toward orgasm, then something happens. They stop. Sometimes quite abruptly. In the blink of an eye, their interest wanes. That decline of interest is directly related to which hormones are governing at the time."

That revelation strikes Gabby close to home. Reaching an orgasm never seemed to elude her with Tim. There were times when she forewarned him that she wasn't likely to reach orgasm. They petted. He entered. Sometimes he climaxed and sometimes not. But never did a hormonal reflex suddenly reverse her ascent toward orgasm. Never, that is, until her lovemaking with Noah Zentner. Zoe Mountolive is moving into a territory that terrifies her. Dr. Crower is not only outlining the bizarre moments in the cycle of passion between two people, but describing what happened with Noah. More significantly, she is also fashioning a scientific explanation for what occurred below deck of the *Dame Cynthia*.

"Could you tell us, Dr. Crower," Zoe inquires, "what triggers a surge in the levels of vasopressin or serotonin inhibitors? What alters a woman's sexual response?"

"Could be many things. Probably a neurotransmitter."

"How about a thought or an idea?"

"Yes. Absolutely. If an unpleasant thought enters her mind, a woman can turn off far faster than she can come on."

"Anything else?"

"Pain, for example. Many woman relate stories how they were making love and their partner inadvertently strikes them with an elbow in the breast or some other tender spot. They tell how they try to recover when the pain subsides, but cannot. Sharp pain can trigger an instantaneous surge of inhibitor hormones and kill sexual desire."

"Please," Zoe interrupts, "let's stop there for just a moment and explore what you said about an idea suddenly reversing a surge of sexual passion. Could a woman's lover say something to release inhibitor hormones?"

"Very possible. We have testimony in which women complain that their partner says something disturbing in the middle of sex. It turns them cold as ice. In an instant. Not minutes, mind you, but quite suddenly."

Zoe cants her head, then lifts her hands, fingers outstretched. "So then it is possible that in the course of making love Mr. Zentner could have said something to Ms. Waller that reversed the direction and pitch of her desire by flooding inhibitor hormones into her body?"

"Not at all impossible. What you describe is quite common, as a matter of fact."

Zoe lets that declaration settle in the minds of those in court. An intriguing thought. "I thank you, Doctor." She looks at the prosecution shuffling notes on legal pads. "The defense is finished," she says directly to Sylvia Junqueira.

For the first time in the trial Junqueira's timing is upset. She is uncertain where the defense is going with this witness and doesn't feel comfortable questioning the medical observations made. The safest approach is to discredit Dr. Crower's expertise. Her questions probe the scientific nature of theories and the authenticity of the medical sources used. She believes that Zoe Mountolive's tour of hormonal physiology confuses more than enlightens and does not regard the sexologist as a threat. Whatever influence Dr. Stephanie Crower might have on the jury, she certainly doesn't disprove the argument that Zentner raped Eli Waller. After Dr. Crower, the lawyers argue about procedure.

Viewers clustered around the TV yawn. It is time for Gabby to leave. That is just as well since she no longer feels like making social conversation. Her thoughts are now jumbled, her feelings raw. Zoe's questioning frightens her. While driving home she admits to herself that she is no longer worried for Noah alone. Her own fate has become inextricably tied to his.

It won't be long before Zoe will be inviting her to Baltimore.

GABBY'S INSTINCTS ARE NOT WRONG. THE NEXT DAY slightly after nine o'clock in the morning, an expected call from the Circuit Courthouse arrives in her office at Ohav Shalom. Zoe is in court and can't place it herself but delegates Andrea Delagnes. Urgent need to talk. Must set up a time during the lunch break to speak by phone. Gabby agrees to remain in her office through the noon hour and not accept outside callers. She knows what's coming.

When Chuck Browner eventually transfers Zoe's call to her there is a long pause while each party waits for the other to open conversation.

"The time for a decision has come, my friend," Zoe says. "It's been nearly four months. I had hoped this wouldn't be necessary. I prayed that Ohav Shalom would appoint you Senior Rabbi first. Didn't want your testimony to injure your chances there. Any news on that front?"

"I've made the short list, whatever that means."

"That means, if you don't know, that you're a serious contender. I'll put my money on you at the finish line."

"Great, because if I testify I'm history in Washington and probably every other congregation in the country." Gabby is cynical.

There is a prolonged pause before Zoe responds. "You understand Jewish politics better than I. Let's hope Jewish leaders appreciate the pursuit of justice. Isn't that a Jewish teaching?"

"In the abstract, yes."

Zoe has no time to equivocate. "Then, will you agree to testify?"

"Depending on what I'm asked." Gabby tries to sound optimistic.

Zoe rallies, "I won't put you on the stand and then blow feathers at you. I need much more than I have a right to ask. Far more than you're obliged to provide. Keep in mind, whatever I ask will be countered by the prosecution. Sylvia Junqueira is a snarling wildcat when cornered. She's likely to probe all the lurid details of your affair with Noah. No slack because you're a respected rabbi in the community. To her, you're the enemy."

"I understand now why you put Dr. Stephanie Crower on the stand."

"We've got to show what happened aboard the *Dame Cynthia*, not just what didn't happen. You're the key, Gabby. I've got four witnesses who heard just about the same words through the open hatch to the cabin. No way to refute such testimony. My only chance is to explain what those words meant at the time they were uttered."

Gabby interjects, "Eli Waller's good on the stand, isn't she? I thought she'd break when you asked her about her previous affairs. She barely showed any emotion. Talk about stonewalling."

"She's masterful. Turns on the charm like a light switch. An artist who disguises her craft. She denies an attack on her character by ignoring it. As far as we can determine, her reputation isn't besmirched one iota because the world now knows she's a sleep-around. Charismatic people are like that, you know. They are adored despite their flaws. Maybe because of them."

"Is she unassailable?"

"Not entirely," Zoe answers. "We're satisfied with limited objectives. We've shown she's sexually active, so she can no longer portray herself as sexually innocent. We don't want the jury to believe she's a saint."

"If I take the stand, what are you going to ask me?" Gabby asks.

"I prefer to go over the questions face to face here in Baltimore. I promise not to ask questions you explicitly prohibit, but I can't promise not to embarrass you. That's a personal matter. Some people are embarrassed easily; others have a higher threshold. Nor can I guarantee what the prosecution will do on cross-examination. They'll be brutal. Did you see how I handled Stephanie Crower?"

"I did."

"Then you'll know the direction I'm headed. With your help, I can make the case."

"Enough to vindicate Noah?"

"Hopefully, a hung jury. One or more of the jurors will have to buy my story. The state won't dare try this case again."

"Why'd the District Attorney try it this time?" Gabby sounds naive even to herself.

"Who knows? Maybe there were complaints and they wanted to show they're tough on rapists. Maybe they wanted to exploit a celebrated figure to advertise that the State intends to prosecute sexual offenders. The case is politically correct."

"How's Noah holding up?"

"The trial's like liposuction, sucking out his guts."

"I'll come to talk with you in Baltimore. Tomorrow evening, if that works for you," Gabby responds. "I owe that much to Noah."

"I'll make it work. We'll have a private dinner in our hotel quarters. I know what you like: vegetarian étouffée, puréed vegetables, with carrots à la mode—that's a cold carrot on top of a hot carrot. The DoubleTree is good with health foods. You know the routine with our security. Be expecting you anytime after 7:30."

Gabby hangs up the phone and sits immobile, her mind pondering the dilemma facing her. She is no longer being asked to present herself in court as a character witness. Nor even as a professional witness. She isn't certain what they call it in legal terminology: *maybe a material witness*?

THE SHADES ON GABBY'S CONDO WINDOW ARE drawn; her telephone is disconnected, though any congregational emergencies will be routed through her pager. She is in no mood to do anything but ponder the spiraling descent of forces around her. Indecision holds her in check. Her brain tells her not to be a fool and testify. But her training pulls in a different direction. Not only is Noah on trial, but Justice itself. If someone else held the key to truth she would gladly allow him or her to open the lock. But she alone possesses it. Seth Greer sacrificed his career for a silly experiment. She, for discovering what turned Eli Waller off when having sex with Noah.

In her office at the condo, she sits to compose a letter on personal stationery in her own hand.

Mr. Zachary Shugoll, President
Congregation Ohav Sholom
27th and Taylor Streets
Washington D.C. 20002

Dear Zack:

This is the most painful letter I have ever written. And while it is addressed to you, it is meant also for the Board of Directors and ultimately the membership of Ohav Shalom.

It is with profound regret that I tender my resignation as Associate Rabbi of Congregation Ohav Sholom and withdraw my name as a candidate for Senior Rabbi.

By the time you read this, my reasons will be public. I will have appeared as a witness in the trial of Noah Zentner. It will become apparent that my relationship with him has evolved into something more than pastor and congregant. Rabbis are not expected to have sexual affairs, especially with members of their congregations, and that I have done.

My testimony at the trial will render me guilty of breaking a sacred rabbinical trust. While I have loved serving the congregation and hope I have been a good rabbi, it is no longer possible to function as a role model. I hope to spare our members and their families additional pain. Since selection of a new rabbi is already in progress and there are many qualified candidates, perhaps one will wish the junior post.

I have no professional plans and can help fill the gap if my services are still wanted or needed.

Most respectfully,
Gabrielle B. Lewyn, Rabbi

Before going to bed she packs an overnight travel bag with toilet articles and two days of clothing in the event she must remain in Baltimore. On the phone that evening, Chuck Browner volunteers to drive her to the courthouse. The next morning, she gives him the letter to deliver to Zack Shugoll's office at Tysons Corner, Virginia.

ON THE DRIVE UP THE BALTIMORE-WASHINGTON Parkway, Chuck regards Gabby in the passenger seat of his Jeep Cherokee. Her eyes are fixed on the thick autumn forest of sycamore and oak bordering the highway.

"Penny for your thoughts." He finally breaks the silence and, when she fails to respond, repeats the invitation.

"Nothing of consequence," she whispers without engaging him further.

"Now, now, Rabbi Gabby, you can't get that by me. In a few hours your image is going to be broadcast throughout the nation. Countless Americans and Europeans will see you. The world will observe your cute nose, dazzling eyes, enchanting dimples. The fate of a person you care about is in the balance. And you want me to believe you're thinking about nothing of consequence. In the immortal words of George Washington, Abe Lincoln, and FDR, 'Oh, bullshit!'"

"Lost in thought, that's all. I can tell you I'm scared to death—terrified if you want to know the truth. I can predict what Zoe Mountolive will ask, but not the prosecution."

"Tell only the truth. That's why they want you on the stand."

For the first time she cranes her neck to look at him and says with sarcasm in her voice, "I'll remember your advice, friend, when I'm conjuring up a juicy lie."

ON THE MORNING DEVOTED TO GABBY'S TESTIMONY, custodians of Lucien Weil's court have failed to adjust the heat.

Courtroom Eleven is hot and clammy. Television lights add to the temperature. The bailiff opens windows to the autumn air, periodically chilling those seated near them with frigid breezes. Judge Weil angrily berates his staff for allowing this situation to occur but is unwilling to postpone a trial that is already behind schedule. The defense is asked to submit its witness and Gabby is called to the stand. Her disciplined eyes avoid Noah.

After being sworn in, she submits to a thorough interrogation about her position, education, experience, and relationship to the defendant.

Zoe Mountolive hangs back from the lectern far from her notes, her hands on her hips, her chin raised high. "Now, Rabbi Lewyn, the court has heard testimony about what was heard aboard the *Dame Cynthia* through an open hatch to the cabin. At the time of the alleged rape of Ms. Waller, witnesses heard slightly different sounds. But they concur on one thing: they all heard the sound EL. Does that correspond with anything in the Jewish religion?"

"Of course." Gabby sounds throaty as she adjusts her volume to reverberations from the microphone. "The ancient name for the Deity is EL in Hebrew. Most often it's found in a less abbreviated or expanded form, ELOHIM."

"Is that the only name for God?"

"Absolutely not. There are several appellations for the Hebrew God. In modern translations of the Bible we usually translate EL or ELOHIM as *God* and the Hebrew description ADONAI as *the Lord*."

"Are these obsolete names for God? Or are they currently in use, say in Jewish liturgy?"

"Oh, very much in use. It's quite rare to have a Jewish prayer that does not contain either ELOHIM or ADONAI or a combination of both."

"Any other commonly used names than these?"

In this field Gabby feels confident. Her response is authoritative. "Yes, there is the tetragrammaton, a technical term for four Hebrew letters of the divine name. This tetragrammaton is generally translated in Christian texts as Jehovah, but Jews tend to shy from trying to pronounce it."

"Why is that?"

"One, because there is a feeling it's unpronounceable and two, because no one today knows what the true pronunciation might be. So the simplest thing is to avoid it altogether."

Zoe inches from her lectern and stares directly at Gabby. "Rabbi Lewyn, we have testimony in this court by Mr. Maximillian Crane that before any of the witnesses heard Ms. Waller say, NO, NO, NO...STOP, STOP, he heard sounds generally associated with lovemaking. I won't entertain the court by trying to duplicate these sounds, but he definitely recalls the words, EL SHADAI. Repeated several times interspersed within these lovemaking utterances. What does this mean in Hebrew?"

"Well, the EL I've already explained means God. The SHADAI is a secondary name for the Almighty. It's used exclusively in poetic Hebrew, mostly in the Books of the Prophets, but can be found in Genesis 49:25. Today, the name is most commonly used to decorate modern *mezuzahs*, Jewish amulets, placed on the doorposts of Jewish dwellings."

"Any other uses of this form of the divine name?" Zoe asks.

"Yes, in Kabbalistic Judaism, that is, the mystic movement of Judaism that arose in sixteenth-century Palestine and later spread to Eastern Europe. Sometimes it's found in incantations to God."

Zoe's palms come together in a clap; her fingers rub each other. "Rabbi Lewyn, you've just identified a possible reference for the words EL SHADAI that Mr. Crane and one other witness heard through the open hatch. Is there any way in which this particular name could be associated with sexual intercourse?"

Gabby forces the court to wait while she collects her thoughts. She is nervous, yet feels in command of the subject. "Yes, Ms. Mountolive, there is. While this is not true for the vast majority of Jews, there are still some who believe sexual intercourse is fundamentally a procreative and not a romantic act. Sex is the fulfillment of a biblical command to be fruitful and multiply. At the moment of orgasm these pious ones recite divine names. They experience a spiritual connection during intercourse. Since God is the creator of life, the devout believe they are acting in God's name when they procreate."

"Which names, Rabbi Lewyn? The EL or ELOHIM, ADONAI or the EL SHADAI?"

"I've heard that all three are uttered. Sometimes in combination with each other. As far as I know there is no prescribed formula in Talmudic literature."

"Both men and women?"

"Ancient and medieval Jewish scholarship deals primarily with the fulfillment of commandments on the part of males. The custom of reciting the divine name during intercourse was practiced exclusively by males. That doesn't mean women were prohibited. Only that there was no religious duty for them to do so."

"So let me see if I get this straight," Zoe declares, sweeping her head around to gaze at the jury. "In limited situations, there is a Jewish custom to recite the divine names of ELOHIM or perhaps EL SHADAI during copulation. This practice is suggested in the Talmud. Kabbalists also observed it."

"That's correct." Gabby nods affirmatively.

"And how about a modern Jew? A man like Noah Zentner? Would he be likely to utter divine names during sexual intercourse?"

"From a Jewish point of view it's most unlikely. This is certainly not a common practice."

"Then are you suggesting that Noah Zentner would not say what two witnesses said he did?"

Gabby hesitates. In the next moment she will depart from the protection of academia and open her personal life to scrutiny. This is her very last chance to pull out and save her career. Her tongue seems to sink into the abyss of her throat.

Zoe waits patiently before repeating her question. "Are you saying, Rabbi, that Noah Zentner would *not* repeat those divine names?"

Gabby's heartbeat accelerates. The abyss is ahead. "No. No. Most contemporary Jews wouldn't, but there are circumstances in which he might."

"And what might those circumstance be, Rabbi Lewyn?"

"Conditioning. Practice. Brainwashing. Repetition."

"That's a very startling statement which requires explanation. Can you accommodate us here, Rabbi?"

"I'm afraid I cannot, Ms. Mountolive. You see, what I've come to learn is privileged information. It was gleaned in confidence between a rabbi and her congregant."

Questioning pauses momentarily while the defense team confers. Noah Zentner becomes part of the discussion. Mortimer Steel eventually moves to the lectern and asks Judge Weil to approach the bar and discuss a voluntary waiver of confidentiality by the defendant. The judge places this request to the prosecution which can find no objection, then leaves his bench to caucus privately with both legal teams. After several minutes conditions of the waiver are worked out. Noah grants Gabby explicit permission to reveal privileged information learned in the privacy of her professional relationship with him. The trial resumes.

Zoe Mountolive returns to the lectern and restates her previous question how a contemporary Jew might be affected by the medieval custom of reciting God's name during intercourse.

Gabby's eyes pass once over Noah but do not linger. There is a small crack in her voice as she gathers the words. "Noah Zentner is separated from his wife, Morgan. As rabbi at Ohav Shalom Congregation I got to know Morgan when she was editing a book on Lurianic mysticism for my senior colleague, Dr. Seth Greer. She invited me to see the manuscripts at her home. Two chapters dealt with *divine synapse*, an attempt to make contact with God through sexual orgasm. While in her bedroom, I saw a sight which shocked me. In place of a bed, Morgan had arranged pillows to look like an altar. Painted on the ceiling above these pillows were letters for the Divine Name, EL SHADAI."

There is a gasp of wonderment in the courtroom. Whispers break out from the audience and creep forward to the clerks. Noah's eyes fall to the desk and quickly jump back to stare at Gabby. When she's on the stand he can rest his eyes upon her without drawing attention.

"Are you saying, Rabbi Lewyn, that in the act of sex with his wife Mr. Zentner read the name EL SHADAI from the ceiling?"

"I cannot say that. I have no information about their sexual lives. I am saying only that Morgan Zentner told me of her interest in *divine synapse*. The placement of the divine name on the ceiling over her bed gives one pause for thought. Perhaps she was trying to contact God while having sex with her husband."

"Did he ever confirm this, Rabbi?"

"Yes, he did, Ms. Mountolive."

"Isn't that an unusual subject of conversation, Rabbi Lewyn? Could you clarify for us how such a conversation arose?"

Gabby glances directly at Noah and for a moment their eyes meet and hold firm. "He confided in me as a friend."

"Isn't that unusual? Here, you're his rabbi. You have a professional relationship with him and, I would think, a professional responsibility. Now you say he's also a friend. Could you explain that for us?"

"Our relationship started on a professional basis. I was approached to be a character witness at this trial. I didn't know him well and suggested we get to know each other. We found we were both joggers. So we started jogging together. This trial has caused him immeasurable suffering. Many of his friends abandoned him. He was isolated and lonely. He sought me out for friendship and I found in him wonderful qualities. Never once did he deny a sexual encounter with Ms. Waller. Said it resulted from frustration with his wife who had become a religious mystic trying to transcend the here-and-now and unite with God."

"Did he ever tell you he recited the divine name EL SHADAI during intercourse?"

"No, he didn't, but I surmised that he did."

For the first time in the trial, Zoe invokes a theatrical gesture, opening her palms and stepping back, as though portraying surprise. "Well now, Rabbi, how would you surmise something as private as that?"

Gabby draws Eli Waller into her vision which shifts to Noah. "My friendship with Noah became intimate. He came to my condo with food to break the *Yom Kippur* fast. This is the season in which we decorate our homes in preparation for *Sukkot*, another holiday which occurs five days later. The ceiling of my bedroom was draped with an heirloom from my mother, a large tapestry painted with Hebrew calligraphy. Noah and I were feeling amorous. One thing led to another and we ended up on my bed."

Exclamations of shock erupt in the courtroom. They are uncensored and sudden. Judge Weil's gavel attempts to quiet them but adds to the din. This is not what anyone expected from the rabbi. It makes good gossip. And good copy for the media.

Gabby stares at Eli Waller, attempting to draw strength from her.

The gaveling continues though Judge Weil understands that he will not restore quiet until the shock dissipates. And that will take a moment or two.

Zoe leans over to whisper with Mort Steel then stiffens and, in an unspoken conspiracy with the Judge, presses to continue her examination.

"Rabbi Lewyn, can you tell the court if Mr. Zentner uttered names for the Almighty while intimate with you?"

"I can, Ms. Mountolive. He did. It totally unnerved me."

"What names did he utter?"

"EL SHADAI. Three times in a row. In a bellowing, possessed voice."

"And what did you do?"

"I lost all sense of arousal. My desire vanished. At first I became angry, reacting as though I had been insulted. I couldn't understand what caused him to do such a thoughtless, insensitive thing. Then I looked up at my mother's tapestry hanging over the bed. The Hebrew letters on it don't mean anything, but they have the same general shape and design as the EL SHADAI painted on the ceiling of his wife's bedroom. One symbol must have triggered memory of another."

"And when you confronted him with this, what was Mr. Zentner's response?"

Once again Gabby gazes upon Noah, this time permitting her eyes to remain on him. "He didn't remember saying it. He was dumbfounded. He could have lied to me, but what was the point? He just didn't know what he was saying. The words meant nothing to him."

"Any idea why that might happen?"

"He once complained that his wife was more interested in having sex with God than him. The experience with Morgan was so painful he blocked the name EL SHADAI from his mind. He wasn't aware of his verbal slip. When I asked him about it, he said there was no recollection at all. Just a blank. If he did make the slip, he was sorry. He didn't intend to be rude."

"Objection, Your Honor," Junqueira stands. "These are not facts, but mere speculations."

"Sustained. Ms. Mountolive, let's refrain from speculations. Please proceed."

"After the incident, did you resume making love?"

"No. I had lost all desire to continue."

"Were you intimate with Mr. Zentner at another time, Rabbi?"

"No, never."

"Why not?"

"It was our last night together before this trial."

Zoe taps her knuckles on the lectern top, ventilates audibly, then tightens her lips. She lifts her reading glasses from her nose and places them where she was tapping. "Rabbi, I'd like to leave your personal experience and draw upon your scholarly expertise one last time. You have explained the use of divine names, such as EL SHADAI. But there's another name before this court which is similar in sound. You've told us the short form of the divine name is EL often translated, for example, in the King James Bible as *God*. What about the given name of the plaintiff in this legal proceeding who calls herself Eli? That's a Hebrew name, isn't it?"

"Yes."

"And what does it mean?"

"*My God*," Gabby translates.

"Now according to Stephen MacNeille's earlier testimony, unlike most people Mr. Zentner did not call Ms. Waller by her abbreviated name, but used her full given name, Elisheva. Is that a Hebrew name, too?"

"Yes, I believe it is. It is the Hebrew name of Aaron's wife. Found in Exodus. The first few chapters."

"And does it signify anything in particular?"

"SHEVA means *the one on whose name I make an oath*. So ELISHEVA means *I make an oath on God*."

"EL SHADAI and ELISHEVA have identical beginnings. Only the second syllables vary, but in both cases they refer to God. Is that not correct?"

"Yes, that's how ancient Hebrew is constructed. Nouns and predicates are often joined."

Zoe pauses and makes a powerful grimace of discovery, then folds the long fingers on one hand into those of another. "Rabbi, you've just told us how Mr. Zentner uttered the name EL SHADAI. You confided in the court the physical effect this had upon you and, without going into the personal details, it's fair to say you felt mention of the divine name in this context was out of place. Is that correct?"

"Yes."

"In your professional opinion, Rabbi, is it possible that Mr. Zentner might have intended to use the name of his lover, Elisheva, but made a verbal slip and said..."

"Objection, Your Honor." Sylvia Junqueira is on her feet. "That is speculative. There's no way Rabbi Lewyn can know what occurred between Mr. Zentner and Ms. Waller!"

"Sustained."

Zoe makes a quick decision to desist from an argument she can't prove and leaves it for the jury to chew on during her summation. She abandons the lectern to move behind the defendant. "Let me thank you for being so forthright, Rabbi Lewyn. While you are obliged to be truthful before this court, your testimony this morning has gone beyond the call of duty. I fear that what you have said here might damage your professional reputation, perhaps your career. I pray your community leaders will weigh any adverse judgments against the service you have provided this court in the pursuit of justice for Noah Zentner."

To Judge Weil, Zoe says, "Your honor, the defense requests a recess at this time for the witness to rest before facing cross-examination. This has been a very stressful time for her."

"Does the prosecution object?" The Judge directs his question to Sidney Hines who is on his feet. There is a brief conference with Sylvia Junqueira who remains seated.

"It does not, Your Honor," Hines answers.

The gavel concludes the day in court.

Gabby lets the bailiff squire her through court officials to adjacent chambers, then out a rear door to a hired limousine in the alley. Andrea Delagnes is waiting in a private room reserved for her at the DoubleTree Hotel. The defense team will return her to court the following day.

A MEMBER OF ZOE'S STAFF SEES THAT ROOM SERVICE delivers a lettuce and tomato sandwich and a pot of tea. Zoe arrives an hour later and greets her with an enveloping hug. Gabby is in a hotel bathrobe and stands on bare feet. She tries to hide the fact that she's been weeping, but red, moist eyes are impossible to conceal. Across the room, a television screen flashes pictures of the courtroom without sound.

"Don't watch garbage on the tube tonight," Zoe warns. "There's a feeding frenzy going on. The networks have gone bananas. They'll probably say a lot of cruel things about us. Can't be avoided. When this is over, people will settle down and be reasonable. But for the moment they can't think straight. In the court we must stick to facts. I hope you have someone running interference for you at your congregation."

"Doesn't matter. I've already sent a letter of resignation."

Zoe grabs Gabby's shoulders, looking mortified. "You what?"

Gabby is matter-of-fact. "Resigned. Our members don't want their rabbi teaching their daughters how to sleep around. No congregation can tolerate a promiscuous rabbi. It's not in the job description."

"Only somebody with scrambled eggs for brains would call you a sleep-around. They've got to understand you weren't obliged to testify. You didn't have to go to bat against this indictment. Nobody commanded you to stand up against a scheming, dishonest woman. You volunteered. They ought to be proud to have a rabbi like you. You can be my Clementine's role model any day of the week. You rescind that resignation immediately, you hear me?"

"You're the best, Zoe. You've done a remarkable job for Noah. There probably isn't a better lawyer in the country. But that's where your expertise stops. Please don't meddle in *my* business."

"I'll do whatever I can to help from a legal point of view. Anything."

"Thanks. I don't think I need legal counsel. This is the last time I want to see the inside of a courtroom."

After Zoe leaves, Gabby sits on the bed and stares at the opposite wall, awash in gloom. When she wakes from her meditation, she lifts the telephone and dials a Manhattan number. The phone on the other end rings four times until an answering machine clicks in.

Tim Matternly's tenor voice is sharp and familiar.

"Hello. We're not in now, but our phone machine is. Sally and Tim are game for playing phone-tag so if you'll just leave a message, we'll get back to you. Don't be shy. Bye-bye."

"Shit!" Gabby slams the receiver onto the cradle. "The witch has moved in with him."

Chapter Seventeen

Chuck Browner watches Gabby's testimony on the television console in her synagogue office, then at his own desk fields an avalanche of phone calls from the media, her friends, colleagues, cousins, civic leaders, two Washington literary agents, and a Hollywood screenwriter. Lights on her two dedicated phone lines flash constantly indicating that many callers are unsuccessful in making contact. There's no way she will be able to return more than a fraction of these, if she has the inclination, which he suspects she doesn't.

Gabby's first day in court is a bad dream come true; her second day is a nightmare. Zoe has tried to prepare her psychologically for cross-examination. Under normal circumstances prosecutors go easy on clergy, but Gabby has stepped out of her rabbinical role and become a foe. Sylvia Junqueira challenges her authority in matters of psychosexual experience, then attacks where she is most vulnerable, her professional conduct.

"How usual is it for a rabbi to have intercourse with a congregant, Rabbi Lewyn?" she asks, rolling her rabbinical title over her tongue in a derisive manner.

There is laughter in the court. Spectators are well aware of the scandal with Seth Greer at Ohav Shalom. The question, while quite proper in a court of law, might be considered anti-Semitic elsewhere.

"Hard to know," she replies. "If it happens, rabbis usually don't advertise it."

There is a mean streak in Junqueira, especially when feeling pressure. This is her opportunity to strike at her adversary. The word she has selected to make her point is *unprofessional*. "Having sex with a congregant is considered *unprofessional*, isn't it?"

"Yes. We don't promote this type of behavior."

"Does Ohav Shalom Congregation in Washington make an exception in this case?"

"I don't know what it has in mind. Since my testimony yesterday I haven't communicated with leaders of the congregation."

"Do you expect approval for what you did?"

"No. I do not."

"Are you saying that having intercourse with the defendant, Mr. Zentner, a member of your congregation, is unacceptable behavior for a rabbi?"

Gabby's eyes do not wander from the interrogator. The question has not taken her by surprise. "It is unacceptable for a rabbi, Ms. Junqueira. It is *not* unacceptable for a woman."

"Since you are a woman would you explain the difference for us, Rabbi Lewyn?"

"There are standards of behavior expected of rabbis, indeed, I would suspect for all clergy. As a rabbi, I crossed that line and will be held accountable for it. Yet rabbis do not take vows of celibacy and are expected to enjoy full sexual lives. Both male rabbis and female rabbis."

"Does that mean extramarital sexual activity as well as marital, Rabbi?"

"Before the sexual revolution it was definitely restricted to marriage. A lot has changed since the Sixties. Old mores are still on the books, so to speak, but sexual conduct has changed. Most women today are not virgins when they marry. I suspect that the female persona of a rabbi falls into the same category."

"Would you say that in your affair with Mr. Zentner you left your rabbinical position to exercise your drives as a woman?"

"I wouldn't described what happened as an *affair*, Ms. Junqueira. It occurred only once."

"Then on the one occasion it occurred, did you abandon your post as rabbi and react as a woman?"

"Yes and no."

"Please tell us what you mean by yes and what you mean by no."

"Yes, I was driven by normal female urges with Noah and in that respect acted as a woman. But no, it was my training as a rabbi that led me to suspect what was happening when he cried out EL SHADAI. I don't believe women who are not rabbis would have been sensitive to that. And it was because I was teaching a course at Georgetown University that Morgan Zentner invited me to see manuscripts in her home where I discovered the name EL SHADAI painted over her bed. It's unlikely I would have been invited to teach that course were I not a rabbi. For the same reason, it is unlikely she would have wished me to review her manuscripts. So the two identities merge."

"Would you describe your behavior as a scandal for Ohav Shalom Congregation?"

"There's a good likelihood it will become that. In religious institutions people tend to spin little things into big things. When a toilet in the synagogue clogs up there is a full-scale debate over the fundamentals of sanitation."

A round of chuckles punctuates the courtroom. What Rabbi Lewyn says about making small things into principal issues strikes spectators as humorous.

Courtroom laughter upsets Junqueira's timing. "Do you believe your actions will harm your rabbinical career, Rabbi Lewyn?"

Zoe Mountolive is on her feet. "Objection, Your Honor. The question is unnecessarily provocative."

"I don't mind answering." Gabby looks at her, then at the Judge who with an uplift of his head gives consent to proceed. "I think it will, Ms. Junqueira."

Zoe leans over to Mort Steel and whispers into his ear. There is a stern look in his eyes as he strokes his chin with thick fingers.

DURING THE LUNCH BREAK, ZOE SHOOS EVERYONE but Gabby out of the defense counsel's office. Two sandwiches sit on the desk along with Pepsis and paper cups. Gabby's chin slumps toward her breastbone, her eyes rest on her lap. Zoe drops down in a chair beside her and takes her hand. "Those questions were in bad taste," she says.

There is a short sigh of recognition from Gabby's lips.

"You were magnificent," Zoe adds. "Dignified. Straightforward. Honest. Thoroughly convincing. Sylvia and Sidney have made a critical mistake. Their questions fortify your credibility. I intend to make the jury ask itself why you would endanger your career to help the accused. Clergy are expected to put the interests of others before their own. That's exactly what you did and exactly what the jury will perceive."

"But clergy are not supposed to sleep with congregants who aren't even legally divorced," Gabby mocks herself.

"It led to a major insight. When good things result, you're entitled to some slack."

"This wasn't a scientific experiment, Zoe. I slept with Noah *first*, and only later figured out what happened on the Chesapeake."

"Perhaps. But juries usually exhibit good common horse sense."

"Have you any idea when the prosecution will finish with me? The last two days have seemed like a year. I'm mentally exhausted. My emotions are so scrambled, I can't say how I feel."

"Don't know. In the seventh inning I was worried. The prosecution seemed way ahead. But it's now the top of the ninth. To get a conviction the state will have to hit a home run. There are too many dubious things about the Chesapeake incident for all jurors to convict. Your explanation of what the witnesses heard will make them think hard. As a rule of thumb, it is better to explain away what witnesses say than to contend with their testimony. And that's exactly what you helped us do."

"Noah is still a symbol of uncontrolled machismo."

"We'll address that in our concluding remarks. Judge Weil will carefully instruct the jury against it."

Gabby unfolds the paper wrapper from the sandwich and scans the contents: processed turkey slices with lettuce and tomato. She refolds the wrapper. No appetite anyway.

THE STATE OF MARYLAND IS RELENTLESS. GABBY'S testimony stretches throughout the afternoon and continues the next day. The prosecution re-examines the link between Hebrew calligraphy and what witnesses heard Noah Zentner say aboard the *Dame Cynthia*. The intent is to emphasize the speculative nature of Gabby's observation, particularly Noah's utterances during intercourse. An afternoon recess to settle a dispute raised by Noah's counsel rolls her testimony into the next day. Grueling, but Gabby gathers strength under stress.

WHEN THE PROSECUTION EVENTUALLY ENDS ITS cross-examination, Chuck Browner is waiting to whisk Gabby away from the throngs of newspeople with their flashing cameras and video camcorders. At curbside, his Jeep Cherokee provides a thin wall of armor. Rude journalists bang on the windows expecting Gabby to provide a statement. Chuck is playing a tape with Prokofiev's Sonata No. 7 in B-flat minor, so loud it mutes noise from the street. To Gabby's mind, nothing could be more fitting. May good music drown out bad manners. As he pulls away from the curb, it is impossible to talk. The vehicle is large for Baltimore's narrow streets. His eyes are constantly in the sideview mirrors hunting for cars following them. After several blocks, he turns down the music and smiles at her, proud of their clean getaway. Just like in the movies.

"I don't want to know what faces me at Ohav," she opens.

"You won't have to. First, you can't get through crowds outside the place and, second, I've arranged with Harold for you to work outside the office for a few weeks."

"They'll find out where I live."

"They already know. There isn't a parking space for five blocks around your pad. People sitting in parked cars all day long. Don't worry, your fan club has it all worked out for you. Harold told me the Board expects you only to officiate at services. The rest of the time you're staying with us."

"Now hold on, pal. Who's *us*?"

"My friends. You're a hero in the gay community. We may not want women in our beds, but we still idolize them. Oedipal, of course. There isn't a gay man in town who doesn't think you're the cat's meow. We have pads all over the city. It's all worked out. Every night you stay in a different safe house. Every day you use a different telephone. Every night I meet with you in a secret place, cloak and dagger style, with whatever you want from the office. We drive you to Ohav, always in a different car with different license plates. To us you're a queen. And you're going to get treatment commensurate with your status."

"That's great. How can I stay with men I don't even know? They'll probably leak everything."

Chuck shakes his head while swerving around a corner, running a red light and accelerating like a hot-rod driver in a drag race. "A car looked suspicious," he apologizes, biting his lower lip. "I doubt he'll be there after the next turn."

His driving terrifies her. When he slows, she asks, "Can I trust your friends?"

"Can you afford not to? Gay men are the masters of secrecy. Men in the closet know the value of silence."

Gabby's eyes are riveted on the traffic ahead as Chuck enters a ramp leading to Interstate 95 south to Washington.

"Why?" She eventually breaks a long silence. "Tell me one good reason why your friends should help me. I don't know them and they don't know me."

"But they do know you, Rabbi Gabby. If you haven't noticed, you're a celebrity."

"Rather like Lady Macbeth after a bad night on the town. In biblical times they stoned to death adulteresses like me."

"My friends appreciate honesty about sex. We respect people who can make a statement about themselves in public. We take care of our own, Rabbi Gabby, and from now on, you're one of us whether you like it or not."

"Hey, wait a minute. Have I missed something? How does an admission I had sex with a married man make me one of you?"

Chuck accelerates around a large trailer rig that blocks his front view, then pulls back into the slower lane. "You revealed yourself in public. We struggle with the same problem everyday. Your fan club admires what you've done."

That seems strange to her, yet she is in no position to turn away friends. How she will manage rabbinical duties in this situation is a mystery. Fortunately, she has only to fill a gap before Ohav Shalom's new rabbi takes charge.

TO HER SURPRISE, ARRANGEMENTS MADE BY CHUCK and his friends work admirably. Each night she is shifted to a different apartment or home, provided with a telephone, room, and bath and served either home-cooked meals or dishes purchased from a neighborhood restaurant. Never once does a host mention financial compensation. On his daily visits, Chuck eludes those who would follow him, sometimes disguised as a telephone serviceman, gardener, soldier-on-leave, or Protestant minister. On the weekends, a team of chauffeurs spirit her to and from Ohav Shalom, always in a different vehicle, many with out-of-state license plates. The media senses there's a big story in Gabby Lewyn, but there's no way to get their hands on it, at least until after the Zentner trial. And by that time it will probably be stale. Chuck is inundated by calls from agents who want to represent the screenplay Gabby has no intention of writing. National TV talk-show producers are relentless in efforts to book her on their programs. *Saturday Night Live* extends an invitation to introduce a show that winter.

The only opportunity for the public to view Rabbi Lewyn is during Sabbath services, that is, if one can secure a seat in the packed sanctuary. The fire department prohibits spectators standing in the aisles during services; thus, only those who come very early are accommodated. At every service countless numbers are turned away. Never has Ohav Shalom experienced such attendance for Sabbath worship. Gabby is neither flattered nor amused. The sanctuary is filled with voyeurs, not worshippers. She avoids any mention of the trial in her messages, compounding frustration in the press.

During the first week, President Zachary Shugoll sends a note to her.

> *I apologize for not responding immediately to your Letter of Resignation. It would have been wholly inappropriate for me to do so without first conferring with the Board of Directors. As you can well imagine, the congregation is in shock. Its leaders are in a state of paralysis. As soon as the smoke clears, I promise a formal reply.*
>
> *Meanwhile, let me say that your efforts to continue functioning under the current pressures are nothing less than heroic. So far, contrary to predictions from our Cassandras, disaster has not occurred. Our members are not leaving in droves, but in fact flood the Board with letters of support. Further, our membership has suddenly swollen with the addition of 29 families and 64 singles. Our critics think we've gone off our rockers, but Ohav Shalom and its rabbi are the talk of the town.*
>
> *We indulge your patience while waiting for a response.*
>
> *Best personal regards,*
>
> *Zack*

Harold Farb comments to her in the cloakroom one Sabbath morning, "We get at least twenty new applications every week.

Mostly from single women. But there are also families with children for our school. In all my years, I've never seen anything like it. Whatever you've got you should first apply for a patent, then bottle it."

"That's how I'm going to make my living in the future," she replies, never certain whether to regard Harold as a friend or foe. The minute membership falls off, as she believes it will after Noah's trial, the sinister side of his personality will emerge. She wouldn't put it past him to say one thing to her and another to Temple leaders.

Morgan Zentner leaves a half-dozen messages with Chuck that she desperately wants to speak with Gabby. Not about Seth's book. But about her husband. Gabby feels obliged not to talk during the trial, but notes that this is the first time Morgan has referred to Noah as *her husband*.

"She sounds terrible," Chuck reports. "She cried on the phone. She is very upset you won't see her. I've never seen you cut off someone in need."

"After what I said under oath, I imagine she wants to wring my neck, same as a lot of other people."

"That's not what I'm picking up. I think Morgan wants to apologize. Or explain herself."

"Between you and me I don't want to see her. Say I'm not permitted to talk until there's a verdict. I'll be out of here soon; with some luck I can avoid conversation with her altogether."

What Gabby wants to hear from Chuck is what he doesn't say. Tim Matternly doesn't call or write.

DESPITE THE OUTPOURING OF SUPPORT FROM RABbinical colleagues, members of the congregation, and the gay community, she is still desperately alone and frightened. Zoe is too occupied to be of support and Seth is far away in Haifa, telling jokes.

Eleven days after her testimony, Ephraim Rothman collects Gabby for a meeting with the Board at his home near Sibley Hospital, less than a quarter-mile from the Maryland state line. It is an understated colonial that his family has lived in for more than thirty years, well maintained with manicured landscaping and an illuminated, cascading fountain in the driveway. For transportation he borrows a friend's Mercury with Maryland license plates.

Board members are seated in his living room, their eyes downcast, their faces expressionless. Customary greetings are subdued. No one tries to engage Gabby in introductory banter.

Zack Shugoll buttons his lips and glances around the room, then for a long moment stares through burning eyes at Gabby. "Well, Rabbi Lewyn, I promised a response to your Letter of Resignation. We thought best to deliver it in person. What we've been looking at the past few weeks is a question of professional standards. We've heatedly argued about them and learned there are major differences of opinion about the expectations of our rabbi. But we've finally come to a conclusion. It is our considered opinion that your behavior is, to be blunt, simply unacceptable."

A lump plunges from her throat to her stomach. Tears well up behind her eyes but do not flood them. Her heartbeat increases, yet her hands do not shake.

"Yes, we take strong umbrage with your behavior," Shugoll continues, "but not about how you discovered what happened to Noah Zentner. We differ about your sexual behavior in that matter. We have agreed to let every individual draw private conclusions. There is no consensus of opinion to take action in the matter. But we have a far greater quarrel with you that transcends all our differences. The resignation letter you wrote, in our view, is unprofessional and patently absurd. As your bosses, we don't want you writing us letters of resignation, Rabbi Lewyn. It's undignified, unnecessary, and entirely unacceptable. If we must take you to court to fulfill your employment contract, we will. We're committed to do whatever it takes to prevent your resignation. And if you insist on leaving us, we'll go to the airport in droves, lie down on the runway, and prevent your plane from taking off."

Gabby is not certain what she's hearing.

"What's more," Shugoll continues, "the Rabbinical Search Committee has unanimously recommended we appoint you as our Senior Rabbi. The search for Seth Greer's successor has been extensive and thorough. The competition was very strong. In the process we learned a lot about what is important to this congregation. First and foremost, how important you are to our families. This wouldn't be a place we'd like without you. Doctrine is not what we're all about. It has something to do with decency. And none of the candidates can hold a candle to you in that department. The Board of Directors concurs with the Search Committee. It remains only for plenary confirmation from the members."

Words fail her. She looks to Ephraim to discern his role in this unexpected announcement. There is so much emotion clogging her system that there isn't room for joy, thanks, or gratification. Is this a challenge to the codes of conduct she broke?

"Give me time to think," she whispers in a weak voice. "It's been a hard time. Noah Zentner's fate is still unclear."

"That's not unreasonable," Ephraim intercedes. "As long as we all agree to keep this meeting confidential and you temporarily withdraw your resignation."

Her throat is dry and she can barely nod agreement.

Farewells are warmer now, but nevertheless stiff.

THE FOLLOWING DAY, NOAH'S DEFENSE RESTS, PLACING his fate in the hands of the jury. Judge Lucien Weil is scholarly and precise in his instructions to the jurors and, as Zoe correctly predicted, he addresses the difference between evidence and symbolism. American jurisprudence demands fairness, not political correctness or support for partisan causes. Women may be very angry about rapists who get away with their crimes. But that is no reason to convict the accused if he is not guilty. A jury is obliged by law to regard the facts and disregard emotion.

The jury deliberates throughout the next two days. Pundits draw different conclusions from that fact. Some point to national statistics showing that a majority of verdicts for innocence come in the first three hours of deliberation, others, that convictions are rarely reached after a jury deliberates for more than two days.

The nation holds its breath.

Chapter Eighteen

Cantor Reuben Blass is a pillar of strength and, as Gabby often claims, the unsung hero of Ohav Shalom. She places a call from her safe house to his home with an urgent request that he conduct worship services on Sabbath. Another call reaches Zack Shugoll in his office.

"I heard the news," he says as soon as the call is routed to his desk phone. "A total surprise. Everybody here is in shock. How could they do it, Rabbi?"

Her voice is hoarse, concealing all but a small fragment of her emotion. "Don't know, Zack. I just can't figure out how twelve people who breathe the same air and eat the same food we do could convict Noah. I'm confused. I want to scream, but this is our criminal system. They tell me it's better than most but fallible. I need a few days to digest the verdict, Zack. I need to get out of town."

"As long as you don't renew your resignation letter."

"Fair enough. Chuck Browner will know where I am in an emergency."

The moment the conversation ends, Gabby sits in silence. A torrent of feeling erupts from deep within. She is angry at the jury. She is angry at the court. She is angry at the system. And she is crying with the abandon of a baby.

The following day, the media analyze the guilty verdict and conjecture about the punishment Judge Weil will give Noah Zentner. There is a day's recess before defense and prosecution make recommendations to the bench. Eli Waller is on television from morning to night, dashing from one studio show to another, each time in a fresh outfit, looking exquisite and stonewalling questions about the relationship between the business of her firm and her sexual conduct.

AT NEW YORK'S KENNEDY AIRPORT, WHILE WAITING for a plane to Tel Aviv via London's Heathrow, Gabby phones Zoe's suite at the DoubleTree Hotel in Baltimore. She doesn't expect to get through, but does get a voice-mail system. "It's Gabby Lewyn," she states. "You were just great through the whole trial. Give Noah a hug for me. And tell Clemmy, if she wants to spend time in Washington, I want to be her surrogate mother. I'm on an airplane. You can probably guess where I'm going."

Once her British Airways 747 has taken off, she hunches into her seat and covers eyes which are sore from crying.

"I know who you are," an elderly gentleman with a silver beard and bulbous nose speaks to her from an adjacent seat. "Bad news about Noah Zentner. We were all pulling for him. It took someone like you to explain it."

Gabby doesn't want to talk. "Thanks. Mr. Zentner lost anyway."

He nods his agreement, allowing her to fall back into her own thoughts. A few moments later a steward arrives with two small bottles of Scotch and a glass with ice. "I thought you might like this," the elderly gentleman adds, opening the flip-down tray in front of her. She sips from the contents of one bottle and stares out into the Atlantic blackness, punctuated by an occasional dot of light.

"HOLD ME," SHE TELLS SETH GREER OUTSIDE BAGgage and Customs in Ben-Gurion Airport. "I'm going to shake. I know I'm going to shake. It will stop eventually but I can't tell you when."

"Then shake," he says, wrapping his muscular arms around her. "I'll hold on for as long as necessary."

He rents a small Japanese car for the drive north to Haifa. "Horrible," he says, glancing over to Gabby in the passenger seat. "I'm thoroughly disgusted. The country will revolt if the Judge gives him a harsh sentence."

"I'm so shocked I wouldn't make any bets. I feel the earth beneath my feet turn to shifting sands. Nothing's stable anymore."

When they arrive in Haifa, he drives to the top of Mount Carmel where the view is spectacular. They stand together watching the midday sun glisten on the bay and observe merchant ships steam from the harbor into the Mediterranean.

"Anything new about Ohav?" he asks.

"They offered me your job. You set me up there, didn't you, Seth? I suspect that you planned for your succession before you resigned."

"Well now, Mazel Tov. You deserve it. A hundred times over."

"You did set me up as your successor, didn't you? Don't deny it."

"In a manner of speaking. I knew how much they adored you there."

"I'd rather you come back, Seth. We could work together as we did before. We could share the senior post. Or I'll remain as associate. I don't really care, so long as you return."

"They'd never take me. Besides, they obviously love you. The time was right for me to move on. Never turn back. Never look back."

"No, that's not true, Seth. It's a different place these days. You've been rehabilitated. People understand your motives."

"You were born for the post."

"I doubt it."

"I can't believe you'd turn it down."

"Let's say I'm thinking it over."

"Got alternatives? Another job?"

"Only the one in Jerusalem as a standup comedian."

He kisses her forehead and she places an arm around his torso, then kisses his neck.

At his apartment, she flings off her cotton jacket and stands foursquare in front of him, speaking in Hebrew, "Well now, Set Gaon, let's start from the beginning. Teach me some jokes."

JUDGE LUCIEN WEIL APPARENTLY DOES NOT CONCUR with the jury's verdict. In sentencing Noah, he recites salient features of the defense, then alludes to the thinness of evidence for conviction. Media attention is responsible for creating an irrational aura around the trial. The difficulty of remaining objective about deeply emotional subjects cannot be overlooked. He implies, but does not state in words, that it is the duty of a trial judge to dispense justice if a jury fails.

There is general relief in the courtroom when he delivers a lenient sentence: a fine of two thousand dollars and a prison sentence of four months at the low-security Eastern Correctional Institute in Westover, Maryland. Eligibility for parole after sixty days.

Zoe Mountolive promises an appeal but, due to the short sentence, requests that her client begin serving his time immediately.

THE PRESS IN WASHINGTON HAS NOT FORGOTTEN about Gabby and, as soon as she returns to Ohav Shalom, jumps on her for interviews. It wants to know her reactions to the conviction and her future plans with Noah Zenter. Her network in the gay community remains steadfast in her protection. Unfortunately, on her first visit with Noah in prison she is ambushed outside the Eastern Correctional Institute and an unpleasant shouting exchange follows.

Prison rules in this low-security facility permit visitors and inmates to sit at tables and hold hands. No separation screens but no embracing either. A single, unarmed guard observes at a distance from the doorway. Noah looks surprisingly well. He continues a strenuous regime of exercise and a controlled diet. There's plenty of good conversation among the inmates who, despite the violation of a law or two, have much to talk about from their colorful lives.

"You need to know something, honey." He eventually stops the introductory banter and inaugurates a new subject. "Morgan is staying in a residential hotel in Salisbury, about fifteen miles from here."

This revelation strikes Gabby broadside, yet she attempts to deflect its impact by answering, "I was rather rude and avoided her in Washington. She's made several attempts to talk with me."

"The trial had an enormous effect on her. Seems like a different woman now. She's renounced all her mystic mumbo-jumbo. Says she's remodeled the bedroom, painted over the ceiling decorations and bought some conventional furniture. Even an honest-to-goodness bed."

The hollowness inside Gabby expands. It begins as a small, dull void which seems to consume her organs, starting from the abdomen and working both upward and downward. She had underestimated Morgan as competitor for her husband's affections. How could she have been so naïve? Story of her life: there's always somebody running on the inside lane.

"Because I knew you'd be here, I asked Morgan not to visit this afternoon," Noah continues.

Gabby's chin drops. Her lower lip drops. She closes her eyes and swallows saliva in her throat.

"I hope this doesn't hurt you, honey. I don't mean to."

She needs a long moment to fashion a coherent reply. "It does. I can't compete with your wife, Noah. I can't do it. And I won't. She rubs his hand against the table top, then slowly lifts herself from the chair. "It's a long drive back to Washington."

"Don't do, honey. We need to talk this out. The trial has drained me." He is on his feet after her. "I don't know where things are going. You were wonderful to me. Your sacrifice was more I deserved. I'm still confused. Please, give me time to let the dust settle. A few weeks, that's all. I'll be home in forty-four days."

She stares at him and shakes her head without a reply.

"Please, honey. Don't go now."

"I'm going, Noah. There's nothing to talk about at this point."

"Will you come back to visit me?"

No. I don't think so. Not while Morgan is nearby. You put it right. The dust must settle first."

THE MEDIA PURSUES. IN A NASTY EXCHANGE ON THE street outside the synagogue, Gabby loses her control. "Look!" she barks. "Noah Zentner and Morgan Zentner are a married couple. I'm not a home buster, understand?"

"But we know that divorce papers have been filed. What's the status?"

"That's not my business. Ask the lawyers."

ZOE AND CLEMENTINE MOUNTOLIVE COME TO WASHington for Gabby's installation festivities as Ohav Shalom's Senior Rabbi. It is a joyous weekend of speeches, singing, and banqueting. People say wonderful things about Rabbi Lewyn. They laud her professionalism and character, her empathy and tireless sacrifice, her devotion to Judiasm. By nature she is a modest person yet she cannot ignore the praise. Deep down she must admit to herself that once in a while it feels damn good. Very soon she will be searching for a new Associate Rabbi to fill her now-vacated position.

Details of the formal ceremony were withheld from her. Organizers of the event left a blank space on the printed Order of Service. This stimulates muffled whispers from those in attendance. Many believe that it was necessary to send the program to the printer before getting final confirmation from the main speaker. What most fail to realize is that the identity of the keynoter is a tightly held secret, even from Gabby. Midpoint in the ceremony, she suddenly understands why. Her blood presssure soars when Rabbi Seth Nehemiah Greer disengages himself from a rear pew and commences to jog down the aisle toward the pulpit. He bounds up the steps to the altar in brisk strides as though ascending the stage of Moadon Baccus in Haifa.

His surprise appearance on the pulpit sends the congregation into confusion. Murmuring floods the Temple. A middle-aged woman in a flower-pattered dress stands, raises her arms and begins a loud clap. In the balcony, a stalwart couple who have been members for more than twenty years also rise and join in her applause. In the first row, an elegant, silver-haired gentleman in a tailored gray suit hauls himself to his feet, then begins driving his palms together. It is unusual for people to clap in the sanctuary. Sounds of their isolated ovations reverberate from the vaulted ceiling. Yes...yes—it is time to forget the past and welcome their errant rabbi home.

But the vast majority of congregants remain anchored in their seats, their hands folded in their laps. For them, forgiveness is not as easily won, nor as willingly extended.

Seth Greer gives no sign of offense. He takes a long, long time before settling himself at the pulpit. Gabby expects him to eexplode with jokes. He doesn't. In fact, he delays an introduction while his eyes hang on the enormous crystal chandeliers above him. When he eventually starts he is soft-spoken, cautious, and rabbinical. "Where?" he asks. "Where do we begin a long, long journey?"

DURING AN ELABORATE RECEPTION AFTERWARD, Clementine and Zoe hug Gabby and hold on for as long as they can. Admirers force them apart, but Gabby whispers into Clemmy's ear, "I'll see you in New York in three weeks."

"Stay with us," Clemmy entreats.

"Best hotel in town," Zoe adds as soon as she is apprised of the visit.

"Absolutely. Wouldn't want to go anywhere else."

"What brings you to the Big Apple?" Zoe asks.

"Got a wedding to attend. At St. John the Divine and a reception at Tavern on the Green. You remember my old beau, Tim? He and Sally are tying the knot. I once promised to strangle him if I didn't receive an invitation to his wedding."

As her attention is drawn to congregants waiting with congratulations, her eye catches Ephraim Rothman and Jonathan Zentner conversing together. She knows they are close friends but cannot recall seeing them in each other's company. It must be a coincidental moment for they are looking straight at her. They awkwardly avoid making visual contact and hide the conspiratorial expressions on their faces.

In that fleeting interval Gabby resolves speculation about their roles in her promotion. One man is the quiet, unpretentious conscience of the congregation; the other its financial benefactor. One is an old friend and admirer; the other a tough, experienced businessman who knows how to pay down an outstanding debt on his son's account.